THE
MYSTERIOUS
PRESS

THE BOMB MAKER

Also by Thomas Perry

The Butcher's Boy
Metzger's Dog
Big Fish
Island
Sleeping Dogs
Vanishing Act
Dance for the Dead
Shadow Woman
The Face-Changers
Blood Money
Death Benefits
Pursuit
Dead Aim
Nightlife
Silence
Fidelity
Runner
Strip
The Informant
Poison Flower
The Boyfriend
A String of Beads
Forty Thieves
The Old Man

THE BOMB MAKER

Thomas Perry

The Mysterious Press
New York

FIRST EDITION

Published simultaneously in Canada
Printed in the United States of America

First Grove Atlantic hardcover edition: January 2018

ISBN 978-0-8021-2748-8
eISBN 978-0-8021-6553-4

Library of Congress Cataloging-in-Publication data is available for this title.

The Mysterious Press
an imprint of Grove Atlantic
154 West 14th Street
New York, NY 10011

Distributed by Publishers Group West

groveatlantic.com

18 19 20 21 22 10 9 8 7 6 5 4 3 2 1

To Jo, Alix, and Ian, with thanks to Otto Penzler

1

The maker's fingers were nimble and certain, never trembling or touching any object or surface without intention. His hands were sure because he had designed the parts to be assembled in a precise order. A bomb was a simple machine. Its only moving part was a switch to complete the circuit running from the power source to an initiator and back. But bomb making was mentally demanding. Creating a potent blast required knowing the chemical processes he could produce by combining particular substances in specific proportions. He had to know how to coax them to transform from inert lumps of matter into sound, light, heat, and brute force.

The switch was enormously important. If he kept the switch open while he assembled the parts, nothing was at risk. The device became lethal only in the instant when the switch was engaged and the circuit was closed. Part of the maker's power was building in the set of conditions that must exist before the switch would close.

He had used barometer switches designed to close when the bomb was at a specific altitude. He'd made time-delay bomb switches from kitchen timers, timers from lawn sprinkler systems, and alarm clocks. He'd made switches that used motion sensors from outdoor lighting fixtures to close a circuit when a person came near. He'd set bombs off with mousetraps, components from children's toys and games, a pressure pad that turned on a laughing Halloween witch when a child stepped on it. He'd made a few from toasters and thermostats.

When commercially manufactured hardware was available that could perform the function he needed, he preferred to use it, no matter what its original purpose. Such components were tougher and more reliable than those built from scratch, and he could test them repeatedly ahead of time to be sure they worked, and then he could buy more or buy other models that worked better. Most electronic components came already tested, with a UL label on them. All he had to do was subvert the will of their designer to adapt them to his own purpose.

For similar reasons, he preferred to use commercially made initiators, preferably blasting caps. Usually he could not obtain manufactured explosives for the main charges of his bombs. Military explosives like C-4 were safe and reliable, but they were tightly controlled. Dynamite was far less powerful, but easier to buy or steal. The drawback of factory-made explosives was that they could be traced. Dynamite even contained tiny identifying tags that would be blown all over the blast area.

His only choice had been to learn to make his own. The planet was full of substances that could be made to explode. Many common materials could be induced to blow up—natural gas, wheat flour, coal dust, nitrate fertilizer. One of the biggest industrial explosions in history had been in a molasses plant. The cars people drove were propelled by small explosions of gasoline in the engine's cylinders that pushed down pistons and turned a crankshaft. A bomb maker's practical problem wasn't that explosions were too difficult. Most of them were if anything too easy, too unpredictable.

Much of the challenge in his current project came from the miniaturization necessary to make a complex set of devices that would work in sequence, but not be noticed before detonation. He had to work with a magnifier on a small stand designed for jewelers and fly fishermen so he could do the delicate work without error.

The idea was to make a device small and familiar enough to be ignored, or at least to remain unsuspected. Right now his stand held a sturdy phone-size black plastic box bearing the white letters of a company logo: Canon, a name people knew. He popped open the case and studied the circuitry. He was pleased. This was an excellent piece of equipment. He could use it. He picked up his soldering gun to make the connections between the device's circuitry and the electrical wires he was expecting the device to supply with power. Each of the wires was stripped to the copper at the end, and the rest of its length was white insulator. Most of the house where he wanted to use the small black box had white walls and white woodwork, so he had decided to start with white. He was intending to keep the device's batteries charging on a wall socket until it was time. And then, even if the AC power source got cut off, the effect would be the same.

After two hours he finished and looked at his device. The circuit was as he had intended, and the solder connecting his twenty-four firing wires looked perfect. He turned off the intense desk lamp, rubbed his eyes with his hands, took a deep breath, and blew it out again. He had been working at this iteration of his idea for most of the day.

He stood and left the garage he had converted into a workshop, went out through the house and into the backyard. He thought of it as a backyard, but it was much too big to be called that. The land was fifty acres of sand mounds, dry brush and pebbles, rocks and yuccas, surrounded by miles more that didn't seem to belong to anyone, and then a range of dry brown mountains on each side like the rim of a bowl.

It was late afternoon, and he looked out on the open land and assessed the period of daylight he had left. The shadows of the Joshua trees were long, but he might still get to his next device after he completed this test.

He had lived alone in the desert for over four years. The desert was a place where he could set off small charges, most of the time without anybody hearing them. Anybody who did hear would attribute the noise to a neighbor taking rifle practice. He did that sometimes too, and the sound was much louder than most of his experiments.

This time he didn't need to make any noise. He had built a silent test device for the circuits he was making for this project. He went back into the shop in his garage and placed the small black box on one end of his long workbench. It had twenty-four coils of white wire attached to it. His test device was a six-foot board that held twenty-four five-watt lightbulbs. He connected each set of wires to one of the light fixtures.

He checked the adjustments on the small black box. Next he set the device to trigger when the electric eye detected motion near it.

He plugged the device into the nearest socket, stepped back about seven feet—too far away to touch it—and brought his hand down like a conductor eliciting the first note from an orchestra. The black box began to tick. With each tick, one of the five-watt bulbs went on. One by one, each of them lit and then went out, so it looked as though the light were a single bright object moving down the board. The effect reminded him of the marquee in front of the old Palace Theatre in Indianapolis during his childhood. He smiled. All twenty-four bulbs had lit and gone out.

He repeated the test, this time with the speed increased, so the light moved down the board much faster, taking only about a second to move the six feet down the board. He slowed it down and played with the timing control until he felt that the speed and rhythm were perfect. He disconnected the wires from the board and gently placed his small black box in a cardboard carton, taking care not to put any strain on the wires protruding from it. He went outside again, feeling he had accomplished something today.

The bomb maker was thirty-five and average looking, with short, dirty blond hair; a thin, sinewy body; and a flat stomach he kept that way with moderate habits and runs in the desert at dawn when it wasn't too hot out. He stretched his back and arms and felt taller than his five feet ten inches. He took a deep breath as he stretched, enjoying the sun and the clear air and the endless blue sky and then decided he still had enough sunlight left to run his next test.

He went back to the workshop, retrieved another device, and set it up a hundred feet away on the range. The last thing he did was make the final connection to bring a blasting cap into the circuit. He retreated to the workshop and picked up the radio transmitter he had taken from the remote controller of a motorized toy car. He had rigged the transmitter to switch on when he stepped on a homemade pressure pad. He set the nearly flat object down at his feet and stepped on it. Instantly the receiver from the toy car received the signal and he heard the satisfying bang of the blasting cap.

Setting off a detonator from a distance wasn't the whole game, but it was a necessary condition for a particular explosion he was planning. He was satisfied. He had five more toy cars in his garage, and tomorrow morning he would begin dismantling the controllers and taking the receivers out of the toys to begin modifying them for his purpose.

As he walked, he congratulated himself on his success. He made weapons, but didn't consider himself a warrior. He was a bomb maker, a person who killed unseen and from a safe distance. All bombs came from a small, scheming, self-protective part of the mind. No bomb came from bravery. At most, bombs were cunning or imaginative, cleverly disguised as something harmless—or even appealing. The Russians used helicopters to drop small delayed bombs designed to look like toys so Afghan children would try to pick them up. The monumental cynicism that led to the design of those devices still excited and amazed him.

One of his specialties was making bombs that came from his observations about human impulses and temptations. He liked small, routine-looking bombs that would beguile a bomb technician and tempt him to try to defuse it. The technician's efforts would then set off a bigger bomb he hadn't seen or imagined was hidden nearby.

He loved the power. He had the ability to obliterate anything he wanted. And he liked the perversity of bombs, the way he could make his enemies use their own skill and intelligence and selflessness and bravery—especially bravery—to kill themselves. When he wanted to be, he was death.

2

Tim Watkins was the senior officer of the team that got the call from the police dispatcher. He and Maynard and Graham had been out to pick up lunch in the truck, and they were within blocks of the address. Watkins had picked up the radio mic and said, "One Zebra Sixty-Three. We're in the vicinity. We'll take it." Bomb Squad teams consisted of two bomb techs and a supervisor, and on this team that was Watkins.

The emergency call had come from David Hills, the owner of the house, who was in France on business. He said he had received a threatening call from a phone in the Los Angeles area. Hills had called the LA police and asked them to check on his house, because the caller had said he was about to blow it up. The suspect had persuaded Hills he was serious: he had the address and described the house—a light gray clapboard one-story traditional Cape Cod with a black front door and white trim, and a Toyota Corolla in the driveway.

The car had clinched it. Hills said he'd rented the car and left it there to make it look as though the house were occupied. That meant this wasn't somebody who had simply looked online and found a picture of his house. Hills had been competing for a big contract with three eastern European rival companies, and he had been getting vague threats from two of them for over a week before the final call.

Watkins stood on the steps of the house and looked at the black front door. He knew this was going to be the last moment when his feet would stand on anything he trusted. The steps were solid concrete, so they were safe. But he was about to enter another universe alone. For a moment he thought about his wife, Nora; and his daughter, Kelly. The resemblance between the two was uncanny. He could see them in his memory, having dinner last night. He was grateful for the sight but then pushed it away so he could keep his attention on what he was doing.

The other two members of the team were sitting in the truck five hundred feet away, the standard distance. Watkins didn't let himself envision Maynard and Graham, because he was intent on clearing his mind of distractions and images that competed for his attention. That was also why he didn't allow any back chatter while he was going downrange on a scene. He reported over the radio built into his bomb suit's helmet, and they listened.

He knelt on the porch in his olive-drab bomb suit. The Kevlar and steel plates made the suit heavy and stiff, but he managed to get down to eye level with the knob of the front door. The boots were like the rest of the suit. The one part of him that could have no protection was his hands, but he seldom let himself think about that because it made him uneasy. He opened his black canvas tool kit and used the lock pick and tension wrench to line up the pins of the cylinder. Then he tried turning the knob. It offered no resistance. He put away the tools. "I've got the door unlocked. Now I'm going to look for reasons not to open it."

His statement brought another memory, this one the image of Dick Stahl, the retired Explosive Ordnance Disposal expert who had promoted him to the Bomb Squad. That was the sort of thing Stahl used to say. He supposed his subconscious was reminding him to make every move the way Stahl had trained him to. He gave himself a few seconds to clear his mind again.

He stood and squinted into the fisheye peephole set at chest height in the shiny black door, but saw no shadows or lines that might be wires—only a miniature image, like a view through the wrong end of a telescope. He saw a sunny room with a brown leather easy chair under a window with translucent white curtains.

Watkins went down the steps and around the house, looking at the lawn in front of him, selecting the places where he could safely put his thick-booted feet free of trip wires or light beams. If there was a bomb, the mind behind it wasn't familiar to him. He couldn't predict or eliminate anything. There could be an electric eye that would set off the initiator if the light beam to its receiver unit was interrupted. There could be a piece of thin wire or transparent fishing line stretched across his path at a level just below the tops of the blades of grass. The trap could be any of a thousand things, or several of them at once, or there could be no trap, and no bomb.

He came to a window that opened onto a dining room furnished with a maple table and chair set. There were two entrances to the room, one a narrow swinging door to the kitchen, like what a restaurant might have, and the other a broad arch that led to the living room. He could see the inner side of the front door of the house from here, and he saw nothing ominous. Once a couple of years ago he had peered in at the inner side of a door and seen a shotgun propped on a coffee table, set up with a wire to fire at the level of a bomb technician's groin. He had wondered why. He still did.

Watkins considered entering the house by breaking the glass of the dining room window and reaching up to open the latch. But beside the front door he could see the glowing panel of an alarm system. Many alarm systems would trigger at the sound of glass breaking, and a bomb could be connected to the alarm circuit. He took the compact monocular out of his tool kit and focused it on the alarm panel. There was a green light to show that the system had power, but the display said: RDY. Ready. It wasn't armed. The panel had no visible wires leading from it, but a tie-in could be anywhere in the house, including at the circuit box, which was usually mounted to the interior wall of a closet. But the fact that the alarm was off made Watkins very uneasy. If this Mr. Hill was in Europe and was worried about an extortion scheme, why wasn't his home alarm system turned on? It didn't fit. Or had an intruder managed to turn it off?

Watkins paused by the window for a moment and looked again intently at several things he had noticed. The door to the kitchen was one. Any old-fashioned house might have a swinging door to the kitchen, but he couldn't recall seeing more than a few like this one in his eight-year career. The door itself was a hazard. It was clad in a layer of sheet metal like the ones in restaurants. It was painted white on the upper half, but the lower half was bare metal. That meant it would conduct electricity. Would a bomber ignore that opportunity?

Watkins studied the chandelier above the dining room table. It was a bowl shape with three layers above it dripping with dangling crystal drops that kept the bulb invisible. An antipersonnel bomb with ball bearings or screws inside the glass bowl would disperse at the right level to kill anyone in the room—about six feet.

Watkins took his time. He emptied his mind and stared, trying to notice anything that felt wrong, anything that would inspire a bomber to do something clever. Watkins moved from window to window, following the same procedure. He tried to see what was plugged into each electrical outlet, searching for commercial timers designed to turn lights on and off and make the house seem occupied. Those were about the most reliable timers a bomb could have, and they could deliver 110 volts to a firing circuit.

Watkins looked for shapes he'd seen bombers use before—pipes, of course, pressure cookers, backpacks, satchels, small suitcases. He scanned for pieces of military ordnance that might have been left inside boxes made for them. Artillery boxes were usually simple, made of half-inch by three-inch wooden laths nailed together and painted olive drab with their contents stenciled on them in black. He searched for the shape, not the color, in case somebody had painted one to look harmless, like a toy box.

Watkins knew if an expert had set this house to blow, there would be at least two charges—the big one to destroy the building, and a smaller, subtler one just for someone like him.

When he had stared into the interior through each of the windows, he found himself back at the front steps. He spoke into the helmet radio. "There's nothing visible from any of the windows. I'm at the front door again."

He stood on the steps beside the door, reached over, and turned the knob. The spring pressure felt normal, and he heard no clicks. He sighted along the jamb as he opened the door a crack. There were no signs of anything held in place by the door or the hinges about to fall or spring away or sever a contact. There were no wires.

He moved his knife along the bottom of the door to locate the magnet embedded in the door to keep the alarm switch under the threshold from tripping. He found it, then took out his own magnet and placed it against the door in exactly the right spot, so when he pushed the door inward the new magnet would replace the one in the door.

He reached inside and lifted the doormat to check for a pressure pad, and then put the doormat into the doorway to prop the door open. He turned and inspected the alarm keypad on the wall. "I'm in," he said. "The alarm is off." A minute later he said, "I don't see any sign of a device yet. I'm going to look for it."

Watkins stepped deeper into the living room, inching ahead in his heavy, hot bomb suit. He had to turn the whole upper part of his body to see anything on either side, because the suit's helmet didn't have a neck. He used his bright flashlight to focus on one object at a time. He didn't want to flip any light switches just yet.

He moved the beam of his light around the room to pick up the shine of monofilament fishing line or any thin wires that weren't meant to be there. Next he turned his light off and searched for thin beams of light from an electric eye in the air.

A glass candy jar filled with multicolored jelly beans drew him to it. The jar was exactly the sort of object a bomb maker would use—harmless looking, transparent, and appealing. He came closer and used his flashlight to search for any hint of an object or a wire hidden among the jelly beans. Maybe it was too obvious for this guy. A professional bomber would know that someone like Watkins would see it as a likely place for the trigger.

The place a bomber wanted the charge was not the first place you'd look. When you looked at the first place, you were still sharp and watchful. The bomber wanted you to work your way to the less likely places. When you got to the least likely place, there it would be. By then you'd be tired and bored, maybe careless enough to open drawers without first checking for contacts, or to step without looking down ahead of your feet.

Watkins refused to rush or get lazy. His mind roamed this nightmare of a house, searching for the other mind, the one that had come here to infuse the building with malice. Watkins had seen bombs go off, and he had seen the aftermath, people simultaneously burned to death and torn apart, charred viscera and brain tissue spilled and limbs wrenched from bodies, blood spattered on pavements and dirt roads. He was aware that in a minute he might experience that destruction. He might already have set off an electronic timer when he opened the front door, and a time-delay relay was about to send the electrical current to the initiator. Maybe now. Or now. Or now.

He went down on his stomach and swept the flashlight beam along the boards of the hardwood floor, trying to spot a single board that was higher or lower than the others. A misfit board could have been lifted and something placed under it.

The floor was perfectly level. Watkins looked up at the ceiling and along the crown molding. He reminded himself that if there was a bomber, he had never seen this person's work before, and didn't know his specialties, his quirks, his favorites. He kept looking.

Bombs were not just weapons. They were something more, expressions of the bomber's thoughts about you, his predictions of your behavior—what you would see, even what you would think and feel. He'd staged a presentation designed to fool you. He didn't even know your name, but you were the one he was really after. Bombs were acts of murder, but they were also jokes on you, riddles the bomber hoped were too tough for you, chances for you to pick wrong when it was almost impossible to pick right.

Watkins turned his attention to the furniture. First he moved his flashlight along the bottom edges of the furniture and then behind it, and then he moved to the couch. The easiest place to put a charge was in one of the seat cushions. The cushions usually had a zipper in the back or underneath so the cover could be cleaned or the stuffing replaced. One couch cushion could hold a pretty big bomb. Three of them could blow pieces of the house all over the neighborhood.

He touched the front of each cushion with his fingers, palpating it to sense whether there was anything hard, or if the stuffing was too full, or there were any empty spaces. He cautiously pushed the spaces between two cushions apart to detect any wires. He worked his way to lifting them up to be sure they weren't too heavy.

Next he moved to the big armchairs and repeated the process. After each piece was cleared, he slid it over beside the couch. When he had moved everything to one side, Watkins surveyed the newly bare part of the room to be sure he had missed nothing. He looked at baseboards and molding, sockets, light fixtures, and lamps. He announced, "The living room is clear." Then he picked up his tool bag and went to the kitchen door.

He took out his mirror and extended its telescoping handle. He slipped it into the thin crack between the swinging door and the jamb, moved it up and down, and rotated it. There was nothing connected to the door. There was nothing on the floor. He adjusted his mirror to reflect the kitchen counters. There were a toaster, a blender, a row of spices, a couple of bottles. One was olive oil.

He saw a small black rectangular box on the kitchen counter. What was that, a phone? A radio? Either could be bad for him. There seemed to be a very thin white cord leading from the countertop to a plug on the wall behind the juicer. He withdrew the mirror, put it away, and picked up the monocular from his tool bag. He leaned into the kitchen, aimed the monocular at the device, and read the brand name. Canon. A camera? No lens, but it looked like camera equipment. As he stared at it, a tiny red indicator on the end came on.

In that silent moment Watkins identified the device on the counter. It was a photographer's intervalometer, a device often planted in the wild to detect movement of an animal on a trail and trigger a camera many times in succession as the animal passed by.

Watkins half turned his body toward the front door to go back, then realized he was not going to make it. The first electrical impulse would be for a charge near the front door, and the next impulses would race around the house, each one setting off a charge where he might take shelter, tearing the house down over him one explosion at a time. "No," he thought. "Toward it."

Watkins pivoted back toward the kitchen, pushed off with his legs and heard the first click of the intervalometer as it sent the first impulse, but there was no explosion. He burst through the swinging door, building speed as he lumbered across the kitchen, dashing for the back door.

The intervalometer's second click set off an explosion at the front of the house, the one designed to kill him if he'd retreated to the front door. The shock shook him and his ears hurt, as though it had damaged his eardrums. He flung the back door open and launched himself off the back porch to the lawn. He managed to remain on his feet in the heavy bomb suit, still struggling to run.

The second explosion punched out the kitchen windows behind him and showered him with glass, and the third took out the windows over his right shoulder. One after another, the charges blew, the next set at the corners of the house. Watkins kept moving, not able to turn and look back, but he heard a crash he believed was the collapse of the roof over the living room.

The house was being imploded, the way demolition teams imploded skyscrapers and apartment complexes. He knew the only thing that had kept him alive for the past ten seconds was the necessity that the last charge to blow was the one near the intervalometer that set off the charges. The kitchen charge would be the biggest.

In another half second it came, knocking him off his feet onto the grass, clapboards and two-by-fours striking his back. Then clouds of white dust obscured the world.

3

Watkins lay still for a few seconds while the debris fell around him, then listened. There was a strange, terrible silence that made him wonder if he'd lost his hearing.

"I'm alive," he said into the microphone, and was relieved to hear himself speak.

"We heard somebody breathing," said Maynard's voice in his earpiece. "Are you hurt?"

"I think I'm okay," said Watkins. It wasn't a perfunctory answer. Some bomb victims had fatal internal injuries and bleeding they didn't detect at first. "Let's get the area roped off before we get overrun."

He recognized Graham's voice. "We're on it."

The voices and the incidental noises in Watkins's earpiece went away. Watkins pushed himself up to his knees, examined his bomb suit for holes or tears, but found it intact. He stood and the layer of debris on his suit fell in a puff of dust at his feet.

The thing to worry about now was unexploded ordnance. He began to walk across the backyard looking for surprises among the pieces of the house. It was unlikely this bomber would have made any bad electrical connections and left a charge unexploded. He was too highly skilled for that. But his work was also devious and premeditated, so it was important to Watkins to be sure he had not left anything intentionally.

As Watkins surveyed the scene he saw the thoroughness of the bomber's work. There were a great many small pieces blown from the house—roof shingles, mostly from the corners of the building, windows and frames, glass, a few sections of clapboard. But the main part of the structure had collapsed into a pile.

Some of the studs and roof timbers he could see had been drilled and wired for charges, so the house would fall in on itself. He found the front door out on the lawn near the street with forty round holes punched through it. He looked at the angles of impact and realized there must have been a bomb or two with ball bearings taped to them placed above the gypsum board of the ceiling to kill him if he tried to run out that way.

He watched his team's black bomb truck stop in the street. It was emblazoned with bright gold paint that said BOMB SQUAD in the hope it would keep at least some bystanders at a distance. Hitched to the back of the truck was a containment vessel on wheels, a steel ball about five feet in diameter with a hatch that could be sealed and a valve for the release of gases. Graham and Maynard got out and began to string yellow tape to keep people away until the scene was found safe and the pieces were examined for evidence.

The team's truck had been only five hundred feet away, so it reached the bombed house immediately, but now other vehicles began to arrive. The patrol cars that had blocked off the street on both ends before he entered the house now admitted two fire trucks, an ambulance, and then another bomb truck towing a containment vessel.

Captain Victor Del Castillo, the commander of the Bomb Squad, jumped down from the truck and trotted up to Watkins. He was lean and tall, a long-distance running enthusiast, and spent months each year trying to recruit his squad members for the annual police endurance races. He said, "Tim, are you all right?"

"A little stressed," said Watkins.

"Stressed? That's it? Then I won't waste my sympathy on you. Did you see anything inside we ought to be looking for?"

"The kitchen was at the back. An intervalometer was on the counter."

"A what?"

"An intervalometer, like photographers use. It was a black box about the size of a cell phone, with the name Canon on it in white letters. I think it was the kind that has a motion sensor that sets off the camera if you want to take pictures of lightning or moving animals or something. I leaned into the kitchen and saw a small red light go on. Then I heard a click. Once the power was on, it ran through a sequence of clicks, each one setting off a charge."

"I'll have the guys start looking for pieces of it. If there's anything left, it could have a serial number or something. The main thing right now is to be sure we don't still have live explosives."

Del Castillo had come with a three-man team of bomb techs, and he assigned them to search the scene for explosives, pieces of detonators, or other bomb components. He repeated Watkins's description of the intervalometer and added it to the list. In another ten minutes two more trucks arrived bringing three-man teams, who were added to the sweep. They had to make sure the danger was over before a crime scene crew could come in and collect evidence.

Their search was difficult and painstaking. Any scrap of metal might be part of one of the bombs. It was essential to clear the area of anything that might explode, and this had to be the priority.

The scene was not quite like any Watkins had seen before. Where the house had been was now a pile of lumber, some of it charred near the ends where small charges had been placed. The roof was collapsed over the pile of wood and siding, its gutters now about three feet above the ground and its peak less than six feet high. The lots on this street were not large, but the houses on either side of this one appeared to be intact.

Watkins looked over the area and realized there were fourteen techs working this scene—exactly half of the LAPD Bomb Squad. After a short time, Del Castillo waved to summon Watkins to the bomb truck parked on the street.

He was carrying a laptop now, and he opened it on the hood of the bomb truck. "Hey, Tim," he said. "Take a look. I got the plans for this house from Building and Safety."

They stared into the screen, shading their eyes from the afternoon sun. The first image was a diagram of the house from above, showing the locations of walls, doors, and windows. Watkins noticed a rectangle with a row of thin horizontal lines. "Is that a staircase?"

Del Castillo looked at it. "Yeah. Looks that way."

"I didn't see any staircase."

"What do you mean?"

"It was a one-story house. Why would there be stairs?" Watkins looked closely and then clicked on the second view of the house's plan, and saw a side-view rendition. The stairway was below ground level.

It took Watkins a second to identify this part of the diagram. There was an underground space, almost square. He spread his fingers on the touchpad to enlarge the image.

A dozen things came clear in an instant. He had not seen the stairs because they were underground, extending down to a small basement. A basement was unusual in Los Angeles, but some old houses had them. The basement was why the charges had all been relatively small, placed high in the skeleton of the house to take it apart and collapse the roof onto the floor. Virtually none of the energy had been focused downward. The bomber was protecting something down below. The bomber hadn't been demolishing some businessman's house; he'd been making it into a trap for the police.

Watkins shouted, practically screamed, "Stop!" He ran a couple of steps toward the wreckage that had been the house as he yelled. "Stop! Don't move! Everybody freeze! Stay where you—"

Later, the video from the camera mounted on Captain Del Castillo's truck that had been recording the search showed Sergeant Timothy Walker running toward the rubble, and picked up what he was shouting. Nobody was able to see later what, exactly, triggered the second device precisely at that moment.

Every bomb technician standing on the lot at 12601 Valkrantz Street could have listed five or six ways to wire that kind of booby trap, but the one who touched the wrong thing didn't see it. This was the big charge, the one Watkins had been expecting but had not found. He'd failed because the large cache of explosives had been, not inside the house, but under it.

The main charge turned the air hard, the shock wave bursting up and out, converting the detached pieces of the house into weapons that cut down bomb technicians where they stood and hurling some of their bodies so they came down on lawns together with the boards, bricks, and hardware they'd been examining.

Watkins, Maynard, Del Castillo, Capiello, and ten others were dead. Many of the police officers who were parked at the ends of the block to keep away the curious, and the firemen who had parked ambulances and pumper trucks farther off, were knocked off their feet by the force of the blast, and a few had minor injuries. The bomb truck Del Castillo had brought was blown onto its side, but its camera kept recording the unchanging image of the blue Los Angeles sky.

4

Dick Stahl had been both a soldier and a cop, two professions that never left a man unchanged. He was forty-four now, but in a suit and open-collared shirt he was still straight backed and walked with a physical authority that made him seem taller than his six feet. He had the sort of tan men like him had—darkened forearms, face, neck, and hands—wherever his shirt didn't cover. His tan was color acquired as wear, one of the things his work had done to him.

He got into his black BMW and looked back at the big house perched near the top of the hill overlooking the ocean. The woman who lived there was standing above him behind a floor-to-ceiling window watching him go. He gave her an unsmiling half wave and then drove.

Stahl's mind was already working on Sally Glover's problem. She and her husband had lived in that house for thirteen years. Every morning Glover had driven to his company offices in Calabasas, and she'd spent her days on the things the wives of successful men did—volunteer work for the homeless, the hungry, and the victims of a couple of favorite diseases—directing the spending of the couple's small charitable foundation. Stahl was aware that the things people distrusted a rich wife for—keeping herself beautiful and capable of intelligent conversation, keeping the big house tastefully decorated and provisioned to entertain her husband's colleagues and customers—were also just chores. The money didn't change that.

The money had brought on their current problem. Her husband had begun to work on expanding his business into Mexico. He had wanted to build a facility for manufacturing and shipping medical imaging machines, and for the past few months he'd been spending weeks at a time in the small towns east of Mexicali, where he had been choosing a site and securing the land leases, permissions, licenses, and permits.

Two days ago Mrs. Glover had received a call from Mr. Glover's cell phone. When she answered, a man with a thick Spanish accent told her that her husband would not be coming home until she had paid for his freedom. If she wanted him back, she should mail a hundred thousand dollars in cash to a mailbox rental business in Mexicali. She was skeptical until the man put Benjamin Glover on the line. He said he had been dragged from a taxicab, beaten, and taken somewhere. He was all right, if a bit hurt and shaken, but she should do as the man asked.

She had called the head of security at her husband's company, who made some calls to friends of his in the narrow world of security and private investigation and found a name and a phone number. There was a man named Stahl who was known to have made some successful extractions from Mexico.

Stahl had come to see the prospective widow and told her to prepare the hundred thousand dollars. He gave her a blue cardboard box and assured her it would hold a hundred thousand dollars in hundred-dollar bills. She must give him the address of the post office box and send the money right away. He took several pictures of the box.

She said she could get a hundred thousand dollars from a personal bank account. Was that all it would take? No, he told her. This was just the kidnappers' way of beginning the negotiations. It would persuade them her husband was worth keeping alive while they prepared to make their next demand. In time they would ask for much more, so she should begin selling stocks, bonds, or property. She had to be ready to respond right away, or they might feel the need to send her an ear or a finger to motivate her.

Stahl said, "I'll leave today for Mexico. I'll do this as quickly as I can." Then he listed some items he would need immediately. One was her husband's most recently expired passport. Another was a collection of photographs of her husband. The third was her current passport.

When she asked about his fee, he said, "I have a flat rate for kidnappings in foreign countries. It's five hundred thousand dollars."

"What if you find you can free him for the cost of a trip to Mexico?"

"I don't give refunds. But if it costs ten times as much to get him back, I won't ask you for more. And no matter what it takes, I won't quit or give up. Here's my card. You can send the check to my office when you have the money in your account. Of course, you can do this another way or contact somebody else."

"No," she said. "I've been told you're the one, and if that's your fee, I'll pay it. This is my husband's life."

As soon as he was on the road he made a telephone call to a man in Ensenada named Antonio Garza, and then another to a woman in Mexico City named Esmeralda Cruz. Next he dropped his car off in the underground parking structure at his condominium building and called to reserve a rental car. He bought all the insurance the rental company would sell him, and packed. A cab took him to the rental lot, and he put his two suitcases into the trunk.

Stahl was on the road to Mexico by noon. He didn't seem to be in a hurry or uncomfortable when he crossed the border at San Ysidro. He told the border cop he was headed for a resort at the tip of Baja. The police made him open his trunk, but they didn't go any further. They just watched him to see if he was nervous, and then waved him on. A man who had spent years rendering bombs safe was not easily flustered. And as a rule, people didn't smuggle anything to the south. It was on the way home that the authorities would be more thorough. He met Antonio Garza in Ensenada, where Garza had set aside a room for him in his house.

Garza was a longtime colleague whom Stahl paid a retainer to remain available to help him in any operations in Mexico. Like Stahl, he had been a soldier and a cop and then had formed his own security company. He had a number of regular clients who paid his company to protect things of value—often a family business, but increasingly, as kidnappings had become more common, their sons and daughters. Garza was about six feet three and 240 pounds, and he conveyed the peculiar impression that he was in life as a kind of referee.

When Stahl and Garza walked into a restaurant near the beach for dinner, Garza took the manager aside and pointed out the spot that would be the best place for him to seat them. The manager seemed to believe this was good advice. During dinner the two men spoke in only the most general terms about the operation. It was only later at Garza's house that they discussed the specific plan. Garza had people watching the mailbox rental store in Mexicali for the blue box, and each of them had Stahl's photograph of the box on his cell phone. There would be a constantly changing group—some men, some women. As soon as they saw the box, they would follow the person who picked it up and try to find the place where Benjamin Glover was being held. When it was time to act, Stahl would do the work and Garza would be the driver. Stahl had been with a great many people in frightening situations. He had learned Antonio Garza was a man who would not let fear overpower his pride. Garza wouldn't get nervous and drive off without him if things turned bad. Stahl knew that if he failed, he wouldn't be alone when he died.

The call came after three days. A man in his thirties had picked up the blue box in Mexicali. He had walked around a corner and gotten into a pickup truck. He drove south and east to the town of Corazón de Maria, then delivered the box to a house in the center of town in the oldest section, near the old church and the town square.

Stahl and Garza left for Corazón de Maria the next morning. Corazón de Maria was a market town with a considerable population, but because there were no luxury hotels, it wasn't a place where American tourists were common. If the kidnappers were expecting an American operative, Stahl would be spotted immediately. Garza dropped Stahl off at a ranch owned by a friend of his and went on alone. He arrived in late morning and rented an office on the top floor of a commercial building across the city square from the house where the money had been taken and then went back for Stahl.

They returned late at night. Garza helped move Stahl into the office and unload the items he expected to need and then drove off to Mexicali to wait. Stahl began his own surveillance. He placed a sixty-power marksman's spotting scope a few feet back from the window so it was enveloped in shadows, and he watched from his vantage point high across the square.

The house was one of the colonial-era buildings that lined some of the streets radiating from the square. There was a wall with a rounded door set into it. The place was like others of that period he'd seen in market towns. Through the portal on the inner side was a garden enclosed by the wings of the house. The rooms were situated in a row, all of the doors opening onto the long covered porch that surrounded the garden.

Whenever the thick wooden door opened, he used the few seconds to stare through it and learn more. Then he focused on whoever went in or out. By the end of the first day he had seen six men and memorized their faces. He had also noticed they brought in a large quantity of groceries, including cases of beer and tequila, and brought out a large number of garbage bags, which they hauled away in a truck. He saw no women or children.

Stahl watched the house most of the time for six days, noting everything that went on. Late on the sixth night, when his office building was empty and there was no chance of being overheard, he called Antonio Garza. "I'm going in tomorrow night. Has Esmeralda arrived yet?"

"Two days ago. I picked her up at the airport."

"Can you be here at two a.m.?"

"Yes. Why tomorrow night?"

"For the past couple of days, men have been leaving and not coming back. It looks like they're getting started on another operation or something. There seem to be only two men guarding the house tonight. It's not going to get better than that."

"What aren't you telling me?"

"They're not taking precautions. They don't hide, and they don't seem to have any defense. I haven't seen lookouts with cell phones watching the place from outside, and nobody seems to guard the door. You know what that could mean."

"Yes. They could have somebody else protecting them. And what about Glover? You haven't seen him yet. How do you know he's not already dead?"

"If he were dead, there wouldn't be much point in leaving any men here, not even two."

"Maybe." Garza didn't sound convinced.

Stahl added, "It's supposed to rain tomorrow night. Rain covers sounds and keeps people at home staying dry. The clouds cover the moon."

"Where do you want the car?"

"Drive up the street by the back of the church, and wait for me to call."

"All right. I'll be there at two."

At 2:00 a.m. the next night, Stahl walked in a light rain on the cobbled street leading off the square past a row of old colonial houses. When he reached the right house, he picked the front door lock, eased it open to keep its hinges from squeaking, and slipped inside. He was wearing a baseball cap to keep the rain out of his face and a gray raincoat to cover the items he was carrying—a short Steyr AUG-3 automatic rifle on a sling that let it hang muzzle downward, a pistol in his belt, and a razor-edge marine KA-BAR fighting knife with a black blade.

He stepped into the garden, which looked as he had expected from his distant surveillance. A low porch with a roof surrounded the grassy space, with tall leafy trees. The porch roof was covered with climbing bougainvillea that had scaled the beams and hidden the clay tiles. He moved along the covered porch, looking in each window.

Stahl was willing to take his time moving through the dark house. If he'd made a noise as he came through the door in the wall, he knew a sleeping man would probably ignore it unless there was another noise that indicated some sort of a pattern. Stahl felt ceramic tile beneath his feet. It made him happy, because he could walk across it silently.

He had gone about two-thirds of the way around when he found the first occupied room. There were two men asleep on beds. The beds were smaller than a twin bed and each consisted of a steel frame with a single layer of interlocking wire links covered by a thin stuffed mattress and a single loose army blanket.

Their quarters were so spare that if he had not seen both men during the week going in and out, he might have mistaken them for prisoners. He thought about the fact that they had bunked together. Every room had its window and door opening onto the courtyard, and he'd looked into every one he'd passed. The house was large, and none of the other rooms had any occupants. Why would both guards sleep here? It made sense only if the man they were guarding was very near. Stahl closed his eyes, waiting a few minutes so they would adjust to the dark, and then he studied the room. He saw a door with a padlock on it. That had to be it.

He couldn't do anything before he made sure the rest of the rooms were empty. He resumed his prowl around the building. He found the second occupied room only two doors away. The man in this room was asleep too, but he looked as though he'd gotten the first choice of beds. His bed was wider and thicker, with box springs, two white pillows, and white sheets. The man had taken off a suit and hung the pants and coat on a single hanger on the door to the bathroom. Stahl could see that the breast pocket of the coat had a leather wallet with a police badge flapped open, the way plainclothes cops sometimes wore theirs to be identified during raids. Now Stahl was sure he knew why the men of this building didn't seem to fear anyone. They had connections.

Stahl paused. He knew he was going to have to get the policeman out of the way before he could return to the room with the two guards. He slowly and carefully opened the door and stepped into the policeman's room. He went to the man's suit on its hanger to see if the cop's gun was in his coat or in a holster. As he touched the coat there was a sudden motion in his peripheral vision.

The cop whirled in bed, his hand coming up from under his pillow with a pistol.

He was reacting like a cop, but Stahl had been a cop too. He had anticipated that this move was one possibility, so he was ready. Under his raincoat, his hand was poised to use the rifle, and he swung it up into the man's face and hammered it butt downward on the cop's head.

Stahl wrenched the pistol out of the man's hand and held it on him for a moment. The man didn't move. He examined the man's skull, then shook him. Stahl was shocked. The blow with the butt of the rifle seemed to have killed him. Stahl had never intended to kill. He had planned to handcuff him with his own cuffs and gag him.

Stahl knew he had to hurry. It was critical now that he get Benjamin Glover out of this house—and out of this town. In a few seconds he was in the other bedroom.

The two men were still asleep. When he came here, he had expected to do what he had done several times before. He had entered a house at night, pointed an ugly-looking automatic weapon into a kidnapper's face, and asked him to consider accepting a smaller ransom than he'd demanded. Stahl had confirmed each time that a few thousand dollars sounded much better to a man who was about to die than it had earlier.

Stahl raised his Steyr rifle with his left hand and prepared to turn on the light. As he reached up, he heard a shuffle, a movement behind him. He turned and a big dark shape hurtled through the doorway behind him and clutched him in a bear hug, trying to pin his arms to his sides. The cop now had the crazy strength of an enraged, hurt man. He swung Stahl around into the wall, but it didn't loosen the cop's grip on him.

Stahl had not forgotten that the man had just awakened. He was still barefoot. Stahl stomped on the cop's instep, and used the second of intense pain to break free. He grasped his razor-sharp commando knife and spun around, slashing the man's throat. The cop fell to the floor bleeding.

Stahl whirled. The two guards behind him were freeing themselves from their blankets. Stahl lunged toward the nearest man, stuck the knife up under the center of his rib cage and found his heart. He snatched the man's blanket, threw it over the second guard and shot him through the head with the rifle.

Stahl stepped to the padlock, used the big knife to pry the hasp out of the wooden door, and opened it.

Inside was a closet with two steamer trunks stored on the floor so that the emaciated, dirty man crouching on the trunks could not stand up and straighten his back.

Five minutes later Dick Stahl walked along the narrow, dimly lit street that led to the square of Corazón de Maria, his open raincoat sloughing off the gentle drizzle. His right hand was stuck in his raincoat pocket and through the slash he had made in the inner fabric so he could hold the 5.56-mm Steyr AUG 3 M1 under the coat. The forty-two-round magazine made the weapon bulky and heavy, but he had removed part of the bullpup stock and shortened the sixteen-inch barrel to make it lighter and easier to hide.

His left hand held Benjamin Glover's arm. Glover was unsteady, almost staggering, because the muscles in his legs had cramped and tightened during the ten days he was imprisoned in a closet that was too low to allow him to straighten them.

"Easy," Stahl said. "We're going to be out of here very soon. The car is waiting for us just past the church. All you have to do is make it that far."

Glover turned his head, trying to look over his shoulder, but Stahl tightened his grip and pulled him forward. "You know better than that, Benjamin. What would you think if you saw a man who was looking over his shoulder all the time? You'd think he believed he was being chased, right? That he was trying to get away."

"I can't help it," said Glover. "I've been in that box for so long. They said if I ran away, they'd ruin my feet."

"Don't worry," said Stahl. "The ones that were guarding you are past noticing. Hey, isn't that something? Just in that time we walked about fifty yards. We're halfway. More, maybe."

Glover was irritated and peevish. "How can you be sure they haven't noticed? They could be awake and coming after us right now."

"No," said Stahl. "Not the three who were guarding you in that house."

"Why not?"

"They ran into some bad luck," said Stahl. "It's a hazard of the kidnapping business."

Stahl tightened his hand on Glover's arm and walked him toward the steps of the old church. At this time of night the town seemed abandoned. All day the square was occupied by food vendors' carts and booths where wised-up girls with bored expressions sold clothing, pirated videos, cheap jewelry, sunglasses, T-shirts, and leather goods. At night the square was an open, empty space where the light rain glistened on the cobbles and the white church loomed against the dark sky.

A car wheeled around the church with its headlights off, and onto the cobbled plaza. The car was not Garza's, but it seemed to be heading directly for Stahl and Glover as they walked toward the church.

Stahl said, "Study this car. Look at the men in the front. If you see a face you've ever seen before, tell me."

He released Glover, reached into the left pocket of his raincoat, and produced a small powerful LED flashlight. He held it in his hand and kept walking, his right hand now gripping the Steyr with the safety off.

The car was close enough now. Stahl raised his left hand and switched on the blinding white light. The two men in the front seats flinched and squinted, and the car stopped with a jerk. The man in the passenger seat ducked, but the seat belt kept him from getting down.

Glover said, "The driver! He was the one who was taking me to Tijuana when the kidnappers ambushed me!"

The driver turned on the headlights and hit the high beam switch, bathing them in light.

Stahl brought the Steyr up and out between the two sides of the open raincoat, and fired. The windshield bloomed with opaque circles of pulverized safety glass.

The men were both dead, held upright by their seat belts, but the car kept coming, gliding along over the cobbles.

Stahl pivoted with his short automatic rifle raised, its sights still trained on the moving vehicle as it passed.

A man in the backseat popped up and raised a weapon that looked like an AK-47, but before he could fit the long weapon out the window, he bumped the muzzle against the window frame. The half second gave Stahl time to fire a shot into the man's forehead.

Stahl saw the dome light of the car go on and held his rifle sights steady.

The car swept by, but the man who had jumped from the far side door was left behind, kneeling with a rifle rising to his shoulder. Stahl's sights settled on him first, he fired, and the man fell backward onto the cobblestones.

Stahl grasped Glover's arm again and said, "Come on, as fast as you can manage." He began to run, dragging Glover along with him. In a moment they made it around the corner of the church into the dark lane that led up the hillside. Stahl pushed Glover into the wall and they both stood with their backs against it in the shadow of the big building. Stahl used the moment to remove the magazine of his Steyr and replace it with his spare, then cycle the first round into the chamber.

He took out his handheld radio. "We're at the pickup location. What are you waiting for?"

"We heard shots."

"Me too. I fired them. Get here now." He sidestepped back to the corner of the church and craned his neck to look out at the plaza.

The car with three of the dead men still inside completed its drift across the empty plaza and slowly pushed its way into the glass front of a long-closed restaurant, bringing the glass down on top of it and coming to rest among a forest of tables and upturned chairs.

In a moment another vehicle with no headlights emerged from the street beside the church and stopped. Stahl threw open the back door and pushed Glover onto the seat, then got in beside Garza. "Go."

Antonio Garza accelerated quickly, his lights still off.

Stahl said, "Stay away from the restaurant on the other side of the plaza, and don't run over that body."

Antonio skirted the plaza, using the open space to gain speed, and passed by a row of ornate government buildings. As he drove, they heard sirens and then saw the lights of the police cars illuminating the upper parts of buildings they passed on the way to the square. Antonio reached the mouth of a side street just before the police cars pulled up in front of the restaurant.

Glover said, "Didn't you see those police cars?'

"We sure did," said Stahl.

"Aren't we going to stop and tell them? They could help us."

"Not on this trip," Stahl said.

Glover was incensed. "That stuff about all Mexican cops being corrupt is nonsense," Glover said. "This isn't some remote village. It's a busy town. Come on."

Stahl said, "One of the men holding you was a police detective. He wasn't there to help you, Benjamin. He was there to be sure that when your ransom got paid the police got their honest cut."

"Look, I know a couple of police captains."

"Then we don't have to wonder about who picked you out for the kidnappers."

Garza drove to the vegetable canning plant where he'd left the other car, and they made the trade. When Stahl helped Glover into the backseat, there was already a middle-aged woman waiting there. She was pretty, with large, lively brown eyes and long black hair with a streak of gray.

She began to talk to Glover rapidly in Spanish, but Glover said, "I'm sorry, but I don't understand you." He said to Stahl, "Who is this woman?"

Stahl glanced over his shoulder and saw the garment Esmeralda was holding up to Glover. "She's asking you to put those on so she can get started on your hair and makeup."

"These are women's clothes."

"She's giving you a disguise. She's very good. She gets lots of work for movie studios."

"Is this necessary?"

"Only if you want to get across the border alive," said Stahl. "At some point they're going to get your picture into the hands of guards at the airports and border crossings. She can make you into a different person, but it takes time, so let her get started."

"What if I don't want to cross the border in drag?"

Stahl half-turned and looked at him. "I haven't had time to explain the whole situation. You're probably really good at what you do, manufacturing things in places where nobody has money and selling them in places where people do. That's a great talent, and I wish I had it. But instead, I learned a trade. I can find and extract a kidnapped American businessman. The bump in the road this time was that I couldn't get you out of the building where they had you without killing the three men who were holding you. That's not something I'd normally do. And you saw what happened at the plaza. Those four men are dead too."

"But—"

"If the police stop us, we die or go to prison for life. I picked that disguise because I knew they would starve you, and being skinny would help you pass for a woman. That's the plan, and I'm afraid I have to insist."

Esmeralda began to work, first pulling Glover's filthy T-shirt off and then pulling the silky blue-flowered dress down over his head. She fitted the wig and looked at him critically. She shaved his face with an electric razor and then began to apply foundation makeup.

Glover said, "What made you do this?"

"A whole lot of money."

"Who's paying you?"

"You are," Stahl said. "Your wife already put up the money with my security company."

"She paid you in advance?"

"It's company policy."

"That's quite a policy."

"It saves my clients from the unpleasant experience of seeing me again."

Glover lapsed into silence while Esmeralda applied foundation and then blush to his cheeks. She said in Spanish to Garza: "Tell me when you're on a long, flat stretch so I can do the eyes. The eyeliner is the hardest."

In a few minutes she finished, and then Glover fell asleep. Esmeralda used a small makeup light on a compact to study her work, and then said, "I like him better as a woman."

Stahl shrugged. "You're the expert." After an hour of fast driving Garza said, "We'll be up on that bridge before long."

"All right." Stahl unloaded the Steyr and then broke down the weapon. When they came to a bridge over the Rio Colorado, Garza stopped. Stahl hurled the receiver over the side to splash into the river. Then he threw the barrel, the trigger, and sear and springs as far as he could, followed by the ammunition and magazines, his pistol, and his knife; got back in; and buckled up while Garza went on.

They drove into the long morning line at the Mexicali-Calexico crossing just before dawn. The line of cars inched forward, nose to tail, their engines idling under the gray, rainy sky.

When they approached the customs booth, Stahl nodded and Esmeralda woke Glover. At the booth, Garza handed the four passports to the uniformed customs officer. As the man's eyes focused on each passport in turn, his expression remained sleepy and bored. When he reached Glover's passport, he studied him for a moment, and then said, "Mrs. Glover. Where were you born?"

Glover said, "Cleveland, Ohio," in a soft, nearly feminine voice.

The customs man closed the passport and handed all four back to Antonio. Then he stepped back and waved the car into the United States.

When they pulled away, Glover leaned forward and said, "Let me see that passport." Stahl took the stack from Garza, then handed one to Glover. He looked at it, scowled for a few seconds, then laughed. "It's my wife's passport. I can't believe you got me across the border on my wife's passport."

When they were leaving Calexico, Esmeralda pulled off Glover's wig and put it back in her kit, and then used wet wipes to remove all of the makeup from his face. She said, "Be careful with the dress. I want to give it to someone."

Glover took off the dress and handed it to her, then put on his pants and T-shirt. "They didn't let me get a shower for the past few days. If the dress is ruined, I'll pay for it."

They headed west toward San Diego. When they reached the San Diego airport, Garza took the freeway exit and stopped in front of the terminal. He and Esmeralda got out. Stahl shook hands with Garza, hugged Esmeralda, and said, "Thank you both. When you get home, check to be sure your money has been deposited in your bank, and then call me."

"Of course," said Esmeralda. "Adios." She set off for the airline ticket counters.

"See you soon, Dick," said Garza. He hurried to join Esmeralda in the airport.

Stahl got back into the car, this time in the driver's seat, and drove toward the freeway entrance. He said, "Your wife is waiting for you at a hotel up the road in La Jolla. I'll leave you there and drive on to LA. Your passport and hers are in that bag on the floor. There's also a wallet with money and a credit card."

"How did you get my passport back from them?"

"The same way I got you back."

"Thank you for my life. I'm sorry I didn't react right to things at first. This has been such a—"

"It's okay. Nobody crouches in a closet for more than a week without getting a little confused."

"I'd like to pay you for the extra . . . trouble."

"No," said Stahl. "Your wife paid in advance, and I would have charged the same for an easy trip. When you get into the hotel, rest for a few days. Don't go back to the house where you used to live unless you have armed bodyguards or police officers with you. Move to a new place far from there, and keep the address a secret for as long as you can. Stay hard to find for the next year or so, and then you should be all right. Whoever is alive back there might like revenge, and might kill you if it were easy, but they won't want to waste a lot of time, and there's no more money in killing you than in leaving you alone."

5

Dick Stahl walked into the four-story redbrick office building on Sepulveda Boulevard. The double doors on the ground floor opened into a glass atrium about forty feet high that enclosed wide concrete steps that looked as though they ought to be outdoors. Somewhere in the glass panels above there were leaks, so drips of water had fallen from above and formed puddles in front of the steps. He could see it must have rained here too while he was gone.

Stahl took the elevator to the fourth floor and walked down the hallway to the steel door he'd had installed. The sign on it said: NO-FAIL SECURITY.

He had a jumpy, uncomfortable feeling today, a hot sensation on his spine. In Mexico he had listened only for the sound of sirens, and then after he and the others had crossed into the United States he'd kept the radio off so he could listen to his own thoughts about his rescue of Benjamin Glover. But a few minutes ago, while he was in his car on the way to the office, he heard something on the radio that shocked him. He thought now that he must have heard it wrong and was anxious to get inside and turn on the television set in his office.

He pushed the door open and entered the outer office. He could see his office manager, Valerie, at the desk behind the glass wall. She was blond and about forty, a person who always moved as though an emergency had been declared, chewing gum as she darted from place to place swooping to pick up papers that had to be fixed or finished. As he watched her she stopped and typed something into the computer at the reception desk, then moved out of the field of the big bulletproof window. He'd had the bulletproof glass installed when he started the business seven years ago and it had no nicks in it yet, but it made him feel better about having employees sitting in plain sight.

Stahl stepped in and caught a movement in his peripheral vision. He looked at the row of leather chairs along the wall of the reception area and saw he had a visitor. David Ogden stood and stepped toward Stahl. Today he was wearing his LAPD uniform with the three stars of a deputy chief on the collar. But there was black tape across his badge.

"Hi, Dick," said Ogden. "Valerie said you'd be back this morning."

"David," said Stahl. "What's going on?" His eyes were on the badge. "I heard something on the radio, but I—"

"It's bad," said Ogden. "It's really bad, Dick. Yesterday afternoon there was a call to a house in Encino. The caller said he was the owner. He said he was away in Europe, and that he'd gotten a threat that his house was all primed to blow up. Tim Watkins and his guys took the call. Tim went in, but they couldn't save the house. Later, when half the Bomb Squad was searching the rubble for unexploded ordnance, a secondary bomb went off, a big one."

"Who got hurt? How many?"

"Not hurt. They're dead, Dick. Fourteen men. Half the bomb techs on the force. Gone. They're calling it the biggest massacre of police officers in national history."

"Tim Watkins? Who else?"

"Maynard, Del Castillo, Capiello, Graham. I have a list." He took a folded sheet of paper out of his pocket and handed it to Stahl.

Stahl stared at it.

Ogden said, “This seemed like a routine call at first. Tim and his crew responded, and then when the place blew up, the ones who went to help clear the scene were the senior people, the most experienced. We lost everybody who was there.” He paused. “I came to ask for your help.”

“You’re asking retired techs to fill in?” said Stahl. “I’ll be willing to help out for a few days, until reinforcements arrive. It’s been a while, but I’ve kept my certification current. You can run into anything in the security business.”

Ogden said, “The reinforcements aren’t arriving. You know how many bomb techs Ventura County has right now? Two. Whenever anybody in Southern California has a situation, they count on reinforcements from us.”

“Have you called the FBI?”

“First call we made. The FBI techs stationed here are going to pitch in. Same for ATF. But transferring anybody to us long-term means taking them from other cities. They’re going to put a rush on getting the first twenty officers on our waiting list trained, but you know how long that takes.”

Stahl knew. The first part of the course that used to be at Redstone Arsenal in Alabama had been moved to Fort Lee, Virginia, a couple of years ago and was still at least six weeks. Thc part after that in Florida was thirty-nine weeks. Stahl said, “It’ll be a year before the first one is back here ready to work.”

“All we can do is get started today. We’re also asking police forces all over the country for lists of bomb techs who retired within the past three years and might still be certified.”

“What a mess.”

“That’s why we need you.”

“Sure. I said I’d help out for a while.”

“We need more than that, Dick,” said Ogden. “You trained Watkins, Capiello, Del Castillo, and half the other senior technicians. You ran the squad for five years.”

"Two years."

"Nobody else who's alive has done it for a day. We need you to run the squad for a while, until we can get a permanent commander. I can get you a rank of acting captain." He frowned. "Whoever did the bombing is still out there. We lost fourteen cops, and we don't know a thing about who did it. No group has taken credit. The recording Tim Watkins left told us nothing."

"Just let me think about it, and we can talk tomorrow."

"There isn't time. My car's outside. You don't have to do anything now but introduce yourself."

Two hours later Stahl sat on the desk outside the newly emptied Bomb Squad commander's office. He was wearing the clothes he had put on to go to the No-Fail Security office this morning—a black sport jacket, a light blue oxford shirt, and a pair of gray slacks. The surviving members of the LAPD Bomb Squad wore work uniforms, essentially dark blue fatigues with badges printed on them. They sat on chairs taken from the conference room down the hall, or sat on desks, or stood.

He said, "I'm Dick Stahl. Like you, I would have given a lot not to be here right now. We all lost friends yesterday. Some of you have lost teachers and supervisors, people who have saved you from dying or taught you how to save yourself. Like you, I want to get whoever did this to them. I'm sure we will. But right now, the highest priority has to be not losing anybody else."

Deputy Chief Ogden, commanding officer of the Counter-Terrorism and Special Operations Bureau, was visible to Stahl in the hallway. He gave Stahl a solemn nod, and then walked off down the hall.

Stahl said, "From now on we will proceed the way we were taught at tech school. A team is three officers—two technicians and one supervisor. Every officer downrange will wear the suit. In most cases that will be one officer only. We'll rely on the dogs to detect explosives, and use robots as much as we can to lift or disrupt them."

He looked at the ten men and four women in the room. "Beginning today, we will work under the assumption that we are not defusing anything, no matter how simple and straightforward a device looks. Everything that can't be detonated in place goes into a containment vessel to be taken to a range and detonated there. I know you want to be able to render the device safe, trace the components to their sources, and convict the bug-eyed creep who assembled them. I'd love that. We just can't be in that business right now. I don't think it's likely this bomber killed fourteen bomb technicians by accident. I think he devised the situation so he could. I don't know why. But we can't let it happen again. Questions?"

A big man around forty years old with black hair and the hint of a tattoo peeking from his left shirt cuff raised his hand. As his shirt came down Stahl could see the design was a rattlesnake coiling up his arm.

Stahl nodded. "Can you identify yourself for me, please?"

"Sergeant Ed Carmody. I was going to ask you the same. You're a friend of Deputy Chief Ogden, right?"

"Yes. He asked me to help out for a while." He shrugged. "I also have other friends on the force, and until yesterday I had more."

"Are you a bomb tech? Everybody here has been through the FBI course at the Redstone Arsenal and Eglin Air Force Base, and then recertified every three years."

"Yes. I was an army EOD man. I did tours in Afghanistan and Iraq, then worked out of Germany on a rapid deployment team for a while. Then I was the NCO in charge of the practical training range at Eglin for a couple of years. Then I came here and ran this squad. Some of the guys we lost yesterday are techs I selected and trained—Watkins, Del Castillo, Maynard, and Capiello."

A small, pretty woman with light skin and her dark hair pulled back in a tight bun said, "How long will you stay?"

“I haven’t had time to figure that out. For now let’s just say I’ll try to help you through this, and then I’ll go away. About a half hour ago the chief swore me in. Here’s my badge.” He took it out and held it up in its identification wallet. “The day you’re back at full strength and running right I’ll give it back to him.”

He took a folded sheet of paper from his coat pocket and consulted it. “Your team supervisors will be the same. If you were one, you still are. There are four teams consisting of three officers, and one team with only two. For now, I’ll join that one to fill in. We’ll call it Team One.” He looked at the sheet of paper. “With officers Elliot and Hines. Raise your hands.”

He saw a couple of the techs look at each other and raise their hands—the small dark-haired woman who had spoken and the tall athletic-looking African American man in his early thirties beside her.

The radios clipped to all fourteen of the uniforms spat and crackled, and the female dispatcher’s calm voice said, “Bomb technician team requested eleven thousand two hundred Moorpark Avenue in Studio City. Officer reports suspicious vehicle chained to the pumps at a gas station.”

Stahl said, “My team will take this one. That will give the rest of you time to return to your stations and stand by for the next. Remember there’s a group or a person out there who seems to want us all dead. Don’t assume what you’re looking at is what it seems to be. Take care of each other.”

Stahl walked quickly out of the squad room with Hines trying to get ahead of him. Elliot followed a few feet behind, on the radio. “This is Sergeant Elliot. Team One is responding,” he said. “ETA approximately fifteen minutes.”

As he followed Sergeant Diane Hines outside to the parked truck, Stahl looked at the new LAPD headquarters building. It was all glass and knife-edge corners, many empty multilevel spaces and hallways with their own views of the Civic Center. The building had won awards, and it had a row of sculptures along its Spring Street side that looked to him like a line of hippos lying down beside a river. The array was interesting, but he knew they were there to keep somebody from driving a truck into the building—maybe somebody like the person who had wired up that house yesterday.

He got in the bomb truck and moved to the back, so Elliot and Hines would take the two front seats. Hines claimed the driver's seat and started the engine while Elliot climbed in. Then she flipped on the lights and siren and accelerated onto First Street. Hines drove with a cop's aggression and speed, and won the game of chicken at each intersection.

It had been a long time since Stahl had been in a speeding bomb truck, but it could never be long enough.

6

It was shortly before noon when Hines coasted off the freeway at the Laurel Canyon exit, covered the last couple of blocks, and then pulled up in front of the gas station. The pair of officers who had arrived at the scene first had strung yellow tape across one entrance and parked their patrol car across the other, and the young male officer was now guarding the scene while he spoke on a hand radio. He lowered the tape to let Hines drive the bomb truck in over it, and then secured it again.

Hines stopped the truck in front of the small store at the edge of the station and she, Elliot, and Stahl jumped down. Elliot knelt to follow the chains from a pump to the car and then to the other pump, examining but not touching anything.

"That's it," said the cop. "There are chains running from each axle and around both gas pumps, so the car stays put."

Stahl said to the cop, "Where's your partner?"

"She's in the store with the owner."

Stahl said to Hines and Elliot, "I'll go in and find out what I can."

He stepped into the small station. There was a counter with a cash register, and behind it a small room that looked like an office. A blond female officer was inside speaking with the owner.

When the cop heard Stahl set off the chime as he came in the door she pivoted. "Sir, the station is closed right now. You'll have to—"

He held up the identification wallet with the captain's badge. "I'm Stahl, the Bomb Squad commander."

"Yes, sir. I was just reviewing the surveillance tapes with Mr. Wertheim. He's the owner."

"Very good. Do they show the car being driven here?"

"The car was towed here about three a.m. The tape shows the car being towed behind a pickup. Then a man steps out of the truck, goes to the cameras, and smashes them, one by one, with a tire iron. He also broke into the store, but I don't think he found anything he wanted. Mr. Wertheim says nothing's missing. He doesn't keep any cash here overnight."

"Okay, thank you, officer. Now, take Mr. Wertheim and your partner and put at least five hundred feet between you and the station. Take the surveillance equipment with you so the recordings are preserved. And please radio a request to stop traffic from coming into this intersection. We'll wait for you to call us before we touch the car."

"Yes, sir."

Stahl stepped outside and walked around the car and gas pumps at a distance of about six feet as he spoke into his handheld radio. "This is Bomb Squad Team One. We have a suspected car bomb at the gas station. Please clear the airspace above Laurel Canyon and Moorpark. And we'll need at least a block on each side of us cleared of vehicular and pedestrian traffic. And please be prepared to evacuate the apartments and businesses on both streets." He signed off and completed another circle of the car, stopping now and then to squat or kneel and look under the car or study the chain without touching it. "A Chevy Malibu, twenty thirteen. Let's get a set of manuals for it on the laptop and get familiar with the parts breakdown, particularly the schematics for the electrical system."

"Yes, sir," said Hines. She stepped to the bomb truck, opened the laptop, and began to search for the manuals.

Stahl's radio came to life. "This is Captain Holman at North Hollywood. You're asking for a lot of space, Captain," he said. "We'll have three or four miles of gridlock."

Stahl said, "If the car is full of explosives, moving everyone a block away won't be far enough. If it sets off the gasoline tanks under the station, four blocks won't be far enough." While he talked, he watched Hines and Elliot looking at the manuals on the computer screen.

"Is that likely?" said the captain.

"I'll let you know as soon as I can. Until then, I think we need to be cautious."

"All right. You've got whatever time you need. Just keep us informed."

Stahl watched Hines and Elliot selecting the equipment for the preliminary examination. Hines carried a small mirror on a long handle, and Elliot had a closed-circuit TV inspection system, a cable scope with a camera lens and light at the end, and a box with a small color video screen for viewing the images. It was designed for plumbers inspecting pipes and other cramped, unreachable spaces.

Stahl went to the corner of the station and looked east, west, north, and south on the streets. The cars had been diverted by police officers to other routes. When he returned to the truck Hines said, "Think we ought to cut the power to the pumps first?"

He could tell she was feeling nervous and scared, but he judged it was the intelligent way to be right now. "Normally I would say yes, but this guy could be the one who booby-trapped the house yesterday. If so, he's after us, and he knows cutting the power is something we'd do. The device could have a solenoid or a magnet that holds the switch in the OFF position until the power is cut. Examine the car first."

"Okay," she said. "I'll take a look."

She extended the mirror and walked around the car, keeping her distance and looking underneath for thin trip wires or filaments, for any additions to the factory-installed parts that might complete an electrical circuit if touched. When she found none, she approached and looked into the interior from all sides, and then the backseat. She looked at her colleagues and shook her head.

She extended the long-handled mirror and slid it under the car again, looking at the reflection for anything attached to the undercarriage, the wheels, axles, gas tank, engine.

"Take all the time you need," said Stahl. "I think this car isn't here to blow up Mr. Wertheim or his customers. No timer, no cell phone, no fuzes. Looks like the bomber wants whatever sets it off to be something a Bomb Squad does."

"You really think so?" asked Elliot. "This setup doesn't look professional."

"I have no proof," said Stahl. "But my theory is that the wired-up house yesterday was done to attract as many bomb techs as possible and kill them. I can't explain it any other way. The guy who called it in wasn't who he said he was, and it's hard to think of anything he could have gotten out of blowing the place up except killing cops. And one day later we get this." He gestured toward the car. "I think this could be a trap set by the same guy, and he wants us to outsmart ourselves. Let's take our time and not touch anything until we're sure we've figured this out."

"Yes, sir." Elliot took his closed-circuit television scope, moved the small camera at the end of the cable under the car, and studied the image on the screen. He moved the camera forward and back, then side to side so he could be sure he saw every square centimeter of the car's underside. He sometimes raised the camera on the cable so it would be an inch or two from the underside, and sometimes he bent it at the end to look sideways along a depression.

"Can you get a look at the wire bundles in the engine compartment?" Stahl said. "Look for ties that aren't dirty. A smart car bomber will try to make his wires look like the car's wiring, and maybe even use the same gauge and color wire. And be sure you trace anything that might be drawing power from the car battery."

"Right," said Elliot.

Hines said, "There are no bundles that look like they've been redone recently, and no boxes or packages that could hold explosives. Now I'm looking for parts that don't look like they were there a week ago, and nuts that have scrapes where a wrench would have slid on them."

"Good," said Stahl. "Keep thinking like that. And don't move anything. This guy probably knows we'd rather not engage with his contraption. We'd rather tow it out of here and detonate it on a range. So I'm pretty sure he will have made it dangerous to try to move it away from the gas pumps."

"Hey!" said Diane Hines. "We've got a hole under the trunk."

"Let me get a look." Stahl stepped close and took the mirror. He moved it around under the car. "I see," he said. "The hole was cut with an electric hacksaw. It looks about five inches in diameter. There's a space up and above that seems to be a tube of silver metal."

Hines said, "There's no visible connection with the ignition system and no direct link to the battery."

"The connection could be to the light circuits in the trunk—brakes, backup, taillights, and the trunk light. That way we wouldn't see new wires."

Stahl went to the bomb truck and got on the radio. "This is Captain Stahl of the Bomb Squad. I need to speak with Officer Engle, from the unit that arrived first at the Moorpark scene."

The dispatcher was on for a moment, calling unit Twelve Mike Seventeen.

"Twelve Mike Seventeen, go ahead."

The voice was Engle's, so Stahl said, "When you watched the security video, did you see the suspect approach the car in any way after he towed it in? Did he open the trunk or the hood or a door?"

"Not that I saw," Officer Engle said. "He drove a truck in with the car on a tow bar. No license plate on the truck. He got out of the truck, then broke the cameras on the outside of the building. You can't see him well because there were no lights on. He looks about average height, average weight, wearing a hoodie over a baseball cap with no markings. After that there was nothing."

"Did you see him look into the car window or under the car or anything?"

"The indoor camera footage showed he knelt down to unhook the two hooks from the undercarriage, got in, and drove away."

"How did the car get chained to the two gas pumps?" asked Stahl.

There was a pause. "I don't know, sir. The outside cameras were broken. I didn't see it happen on the recordings from the cameras inside the building."

"Okay. Try to remember. Was there a point in the recording from the inside cameras of the building where there was a jump in the action, or a period of static where you couldn't see anything?"

"There was some of that—once when the car had just arrived, and then later too. But most of it was clear."

"All right," said Stahl. "I think that may be what he wanted when he broke into the store and the office. He erased some of the recording. He may even have intended to erase it all. We need to have you see what's missing. There may not be anything. But beside the gas station is an apartment building. Across the street from me there's a strip mall with four businesses. There's another business across the other street. If there are surveillance cameras in any of them, they may have something. We need to know if the man who brought the car did anything to it just before he left. Understand?"

"Affirmative."

Stahl hung up.

Elliot said, "What are you looking for?"

"The guy towed the car in here," said Stahl. "Maybe he set a timer or a switch after the car was in place. If one of the cameras caught him doing it, we'll know where to look for it, and for the arming circuit."

"You think he put in a master-arm switch like in aircraft firing systems?"

Stahl shrugged. "He towed the car here. He could have driven it here, or booby-trapped a car that was already here. What does that say to you?"

"That the bomb is too big for him to make on the spot or carry here by himself."

"And maybe once it's armed, it's too sensitive to move," Stahl said. "I think this guy wants us. He was hoping we'd drive up, see we probably had a car bomb, think we knew exactly how it worked, and guess wrong. Maybe we'd look at the chains to the pumps, just cut them and try to tow the car away, and set it off."

"Maybe we haven't found the connection because it's on a timer," Hines said. "Maybe he wants us to stand here paralyzed until it blows. Or maybe he's got his initiator connected to a cell phone or the remote control of a garage door motor."

Stahl said, "If he just wanted to set off a bomb on a gas station, he could have done it last night. Why build a trap unless you want to catch someone?"

Hines said, "You're saying the priority should be looking for whatever springs the trap?"

"That and keeping other people away from here," Stahl said. "If he has a way to set it off remotely, he'll wait until there are enough people to make it worth his trouble."

"So we're on our own," said Hines. "No reinforcements."

Stahl didn't answer her question, which wasn't really a question. "While we're waiting for the word from Engle, let's step back and try to understand what's happening. He chose a gas station. If he blows up a car by a gas pump, there will be a fire. But a gas pump is like a faucet. The gasoline isn't stored in the pump, it's in the underground storage tanks."

They walked through the station, inspecting the round caps the gasoline delivery truck drivers opened to refill the storage tanks. Stahl said, "There are supposed to be three tanks in one place, and three in another place. The station has to be laid out so the fuel truck can come in, stop, fill the tanks, and drive off without ever backing up. And by law the tanks can't be right below the pumps."

The radio came alive. "This is Twelve Mike Seventeen for Bomb Squad."

"Officer Engle. Did you check the tapes?"

"The store across the street has its recordings on a computer," she said. "I just watched what was happening while the other tape was blacked out. The man used two chains to chain the car to the pumps, then went to the trunk of the car, opened it, reached in, and then closed it. Then he drove off."

"How long did he reach into the trunk?"

"Seven and a half seconds."

"Thank you. Great work, Engle." He made a call to the captain at North Hollywood. "Hello, Captain. Stahl again. I'm afraid we've verified that the car is a bomb, and so we'll need to keep the streets shut down for at least a few hours."

"Understood. Do you need anything else?"

"Yes," said Stahl. "I need a set of steel plates one inch thick, like the ones the DPW uses to cover holes in the road they make during underground repairs. Maybe four plates, each at least four by six. We'd also like a load of sandbags—enough to make a wall about six feet tall around a Chevy Malibu, and two car jacks."

"I'll get the Department of Public Works going on that right away."

In less than an hour a truck arrived with the items Stahl had requested and a trailer carrying a forklift. The crew used the lift to unload the items, and then to help move them into place. They pushed two plates under the trunk of the car, and one in front of each of the two gas pumps to form a hard shell for the layer of sandbags they stacked against them. Then the DPW truck left.

Stahl placed a pair of sandbags against the front and rear of each of the car's tires so the car could not roll. Then he had Elliot set one car jack on the left side of the Malibu while he set one on the right. He had Hines count while he and Elliot raised the two jacks simultaneously so the car wouldn't rock from side to side.

Stahl opened radio contact with the Bomb Squad members at police headquarters while he, Hines, and Elliot put on the heavy bomb suits. "This is Stahl. Be sure what I say is recorded."

"Recorder running."

"All right. The car is chained to both pumps. I think that is mostly a deception, to make us think if we cut the chains we can move it. We can't. We're going to try to get a flexible closed-circuit television camera into the trunk of the car and see what it has inside that blows up. The floor of the trunk has a hole that's blocked by something, so we've got to make another hole to inspect the trunk."

"Good luck."

"Thanks. We'll report from time to time. If this doesn't end well, send copies of the recording to the FBI and ATF, so they'll know what we learned about this guy, and what we tried."

"Yes, sir."

"Sergeants Hines and Elliot are sending photographs of the car, the layout of the gas station, and the nearby buildings. We've stabilized the car, and now we're going to drill into the trunk."

Hines had fitted an electric drill with a cylindrical bit with a wider diameter than the lighted camera. She said, "Where do you want me to drill?"

"On the side away from the gas cap," Stahl said. "He could have a circuit with an initiator inside the gas tank, and we don't want to make contact with it."

"All right," she said. She wrapped a bit of masking tape around the drill bit so she would know how deep she was drilling.

"How deep are you going in?"

"This is an eighth of an inch," she said. "I'm hoping that won't be too deep, but it should make a hole we can use to insert the camera."

"Okay," said Stahl. "Not a lot of pressure, and stop every few seconds to cool the bit in water." He brought a large bottle of water and a bucket from the squad truck, and poured some water in. "Lots of drilling, not much pushing."

She nodded and began drilling. She would take the drill off the car now and then, and immerse the bit in water so it wouldn't get hot enough to set off an explosive. After the second break she poured some water on the car's surface. She said, "Are we filming this?"

"Yes," said Stahl. "The camera in the truck is on."

"Maybe it will pick up this guy watching," said Elliot.

"I hope it does," Stahl said. "The smart ones don't come in person, but maybe he's got a weakness."

Hines stopped and pulled back. "There it is. We're through." She dipped the drill bit and then poured water around the hole she had drilled without letting any into the hole. Then she pried out the small disk of metal she'd cut out.

"I'll get the scope in and take a look," said Elliot.

"Okay," Stahl said. "Just don't get impatient. If you can't see we can try something else."

Elliot put on his helmet and tugged it down so his face appeared behind the Plexiglas front. Elliot inserted the end of the flexible scope into the trunk and began to move it around. From his helmet radio the others could hear his breathing, and the fan that kept the helmet's window clear of condensation. They listened to his breaths, trying to guess what he was seeing.

Stahl hadn't been in a suit in years. It felt familiar, but not pleasant. The suit weighed eighty-five pounds, and the armor plates in it made it stiff. He watched Elliot kneeling, looking down at the closed-circuit television monitor as he held the flexible cable to move the camera and its light.

Elliot's voice in the radio said, "It's a mess."

Hines said, "What do you mean?"

"The trunk is full of what look like plastic explosives. I think it's homemade Semtex or C-4. There are bricks of it, each one about a foot long by four inches by four inches, but they're not even close to identical. Probably each one was a batch. There are wires going to each one, so it's like a rat's nest. Each pair of wires I see looks like the leads of a blasting cap. If only one circuit works, it will set off everything. At the center of the pile is a vertical tube about ten inches in diameter. It seems to be right above the hole that was cut into the bottom of the trunk."

"Shaped charge," said Stahl.

"That's what it looks like," Elliot said. "I think it's set up to do what you said—blow downward through the pavement to breach the gas tank below."

"We've put two inches of steel between the trunk and the pavement, but if a shaped charge that size is made correctly, it might still blow through the pavement under it and set off a tank. The rule of thumb is that a shaped charge can penetrate through steel plate seven times its own diameter. That might be why the car is chained there—so the trunk will extend over that set of tanks."

"The tanks under the station could make a hell of an explosion."

"Look at the trunk itself," Stahl said. "Is the lid rigged?"

"I don't think so," said Elliot. "But he's built in lots of ways to set this off. He must have fifteen or twenty sets of blasting cap leads, and they don't seem to be wired to one power source. They run in every direction."

"One more thing. Is there any ceiling space between the top of the explosives and the underside of the trunk lid?"

"Just a second." There was more shallow breathing, and then: "It amounts to about three inches in most places, but only about an inch above the shaped charge."

"Mark the spot on top of the trunk directly above the shaped charge."

Elliot stood, still holding the screen, moved the cable a little, and then took off one of his gloves and set it on the trunk lid. He went down on his back and looked at the hole under the trunk. Then he stood up and moved the glove an inch back. After a moment Elliot said, "Done. The shaped charge is directly below my glove."

"Come back."

When the three were standing on the far side of the truck from the booby-trapped car, they all removed their helmets. Their faces were covered with sweat. Elliot and Hines stared at Stahl, who seemed deep in thought. After a moment he looked up at them and noticed they looked worried, apprehensive, scared. "Don't worry. We can do this."

Hines said to Stahl, "How do you want to go about this part?"

"Popping the trunk lid will probably set off a trap initiator, but we just found something else we can do to get into it," said Stahl. "We take part of the trunk lid off, so we can reach the explosives." He took a black grease pencil from the tool kit in the truck, and then walked to the trunk of the car. He drew a ten-inch circle around Elliot's glove, then made a two-foot square centered on it. He picked up Elliot's glove, carried it back to the truck, and handed it to him.

"Thanks."

Stahl said, "Before we do this, we've got to think of a way to cut into the lid without throwing sparks into the trunk full of explosives."

Hines said, "I think I know how to do that. An electric saw can open a hole in the trunk. But first, we use the hole we drilled to insert a layer of something over the explosive."

"A layer of what?" said Stahl.

"I was thinking of that foam insulation they use in attics. They spray it into walls and things."

He looked at her. "That's not a bad idea. Call Engle and see if she can find us some."

In a half hour, Officer Engle drove up without her partner and opened the trunk of her patrol car. "A hardware store on Ventura had it." She lifted a tank out of the trunk and handed the box of attachments to Elliot.

"Thank you, Officer Engle," Stahl said. "Now you'd better pull back."

Stahl, Elliot, and Hines went through the procedure of drilling a second hole through the other side of the trunk, cooling the bit and the car over and over. When the second hole was finished, Elliot inserted the flexible video camera into the trunk again, then the small hose from the insulation tank, and began to spray. The foam came out steadily, but not too quickly as he applied a layer of polyurethane foam over the surfaces of the bricks of explosives. The insulation expanded to fill the available space. Elliot had to pull out the camera quickly to keep it from being covered. He repeated the procedure on the other side of the trunk to be sure all of the explosives were protected.

"Is everything ready?" said Hines.

Elliot looked at her and then Stahl, his expression tense. "Let's hope that stuff works."

Hines drilled a hole at the edge of the square Stahl had drawn, then picked up the electric hacksaw and began to cut along the outline. Every few seconds she stopped to cool the blade in water, but the work went quickly. In time there was a square of the trunk lid ready to be lifted out. They pried one edge up so Elliot and Stahl could get their gloved hands under it. They paused for a second, their eyes meeting. Stahl said, "Lift."

The metal square was out. They set it down near the bomb truck and came back to the now open trunk and began carefully lifting out pieces of foam insulation to reveal what was beneath. They all saw the switch, but Hines got the words out first. "Mercury rocker switch."

The switch was resting on the off-white layer of explosive bricks in a handmade wooden frame about six inches long. The frame held a glass tube tilted at a twenty-degree angle. Inside the tube were two copper wires glued on opposite sides of the upper end. An inch of silvery mercury pooled on the lower end. If the tube were tilted, the mercury would, for an instant, connect the two contacts.

Elliot said, "If we hadn't stabilized the car before we went to work on it, we'd be dead."

Hines touched his arm. "But we did."

Stahl said, "Let's get the best and closest possible look at the switch and the frame to be sure it's not wired to another switch before we remove it."

They examined the device with flashlights and magnifiers. Then Stahl reached down and cut the wire to one of the contacts. "Wrap that, will you, Hines?"

She leaned close, took an insulated cap, twisted it over the wire, and then waited while he cut the other wire and capped that one too, so they couldn't come together and complete the circuit accidentally.

Stahl put the mercury switch in an evidence bag, took it to the truck, and then returned.

"What's next?" Hines asked Stahl.

"Now we start taking away some of its muscle. As we remove the Semtex, keep running your flashlight along the edges of the bricks. If there's another tilt switch or pressure switch somewhere, find it before it finds us. Look for springs, any thin piece of metal that might touch another if you move a brick. I'll do the first one, and we'll take turns."

Stahl lifted an end of one of the bricks from the left side a quarter inch, used his flashlight to look under and around it, then cut the lead wires and extracted the blasting cap from the claylike object. He then carried the brick of explosive to the containment vessel and placed it inside.

The next brick had no lead wires for a blasting cap, and Elliot carried it to the containment vessel. The third one was the same, and Hines carried that one. They were beginning to feel hopeful. They were decreasing the size of the potential explosion with each brick they removed. They removed six and set them in the round vessel. The vessel had two relief valves for venting the gases from an explosion slowly, and he checked to be sure they were both open before he closed the hatch.

Stahl said, "We'd better stop now. This is a lot of high explosive for one load, and somebody's got to drive it out to the range and detonate it. Hines, can you call to tell the nearest squad to get somebody out here to pick it up and bring us another containment vessel? If they've got two, they'd better bring them both."

"Yes, sir." She took off her helmet, went to the driver's seat of the truck, and made the call.

In ten minutes, Team Three's truck came and took away the first load.

Team One restored their helmets and went to work again. Stahl said to Hines and Elliot: "I want to get everything else out before we touch the shaped charge. That means every brick of plastic and all the wires we can see before we move the big one."

They followed the same procedure as before, using lights and mirrors in the trunk to be sure there was nothing to actuate a detonator, no spring or metal clip ready to move and bridge a gap in a firing circuit. Whenever they had a sufficient number of bricks free of the trunk they called for a pickup and started on the next containment vessel. After an hour there was a radio call from headquarters. Stahl went to listen.

He said, "Stahl."

"Bomb Unit Three just called in from the range. They set off the first few bricks of explosive. There were no duds. The plastic is well made, very high power."

"Thank you," said Stahl. "Ask them to come back and pick up the next load." He went back to work on the trunk of the car.

"Anything we need to know?" asked Elliot.

"No," said Stahl. "You know how it is. If you're not the one downrange, you get impatient and want to chat."

"Right," said Elliot.

A few minutes later, they reached the last four bricks around the shaped charge. One by one, they removed each explosive brick and replaced it with a sandbag to hold the shaped charge in place. The last bricks were now in the containment vessel.

The three stood back and studied the device in the trunk. It was a ten-inch pipe with a funnel-shaped cone of metal welded on the lower end, aimed down through the hole that had been cut in the floor of the trunk. The pipe had been held upright by a frame consisting of circular pieces of plywood with four legs, and by the weight of the plastic explosives wedged around it. There was a matching cap on the top end like what a plumber would use to cap a pipe, with two holes drilled into it for the leads of a blasting cap. The two leads were spliced to a pair of wires that led to a hole drilled in the forward end of the trunk. The wires would lead under the car's seats and the carpet toward the dashboard, engine, and battery.

Stahl said, "Let's cut those leads."

Hines leaned into the trunk and clipped one of the wires with wire cutters, capped it, cut and capped the other, then stepped back.

The three looked at the structure, and then Stahl said, "The frame is anchored with screws to keep the charge vertical. But the guy didn't build the frame around the bomb. He prefitted it to the pipe, and after he built the bomb he just set the bomb down into it. I'll bet we could lift it straight up if we wanted to."

"Do we want to?" said Hines.

"Not yet. I'm a little more interested in the cone right now. It's just a steel cone with air inside and some kind of liner—probably copper, maybe tin and lead—but it's designed to focus the force of the blast straight downward through the pavement to the gasoline storage tanks. If the cone is built right, the liner will become a jet of molten metal and blow downward through the steel plates we put under the truck, the pavement, and a few feet of ground without any trouble."

"Should we take the cone off?" said Elliot. "If we take the cone away, the rest of it is just a bomb. If it goes off, it'll blow up unfocused, in all directions."

"True," said Stahl. "Removing it won't change much for us. Look at the size of the charge. But if the cone is gone, it's less likely to set off all that gasoline. We might be the only ones killed."

"I'll buy that," said Hines. "We'll take away most of his victims."

"We can't move the main charge like this unless we know what's meant to detonate it," said Stahl. "So let's do this without moving it."

Stahl said, "Slightly different method this time. Let's get some ice from the freezer in the station's store. We pack the outside of the tube with ice. We leave the bomb in its cradle to help keep it steady, and then saw the cone off. But first we drill the cone to be sure it really is there just to focus the blast, and there's nothing in it."

Elliot went into the store and brought back three bags of ice, but they didn't open them, because water from the melting could short-circuit any stray wires and set off the device. Hines was the one to drill into the cone. When she finished, they held the flexible camera up to the hole and looked in. Elliot said, "It's empty. All the action is upstairs."

Hines used the electric hacksaw to remove the cone. She picked it up, looked at the inner surface, and said, "Copper it is."

They cooled the outside surface with the ice bags, and then Stahl removed them and stared at the bomb. "You know, that end cap at the top looks like it might be threaded. Let's see if we can unscrew it."

"How?" asked Hines.

"You two hold the tube tight as you can, and I'll try to unscrew the cap."

The three assumed their positions, and Stahl tried to turn it.

"It won't budge," said Elliot.

Stahl leaned into the trunk to get his helmet's faceplate close to the end cap and ran his flashlight around the cap. "There's some residue here." He touched it with his finger. "It looks like epoxy. That could be part of what the guy spent seven point five seconds doing in the trunk. He didn't need seven seconds to flip a switch. He probably put epoxy on the rim of the tube to form a seal before he closed it."

Elliot said, "Once he had the tube packed and wired, he wouldn't want anybody to open it again."

Hines said, "What do you want to do?"

"I'll be right back." Stahl went to the truck and took the microphone. "This is Stahl."

"Yes, sir. What do you need?"

"I need to detonate a bomb in the Los Angeles River. It has to be close, within walking distance of this gas station."

"A bomb? In the river?"

"Yes. There's very little open space around here. We're in the middle of the city, and we have a bomb we'll need to detonate. The bomb is high explosive, and far too big and powerful to be transported in a containment vessel. I believe it has a fuze so sensitive that towing it will just convert the containment vessel into shrapnel. The riverbed is concrete, the sides are about twenty feet deep, and it's dry right now. That's the only place that makes much sense to me."

"I don't know. We'll have to get permission."

"Call Deputy Chief Ogden. Tell him what I want, and have him handle the permission. I just need the maintenance gate in the fence opened. Got it?"

"Yes, sir."

Two minutes later, David Ogden was on the radio. He said, "What's wrong with a robot? That's what a robot is for—to carry dangerous stuff."

Stahl said, "Dave, the main triggering device we found in the car was a mercury tilt switch. If we had moved the car, there wouldn't be much left of this neighborhood. The stuff we took out and the other team detonated seems to be homemade Semtex, and it all worked as well as the real thing. What we've got is a vertical tube, ten inches in diameter and over two feet long, filled with more Semtex. The cap on top is epoxied shut. What I think might be under there are a battery and a second mercury switch, placed there just for people like my team, who might be stupid enough to try to remove it."

"Okay. Wait for my call."

Stahl looked down from the cab and saw Hines and Elliot standing a few feet away. They had both removed their helmets, and their hair was drenched with sweat. They looked shocked, their eyes wide.

"What can we do?" said Hines.

"Help me rig a harness for the device. It should be in front of me, so the weight hangs on my shoulders, but not strapped tight. I'll need to use my hands to keep it level."

"We can use one of the backpacks for the straps and the body," said Hines. "We'll add a floor so the bomb can't shift."

Elliot said, "Boss, I'd like to be the one who does this."

"No," said Stahl.

"I'm younger and stronger."

"Better looking too," said Stahl. "But I'm older, and I outrank you by so much I can barely see you down there. So forget it and help me get ready."

Stahl got out of the driver's seat, went to the toolboxes along the side of the truck, and opened each until he found a carpenter's level. He held it up. "The secret weapon."

7

It was late afternoon now, and there was a procession moving north in the center of the empty pavement of Laurel Canyon Boulevard.

As in many parades, the first cars were four black-and-white patrol cars with their colored lights flashing. They went at the speed of a slow walk five hundred feet ahead of the procession. Two of them stopped across the blocked entrance ramps to the 101 Freeway and the others parked across the lanes beyond. The next vehicle was the Team One bomb unit truck towing a containment vessel behind it.

Then, about two hundred feet behind the Bomb Squad's truck, walked a single man wearing a harness made from a backpack that had once held a professional first aid kit. The spirit level was taped to the top of the rig, so the bubbles in the three glass tubes of the level were directly under his eyes as he walked.

He was five hundred feet ahead of the next pair of police cars. Behind them came a fire truck: a pumper that carried water and fire extinguishing chemicals. Next there were three ambulances, and after them, four more police cars. The whole procession was more than a block long, most of it shiny official vehicles with colored warning lights flashing.

The convoy to conduct Dick Stahl to the gate leading down to the concrete riverbed made a strange, dreamlike parade. All the police officers, firefighters, and paramedics in their powerful specialized vehicles were silent, rolling along before and behind the solitary walking figure of the man harnessed to the bomb. When Dick Stahl arrived at the station this morning he had been wearing a plain black sport coat, gray slacks, and casual walking shoes. Much of the day he had worn the heavy bomb suit. But now he wore his civilian shirt and slacks again. His clothes made him look like an outsider, maybe a penitent or a prisoner—certainly not a bomb expert. A man carrying fifty pounds of plastic explosives packed in a metal pipe was not going to be any safer wearing a protective suit.

Stahl moved with great care, his gait like a slow-motion version of the heel-and-toe steps of a tightrope walker, his eyes on the small glass tubes of the carpenter's level. Now and then he made minuscule adjustments in response to the positions of the bubbles in the tubes of the level.

Stahl had been the source of the neighborhood evacuation order before. He hoped nobody had been foolish enough to stay in any of the nearby wood-and-stucco apartment buildings to hide behind blinds or curtains and watch him make his walk. If this bomb were triggered, many of the buildings within five hundred feet—just where he would be close enough for an occupant to see him clearly—would be heavily damaged.

The explosives he'd seen seemed to be a form of Semtex. Factory-made Semtex had a detonation velocity of twenty-six thousand feet per second and at the explosion's center produced heat of three thousand degrees. These numbers renewed his alertness and his patience, two conflicting feelings. He used both to focus his concentration on keeping the bomb level.

Stahl could visualize the mercury tilt switch he believed had been placed under the cap of the device. It would be just like the first one they'd found earlier. There would be the glass tube, the shining slivery blob of mercury at the bottom, the two copper wires glued to the inside surface, connecting to a battery and to a blasting cap embedded in the explosive. He kept his eyes on the bubbles in the level as he walked.

Stahl reached the gate, which had been opened. It was a few yards past the wide bridge carrying the six lanes of Laurel Canyon Boulevard over the Los Angeles River. He had reached his first goal, but now he faced the most difficult steps, carrying the bomb down into the riverbed.

He paused at the gateway and looked down. He saw the bomb truck waiting in the concrete trough of the riverbed. Hines and Elliot had unhitched the containment vessel from the back of the truck and opened the lid of the vessel for him.

The other vehicles, the ones behind Stahl, were assuming their places, where they would not be in a direct line of fire if the bomb went off in the concrete channel. He looked at the ramp that led into the dry river. The ramp was wide enough for a dump truck to come down safely, but there were places where gravel or stray pebbles lay on the surface. He memorized them and the uneven spots, then took a deep breath and began to walk again.

He took each step so slowly that he imagined the people watching him must find it difficult even to detect his progress. He stopped occasionally to recheck the surface ahead, and then went on.

Finally, he was at the bottom of the ramp. He advanced two small steps and stopped to watch the bubbles before he took the third step down.

On solid, level pavement now, he walked steadily to the bomb containment vessel, where Hines and Elliot waited.

"Well done, boss," said Elliot. "Let me steady the bomb while Hines helps you out of the harness."

"Okay," he said. "Just keep your eye on the level."

Hines gently undid the clasps and lifted the rig, and Stahl slid the straps off his shoulders. Keeping the bomb vertical with Elliot's help, he said, "Have you got the rack inside to keep it from tilting?"

"Yes," Hines said. "I'll help steady it. You and Elliot can lift it and then lower it into the rack in the containment vessel. I'm going to count to three, and you'll both lift it slowly and together. Ready?"

"Yes."

"One. Two. Three."

Stahl and Elliot lifted the cylinder, moved it to the opening of the containment vessel, and lowered it into the bomb maker's wooden frame. They both held it there for a few seconds, not quite ready to call it safe. Then they released it and slowly withdrew their hands. Hines closed and latched the lid of the steel vessel.

Stahl closed his eyes, shrugged his shoulders a few times, and then laughed. "Nice job. Thank you both."

"Thank you, boss," said Hines. "We still have to detonate. Do you want me to put a charge in there to initiate it?"

"I think we need to know if we were right about the way it works," Stahl said. "Let's lay out a few hundred feet of rope. Then we'll attach it to the containment vessel and give it a tug."

The bomb truck had a rope on a reel near the rear doors. Elliot paid out rope as Hines drove along the riverbed. They came to the spot where the concrete LA River met the concrete bed of the Tujunga Wash and turned a corner. When they had gone another two hundred feet, they set the reel on the concrete surface of the wash and drove back to the containment vessel. They tied the rope to the tow hitch of the containment vessel, drove back, returned the reel to the truck, and then set the reel so it wouldn't turn. Stahl got on the radio.

"This is Bomb Squad Team One. We're ready to detonate the explosive device in the riverbed. We'd like to make our first attempt as soon as possible. Please alert all units in the vicinity of the river, and make sure they're clear of this area. The vessel is seven hundred feet east of Laurel Canyon Boulevard, near the spot where the Tujunga Wash meets the riverbed. Please advise when all units have responded."

In a moment they saw fire engines, ambulances, and police cars moving. From where they were they could see that the bridge was clear, Moorpark was empty, and Laurel Canyon to the south looked clear. Most of the official vehicles had gone north under the freeway overpass, where they couldn't be seen from below the street. Five minutes later, the ranking police officer on the scene, the North Hollywood captain, said, "The scene is clear and vehicles are blocking any access to your location. You may detonate at will."

"Roger." Stahl looked ahead at Hines in the driver's seat and Elliot in the seat beside her. "Are you both ready up there?"

"Ready," she said. "How do you want this to happen?"

"I think as soon as the vessel moves an inch, the detonation will be instantaneous. When I say 'fire in the hole,' drive and take up the slack at fifteen miles an hour. Start the engine and stand by. And put your ear protectors on."

Hines started the engine and the two fastened their seat belts, put their earphones on, and squared their backs against their seats.

Stahl said, "This is Bomb Squad Team One. We will attempt to detonate in five seconds." He waited five seconds and then announced into the radio: "Fire in the hole. Fire in the hole." He put on his ear protectors and sat back in his seat.

Hines drove, accelerating as she went. When they ran out of rope, they never felt the drag, or had time to see the rope snap taut. Instead, there was a deafening roar, and a shock wave that rose from the earth beneath the concrete and bounced their truck on its springs. They felt the shock in their bellies, like a punch.

Hines let the truck coast for a moment, holding the steering wheel straight, then braked to a full stop. She looked over her shoulder at Stahl. "Yep. Another mercury rocker switch."

Stahl said, "The battery and the rest of the circuit were all under the cap where we couldn't get at them. We'll have to make sure everyone knows he does that."

8

The maker watched the idiotic report on the eleven o'clock news. The commentary from the reporters was so ill informed and full of false authority that hearing it was like listening to a child trying to repeat an adult conversation he'd overheard from a distance.

The bomb maker muted the television set. He had no need of the report even if it had been accurate. He knew the mechanisms found in the car because he had built them.

But seeing the odd procession of vehicles with the one man carrying the shaped charge like a baby in a sling amused him a little. He wondered if that man had known exactly how sensitive the mercury switch had been, and how close he had been to becoming a whiff of smoke. Watching that one man walk alone down the street followed at a safe, cowardly distance by the enormous trucks and heavily armed cops made him laugh. What a fool that man was.

He was mesmerized and ecstatic watching the footage of the explosion when they detonated his device. There was a terrific blast that sent fragments of the containment vessel and pieces of shrapnel up and outward. The bomb technicians had turned his shaped charge into a standard bomb before they set it off, so the twenty-foot-deep concrete trench of the dry riverbed had caught the punishment. That was too bad, but the explosives had been great. He pressed the reverse button to watch the explosion again and again, slowing it down and watching objects in the background, the movement of the flying metal, the cracking of the concrete walls of the river.

The pictures of the windows blown inward in the buildings on Laurel Canyon and Moorpark Street, the bottles and cans shaken off shelves in the stores along Ventura Boulevard, and the incidental, comical things that had been swept over by the force of the blast—a few trees along the river, a stop sign, a couple of fences, some tables with umbrellas, a row of parked cars—delighted him.

When the reporter interviewed the locals about their reactions to his device, he couldn't resist turning the volume up. Several people said they thought it had been an earthquake. They were from Los Angeles, so everything big and scary felt like an earthquake to them. Two of them thought a missile had hit nearby, and another thought a house with a gas leak had blown up.

Listening to these people lightened his mood. And even the fact that there had been no casualties didn't depress him much. His car bomb had tied up a bomb team for a whole day, held thousands of cars in traffic for about nine hours, dominated the national news, and made the entire country aware that Los Angeles had a problem. And whether the general public knew it or not, the Bomb Squad knew they had survived only by making lucky guesses about twenty times in a row. Only one day ago he had killed half the LA Bomb Squad. He'd accomplished the largest police kill-off in history.

And today, just like yesterday, everything had worked. His plastic explosives hadn't been manufactured by a company in the Czech Republic. He had made the whole supply himself—over two hundred pounds—and it had been as good as the factory-made version. It was stable, easy to detonate, powerful, uniform, and reliable.

He had made the PETN with nitric acid, pentaerythritol, lye, and acetone—measuring, mixing, cooling, heating, and filtering. He had fabricated the RDX crystals and crushed the two mixtures into powder with a wooden rolling pin and mixed them in a jar. Breaking them down and combining them any other way would have detonated them. He had made a paste of the powder with petroleum jelly, shaped the explosive paste into bricks, and wrapped them, leaving them to solidify further like bread in baking pans until he needed them.

Making the plastic explosive successfully had liberated him. He didn't need anybody to make him powerful. He could make his perfect weapon himself. There were many men who had attempted these same procedures—mixing and agitating these highly explosive compounds to combine their power—who had died in the process.

He had built his own mercury switches to set off the shaped charge. During the day he had wondered if he had somehow botched the switches. But then, when the bomb technicians detonated the bomb by moving the containment vessel, he knew his workmanship wasn't the problem. Still, he resolved to start using more ready-made components to avoid uncertainty. Mercury switches could be purchased, or he could take one from any of a number of junked machines—the trunk-lid lights and braking systems of cars built before 2003, the anti-tilt mechanisms in vending machines and pinball machines.

He had also built in other ways of producing an explosion in a car bomb. He had connected the blasting caps in the bricks of Semtex to the car's mechanical and electrical switches so they would complete a circuit if any one of several things happened—lifting the trunk lid, opening a door, starting the engine, turning on a light, stepping on the brake pedal. But the bomb technicians had resisted doing any of those things and evaded his traps.

He hadn't needed ready-made blasting caps, really. He was good at making initiators too. They could be very simple—two wires soldered to the inner sides of a spent bullet casing, a small amount of explosive material between them—black powder or fulminate of mercury, maybe, and then a seal at the end. He had once even used a small Christmas lightbulb with the tip ground off so he could fill it with acetone peroxide and seal it again. All it took was a nine-volt charge to set it off.

But he wasn't experimenting to amuse himself now. He was making bombs to kill people, so using homemade components was just vanity. That was why he had switched to using commercially made blasting caps. They were reliable and safe. They always required a current of 0.25 amp to set them off, not more—and even more important, not less. And he could use a variety of different power sources to produce that current.

He had plenty of blasting caps. Only a few months ago he'd taken a trip to replenish his supply. A person had to fill out Form 5400 and have a blaster's license to buy them, so it was much safer to get them in other ways. He had begun by searching for trained and certified blasters who might need money.

Many blasters worked in coal mines. A few Internet searches gave him a list of coal mines that had closed in the past year or two. There were some in Boone County in western Kentucky; some in Wyoming County, West Virginia; and some in Knox and Pike counties, in Indiana.

He searched the online newspapers from coal-mining counties. He found his first three prospects by looking at ads placed by people offering themselves for employment. He found three more by looking up "blasting services"—road clearing, stump removal, demolition. They had clearly tried using their best skills on a freelance basis, but he was almost certain there couldn't be enough work for the number of blasters living there now that the mines had closed.

When he had ten names of men who had placed ads saying they had blasting licenses and recent coal-mining experience, he flew east and drove into West Virginia. He started with a man named Carl Mazur, who lived in Wyoming County. He called Mazur and met him at a diner.

Mazur was a big man in his forties who wore a flannel shirt, Carhartt canvas work pants, and a pair of steel-toed boots to the meeting, so he looked like a lumberjack. He handed the bomb maker a neatly typed résumé when they sat down. The bomb maker glanced at it only long enough to see the blaster's license and said, "I'll read this later. Right now is our chance to talk." Then he put the résumé into his briefcase and said, "How do you find yourself out of work?"

Mazur explained that the Dall River Mine had closed. He said the closing of the mine had been a gradual process. The number of tons shipped had been decreasing for years, and according to the company, so had the profit margin. Closing down had been discussed vaguely from time to time, but then it was brought up one year during contract negotiations. Many miners had insisted it was a hoax, a trick to get them to work for less. In the end, the union tried to save the jobs for a few more years by giving in on health insurance and pensions. All that accomplished was to give the owners a chance to slip in new clauses to make it easier to lay off everybody, starting with the men who had black lung or silicosis or cancer.

The bomb maker nodded in sympathy, then made his proposal. He said he was a successful developer who had planned to make more money by buying up some wild land in Missouri and building gated housing developments. In order to get started, he would need to clear and level several thousand-acre parcels and build access roads. The land was high and rocky, but beautiful and surrounded by thick forests. Three of the parcels even had lakes on them. The blasting job was big, and would probably take six months to a year. He offered to pay Mazur his regular fee plus an additional fifty percent bonus for working out of state.

Mazur asked, "Would I be an employee of your company?"

"Not unless you want to be. It's always suited me fine if somebody wanted to be an independent contractor. That gives you a chance to get paid by the job, not the hour. I just want your assurance that you won't be careless and endanger my men."

"What kind of explosives are we talking about?" said Mazur.

"It's basically a dynamite job. But I figure nearly all of these blasts can be done with nitrate fertilizer mixed with motor oil and set off with blasting caps. We have men to drill the holes for you wherever you say and clear the rock away after. I'll leave the blasting details up to you, but we'd like to keep the costs down. We have investors, and once they hand me their money they start asking when payday is going to be."

Mazur nodded. "I'll do it."

"Does your résumé have all the information I need? Your blaster's license number and your contact phones and everything?"

"Yep," said Mazur. They made a handshake agreement and the bomb maker gave Mazur twenty thousand dollars to start ordering the supplies he would need to clear the first parcels. Then he gave Mazur one of the business cards he'd made for this trip and they parted in the parking lot.

After a couple of weeks, Mazur called the cell phone number on the card and said he was nearly ready. He had purchased most of the supplies he would need.

The bomb maker arranged to meet him in a place called Little Blank Lake, Missouri, in four days. He said he had hired a crew to work on the clearance, and they would get started that Monday on the first parcel.

They met on a remote forest road on Sunday at noon to look the place over. The bomb maker chatted with Mazur about the project and waited until Mazur took out a key and opened the lock on the big built-in storage box on the left side of his pickup. Then he raised his pistol toward the back of Mazur's head and shot him. The bullet went through and emerged from Mazur's forehead, spattering the white truck with bright red blood.

Shooting Mazur had been a gamble, but he liked to make these small bets with himself about how people would behave in response to a stimulus he'd provided. If he'd been wrong, his penalty would have been to start over again on another licensed blaster. This time he had been right. When he looked inside the big storage box, he found the whole space was neatly packed with new boxes of number eight blasting caps. In the storage box along the other side of the truck bed were reels of insulated wire, a blasting generator, a multimeter, and a toolbox with insulated wire cutters, gloves, wire strippers, and connectors. A hard hat, ear protectors, goggles, one box of dynamite, and four more boxes of blasting caps took up the rest of the truck.

He left everything but the blasting caps, the dynamite, the money Mazur had left from the twenty thousand dollars he had given him, and the business card he had printed with the name of an imaginary developer.

9

Dick Stahl lay on the couch and closed his eyes to ease his headache. He had been too tense, too alert for too many hours. He had spent the time since disarming the car bomb going over all the information he could collect about the two booby-trapped sites of the past two days.

The trap at the house in Encino that killed Tim Watkins, Del Castillo, and the dozen others had not been an attempt to harm the house's owner. It had been a way of luring as many bomb technicians as possible to one site and murdering them. The man who had called the 911 line was either the bomber or someone working for the bomber. Stahl knew a bomber called the police only if he was trying to kill the police officers who would respond.

The car bomb today had been a second attempt to wipe out cops. Chaining the car to the pumps was a sign to the gas station manager that something was going on that was beyond him, and he should call the police. The owners of the gas station in Studio City and the house in Encino had no connection and nothing in common. The two common elements were the police and the bomber.

He had listened to the recorded 911 call that had summoned the fourteen to their deaths and watched the video of the man delivering the packed car to the gas station. Both the caller and the video image were unidentifiable, but the evidence did indicate that this was probably a single man, not a group of conspirators. In his experience, terror bombings usually worked this way. There was a single person, usually male and over thirty, who conceived the idea and made the bomb. If there were a second person, he or she drove the explosive-packed car and parked it in a marketplace or in front of a government building, or wore the explosives on his body, or left the briefcase on the crowded floor of the station, or buried the IED in the middle of the dirt road. This time there was no sign of a second person, and there was no hint of why the lone man wanted to do this.

Stahl had spent years studying explosive devices. He couldn't think of a single instance of anything resembling these two incidents. Everything was contradictory. The devices themselves were a mixture of the crude and the sophisticated, the rudimentary and the complex.

The bomber seemed to be an amateur. He had made his own mercury rocker switches, and appeared to have made his own explosive charges. To Stahl this meant the bomber had no access to ready-made materials. On the other hand, only a few professionals were able to make such powerful high explosives. Military demolition people—no matter how deep undercover—seldom had a need to learn practical chemistry well enough to produce explosives from scratch. The al-Qaeda operative who made the shoe bombs and the underwear bomb had been reduced to using peroxide explosives, which were much easier to make than military plastic, but far less safe to work with, and less effective.

Having an unknown enemy in Los Angeles able to make his own C-4 or Semtex was a disaster. This one understood methods like using shaped charges to penetrate hardened targets, and imploding buildings with dozens of small charges. Stahl had consulted the ATF's list of recent bomb incidents and found nothing remotely like what he'd seen at the gas station, or what had killed the men in Encino.

Stahl had not been ready for this. The rescue in Mexico had been a catastrophic case of overconfidence that he'd survived only through ferocity. Before he even had time to catch his breath, there was Dave Ogden.

It actually crossed his mind that Ogden had come at the head of a squad of cops to arrest him and extradite him to Mexico for murder. Instead, Ogden had come to ask him for a favor that might, ultimately, be worse. And he could not refuse.

Ogden had been a sergeant when Stahl came out of the police academy. He had been assigned as training officer during Stahl's probationary period. Because Stahl had enlisted in the army about the time Ogden became a cop, they were almost the same age in spite of the difference in ranks. Ogden had been fair, and Ogden had taught him about police work. Other supervisors had done those things too.

What had made the difference was one late night in the north Valley. Ogden and Stahl drove past a shipping warehouse in Northridge, and Stahl saw a moving light under a garage door. They drove around the property and found a spot near the back where the chain-link fence had been cut and rolled up in both directions. The barbed wire at the top had been removed and tossed into a nest of coils nearby.

Ogden and Stahl went through the breach on foot and saw a dozen men taking cases of liquor out of the back of a big semi and setting them on the tarmac nearby. Rather than attempting to steal the truck, they were loading its cargo into a line of vans, SUVs, and pickups. Ogden called for backup and waited, but someone had already spotted the police car. In less than a minute, the small trucks had begun to pull out through the hole in the fence onto a side street and accelerate onto the boulevard to escape.

Three SUVs pulled up near the police car—one behind, one in front, and one to the side. They found the police car was empty, so they kept coming. They swept the area outside the fence, and then pulled in through the opened section of fence. Ogden and Stahl retreated toward the warehouse for cover, but the first shots were fired before they could reach it. Within the next three minutes, Ogden had been wounded in the leg, and Stahl was using up their supply of ammunition trying to keep the attackers' heads down on the other side of the lot. Then, without warning, Ogden drew a .380 backup pistol from his ankle holster and fired over Stahl's shoulder. The man who had crept up behind Stahl to kill him fell dead. Other police units arrived in another three minutes, too late to affect the outcome.

He knew that when David Ogden came to his office he'd had mostly noble motives. But there had been a little bit of self-protection too. As of this morning Ogden couldn't be held responsible for whatever happened next. Nobody could blame him, because he had immediately brought in a former commander of the Bomb Squad, and turned the problem over to him.

On the way home from the station this evening Stahl had already heard a radio news report giving him credit for outsmarting the car bomber. That was unspeakably stupid. Moving a bomb and detonating it didn't defeat the bomber. The bomber was fine. He wasn't in custody, nobody knew anything about him, and he was probably busy building his next bomb right now.

While Stahl had been at the scene the mayor had apparently been interviewed and given his amateur diagnosis of the bomber as "insane, mentally ill."

In Stahl's experience, men like this bomber never showed any sign whatever that they were mentally ill. They looked like anybody else. They exerted great self-control. They had to obtain substances and devices that were hard to find, hard to buy, and hard to use. They were patient and careful. They had to be the ones who weren't noticed, weren't seen, and weren't remembered.

And this one scared Stahl. He wasn't sending out grandiose messages or threats. He hadn't issued demands. If he had a plan, it was hard to figure out what it was. Stahl was sure he was actively trying to kill off bomb technicians, but why? And what did he have in mind after that?

Stahl knew he couldn't sleep. He wanted a drink to loosen his muscles, get rid of his tension headache, and make his eyelids heavy. But if the next call came tonight he would still be under the influence. He had to endure whatever his mind did to him tonight. He was in a fight.

His cell phone rang and he looked at the display. He didn't recognize the number, but he had moved into a new environment today, so it could be anyone. "Stahl," he said.

The voice was female. "Hi, boss. This is Diane Hines. You're not asleep."

"Apparently you're not either."

"No. I tried taking a hot bath until my fingers and toes got all wrinkled and the water got cold. I tried watching television, but they kept interrupting my sitcoms and showing us at the gas station and the riverbed. You have any ideas?"

"I'm surprised you're asking me."

"You're my team supervisor. It's your job to get your troops through."

"What I'd normally recommend in these situations is to have a glass of single malt scotch to take away the agitation and relax the tension. But that only makes sense when the danger is over."

"The danger is over for tonight. I don't know if they had the rule when you were still working, but neither of us is supposed to go on another call for the next shift."

"I doubt that applies now. We're too short staffed." He paused. "By the way, I don't know if I had the presence of mind to say this earlier, but you and Elliot did a terrific job today. You're smart, you have great self-discipline and composure, and I was proud to work with you."

"What a nice thing to say. Thank you."

"I'll write it down and put it in your files tomorrow."

"Thanks. But I was hoping the next thing you'd say was that you were inviting me over for that drink. I kind of need to talk."

"I don't think that's a good idea. I'm your commanding officer, at least for now. If you were with Elliot, then it could be a team meeting, but—"

"Not likely. Elliot is married, has two kids, and doesn't drink."

"Diane," he said. "You know there are police regulations about conduct between us."

"Of course. Do you think any female cop doesn't have Police Regulation 271 memorized? But this is an exception. I'm scared shitless. I could die tomorrow. And you told us all you're just filling in for a while. I'm not worried that your two-week second career in police work is going to be ruined by having a drink with me. Are you?"

"To be honest, no. I'm not."

"And you have a security company that must pay really well, judging from what your condo is worth."

"How do you know what my condo costs?"

"I have a good eye, and I know the neighborhood," Diane said. "I'm in my car sitting outside your window. I've been watching you pacing in there while we've been talking."

"If you're already here, then you might as well come in."

She walked up the steps to the high iron security gate and looked into the camera while he buzzed her in. Then she climbed the steps to the steel security door that had been shaped and colored to look like wood. She reached up to knock on his door, but Stahl opened it first.

She stepped inside and he closed the door behind her. Diane Hines didn't look much like the woman he had seen in uniform today. She was wearing a gray skirt and black silk blouse that might have seemed plain except the fitted cut emphasized her breasts and thin waist.

"You look very nice in civilian clothes," he said.

"Everybody looks fat in a bomb suit." She smiled at him, reached into the oversize bag she carried, and pulled out a bottle.

"Macallan," he said. "Very thoughtful of you." He didn't take the bottle. "Come in and sit." He pointed at the couch. She walked over and sat, then watched him take two glasses from a cupboard and an identical bottle of Macallan Scotch from a cabinet. "This one's already open. Ice? Water?"

"About an inch of ice, please."

He prepared her drink and poured one for himself. He brought them to the couch and set hers on the coffee table in front of her where she could reach it. Then he sat in the armchair across from the couch and lifted his glass. "To the duds."

"To the duds," she said.

"You said you wanted to talk?"

"I think I said I *needed* to talk. I'm sorry to come here like this, but it was kind of inevitable after today. If you hadn't tagged along on that call, I'd be dead. When I got home I watched that explosion in the riverbed about forty times, and it scared me even more each time." She took a sip of her drink.

"It was a big charge," he said. "You must have known it would be at the start. Nobody needs a car to deliver a pipe bomb."

"It's that retroactive feeling that got to me tonight," she said. "You can do what you have to do at the time. Some combination of training and focus and caution gets you through. But later you start to shiver and feel weird and feel panicky, and you look for ways to get back to normal. As I was thinking about that a few hours ago I noticed I had developed an interest in seeing you."

"So you came over for a drink. It was probably the right thing to do. A drink and a talk will probably help us both work through what happened today and yesterday."

"I think so," she said. "You're a reassuring presence."

"I cultivate that for my business," he said. "I make faces in front of the mirror until I hit on one that will make people think I'm the guy who can solve their problems. It makes them pay my outrageous fees."

Diane laughed and they both sipped their drinks and set them down at the same time. Diane took a deep breath and then started again. "Here's my problem. When I was working with you today, I was doing things—cutting steel, disconnecting circuits, moving explosives, searching for signs of tampering or components that didn't belong. But I was just an extra set of hands for you. I wasn't doing the thinking. You were. I could see right away that you knew things Elliot and I didn't. I need to know those things. I could tell today that my life depends on it. This guy has hit two days in a row. I don't think he's going away."

Stahl shrugged. "I think I know what you're feeling. You haven't seen anything quite like the one today. And yesterday was pure horror—friends and teammates killed for no apparent reason. We lost people who were part of our lives. If I tell somebody a funny story, there's a good chance one of those fourteen guys made it up. Whenever I remember the years I spent on the force, some of those faces will be part of the picture in my mind. And today you did what you were supposed to, but it cost you. It might take you a little while to get past the shock and the loss. If you need a couple of extra days to recover, I'll do my best to get them for you."

"That's a lot to ask of you, and it's not what I want."

"I'm trying to be a reassuring presence," he said. "How do I do that?"

"I think you've figured out some things about this bomber. Tell me."

He took another sip. "Judging from the surveillance tapes, he works alone. He wasn't sent by some foreign government that supplies him with factory-made explosives or sophisticated gear. The house in Encino was initiated by a photographer's intervalometer he could have bought at a good camera store, and the car was full of homemade switches and explosives. The devices at the Encino house made me realize that what he intended was to kill bomb technicians. That was all his complicated trap was good for. So today I guessed that the next device I saw was going to be an attempt to get rid of a few more of us. That meant each component would be designed to mislead and deceive a technician."

"So what are we supposed to do with that information?" she said.

"Don't think in terms of devices made to kill some guy's enemy as he checks his mailbox one morning. This is not about civilian victims. It's about predicting what a trained bomb technician will do to render the device safe, and turn that action into a trigger. You have to think about the logical procedure you would usually follow with his device, and then dismiss that option and think of some other way around the triggers he might have built in."

"That explains something," she said. "Part of what shook me today was that sometimes I thought I knew what to do, and you kept choosing the opposite, and each time that turned out to be right. I guess what I want you to say next is that it's going to be okay, and we're going to be able to handle whatever this guy is dreaming up right now, arrest him, and walk away."

"I'm going to try," he said. "I'm confident you will too." He shrugged. "It's a great advantage to have somebody on the team who's got small hands, thin arms, flexible joints, and a quick brain."

They talked for a long time about the events of the day, going over each component they had found in the car and the decision Stahl had made about how to circumvent or neutralize it, and what other choices there had been.

Later their talk turned to fighting back—the various items they had found and saved, the images that had been preserved on surveillance video, and all of the other paths that could lead to the identification of the bomb maker. Stahl said, "At the Encino house everything got destroyed. But we bought ourselves some chances today. At the gas station nothing got destroyed except the explosives. We have everything else he brought to the scene."

At midnight he said, "It's getting kind of late. Are you okay to drive home? If you're not, I have a guest room."

"I could drive, but I don't want to."

"You're sure?"

"I'm sure. I'm not sleepy. I'll even make you breakfast before I take off."

He went back to the kitchen counter, brought back the bottle, refilled their glasses, and set the bottle on the coffee table. Then he sat down in the armchair again.

"Why over there?" she said. "You're not going to make this easy for me, are you?"

"What?"

"You know. Getting you interested."

"I was interested as soon as I met you, but I figured I could wait until only one of us was still a cop. I sat here so I could see you better. I like watching your eyes. They're beautiful."

She sipped her drink. "I know. I have a really cute body, too. I think it's from the stuff they make you do in the academy. I've been doing the workouts ever since." She held him with her eyes. "You know, I think I've talked enough for now. Have you?"

"For now. Would you like to finish your drink in the bedroom?" he said.

"At last. An invitation that came from you."

10

Stahl opened his eyes. The curtains dimmed the room, but he knew the world was light beyond them. He heard the shower come on, and then he thought about the way the night had ended. He let his hand run along the top of the sheet beside him, even though he knew where she was.

He reached in the opposite direction and picked up his phone from the bedside table. It was six o'clock. The shifts would change at eight. There were no missed calls on the screen, but there were plenty of other things—e-mails, tweets, text messages. He scanned the names and knew he was free to ignore them. They were reporters and acquaintances, and one text from Valerie, saying only that she was glad he had made it through the car bomb, and that the check from Mrs. Glover had cleared. None of them were police business except a reminder from his new assistant, Andy, about the police funeral at eleven.

The door to the bathroom swung open and there stood Diane Hines, naked, twisting her hair into a professional-looking bun. Her eyes focused on Stahl's. "What?" she said. "There's nothing you haven't seen several times, close up."

"I was wondering if my luck would hold."

She lifted the edge of the sheet, slipped into the bed, and slid to the middle beside him. She put her arm over his chest and kissed him. "Yes."

Then she said, "But right now we've got to get ready for work. I remember promising I'd make breakfast. While you get your shower and dress, I'll do it." She swung her feet off the bed and stood again.

He said, "The memorial service is this morning at eleven and I don't have a new police uniform yet." He got out of bed.

She turned toward the hallway. "I'm sure you have a nice dark suit."

"Hey," he said. "Aren't you going to ask me if there's anything I don't like?"

"If you don't like it, why would you have it in your kitchen?"

"Good point. See you in a few minutes." As she started to move again he pulled her back and held her for a few seconds, kissing her one last time.

"No hurry," she said. "I can be late. I'm screwing the boss."

He released her.

"I am, right?" she said. "If I came to your door some other night after work, you wouldn't lock your paranoid locks and gates and pretend you're not home?"

"Never. If you still want to face the risk now that you're sober."

"I'll take the chance. As you said, in a couple of weeks only one of us will still be a cop."

"So come back tonight." He walked toward the bathroom.

"I will." The door closed. She whispered, "If we're both still alive."

When she heard the shower she went back into the bedroom and put on the clothes she'd left there. Then she stepped into the living room and picked up the unopened bottle of Scotch on the coffee table and went to the kitchen to see what he had in his refrigerator.

Within a few minutes she had the table set, eggs and bacon cooking on the stove, bread in the slots of the toaster, and fresh-ground coffee burbling through the filter.

Stahl came out of the bedroom in a black suit that was too good and too expensive for a cop to wear to work. He looked into his kitchen, saw the food, sniffed the smells, and said, "Thank you, Diane. This is wonderful."

When they finished eating breakfast, Stahl sat back drinking coffee. "How do you want to handle work? Do you want to be moved to another team?"

She shrugged. "No. I'll go in my car and you go in yours. We spend our shift doing our jobs. Neither of us drops a clue about us to anyone. We go home. When I get cleaned up and feel human again I'll give you a call."

"That will do."

"I'd better get to work. Can you handle the dishes?"

"I can put them in the dishwasher and start it."

"That'll do. See you later. Now push the buttons on your console so I can get out of the cell block."

He went to the door with her. "I want you to know I designed the security for this building, and I'm proud of it."

"You must have some amazing enemies."

"I do," he said. "And if you keep hanging out with me, so will you."

11

When Dick Stahl reached the First Street headquarters, Andy had a message for him. The Encino bomb murders had been assigned to Homicide Special. They were meeting to develop strategies for solving the case, and Stahl had been summoned.

Stahl was not surprised that the case had gone to the elite Homicide Special section. The murder of fourteen cops in a fraction of a second was a national tragedy, and the department would do everything possible to ensure that nothing like it ever happened again.

When Stahl was a cop, headquarters had been in the old Parker Center. The new headquarters had been completed since he left, so he was not yet familiar with the building. He walked to the Robbery-Homicide Division and asked the first plainclothes cop he saw where the Homicide Special section was. He could have walked to it with his eyes closed in Parker Center. The plainclothes cop saw Stahl's captain's badge at his belt and stood up. "This is the right office, sir. Whom can I get you?"

"I'm Dick Stahl, Bomb Squad. I got invited to a meeting with Homicide."

The cop said, "I thought I recognized you from television. I'll take you."

He led Stahl into an open mezzanine and up to a conference room door. He opened it and stepped inside, then returned with another detective with a captain's badge and a white shirt.

The captain held out his hand. He was a few inches shorter than Stahl, with expertly barbered black hair and the broad shoulders and thin waist of a wrestler, as though as a young man he had built muscles to make up for his short stature. "I'm Bart Almanzo. Welcome back to the force. You had a hell of a first day yesterday."

"I'm glad you got the case." Stahl was sincere. Homicide Special included the best homicide detectives in the department, whoever they happened to be at the moment, and the best was what this case deserved. "Some of those guys were friends of mine, and others were technicians I hired. How can I help?"

Almanzo said, "We're having a meeting to share the first technical reports on the bombing, and if you're able to spare the time, we want to hear anything you'd like to say."

"I'll tell you the little I know so far."

They stepped inside and Stahl saw a dozen plainclothes officers in white shirts and ties, some wearing shoulder holsters and others wearing their weapons on their belts. The conference table was crowded with laptop computers, file folders, densely printed papers, and enlarged photographs. There were four women, two more than there would have been years ago when he'd last met with Homicide Special. Otherwise they looked about the same—cops in the middle of their careers, people who had learned a great deal and were ready for the next thing.

Almanzo said, "Captain Stahl, would you like to start?"

"All right. Here's my interpretation of what I've seen. The surveillance tapes from yesterday's attempted bombing make me think this is one man who works alone, not a political or religious group. This bomb maker is good. He has a sure hand and a very sophisticated sense of what a bomb technician is likely to look for and how he'll go about making the bomb safe. That argues for some experience. He's not at a point in his life where he can get military explosives—C-4 or Semtex. He's had to make his own. That adds to my impression that he's working alone."

Stahl looked at the detectives, who were paying close attention. "That's very bad news, because it makes him more independent and more dangerous. We think the explosive he's been using is a homemade version of Semtex. Making it is a tricky task, because the main part of the formula is to mix two already powerful explosives, RDX and PETN. Since he can't buy either of them, he must be making them. But because the ingredients are not perfectly controlled, he can make an unlimited supply. If an ingredient becomes scarce, he can simply move back a step in the process and make the components of the ingredient."

"What do you suggest we look at first?"

"He used number eight commercial blasting caps for his car bomb. We took some out unexploded, so they can probably be traced to a source using model numbers and lot numbers. I don't imagine tracing will lead directly to him, but it may give us something else—a licensed contact, a supplier. The car he left at the station has to have a history. He either bought it or stole it from somebody. He was all over it, touching many parts of it to turn it into a bomb. If we're really lucky he might even have left a fingerprint. His switches are often the simplest kinds of devices to complete a circuit—wires attached to metallic surfaces that will connect for an instant if a door is closed or a spring is released or a button is pressed. But one thing he really loves is a mercury tilt switch. He knows we don't want to defuse any bombs. What we want to do with a bomb is move it away from a populated area and detonate it. A mercury switch means that trying to move it will kill you."

"Is he military trained?"

"I don't know. There are signs he's self-taught. His designs are eccentric, made for a single use on a single day. He's good at improvising. He likes to build in redundancies like backup switches and separate charges, so a bomb will have several ways to detonate. That tendency is often part of the amateur mentality. Think of the guys who send mail bombs. The amateurs overwrap them. You know. It would look just like a normal package but it has layers and layers of tape around it. But it's too early to assume this guy is untrained. He might be doing some of this to point investigators away from himself."

"Could this man be a former Bomb Squad member who has a grudge?"

Stahl shrugged. "I can't rule it out yet. I would definitely take a look at a rejected applicant who was angry, or a person who has served time for planting a bomb or possessing explosives in Los Angeles. It won't hurt to look at the lists of men and women who have been in the FBI bomb tech school at Redstone, Alabama, or Fort Lee, Virginia, particularly if they washed out. But first I'd look at people who have been through demolition school in a foreign military service. An American graduate might make C-4, because he's used to handling it. A graduate from some other country might make Semtex for the same reason. Semtex was bought and used by all of the former Communist countries, the Irish Republican Army, and terrorist states like Libya. You might say any country where soldiers were issued Kalashnikov rifles probably used Semtex for demolition."

"Any indication of what he's trying to accomplish?" Almanzo asked.

"He made a phone call to report the rigged house in Encino. There was no reason to report his own bomb unless he wanted bomb technicians to come to the scene. I think chaining the car to the gas pumps yesterday was also intended to lure bomb technicians to a trap. If what he wants is to kill every bomb technician, he's halfway to total success already." He paused for a second. "We're losing. I can honestly say that my own team of three is about as good as any bomb team I've ever seen. But it's unlikely we would be able to pull off what we did yesterday a second time. This bomb maker knows that, and he'll keep giving us opportunities to fail."

The homicide detectives looked shocked. There was a brief silence while they stared at Stahl. Almanzo said, "Do you have a plan?"

"I'm hoping we'll get reinforcements from the FBI and ATF, but they're not going to be any better than the technicians we already have. Their presence is welcome, and they'll give me a chance to keep my teams from getting exhausted and making mistakes. But some of the reinforcements won't have served here before, and learning to be a good LA cop takes longer than training to be a competent bomb tech. Our only possible strategy is to try to keep this guy from killing us as long as we can."

Almanzo said, "We've been told that often bomb experts can recognize a bomb maker's work. Any chance some bomb squad in some other city has seen this guy before?"

"It's made national news and no agency has called. I spent part of last night looking through the ATF's summary descriptions of explosive-related crimes, but there's nothing listed that's remotely like this guy's work. I went back about ten years."

There was a buzz and Stahl looked at the screen of his phone. "That's my alarm."

Almanzo looked at his watch. "I guess that's all we can cover for now." He reached to the back of his chair for his coat. "Anybody else who's going to the funeral, it's time. The rest of you, keep at it."

Stahl drove to Forest Lawn alone and joined the mourners already assembled. There were a large number of civilians who continued to arrive for a long time—fourteen dead men had many friends and relatives—and the police presence was overwhelming. There were contingents from various parts of the state, and even from a few other states that touched California on the north and east.

Parked on a single winding piece of pavement were a dozen news vans with satellite dishes on booms, and camera people recording with telephoto lenses.

Stahl had been present at too many funerals of men in uniform—men who had served with him in the army, police officers who had died chasing getaway cars in LA traffic, victims of shootings. They had become almost interchangeable to him, casualties of battles that seemed to be parts of one struggle. During the previous evening he looked at the photographs taken at the scene in the hope that his practiced eye would see something new, but they were the same as what he'd seen in Iraq and Afghanistan and other places. High explosive shock waves tore people apart and heat burned them. He recognized a couple of the victims as old friends, but there was little to be learned from this horror that he hadn't already known.

Stahl listened to the words of the chaplain, the several priests, and the ministers who were there to represent their versions of God. He listened to the mayor and the police chief. His cell phone was in his shirt pocket. He was aware it might vibrate with an incoming call related to a new bomb threat at any time and felt relief with each passing minute when it didn't.

He had scanned the ranks of uniformed police officers in the cemetery when he arrived, but he didn't spot Diane Hines. She was probably somewhere in the rows behind him. The fourteen technicians who had not been at the Encino house would all be sitting together.

When the ceremonial talk ended, a police honor guard fired the customary rifle salute, and a lone bagpiper played a sad, wailing tune from a few yards higher on the hillside that looked out over the flat valley below. Stahl waited for the final prayer to end and turned to look behind him. He saw her about fifty feet away with Elliot and Team Three and Team Four. She looked very solemn and beautiful. Her eyes never glanced in his direction as she pivoted and walked along the row of chairs with the others.

At that moment his phone began to vibrate in his breast pocket. He saw the number was his office, and he moved off quickly to be able to talk.

As he hurried toward the road where his car was parked he called Andy. "This is Stahl."

"Second team is out on a suspicious package call, but Sergeant McCrary, the supervisor, just called to talk to you. He said he's got something."

"Can you connect me?"

"Yes. Hold on."

When he heard the connection go through he said, "This is Stahl. What have you got, Sarge?"

McCrary said, "A pipe bomb. It was left outside the front door of the women's health building at Kaplan and Steers in Van Nuys this morning. It looked like a routine delivery, but when a security guard went to pick it up, the box was just an empty cover slipped over the bomb. When he ran inside to get something to keep people from touching it, the phone was already ringing at the front desk. It was a guy warning him he had five minutes to clear the building."

"Did he?"

"Hell yes. He got everybody to go outside like it was a fire drill."

"Why did the bomber call?" asked Stahl.

"What do you mean?"

"The pipe bomb was right outside the front door, right? The guard lifted the cardboard box and saw there was a pipe bomb under it. The bomber knew one of two things was going to happen: either the guard would blow himself up or he'd know what it was."

"Yes," said McCrary.

"So why call?"

"Maybe the guy wanted to scare people, but didn't want to kill them, or lost his nerve, or just changed his mind. I don't know. But it's a routine-looking pipe bomb, put in an unsurprising place. You know how many women's clinics have had bombs in the past ten years. I'd like to render it safe and then take it out of here in the containment vessel for detonation."

"Don't do anything yet," said Stahl. "Let it sit until I get there. And above all, don't let anybody back into the building. If this is a bomb that's not related to the others, we'll do just as you say. But right now the call doesn't feel right. It feels like our bomber used the pipe bomb to get them to evacuate the building so he could go inside and plant something worse. And it seems he might have picked a women's health center to make it seem routine to us."

"Yes, sir," said McCrary. Stahl could hear in his voice the patient resignation of a man who was used to obeying superiors because they were superiors, not because they were right.

"You said Kaplan and Steers, right?" Stahl said.

"Right."

Stahl hung up, trotted the rest of the way to his car, and drove to the women's health center. The center was a four-story brick building with two rectangular wings and a central lobby with glass doors on the edge of a huge parking lot. Stahl could see the bomb truck, the only vehicle within a hundred feet of the front of the building. There was yellow police tape strung around the building's entrance, and a second tape beyond the bomb truck to establish a perimeter. Stahl approached the nearest cop and showed his badge so he could pass.

He ducked under the tape, walked straight to McCrary, and shook his hand. "Good," said Stahl. "You've got a good perimeter set up and everybody out of the way. I assume you made a Code Five Edward call to clear the airspace?"

McCrary nodded.

"Then let's take a closer look."

McCrary and Stahl walked to the front of the building, where they both paused a few feet from the device. Finally they approached the device cautiously. When they were near it, Stahl could see that the device looked like most pipe bombs. It was a two-inch metal pipe about a foot long with screw-on caps at both ends. Two holes had been drilled on one end and a pair of wires that looked like the leads to an initiator ran out to a lithium-ion battery. The trigger switch was not visible, but a switch could be any size, and there was a layer of tape around the pipe that Stahl could see was thick and lumpy and looked as though it held ball bearings. The tape could also hide the switch.

"It's too big to detonate here. We've got to take it away," said Stahl. "We still use the Mark V-A1, right?"

"Andros?" said McCrary. "Yeah. We don't have one with us right now, but I'll call for one."

"Okay," said Stahl. "While we wait we can get the containment vessel ready to take the bomb and start having the officers move the bystanders back another two hundred feet. That device has a couple of layers of shrapnel taped around it."

While McCrary was on the radio to headquarters and to the police officers guarding the perimeter, they walked to the bomb truck. As they approached the truck, McCrary said, "Gentlemen, you've met Captain Stahl."

Stahl shook hands with the two. "Curtis, Bolland, nice to see you."

"The captain has given us the go-ahead to get the pipe bomb moved out of here, and I've called for an Andros," McCrary said. "Let's get the containment vessel moved up close so the robot can get the bomb into it by carrying it a few yards. No bumpy areas, no inclines if we can help it."

Curtis and Bolland got into the truck and towed the five-thousand-pound containment vessel close to the device lying on the concrete in front of the entrance. They secured it so it wouldn't roll, then opened the vessel's hatch. They pulled the truck back to where the others stood in the parking lot, and then began checking with the police officers in the area by radio to be sure all civilians had been moved back to a distance of five hundred feet.

The Team Three bomb truck arrived with the robot. Two of the bomb technicians jumped out and dragged out the ramp at the back while the other, Alice Terranova, brought out a small control device and began using it to direct the robot down the ramp to the surface of the parking lot.

Stahl said, "Thank you, Terranova. Nice to see you, Moss." He was making a point of addressing everyone directly for the moment. It wasn't too much to expect for him to remember the names of the living fourteen people on the Bomb Squad, officers who would be risking their lives with him each day. He waved at the man driving the bomb truck. "Hey, Townsend."

Stahl said, "This is Sergeant McCrary's operation. I'm just here to hang around and see if I can learn anything about this bomber. Team Two has done a great job of setting up a perimeter, getting everybody back far enough, and so on. The first mistake was mine. Because of me, this bomber has managed to get seven of us here at one time. That's half the Bomb Squad at current strength. So I'm going to ask Team Three to turn around and return to your station. Team Two will take it from here. Thanks for the robot."

"Yes, sir." Terranova handed the control console to Curtis, and she and the others climbed back into their truck and drove off.

Stahl nodded at McCrary, then stepped back to stand by the truck while Curtis maneuvered the robot across the asphalt parking lot toward the entrance to the building.

The work went quickly. The robot's top speed was three and a half miles an hour, about the normal walking speed of a man. As the robot approached the pipe bomb, Curtis slowed it considerably and transferred all of his attention to the screen of the control box so he was seeing the bomb and the pavement from the point of view of Andros's video camera.

Stahl stood by the truck and called his assistant, Andy, at the station. "Andy, this is Dick Stahl. Get in touch with the building manager of the women's health center at Kaplan and Steers and find out what you can about the security cameras outside the building and inside. Find out how we get the footage. What I need to know immediately is whether, after the people were evacuated from the building, the bomber went inside. Thanks."

He hung up and called Bart Almanzo at Homicide Special. He told Almanzo what was happening and said, "I think this is our guy again, but don't send anybody here until we've checked the whole building. If I'm right, this isn't going to be safe for a while. But we know this bomber was here in person. If there's any surveillance footage that will help identify him or his car or any witness, it might make the difference. Our people have already requested whatever this building has to help us clear the place. But any building in the neighborhood might have caught something."

"Thanks," said Almanzo. "We'll get people collecting it. Good luck."

Stahl hung up and watched the robot. The robot was equipped with a two-thousand-foot cable, but they were using the remote control for the moment. Either this would work or it wouldn't, but it would be quick.

The robot was directly over the bomb now, and Stahl and the technicians studied the video image closely, scrutinizing the bomb for anything that might be a trap's trigger: a wire or filament, a sensor of some sort, a pressure device or spring that would hold the switch at the OFF position until it was lifted, a remote control receiver.

"Anybody see anything?" said Curtis.

"No," said Bolland.

"Nope," said McCrary.

Stahl said, "Agreed."

The robot reached down, closed its grasping claw over the pipe, and lifted.

There was a bright flash as the bomb tore itself apart and fired hundreds of projectiles in all directions, blowing the glass front into the building and sending a shock wave toward Stahl. A half second later the sharp bang slapped his ears and collided with his body, a flat, hard force that felt to him like something solid pounding his chest and stomach.

At the same time, he saw the robot thrown outward from the building into the parking lot. It flew about fifty feet—not lifted but swatted—spinning and hitting on its side. Then it slid across the pavement to a stop. Some part of his mind noted that the arm was missing.

Immediately Stahl's eyes sought the sight of Curtis, McCrary, and Bolland. When he spotted them, Curtis was lying prone on the pavement of the parking lot and the others were kneeling over him. Stahl gasped and took a running step toward them, then saw they had not been hit. They got Curtis up, then stood. McCrary brushed invisible dust off his uniform pants from his knees to his waist and then the front of his shirt while Curtis picked up the control unit. After a few seconds he turned it off. Bolland began walking toward the front of the building to see if there was any part of the bomb left to be collected for evidence.

Stahl walked up to Curtis, smiled, and patted his back gently. "Don't worry about the robot. That's what it's for. This guy's objective was to take us all out and maybe incinerate a few civilians as a bonus. He got nobody."

Curtis managed a faint smile as Stahl passed him on the way to McCrary.

Stahl said, "We still have to clear the building before we let anybody in."

"I know," said McCrary. "This time that's got to be my job. I'll get suited up."

"Have you got a suit I can borrow?"

"Sure, but I thought we were going to send only one tech downrange from now on."

"This time looks like an exception. I think this might be the same guy who did the house in Encino and the car at the gas station.

What you see is something simple—today, an ordinary pipe bomb. But in the other two what we got was a second charge that was bigger. I want to see if there's something else in the building."

McCrary shrugged. He went to the truck and took out a suit with his name stenciled on it and found another labeled with the number 2. He handed it to Stahl.

While they put on the bomb suits, Stahl called Andy at the station. "It's Stahl. What do we know?"

"We've got some video from the building across the street from you. You were right. A man went into the clinic building during the evacuation. He was wearing some kind of uniform, maybe a janitor's uniform—dark blue shirt and pants, no badge. About five ten or six feet tall, average weight and build, baseball cap. Nobody stopped him or even looked closely at him. He was going in as they were going out."

"Of course," said Stahl. "Was he carrying anything?"

"Yes. It looks like a gym bag. That size, anyway. Dark, probably black."

"Any luck getting the interior video from the clinic?"

"Not yet. The security guy who has access to the system took charge of evacuating people, so now a unit is working with him and with the equipment manufacturer to set up a remote feed from the Van Nuys station."

"All right. Keep trying."

Stahl cut the connection and left his phone with Curtis. "If there's a call, answer it. If it's about the indoor surveillance cameras, call me on the helmet radio frequency."

As Stahl and McCrary walked toward the building, Stahl told McCrary what he'd learned. When Stahl and McCrary reached the entrance they examined the damage. There were impact holes in the concrete like a pattern of little craters where ball bearings had hit. Stahl said, "Antipersonnel. I guess he was hoping for a few extra bodies. But he mainly wanted everybody out, so he could go in alone."

McCrary said, "What kind of trap do you think he put inside?"

"Something new," Stahl said. "Something we haven't seen him do before. We'll have to go through each room and clear it. He knows there won't be more than one or two bomb techs inside the building at first. Maybe he wants to injure us so more cops have to go in before he drops the roof on our heads. We'll have to take our time and look at everything."

When Stahl stepped in over the fallen glass, he appreciated the architectural design of the women's health building. The concrete and steel stanchions in a row in front of the glass entrance had apparently been intended to keep a vehicle from crashing through. The freestanding wall behind the glass front of the building had provided more protection from the blast.

The wall had been covered in a layer of plasterboard and painted like plaster, but behind that layer was structural concrete. The bomb's ball bearings and pipe fragments had swept the glass inward. They chewed up the plasterboard, but did nothing to the wall behind it. The reception area inside looked untouched and intact.

"One more thing just occurred to me," said Stahl. "Nobody has said they've seen video of this guy leaving the building. We've been assuming he left as quickly as he could, because bomb makers do that. But he could still be in here. The building has four floors to hide in."

"I'll keep it in mind," McCrary said.

The two men searched the lobby for any of the signs of a booby trap—fine trip wires, a gym bag like the one seen on the video, devices plugged into electrical outlets that didn't seem to belong. Stahl knew their job was especially risky today because dozens of people had evacuated the building in a hurry, and might have left things like briefcases or equipment bags anywhere.

When they made sure the lobby was safe, they began to move from room to room on the ground floor. The first offices they came to were administrative. There were signs that people had been interrupted—pens dropped on half-completed forms, computer screens that had gone dark or displayed screen savers since their users left.

Farther on were medical examining rooms. There were tables in some rooms with white paper on them that was puckered and wrinkled by the last patient, white coats that still hung behind the doors. There were even a couple of telephones left off their cradles.

Stahl and McCrary found nothing dangerous in any of the rooms. They examined the phones, particularly the ones that were left beeping with the off-the-hook signal. This would not have been the first time placing a phone in its cradle had set off a bomb.

They moved across the lobby to the other wing of the building, where there were a few offices with big filing cabinets that looked as though they held medical records. There was a large conference room with a big video screen, video recorders and players, and a computer. They spent some time examining the equipment for suspicious wires or components.

When they finished their sweep they went back to the central lobby. There was a big steel door labeled STAIRS, the reception desks they had already examined, and a pair of elevator doors. McCrary headed for the elevators.

As McCrary reached up toward the panel between them, Stahl shouted, "Freeze! Don't touch the button!"

McCrary had to turn his whole body to look back. "What is it?"

Stahl hurried close to him. "Something's wrong," he said. He pointed up at the panel above the elevator doors. "See that? The number lit up is four. Everybody has been evacuated. There was nobody up there on the fourth floor to hit the button. Both elevator cars should be down here."

"You think the bomber went up there?"

"Yes. But I don't think he's still there. He knew the first ones back in the building would be the Bomb Squad. He knew we'd be wearing eighty-five-pound bomb suits. Probably he even knew that searching the ground floor would tire us out. He knows the last thing we want to do right now is climb stairs under all this weight, but he also knows we have to go up to check, floor by floor."

"So what do we do?"

"I think he rigged the elevators to explode. So what we should do is climb the stairs to the fourth floor. First, we've got to call Curtis and Bolland to explain what we've done and what we're about to do. If we die, no information dies with us, all right?"

"Agreed." McCrary made the call to his teammates who were waiting outside.

Then Stahl pulled open the door to the stairwell and began to climb. As he did, he took his mind off the sheer dull strain of lifting one foot after the next by thinking about elevators. Since his first years as an EOD man in the army he had studied the ways buildings, bridges, towers, vehicles, ships, and airplanes were constructed. It didn't matter how much a technician knew about explosives if he knew nothing about the places where they were hidden, how they could be disguised, and the electrical circuits or physical features that could be used to detonate them.

As he climbed he constructed a blueprint of an elevator in his mind. There was a vertical shaft. At the top, above the upper range of the elevator car, there was a motor that turned a wheel called a sheave, which operated a pulley. On one end of the cable was the elevator car, and on the other was a counterweight about equal to the weight of the car. That way the force required to turn the pulley to raise or lower the car was minimal.

He studied the mental image to figure where the gym bag full of explosives would be placed and how it would be triggered. The elevator car was at the top floor right now. The bomber would expect the first bomb technician to arrive at the doors on the first floor and press the UP button.

The controller above the fourth floor with the pulley and sheave would switch on the electric motor to simultaneously raise the counterweight toward the fourth floor and lower the elevator car toward the first floor. When the counterweight reached the upper limit switch in its track and the elevator car reached the lower limit switch, the motor would stop. The doors would open, and the passenger would step inside the elevator car. After a few seconds the elevator doors would close, and the elevator would be ready to rise when any of the numbers—2 , 3, or 4—was pushed.

Stahl reached the second-floor landing. He and McCrary were both panting. Stahl stopped there and said, "Have you ever worked on a bomb in an elevator before?"

"Never," McCrary said.

"Okay. I'm going to do something that's going to look stupid. But it isn't."

He began to take off his bomb suit. He put down the heavy helmet with its Plexiglas window and whirring fan. He was drenched with sweat from the exertion of the past couple of hours. "I just realized we're doing this wrong. The bomb has to be in the shaft. I won't be able to go into the shaft and climb around with this thing on. And the charges this guy sets for us couldn't be stopped by a bomb suit anyway."

"A gym bag full of high explosives? No."

"The bottom of an elevator car is thick, made of steel to take the weight of the riders. The top of an elevator car isn't. There's even a hatch in the ceiling that opens for maintenance."

"Yeah. I've seen those."

"There are a dozen safety devices on an elevator. It can't free-fall, even if you cut the cable. It can't even pick up speed. But there's no protection from a bomb placed on the roof of the elevator car."

"You're right."

"So if he rigged the elevator, that's where the device probably is. Now I just have to get up there and see what triggers the charge."

"Why not the buttons inside the elevator?"

"It's possible. No matter what the switch is, the charge has to be on the roof of the car."

"What can I do to help?"

"Go back down to the lobby. Stay near the elevators, but not in front of the doors. If I screw up they'll blow outward. But guard the buttons. Don't let anybody get near them. We don't have proof yet that the bomber has left the building."

"Yes, sir."

Stahl removed the suit, took his tool kit, and climbed the stairs. When he reached the fourth floor he studied the area around the two elevators. The elevator shafts were in a recessed rectangular space. He looked for the plain unmarked door that must provide access to the working parts of the elevators, but there was none.

He reentered the stairwell and climbed. There was only one flight, and then, on the next landing, there was the plain steel door he had been expecting. He tried the handle, but the door was locked.

Stahl set the canvas tool bag down and found the electric lock-pick gun. He inserted the tension wrench and the gun's needle nose into the keyway and pressed the trigger, and when he felt the lower pins jump to make a space below the upper pins, he put pressure on the tension wrench and turned the knob.

The door opened to a level above the two elevator shafts. As he approached the first shaft, he saw an empty black gym bag that had been discarded on the floor a few feet away. Above the shaft, at about waist height, was the platform that held the controller and the motor. He could see downward past the sheave and pulley to the roof of the elevator car.

The bomb on the elevator roof didn't look like much. There were three separate metal canisters, each about the size of a liter of liquid, taped onto the access hatch with insulated wires connecting them.

Stahl lowered himself onto the roof of the elevator and followed a thicker wire toward the top of the shaft where it was attached to the stationary platform that held the motor. He followed the wire back down to the roof of the elevator. There he could see that a switch had been installed. The double wire of the firing circuit had been split and its two copper strands were screwed onto the two contacts of the switch. It was a simple knife switch with a metal lever that when closed would be pinched between two copper contacts and complete the firing circuit.

But the switch had been modified to work in reverse. The lever, the "knife" of the switch, had been removed, and the two contacts had been squeezed together so they would always touch. Then the knife had been replaced by a thin sheet of fiberboard insulator between the contacts that held them apart. Attached to the insulator was a coil of wire that would uncoil as the elevator descended. Just as the elevator reached the first floor, the wire would reach its limit, and the fiberboard insulator would be tugged from between the two contacts.

Stahl looked to see what else was in the circuit and saw a small electric timer set at seven seconds. It gave the person on the first floor seven seconds to enter the elevator and let the doors close. And then the timer would run out and the bomb would detonate.

The power for the firing circuit was a splice that tapped into the circuit that powered the elevator's lights and switches. But he was not positive that was the only source of power. With this bomber there could be other secondary firing circuits powered by batteries. This bomb maker was obsessed with backups.

Stahl took a screwdriver, loosened the screws that held one of the wires to the firing circuit, and pulled it out. He capped the end. Then he disconnected and capped the other wire. He had now disabled the main switch, but he was beginning to know this man's work. There would be a second circuit somewhere designed to kill any bomb tech who neutralized the first one.

Stahl found it almost immediately. If he had been in a hurry to lift the canisters of explosives he would have set them off. Lifting any canister two inches from the elevator roof would have pulled another nonconductive fiberboard strip from between two contacts, and the internal batteries in the canister would have set off the blasting cap inside.

He disconnected each wire that led to a power source and capped it, removed all of the switches and canisters from the roof of the elevator, set them on the concrete floor away from the shaft, and climbed up after them.

He sat still for a moment, collecting his thoughts. Then he stood and went to the top of the second elevator shaft. The knife switch attached to the counterweight's track was the same. The backup switches under the three canisters were the same. There was no new switch that was designed to make a bomb technician who had gotten this far get overconfident and kill himself. He supposed the bomber had needed to come in with everything ready to take out of the gym bag and attach to the two elevators and then go.

When Stahl brought the explosives out of the elevator maintenance room and set them on the floor outside the steel door, he called McCrary. "Hello, Sergeant."

"Should I still be holding my ears?"

"Not anymore. I've got six canisters of explosives and some disconnected wires and switches on the roofs of the two elevators. Your team can come and get them now."

When Stahl hung up, he went to the fourth-floor elevator doors and pressed the DOWN button. The elevator doors opened to show him a pair of pristine, empty elevator cars. He took the first, pressed 1, and watched the doors close. In a moment it was taking him down.

The doors opened at the lobby and he stepped out to see McCrary and Curtis walking in around the false wall with their bomb suits on. As he walked past them toward the gaping hole that had been the front entrance he said, "Thanks, guys. It's safe to take the easy way up, but clear the upper floors before you let anybody back into the building."

12

As soon as Stahl made it back to the office, he began to work with frantic determination. He couldn't let this bomber keep probing the Bomb Squad's defenses, booby-trapping one spot after another and waiting to see whom he could kill.

Stahl recorded a computer presentation for all four teams, and put them through a quick online course that would show them everything he'd learned about this bomber so far. He showed them the surveillance video from the car bomb at the station and the one at the women's health clinic. "We can't see his face, but we can see the way he moves, and roughly his height and weight. This is definitely the same man. He's about five ten to six feet, and weighs around a hundred and seventy. Here is his voice." Stahl played the audio recording from the 911 call that had lured the team to the Encino house. Next Stahl played the audio recording of Tim Watkins's voice as he walked his way through the house, describing each thing he saw.

Stahl hoped, not only that the remaining bomb techs would develop a sense of the way the bomb maker's mind worked, but also that watching him move around on the dim, grainy surveillance videos would trigger a memory if any of them ever saw him. Stahl included the photographs that were taken of every component of the devices that had been removed intact, including the ones on the elevators he found only hours ago.

Stahl concluded: "When you're on a call, look for anything that reminds you of these pictures. He likes devices that look conventional, but actually have something bigger behind them or under them or inside them. Most of his components are simple, and nearly all are homemade. You notice I avoid the term 'improvised.' He never improvises. He plans each device meticulously and thoroughly. And so far he's made nothing that wouldn't have worked. He's been planting devices at the rate of one a day. I'm hoping it's impossible for him to keep up that pace much longer.

"At the LAPD most of the calls you'll get are still going to lead to devices made by somebody who thinks he was cheated by the phone company, or wants his business partner out of the way, or hates the government. About two-thirds of them won't work.

"But while you're handling those calls, look for signs that you're dealing with this bomber. He's been using a handmade version of a plastic explosive resembling Semtex. His main signatures are a secondary charge and multiple ways of triggering his initiator. In the last two devices, I've seen number eight blasting caps. Study the pictures of the lead wires in these photographs so you'll spot them easily. Take no chances. If you see an obvious way to render one of his devices safe, you're probably wrong. We will continue the policy of detonating devices in place or, if you can't do that, removing them for detonation elsewhere. Good luck."

Stahl ordered Andy to be sure that every member of the Bomb Squad saw the e-mail with the online presentation attached. Then he walked briskly to Almanzo's office in Homicide Special. He gave Almanzo a thorough description of what happened at the women's health center and sat down at a computer in the Homicide Special section and transferred to Almanzo the photographs of the devices hidden on the roofs of the elevators.

Almanzo and two of his detectives had been studying the video recordings of the man at the health center. One thing that had not turned up, he said, was anything indicating how the man had gotten out of the building. It must have been a door or window at the side of the building where there were no security cameras. The man apparently had worn surgical gloves, because no prints or DNA had been found on any of the components in the car at the gas station or the health center. A detective was trying to find a single car that had been photographed in the neighborhoods of more than one crime, but so far none had turned up. The next task was to see if the bomber had rented cars to come and go. They were also working with cab companies and with Lyft and Uber to gather information on men who got rides at the right times on the right days. In the midst of Almanzo's recitation, he stopped. "You holding up all right?"

"I'm okay," said Stahl. "You?"

"Seriously, three bombs in three days."

"Three days could be just the start. I've worked shifts longer than that."

"Where?" Almanzo asked.

"Iraq, Afghanistan, Kenya, Tanzania, England."

"England?" said Almanzo. "Really?"

"London, two thousand and five," said Stahl. "I was part of an EOD team that flew out of Germany whenever a big one happened. We'd work a scene until there was no point in working anymore."

"And then you decided to become a cop?"

"It made sense at the time. The pay was better than army pay, and I hadn't been at home much. The department Bomb Squad needed somebody who was already trained, and at that time I was one of the guys who trained people at Eglin."

Almanzo nodded. "You mind if I ask why you left the department after only a few years?"

"It took a couple of years to hire and train a bunch of guys like Watkins and Del Castillo, guys who had the temperament and minds for the work. Then there were a couple of years taking black powder letter bombs out of mailboxes in the suburbs and blowing up a lot of empty suitcases left on the sidewalk at LAX. I got restless. By then we had plenty of guys who could handle just about anything."

Almanzo nodded. "I'm sorry we lost those guys. I know it hurts."

"It hurt worst in the first couple of hours, but it still hurts. I wake up at night thinking about them. And I get mad."

"I wish we had a breakthrough to tell you about, Dick. We're trying hard, following up on everything we have. We've got detectives working on the car he rigged. It was stolen, of course. But we've got the car's history, backgrounds of the owners, the maintenance records. The crime scene people are examining every single thing on it from the prints to the road dust. We've set up a hotline, and the city council is offering a hundred-thousand-dollar reward. Within a week it'll be half a million. We're getting video of the route he must have taken after he stole the car, and more of the routes he could have taken to tow the rigged car to the gas station a day later. The FBI is interviewing the best bombers in federal custody to see if any of them ever gave anyone lessons. We've got other detectives following up on calls and tips. Eventually we'll get him. It's early yet."

Stahl glanced at his watch. "But tonight, it's getting late. I'd better get going."

"I'm going home soon too. We'll try again tomorrow."

"I'll be here."

Dick Stahl pulled into the entrance of the driveway to his building but stopped there until he pressed the remote control button and the iron gate opened. He pressed the second button to open the garage door, and he was about to pull in when he glanced in the rearview mirror and saw Diane Hines arrive on foot at the edge of the driveway.

He rolled down his window and she stepped close.

"Hi," he said. "Where's your car?"

"I parked right over there."

"Get it and follow me in. I'll wait."

She turned and walked off, and in a moment he saw her Camry appear behind his car. He drove ahead, turned to the right, and coasted down the ramp into the cavernous parking garage beneath the building and into his space. She pulled into the space beside him because they both had the number 3 painted above them on the wall.

Stahl got out of his car and opened her door. "I'm a little late. I'm sorry."

"I know you have a job," she said. "I have one too. This just gave me a little longer to clean up and change. It was good timing. I didn't dare think I'd be invited over the drawbridge and under the portcullis and down here to the dungeon." She got out and looked around. "Actually, this is pretty nice," she said.

"Yeah. It keeps your car clean and your radio inside it," he said. "You have anything I can carry?"

She pulled a leather bag off the passenger seat and let him take it. This one was unambiguously an overnight bag. He took it and led her up a flight of stairs to a door marked with the number 3, then unlocked the door to the small foyer.

Stahl unlocked an inner door and held it open for her. She paused to give him a peck on the cheek and went past him into the kitchen.

"You said you designed the security, right?" she said. "I have to wonder why you need this much. Lots of tall iron and impervious concrete, with straight lines of sight and no hiding places."

"I have a crappy personality."

"No, you don't. You're a philosopher-king. I'd vote for you to be class president."

"I appreciate your support. What happened was that a developer hired my company for a security job and liked my work. About a year later they asked me to design the security for a new building they were planning. They said they wanted to rent to people who didn't like to be visible to the public. I have a few security issues of my own, so I said okay, but that I wanted a deal on a condo for myself. They seemed relieved that I didn't want actual money. So here we are. I anticipated they'd sell to celebrities, but so far there seem to be more rich people who don't want to be kidnapped for ransom."

"Does that happen often?"

"More often than you'd think," he said. He took her into his arms and held her there for a few seconds. "I'm really glad to see you."

"I heard that joke in middle school," she said.

"I didn't mean it like the joke. What time is it?"

"It's after nine."

He glanced at his watch. "No wonder I'm hungry. Want to go out for dinner?"

"Of course I do, but we can't. You remember Police Regulation 271."

"You're the one who said the regulation was—"

"I'm not worried about breaking it, just about getting caught." She leaned back in his arms. "You seem to like my cooking. If you've got anything that's nontoxic in your refrigerator I can make something edible out of it."

"Thanks, but I know a few places we could go without being noticed. I'll call one and see if they've got a table for two at the last minute. What do you like? Oversize freshly murdered steaks? Snobby French? Dark and wine-cellary Italian? Slippery creatures from the ocean?"

She shrugged. "If you want to impress me, you'll have a leg up with snobby French."

"Well, let's see." He used his thumb to slide through a series of phone numbers on his phone, then hit one. "Hello. This is Dick Stahl. Is it possible to speak with Roland?"

A moment later he said, "Hi, Roland. Look, I have a beautiful woman here with me, and I'd love to impress her. Would you do me a—" He grinned. "Thank you. When can we come? Wonderful. See you in a few minutes." He pocketed his phone. He saw the odd expression on her face—a skeptical squint. "What?"

"That's not *the* Roland, right?"

"Gallimard."

"You have Roland Gallimard in your phone."

"You wanted to be impressed." He took her hand to get her moving, and then guided her toward the door to the garage.

"I had butterflies when you said 'beautiful woman.' Now I'm weak in the knees. I'm such a pushover for your bullshit I'm ashamed of myself."

"Weak in the knees?" he said. "It's probably just hunger."

"No, it's being in the power of a manipulator."

"The compliments never stop. Roland is a friend. He'll take care of us and make sure we're not noticed."

She looked in the mirror of his car. "Gallimard," she repeated. "Do I look all right?"

Her long, dark hair was silky and shone in the light, and her very simple blue dress made her eyes look a deep sapphire. "You don't look like a cop. Get in."

She got into the passenger seat and he shut the door on his way to the driver's side. He drove back up the ramp, pressed the buttons on his remote control unit, and went under the rising garage door, past the opening gate, and out to the street.

She said, "I have to tell you I heard about the elevator bombs today—which you haven't mentioned. So I was kind of emotional already."

"Really?" he said. "I didn't think you'd had time for gossip, since you were downrange yourself today. Which you haven't mentioned."

"You know about that?"

"I'm the commander of the Bomb Squad. People think they have to report things to me."

"It was nothing."

"No, it wasn't nothing. The grenade you picked up and destroyed was live. I watched the video before I went home. When the detonation charge went off, the grenade did too."

"The problem was stupidity, not malice. The grenade was a priceless family treasure, a souvenir from Vietnam. An heirloom."

"It held up pretty well," said Stahl. "I got a little concerned while I was watching the video. You did it right. I watched you twice."

"More pressure. I'll have to try to look attractive in a bomb suit from now on."

"You looked fine."

They pulled up in front of Restaurant Gallimard, which looked like an old brick mansion behind an ivy-covered wall. There was no sign, only a valet parking attendant. He said, "Good evening, Mr. Stahl," and then got in and drove the car away.

The maître d' opened the restaurant's door for them and then almost magically reappeared ahead of them in the foyer. He led them past a large room with a long bar and twenty tables, then along a narrow side corridor to a second smaller room with eight tables, all occupied but one. Diane's cop eyes scanned the faces in a second on the way in and recognized four actresses, two singers, and a couple of rich-looking older couples she knew she would place when she had time to think.

The maître d' led them to the empty table. He pulled out Diane's chair and said, "Is this acceptable, sir?"

"It's perfect," said Stahl. "Thank you."

"Good. I've let them know you're here. Your waiter will be here soon." He turned and disappeared along the corridor.

Diane stared across the table into Stahl's eyes for about four seconds—and then broke into laughter until he laughed with her. She shook her head. "I don't know what I expected Gallimard would be like. Of course it would be like this. The big room like a bistro is the one you see in magazines. But now I realize there would have to be a place like this too, so people who get bothered by fans and paparazzi can lie low."

A voice came from behind her. "I thought you and Dick would like it. He warned me that you were beautiful, and he doesn't like attention."

She turned and saw the tall, thin figure of Roland Gallimard. His face was long and thin too, with a sharp nose, thinning blond hair, and a sculptured forehead. He bowed slightly, took her hand for a moment, then released it.

Stahl stood and shook Gallimard's hand. "Thank you, Roland. My friend's name is Diane. I brought her here because I knew nowhere else would mean as much."

"It's a pleasure to have you both." He turned to the waiter, who was about as tall and elegant as Gallimard. He said to Stahl, "You know Raymond. I chose him to serve you. Have fun." He turned and moved off. He smiled and waved to a couple of other customers, but did not stop again.

"It's nice to see you again, Raymond," said Stahl. "What do you recommend?"

The meal was two and a half hours of indulgence. Gallimard had chosen common, traditional dishes for them, but each dish was the response to this challenge, an implied promise that this would be the best sole, the best duck they would ever have. The dessert would be the one they felt wistful about someday when they couldn't have dessert.

Their table conversation was unlike those of the other diners. Diane said, “Tell me about the elevator charges.”

Stahl described the devices, particularly the backup triggers, specific in each detail, how they were disguised, wired, and positioned. He explained how he had gone about selecting his approach and executing his plan to render the bombs safe.

“When did you decide to go downrange again yourself?” she asked.

“When I was in the parking lot observing, and the robot set off the pipe bomb’s antitampering trigger. It wasn’t intended to get some civilian. It was designed to go off only if it was lifted. Nobody does that but the Bomb Squad. I wanted to learn more about the man designing these things.”

“What did you learn?”

“He’s trying something new each time. First he took down a house with small charges—imploded it, really—but planted a big charge to kill the bomb techs. Then he left a car bomb at the gas station, also a way to kill bomb technicians—you and me, to name two. If it had gone off, there would have been a huge fire and plenty of other casualties, but that was really just a way to be sure we couldn’t do something easy to neutralize it. We had to get our hands in it.”

“And the elevators?”

“I knew there would be a trap, but I didn’t realize what the trap would be until I saw McCrary heading to the elevator to press the button. If what the bomb maker wanted was just an explosion he could have broken in some night and planted charges that would have taken the whole medical building down. But he’s not after a bunch of women and their doctors. He picked a women’s clinic because bombing them is a familiar crime. There are also many false threats to them. And he picked a big clinic, hoping we would commit more bomb technicians.”

“Why did he put a pipe bomb right in the open in front of the doors?”

"I think he wanted the medical people and patients to be evacuated so he could get in alone and leave a trap specifically for us, and then get out. He knew we'd be the first ones into the building after the explosion—the only ones—and that we would have to clear the floors, first level first. Then we would have to move up. We would be wearing heavy bomb suits and carrying tools and equipment. We would want to use the elevator, not climb stairs. He knew that before we stepped into an elevator we would look inside, so there couldn't be anything visible. The bomb had to be outside, and the roof of the elevator car was the best place—the hardest to see and structurally the weakest."

"What do you think he's going to do next?" she said.

"Something he hasn't done before. He wants to keep putting us in new situations where we'll have to guess right over and over again. He's giving us chances to fail."

She fell silent, and then he did too. They were both trying to clear away thoughts of the bomb maker and what he might do tomorrow.

After a few minutes she spoke. "How do you know Roland? Tell me the truth."

"The security business puts you in contact with people who have things to protect—safety, money, or privacy, usually. Some are nice, and some are awful. I met Roland a few years ago at a party thrown by one of the nice ones. I was working, and he was catering the party as a favor to the host. We talked and liked each other. We still talk occasionally. That's the whole story."

When Stahl paid the bill and handed the folder to Raymond he said, "Please tell Roland I'm indebted to him for this evening."

Stahl and Hines got up and went back out through the long corridor. Stahl's car pulled up quickly. In a moment they were away again.

"That was amazing," she said. "Thank you."

"I'm glad you liked it. Besides, now I'll get to go again. From now on, he'll hope I bring you too."

"Wow. Your bullshit machine never shuts down. You know what the worst part is?"

"What?"

"I do get fascinated when a grown man goes to the trouble of making this stuff up and saying it out loud. I wonder, 'What can this man want to accomplish? What's he hoping for?'"

"I'm a simple guy."

"You don't have to hint. You carried my overnight bag in. You were going to get laid if dinner had been sharing a can of tuna," she said.

"Then I'm glad dinner was a success, so I didn't change that."

"It took my mind off dying for a while," she said. "That's a gift."

"People in danger do things to grasp a lot of life all at once. And we instinctively huddle together for strength. If you start to feel you've made a mistake, or that it doesn't work anymore, please don't think you're stuck."

"This bomber does have a way of bringing people together," she said. "But I know what I'm doing. I'm not just here because you're older and stronger and know more. Although, come to think of it, I like those things. Yeah, maybe I am doing that, and you're taking selfish advantage of my innocence and fear."

"Great," he said. "I'm glad we cleared that up."

As they pulled into the driveway and the gate slid open she said, "Why no guards?"

"Guards attract attention. You don't want a building to look like it's worth breaking into."

She looked at him with narrowed eyes. "So there are guards, aren't there? And they're armed and hidden somewhere."

He smiled. "They sit in a comfortable office downstairs and watch the video monitors. If they're needed, there are a few places where they can come up and out."

When they got out of the car and climbed his private stairs, he closed the door and locked it. As he turned around, she began to unbutton his shirt. She pulled him into the living room, and then started on her own clothing. In a minute they were both naked, and they made love in the middle of the living room. A while later they lay together on the floor, where she had tossed their clothes, letting their hearts slow down. She said, "I thought we should get started right away if I was going to impress you."

"You have," he said. "Almost as though you'd planned it."

"Premeditation keeps my mind occupied."

"Any other plans?"

"We need another drink."

"We do. What kind?"

"The single malt Scotch has been kind of fortifying. Do we still have any?"

He got up, walked to the counter, and lifted the unopened bottle she had brought last night.

"Thank heaven for me."

He took down two glasses and filled them. He brought the Scotch back with him and they sat on the floor together, leaning against the big couch and sipping their drinks. She leaned on him and he put his arm around her.

He stood up. "Hold on for a second." He went into the bathroom and came back with two white terry cloth robes. As Diane leaned forward he slipped one robe over her arms and up to her shoulders. Then he put on the other.

"Two bathrobes?" she said. "Why would you have *two* bathrobes here? If you say it's for visits from your old granny, I'll hit you. Are you screwing everybody in the police department?"

"Not yet," he said. "You told me this morning you were coming over tonight. There's a linen service here, just like in a hotel. I called and changed my order to two bathrobes. Now you know my secrets."

"Not enough." She stared across the room, her eyes focused on something far past the wall.

"Something wrong?"

She sipped her drink. "I'm sorry. I've had so much fun tonight, but then our day jobs just drifted back into my mind. I'm really afraid of this guy."

A moment passed while they sat in silence. Then he said, "Anybody who isn't scared would be a flat-out idiot. Being scared helps you pay attention and sharpens your focus. But he'll get stopped, one way or another."

"How?"

"We'll do our jobs. Tomorrow we get our first reinforcements from the FBI and ATF. They'll be competent and well trained, and they'll bring us almost up to strength. But they won't know a few important things. They'll assume the men they're replacing died because they weren't any good. We have to make sure they know how good the guys we lost were, so they won't get overconfident. I asked for people from the LA offices, but I don't know who we'll get. Outsiders will have to be taught how to navigate the city the way an LA cop does—how to get to a scene in a city choked with traffic, how to interpret what's there when they arrive, and recognize signs that something is wrong."

"I just want to get this guy before he does anything else."

"Me too," he said. "But we have to take our time, study everything we see, wait him out."

"Wait him out?"

"At some point, he'll make a mistake. In order to finish us, he has to keep trying things we don't expect. Maybe he'll stop using stable, practical explosives and reliable commercial detonators, try things that are less familiar and more volatile. He could make home-brewed nitroglycerin, or mix up a peroxide bomb. Either one can blow up spontaneously, even if he doesn't make a mistake."

"What do you think he's doing right now?" she said.

"Right now? He's thinking about us."

13

In the morning the alarm on Stahl's nightstand woke him, and he realized he was instantly alert because he had been dreaming about ways the bomb maker might be devising firing mechanisms. The bomber had not used any mechanical methods yet—no spring-loaded percussion hammers, no pull-out pins, no burning fuses—so Stahl's mind had been devising some in his sleep. He sat up and saw Diane was already gone from the bed. He heard the shower start, and he got up.

He cooked their breakfast, and this time they sat next to each other at the table to be closer together. He said, "Do you plan to come back tonight?"

"If I'm not taking up the next girl's turn."

"Good. I left a spare remote control by your purse over there with your keys, and I put a key to the door on your key chain."

"You're so sweet," she said. "And I promise to return them after I've used you up and left you a hollow husk of a man in your lonely condo."

"Very considerate of you."

She leaned close and gave him a lingering kiss. "I'd better go. I want to stop at my apartment on the way to work and get some clothes and stuff."

"All right." Then he said, "Look, if you want to leave some clothes here, there's a closet I don't use."

"Thanks. I'll have to think about it," she said. She picked up her overnight bag, put the remote control into her purse, and went to the door.

"What's there to think about?"

"What I would need clothes for if I'm over here. I'm always taking them off." She opened the door and closed it behind her. He heard her put the key in the dead bolt lock and then heard the bolt snap into place.

A few minutes later Stahl went out the same door and headed for police headquarters downtown. On the way he called Almanzo's office at Homicide Special and asked Almanzo's assistant whether there had been any developments overnight. But he was told there was nothing new.

When he reached headquarters he spent the first half hour going over the reports filed in the last shift, then listened to Andy explain the details of the temporary transfers of the federal bomb technicians. Andy had worked out their individual schedules and prepared the paperwork for Stahl's signature.

They were still at it when the new people came in. They were ten men and four women, all in their thirties or forties. Eight of them were on loan from the FBI and six from the ATF. He led them into the large conference room to talk.

"I'm Dick Stahl, acting commander of the squad. Thank you all for agreeing to fill in for a while. I just looked over the information about you that your home agencies have shared with us, and I'm pleased to serve with all of you.

"What I'd like to do is get you out on the line as quickly as possible. A normal LAPD shift is twelve hours, three days a week. For this week only I want each of you to stay on the schedule you're used to: work five eight-hour shifts. We have two teams on duty at all times. You'll work the first four hours with one team and the second four with the other. The next day you work four with the third team and four with the fourth. So after two days you will have met everyone and seen how all four teams operate.

"At the end of the first week you'll form your own teams. The only exceptions will be the six of you who have come from offices in other cities. We'll want to attach each of you to a team of our own officers for a bit longer. I have no doubt about anyone's qualifications. But this is a city that's essentially eighty miles east to west and sixty north to south, and some of it is more densely populated than New York. The term 'rush hour' isn't used here anymore, because the roads are packed every hour of every day and night. You'll need some time to get your bearings, learn the map, memorize the LAPD radio codes, and get used to our equipment."

None of the bomb technicians betrayed surprise or doubt or discontent. They were professionals, ready to get to work.

"Just a few quick remarks on our situation. I'm a temporary recruit also. As you know, you and I were brought in because of the worst disaster in LAPD history. We lost half the Bomb Squad, including its commander, in a single explosion. Based on video recordings and a similarity of explosives and methods, I believe that we're up against one bomb maker who is systematically targeting the Bomb Squad, and he's tried twice more in the past two days. The bombs he makes are designed to force us to take risks and make guesses instead of doing what we were taught." He looked around at their faces.

He said, "While this is going on, there are also about three routine calls each day to render a suspicious device safe. About twenty percent to one-third of the calls involve devices capable of producing an explosion. For now, we're trying to detonate devices in place if we can, and transport and detonate if we can't. Do not take any unnecessary risks. Anything you see that looks amateurish might be an amateur's work or it might be this guy trying to fool you. Do not get fooled."

He nodded and Andy came to the front with the schedules. As Stahl turned and walked out of the conference room there was a wave of applause. He ignored it, walking away as though it were an unrelated noise from down the hall. He supposed the agents must have seen the excessive news coverage of his two render-safe incidents. But the last thing he wanted was a squad built around loyalty to him. In a week he could be dead, and what they needed to trust wasn't a boss. They needed to rely on their training and each other.

Stahl kept going all the way to Almanzo's office in Homicide Special. When he got there Almanzo wasn't at his desk, so he looked for the nearest detective. There was a tall black cop in a summer-weight suit sitting in a cubicle with his phone to his ear. "We're trying to speak with all of the merchants and professional offices in the neighborhood to find out if you have any video recordings from surveillance cameras. The period we're most interested in is yesterday from midnight until noon. Yes, sir. Anything. It might be extremely important in a homicide case. We'd like to see it all. No, sir. There won't be anybody who would harm you, and your name would not be made public. We don't even have a suspect yet. We're trying to get one."

Stahl saw Almanzo's head pop up from a cubicle where he had been talking with another detective. As Almanzo approached, Stahl reflected again that Almanzo's short, sturdy frame showed the results of a great deal of effort. It occurred to Stahl that there must be a long succession of suspects in Almanzo's career who had found resisting arrest brought unwelcome surprises.

Almanzo said, "Glad you're here. The number eight blasting caps were purchased by a licensed blaster named Carl Mazur. He bought eight hundred with that lot number in February. He had worked in coal mines for seventeen years."

"Coal mines?" Stahl said. "What coal mines?"

"He spent most of his career in West Virginia. He's dead. His wife told the FBI he was hired by a man who wanted him to clear land for a housing development, and he was supposed to start by blasting the way for a road to the site. The man gave him money and he ordered a supply of explosives, including the blasting caps."

"What are the other explosives?"

"Dynamite and different kinds of electrical initiators and timers. He loaded up his truck and drove to meet the contractor in a relatively remote area of the Ozarks in Missouri. He was shot and his supplies were stolen."

"Of course they were," Stahl said. "Damn. We'll probably be seeing whatever else was taken before long. Do the Missouri cops have anything?"

"Nothing yet," Almanzo said. "They were thinking it had been a robbery, and the thieves who got the explosives weren't looking for anything in particular. When we told them about the blasting caps turning up in bombs here, they said they'd start looking for people who might have seen the victim and another man together, or any pictures of them in the same truck on the interstates."

"This happened in February. Three months ago?"

"I know. There's not much hope of anybody suddenly remembering anything now, but it happens."

Stahl said, "Has the FBI found anything on the people who attended the advanced bomb course at Eglin while I taught there?'

"Not yet," Almanzo said. "Is there somebody you have in mind? Are you remembering somebody who didn't seem quite right?"

Stahl shook his head. "No. But this guy thinks the way insurgents think. He's hiding booby traps, building in antiwithdrawal mechanisms, setting bombs that attract technicians and secondary bombs to kill them. Bombs are crude, brutal weapons. What's complex is the deception, using people's mental habits against them."

"Is bomb technician training the only way he could have learned that?"

"You can teach people a hundred ways of making bombs so they'll watch for them. I don't know if you can teach a person to love murder so much that he'll risk the danger to himself to keep doing it."

Stahl felt his phone vibrating and looked at the screen.

"I know," said Almanzo. "You've got to go. Me too. Good luck to both of us."

14

The bomb maker was in his garage workshop drawing new designs. Making bombs was imagining, building, and testing. The past few months had been a time of preparation, building devices and planning where and how to use them. Now, he'd realized, he had to incorporate new ideas if he wanted to kill bomb technicians.

The LAPD Bomb Squad had surprised him. They were competent and sure. They were sometimes wrong, but they were never careless or baffled. He had read somewhere they were about the best outside the military. They had invented many of the now standard ways of rendering bombs safe. He had hoped the current technicians were an inferior group living on a dead legacy, but they weren't. They had found two of his devices, handled them expertly, and destroyed all the work and preparation he'd invested in them.

He had originally decided his best strategy would be to design and install a device that would bring a large portion of the Bomb Squad together and kill as many of them as possible. He'd killed half of them, and he'd been confident the rest would succumb in time.

His problem now was that the survivors were more wary and observant. They knew he was trying to obliterate them, so they were difficult to deceive. Everything that looked like an explosive device was considered to be one, and no device was treated as routine. The next two had been destroyed without mishap or casualties.

He had been working all morning on new designs. He'd drawn schematics and sketched bomb triggers, dreaming up components that didn't look like what they were, or could be hidden inside the housings of other objects. When he began to get tired and stiff from sitting at his drafting table, he gathered all his diagrams and schematics and took them to his workshop safe. He had to be careful.

He knew anyone who wanted to break into his safe would have to subject it to heat from a cutting torch or blow the lock open with explosives. He had placed a plastic container of white phosphorus inside so any application of high heat would melt the plastic and allow the phosphorus to burn everything in the safe, and probably injure the safecracker.

When he had put his workshop in order he went to his gun cabinet and selected weapons for the afternoon's trip to Los Angeles. He took an M9 pistol and a .223 Remington Bushmaster rifle with a six-position telescoping stock and a thirty-round magazine. He put the pistol on his belt where it would ride under his sport coat and collapsed the rifle's stock so it would fit in the briefcase he'd modified to hold the weapon and a second magazine.

He had selected a reusable grocery bag to hold the bomb. As he put the device inside he admired it. His creation looked like a bomb. He had strung together a dozen sticks of Carl Mazur's dynamite and sewn them into a vest created by cutting away the sleeves of an old denim jacket he'd taken from the lost-and-found basket in a Laundromat. The bomb looked like a suicide vest, and could have been used as one if he'd wanted. He had sewn in lithium-ion batteries and a switch that could be activated by a clock.

The clock had been a wonderful find. If it was possible to have a clock face that looked made for a bomb, this was the one. The clock had been intended to be started and stopped by an electric eye aimed across the finish line on a track. He started the clock manually, so it began to tick and move the hands around the dial. The entire presentation of the bomb was a bit of theater, and it was dramatic enough to make him laugh.

The bomb looked like a bomb, but it wasn't the kind of bomb it appeared to be. The clock would complete the firing circuit to set off the dynamite and the layer of plastic explosive he'd sewn under it in a few hours. He had also placed a layer of Tannerite next to the main charge. Tannerite was the substance used in exploding targets. It was harmless and inert until a high-velocity projectile hit it, at which point it would explode.

Usually he planted his devices at night, between 2:00 a.m. and 4:00 a.m. He was going to plant this one while the afternoon sun was still high, so he could put himself where the sun's glare would half-blind the eyes of his enemies. Today he would be near enough to the bomb so he would see everything.

He had rented a gray Toyota two days before and then put on it stolen license plates that he altered with black paint, so the numbers were changed. He drove the car to a parking structure off Hollywood Boulevard he'd selected a week ago. The structure was privately owned—and old enough not to have been fitted with security cameras. He walked along Cherokee south to Selma and then near the building that housed the office he had rented. He didn't stop there, but kept walking. He came back on the other side of the street, and as he passed an alley he took the bomb vest out of the shopping bag, left it in the alley's mouth, and kept going.

He came around the next block and into the rear of the office building. Then he climbed the back stairs to the office he had rented. He opened the window and looked down at the sidewalk to be sure the vest was still where he left it. He opened his briefcase, took out his rifle, adjusted the length of the stock to fit him, inserted the loaded magazine, and looked through the scope. Then he positioned the desk so he could stand on top at the proper angle to see the vest from above, but far enough back from the window not to be seen from below. He pushed the conference table in front of the desk, and then tipped it up on its end to serve as a blind. He could rest the rifle on the edge of the table and steady his aim while his body was hidden behind it. When he was ready and comfortable, he sat down by the window to wait.

The 911 call came in at 4:57 p.m. Team Two was out, and Team Three and Team Four were scheduled to come on shift in two hours. Team One would take the call.

Today Team One meant Elliot; Hines; John Crowell, one of the agents on loan from the FBI; and ATF agent Judy Welsh. Since Dick Stahl was moving from team to team to observe the replacements, Elliot had by seniority inherited Stahl's slot as supervisor of Team One for the day.

The team scrambled into the bomb truck and Hines took the wheel. As they left the headquarters building, most of the traffic was flowing north through Hollywood toward the Valley, in the same direction they were going. They could hear a constant stream of radio chatter, with the regular patrol units announcing that they had arrived and closed off one intersection after another to incoming traffic. When Hines reached the final block, there were already two police cars parked at angles at each end of the street. They pulled apart only long enough to let the bomb truck pass.

Hines parked the truck a hundred feet up the street from the alley entrance, and the four bomb technicians climbed out. Elliot looked through binoculars and said, "The responding officer was right. It looks like a suicide vest." He handed the binoculars to the nearest technician, Agent Crowell.

Agent Crowell said, "I've seen a couple of them before. There was a guy named Hamid who made them for Hamas while I was in Israel years ago. It's good to see one that's not strapped to anybody."

Agent Welsh said, "Maybe somebody got cold feet?"

"Maybe," said Crowell. "And maybe it's fake."

"Time to go downrange and take a closer look," said Elliot. "Anybody else ever work a bomb vest?" There was silence. "I guess you're it, then, Crowell."

"Honored," said Crowell.

Elliot said, "I'm going to suit up too, and go with you for the first look."

The two began putting on their heavy EOD suits. As he stepped into his, Elliot said, "Hines, as soon as we go, get the truck into position at least two hundred feet back. Better call in a Code Five Edward too. We don't want any helicopters hovering over us if this goes bad."

"Will do."

"Welsh, let the officers in the area know we're going downrange. They should get ready to get people out of these buildings if we have to disturb the vest."

"Yes, sir." Welsh stepped off down the block with a hand radio, checking to see where the units were and which buildings might have to be emptied.

Diane Hines moved the truck back two hundred feet. Then she ran tests on the communication equipment in the helmets of the two men wearing the suits. "This is Hines, testing. Please respond."

"Elliot here."

"Crowell here."

"I'm reading you both," she said. "You're good to go. Hines out." She turned on the recorder and checked to be sure the truck's camera was running. She listened to the talk between Elliot and Crowell as they clumped along toward the alley entrance.

"There seems to be a manual switch over there on the right side of the vest." That was Crowell's voice. "See the wire and then the plastic oval with the thumb switch? Beside the pocket."

"I see it. That would support the idea that it really was intended as a suicide vest," Elliot said. "But it's odd that it has a clock."

"I don't know. Maybe that's a backup. If the bomber got disabled or killed, the vest would still go off."

There was a pause, and then Elliot said, "Move back a little so I can photograph the device out of your shadow." Then he added, "Can you see the place where the clock is connected to the firing circuit?"

Crowell said, "It's got to be this wire here. And there's one on the other side of it too. Want me to cut it?"

"I'd love to get the timer issue off the table at the start, but no. We're not dismantling it unless we have to. The clock looks as though it's set for seven o'clock, and that gives us time."

His voice rose. "Hines? The vest isn't attached to anything bigger. Let's get Andros out to pick up the device and put it into the containment vessel."

"Roger," said Hines. She opened the truck door and climbed down, then opened the rear of the truck to pull down the ramp. She climbed up and detached the robot's mountings, then picked up the control unit, steered the robot down the ramp to the street, and lifted the ramp back up. The robot was an older model that had been refurbished to replace worn parts. To Hines, the control mechanism seemed slightly stiff, and she knew that in this situation she was most likely to be the one to pilot the robot. She tested the control by making the robot wheel around in a circle and zigzag. She moved its arm and opened and closed its gripper, looked at the image that appeared on its screen, and then brought it back to the rear of the truck.

Across the street from the bomb, the maker looked out the window and watched the two men in bomb suits. They knelt close to the vest. He could tell they were communicating as they studied his device. He kept hoping one of them would reach out and try to cut one of the obvious connections he had made, and then try to remove components. He couldn't see their hands because the suits exaggerated their bulk, and their hands were in front of them. All he could see were their elbows.

When the two technicians turned their bodies to look at something down the street, he moved back in the shadows, then to the side of the window so he could see what they were looking at. The Bomb Squad truck was near the end of the block. It faced in the direction of the bomb vest. That was unusual, but he decided it was because the street was too narrow to turn a truck sideways. A moment later he saw what the technicians were watching for. The Bomb Squad robot came around the back of the truck and rolled past it. Someone was operating the remote control to bring the robot forward.

The robot meant the bomb maker was running out of time. Things were happening too soon. This had just begun. The two men standing near the bomb had just begun to examine the vest. They hadn't so much as opened a tool bag. They weren't trying to render it safe or carry it to the containment vessel.

He had to do something. He climbed onto the desk behind the upended table, rested his rifle on the edge, and looked through the scope. He could see they both wore new-style EOD suits, the very best available. The helmet could withstand a bullet traveling 2,000 feet per second. The front of the torso would stop a projectile at 4,500 feet per second. The arms and legs would not be penetrated at 1,850 feet per second, and the joints all overlapped. There was no point in shooting at a man in a bomb suit. What the bomb maker had to do was set off the high explosive in the vest, which would propel shrapnel at them at 26,000 feet per second from just a few feet away.

The maker took careful aim at the bomb. He had embedded a blasting cap in each of the twelve sticks of dynamite. He had attached a plastic container of mercury fulminate to the inside of the clock behind the face. All he had to do was hit the clock, and everything would explode. Even if he missed the clock, he would hit the Tannerite, set it off, and the shock would set off the main charges. The two technicians would be torn apart.

He watched them through the scope. The two oafs were standing in front of the alley, blocking his view of his bomb vest. He must get them to move. He decided he'd have to bet on their reflexes and impulses. He squeezed the trigger.

The man who had been blocking his view was hit on the ankle, and the impact made him fall onto his side. There was no hope the bullet had pierced even the outer layer of the suit, but it had hurt him. The problem now was that the damned idiot had fallen in front of the vest, so his stupid body still blocked the bomb maker's view.

He fired again and the bullet hit the arm of the suit. The man clutched the arm, but didn't get up. But the shot made the man's companion squat, bring his arms around the man's torso, and practically lift him to his feet. They turned, as though to look for the shooter, so he fired four more shots, hitting the tall one who had helped the other in the front of his helmet, his leg, and his helmet again. They hobbled out of his way.

The bomb maker placed the crosshairs on the clock face and fired, but there was no explosion. The blast should have been instantaneous. He tried to adjust his aim, but all he could see through the scope was a featureless black surface.

He lowered the rifle to look over the scope and saw what had happened. In front of him, blocking his view, was the bomb truck. Another bomb technician had heard his shots, seen the two men in suits under fire, and driven the bomb truck forward to put it between him and his bomb.

He had to get the bomb technician in the truck to panic and drive away. He fired on the truck's cab. The first bullet slammed into the truck's door. The second shattered the side window, and then he saw the driver. It was a young, dark-haired woman dressed in a navy-blue police uniform. She ducked down, slithered out the passenger side door, and disappeared.

He collapsed the rifle's stock, put the rifle in its case, closed it, and ran to the stairwell. In seconds he was out the back door of the office building. He moved down the alley behind the building and reached the parking lot on Cherokee where he had left his rental car. He got in and drove up Hollywood Boulevard toward Laurel Canyon and the San Fernando Valley, spitting out a string of twenty expletives about the woman who had taken away his kill.

15

Stahl watched the footage from the bomb vest incident for the third time. This was a completely different kind of attack from the others. The fact that Stahl had predicted a change in methods didn't reassure him. He had guessed the bomb maker would keep presenting the squad with new kinds of devices in new locations. Right in the middle of Hollywood was not like the other crime scenes.

The idea that there would be a person with a suicide vest just off Hollywood Boulevard was chilling to a bomb technician. The crowds that gathered in front of the Chinese Theater to see the hand- and footprints of movie stars, or at the Hollywood and Highland complex, would make a mass murderer drool. The plan had worked exactly the way the bomb maker wanted. He'd had four bomb technicians there within fifteen minutes after the bomb turned up.

The device itself was worse than a suicide vest. There were about five ways to get it to detonate, and while the vest had twelve sticks of dynamite displayed, the explosives hidden inside the vest were much more powerful.

Only two aspects of the event pleased Stahl. The technicians of Team One had sent for the robot and had not been tempted to dismantle the vest. And when they came under fire, a quick-thinking technician had reacted instantly to put the truck between them and the shooter. What didn't please him was that in order to do it she'd had to put herself in the line of fire, where she could have been shot. And it didn't please him that the one who had put herself in danger was Diane Hines. He wondered if he would have the same contradictory feelings if it had been another bomb tech—say, Crowell. Probably not.

Andy knocked on the door frame to announce his presence, and Stahl stopped the image on his computer. "What's up?"

"Deputy Chief Ogden wants you for a conference."

Stahl stood and started for the door. "Where?"

"Room Two Thirty-Nine."

"What's that?"

"The pressroom."

"Get Ogden on the phone for me, will you?"

After a moment Andy came back into Stahl's office. "He's already on his way to Room Two Thirty-Nine."

Stahl got up. He hurried along the broad corridor toward the pressroom. When he spotted Ogden and his aide, Perkins, up ahead, he trotted to catch up. Ogden said, "Great to see you, Dick. I haven't dropped by because you're doing a great job. I don't have time for people like you."

"That's okay. But we need to talk for a second."

"And congratulations on that that incredible girl you've got."

Stahl froze. "I don't know what you mean."

"You know," said Ogden. "What's her name." He looked at his aide, Perkins.

"Hines," said Perkins. "Sergeant Diane Hines."

"Right," said Ogden. "She's going to be a real help in this fight. Right now people are still thinking about the fourteen men we lost. But sympathy doesn't lift people's spirits. We need the people to know we still have officers like her. She's a hero, and she looks like LA: young—half athlete, half actress. And the other one too—who dragged his partner out of danger. He gives us diversity."

"Elliot," said Perkins. "Sergeant Robert Elliot."

Stahl said, "Look, Dave. That's a problem. We can't have members of the Bomb Squad at press conferences."

"Not normally," said Ogden. "Not unless one of them earns a medal. But this time we can't wait for that. The city has been in fear for four days. There's been growing talk in the city council that we aren't prepared for terrorism, and we have a mayor with ears like a rabbit. He'll turn on the chief in a heartbeat. Having Hines and Elliot on the stage with the chief will raise department morale and reassure the city that we're not defeated. We need to make people admire and identify with the police, and keep their eyes and ears open to help."

Stahl turned to Perkins. "Would you give us just a second?"

Perkins glanced at Ogden, who shrugged at Perkins, who then walked alone toward the pressroom. Stahl stepped close to Ogden. "Dave, you know better than this. Putting their faces on television would tell this bomber who they are. None of us should be on television now. The department never used to do this."

"The chief was the one who called this conference. Look, Dick. I haven't forgotten that you can walk away from the department whenever you feel like it, and nobody could blame you. But Hines and Elliot can't. They're career officers. And they've behaved heroically about three times in four days. They're perfect. And they're subject to the lawful orders of the chief."

"It's too dangerous. I think this bomber is a guy who sees everything as a battle between him and us. If we start showing off the people who deflected his attacks, he'll want to punish them. When this guy is in custody or dead, I'll put all these officers up for commendations and decorations before I resign. I promise."

"They're already targets."

"But until they get on-screen, they're still nameless, faceless cops to the bomber."

"You think he hasn't seen them?"

"Not close enough to recognize them. They've been in bomb suits or in the squad truck or too far away for the news cameras to distinguish their features."

"He won't know where to find them," Ogden said. "Addresses are never released. We've never had a cop attacked at his home during my time on the force."

"Maybe it's because they were mostly kept anonymous until there was a trial," said Stahl. "Look, let's postpone this. If we had a day or two, we could think of a way to use a press conference to mislead or trap the bomber. We could dream up an imaginary event he'd want to hit. Or we could tease him with the press conference itself. If he knew about it in advance, and it were somewhere other than police headquarters, he might try."

"The conference is in three minutes, Dick. This is the plan we've got." He stared at his watch. "Make that two minutes."

Ogden walked off toward the press conference while Stahl hung back for a moment and then ducked into a restroom. He took out his phone and dialed Andy.

"Captain Stahl's office."

"Andy, I need to have a bomb call come in right away. I don't care how. And it must be assigned to Team One."

Stahl walked into the pressroom just in time to beat the chief. There were about twenty television reporters, a dozen camera operators, and a few print reporters seated or standing around the room.

The various aides and deputy chiefs and other police dignitaries stood in a row along the wall at the rear of the stage. The chief moved into place on the podium and looked out above the crowd. "Ladies and gentlemen," he said.

The audience sat up straight and there were quick movements to aim microphones and cameras in his direction.

"We're all painfully aware that the people of this city and this department suffered a terrible loss a few days ago. Fourteen noble and courageous officers of our Bomb Squad lost their lives in a cowardly and vicious ambush. Since then the surviving officers of the squad and the temporary reinforcements from the FBI and the Bureau of Alcohol, Tobacco, Firearms and Explosives have thwarted the attacks of this murderer. The latest was only a few hours ago. I'd like to show you some video recordings of the incident, taken from the bomb truck's cameras and the camera in the robot they use."

The large projection screen above the chief's head lit up, and Stahl recognized the video of this morning's bombing. He saw Elliot and Crowell approaching the bomb on the sidewalk wearing their EOD suits. They knelt before the bomb vest and then came under fire. At that point the truck's camera began to bounce up and down as Hines drove into the line of fire. From there, the video switched to the robot's camera, taken from where Hines had left the robot on the street. It showed Elliot dragging Crowell away from the bomb, the truck arriving to shield them and the bomb from the rifle fire, Diane's window being blown in, and Diane diving out the passenger door and scrambling to take cover behind the front wheel of the truck. The intensity of the rifle barrage was evident as the bullets pounded the pavement and the truck. The video stopped and the screen went black.

The chief said, "Because of the bravery and quick thinking of the Bomb Squad members, there were no casualties, and the device was removed and destroyed safely. And now I'd like—"

Deputy Chief Ogden appeared at his side and whispered something with his hand over the lectern's microphone. The chief nodded and replied and then said to the crowd: "This is inconvenient. I was going to introduce the two officers and one agent you just saw on camera. But it seems they had to leave to answer another emergency call. The squad has received reinforcements, but we're still short staffed, and must continue to rely on our regular officers to keep the city safe. I hope to make them available soon." He looked around. "I see we've got acting captain Richard Stahl of the

Bomb Squad with us. I'd like to give him the job of answering any questions you might have."

The chief waited while Stahl made his way to the podium. He shook hands with Stahl and then joined the others at the back of the small stage.

Stahl looked out over the audience of reporters and camera operators. "I'll try to answer any questions now."

A blond woman reporter Stahl recognized as Gloria Hedlund from Channel Ten said, "Can you give us the full names of the officers involved in today's operation?"

"As a rule, departmental policy is not to release personal information about individual police officers, particularly when they're engaged in very dangerous cases. It can put them in jeopardy from unknown suspects, and open them to retaliation later. I've been back on the force for exactly four days, so I'm not aware of how much I'm allowed to say." He glanced behind him to look at the chief, but the chief had already left. "I'd like to defer that question for now, and let the press office provide what they can when we're done here."

She said, "Follow-up?"

"Sure."

"Doesn't that policy apply to you too?"

"I'm temporary commander of the squad, not one of the regular officers. I'll have to take my chances."

He pointed at a young African American male reporter, who said, "Is it true you're only here because a deputy chief is a friend of yours?"

Stahl said, "I'm here because every cop is a friend of mine. Deputy Chief David Ogden—that's O-G-D-E-N, age forty-five—is an old friend and also a cop."

There was laughter from several of the reporters.

Stahl continued. "He remembered I was once the commander of the Bomb Squad. Deputy Chief Ogden asked me to fill in until this special trouble is over and the situation returns to normal trouble."

An older male reporter said, "That doesn't really tell us whether your hiring was an instance of cronyism. Aren't high-ranking jobs in the LAPD subject to strict appointment procedures? Tests, interviews by committees, background investigations?"

Stahl looked at the young man who had asked the first question. "Was that what you were asking about? Cronyism?"

"No," he said.

"Good. I thought I missed something." He turned to the second man. "I've been given a temporary appointment as a captain so I can accomplish a task. Then I'll go away. Whatever salary I earn during the period I plan to donate to the fund for the families of the fourteen murdered officers. I assure you I hope I'll be gone quickly."

He looked up at the other reporters. "Anybody else?"

A woman stood. "What can you tell us about the perpetrator of these crimes?"

"I'm sorry, but there's nothing yet. When we catch him, I'm sure you'll be told. Right now the Bomb Squad's job is to respond to reports of suspicious devices. Other parts of the department will be doing the investigating."

"Then tell us about the bomb part," she said. "Was the incident we just saw the work of the same perpetrator?"

"I can't answer that," Stahl said. "Anyone else?"

There were a number of people on their feet with their hands up, but he felt his phone buzz. He looked at the screen and said, "I'm very sorry, but I've got to get back to work now. I appreciate your patience." He stepped away from the microphone. He saw David Ogden step toward it as he walked off through the side door.

As Stahl reached the hallway, he glanced at the text again. It said, "Dodgers 6, Mets 4, FINAL." He erased it as he headed back toward the Bomb Squad office.

16

When Stahl drove into the underground garage at home, Diane Hines's car was in his second parking space. He parked beside it, but sat still for a moment. Her car set off a train of thought he had been pushing aside for most of the day. He'd told himself he would think about it later, when he wasn't handling a crisis. Now he had run out of reasons not to think.

The car meant Diane was in his apartment waiting for him. Coming over four nights ago had been her idea. But tonight she was here because he made sure she would be—or at least made it clear that was what he wanted. He was living with a woman he had met four days ago, and who was fifteen years younger than he was. And he was in a romantic relationship with a woman he was supervising in a public job.

Being with her was against the rules, and he was also reluctantly coming to realize it was unethical. He was endangering her career, or helping her to endanger it, which was the same thing. He'd had many relationships with women, but never one like this.

What was he doing? The first night, he supposed, had been an instinctive attempt by both of them to counteract their near collision with death with a bigger dose of being alive—companionship, liquor, lovemaking. Those were things human beings turned to after a brush with danger, especially if they knew death hadn't gone away.

But nothing had ended. Neither the danger nor the antidote to danger had changed. They'd become more intense each day. Their camaraderie and their affection had stopped being transient. Worse, they had become necessary.

Today he had watched a video recording of four people under his command behaving bravely under fire. He had been concerned for all of them. But for one he'd felt terrified, wanting to protect her. He cringed each time he saw a bullet pierce the side of the truck she was driving. He wanted to shout at her to get down, to get away.

He tried to put his feelings for Diane in the context of his life. When he was twenty-one he had married a woman he met in the two-year college he attended. Her name was Melanie. They had bonded, partly because they were both poor kids and looked at life the same way. Her father had left when she was five, and his had died in a car crash making pizza deliveries when he was ten.

Dick and Melanie had both grown up avoiding mistakes. Poor kids knew that even small mistakes destroyed people, because they'd seen it happen. Lawyers and doctors and second chances were things rich people had, but help was never on the way for people like the ones they knew.

They'd both needed to work when they were in high school, and in college they had to work more. They were very earnest and focused on forcing the future to be better because the past was unthinkable. They worked for their lives, and for each other.

Now, twenty-three years later, it was not hard to find reasons why the marriage hadn't succeeded. They had been drawn to each other by a mutual attraction that seemed like fate. She was beautiful and good. He was strong and smart. How could they lose?

They turned themselves into sleep-deprived drudges who barely saw each other between classes and jobs. They'd both been inexperienced and not very adventurous, so sex was tame, quick, and perfunctory, another chore to be performed efficiently and crossed off the list until next time. Increasingly it came at the end of the list, almost the only chore they could put off without having disaster overtake them.

Stahl was the one who cheated. But neither of them was the sort to wait for a second slipup, so when she mentioned divorce he agreed it was fair. Their divorce was quick and cheap.

By the end of the waiting period for the divorce he was prepared to enlist. When the marriage collapsed, he had found himself with little concern for his own welfare. The feeling influenced his choice of Explosive Ordnance Disposal. Now, on the rare occasions when he thought about this decision, he believed he had been discarding the illusion that he could control everything. In working with explosives, if he did badly, he would die. If he did well, he might die anyway. He did well, and as he got more skillful and knew more, he learned to control more and more. Every living EOD man's failure rate in the field was zero.

Stahl's life since then had not made it easy to have long relationships with women. He had spent years in war zones, then more years on a ready response EOD team based at Wiesbaden, Germany, that flew to trouble spots when the need arose. Then he spent more years at Eglin Air Force Base in Florida before he went home to California to take a job with the LAPD.

His first night with Diane Hines had been like most of his other first nights with women. They were affairs rather than relationships, ignited by chance and proximity. He and an attractive woman would be thrown together, pursue the attraction, and then weeks or months later, one of them would move on to the next job or the next station or the next city. The problem this time was that because of the bombs every feeling had been magnified and intensified and sped up. Some part of his mind seemed to be on Diane all the time.

Stahl got out of his car, took a step, and put his hand on the hood of Diane's car as he walked past it toward his apartment. Warm, not hot. She had been in his apartment waiting for a while. He went up the stairs and let himself in.

He moved through the kitchen to the living room, and then into the back hallway. He found Diane in the spare bedroom. She had a suitcase open on the floor, and she was taking clothes from it and hanging them in the closet.

She looked up at him. "Caught me. I was hoping you'd be a little later tonight. I wanted time to make your condo swallow my stuff without a trace, then get a bath and be waiting for you, like the vision of loveliness I really am underneath the road grime and dried sweat."

He came over and kissed her. "I'm glad to see you took my invitation and brought some extra clothes."

She held on to him so the kiss didn't end. "I found none of the other girls' stuff fitted me, so I threw it out."

"You'll have to work that out with the rest of the harem."

She said, "I'll rent an auditorium so we can all have a meeting."

Stahl said, "You went on a call again. Tell me what you learned in the bomb call today that might help us."

She pursed her lips. "He was different today."

"Different how?"

"Different than I thought he'd be. In the first few calls, he was just a set of plans for a device. Everything was thought out and cold and intelligent. But today I could feel his rage and frustration aimed at me. He had to know that once the truck was parked in his line of vision his chance of hitting his bomb with a rifle was zero, and hitting me was near zero, but he kept firing."

"Do you think he's getting reckless, or is he trying to get close so he can see his device go off?"

"I don't know."

She closed the empty suitcase, put it on the floor inside the closet, and shut the door. "There. Now the day of our big fight I can just toss it all back in the suitcase and walk out within three point six minutes. No fuss, no embarrassment."

"Good breakup planning. Odd that you're not more self-protective about getting *into* relationships."

"I can't resist a man who would make my mother scream."

"I'm grateful for that."

"Besides, I'm learning from you," she said. "This is on-the-job training."

"So you're studying me?"

She laughed. "I don't want to be you. I want to be able to do what you do." She looked at him and smiled. "You get that, don't you?"

"Sure. But if I die on a call tomorrow, you'll get a few surprises."

"I hope the other surprises are better than that one."

"You'll suddenly realize you're about as good at this as I am. You just haven't given yourself permission to know it yet."

"That's because I don't think it's true yet. I think I need more time with you."

"You'll get tired of me," he said.

"Maybe," she said. "But there's no longer much of an argument against living for the moment. And this is what I want to do for the moment."

"Me too."

That evening he had dinner delivered to the condo. The food was from an old-fashioned steak and chops place where he was a regular customer, but the restaurant had no private entrances or even quiet, out-of-the-way tables. As soon as Stahl had called in their order, he walked through the living room and dining room to search for signs that he had a woman visiting. They had both been too visible lately, and he didn't want Diane recognized.

When he heard the buzz at the gate and looked out, he recognized the man carrying the bags and boxes. He was a busboy at the restaurant. He asked the man how he was, thanked him, and gave him a generous tip. Even though he knew him, he didn't leave the door to put away the food until he had locked it again.

Stahl knew there was no doubt in the man's mind that Stahl was entertaining a second person, or who was going to eat the second meal. But since he had not seen her or her car or heard her name, he had no way of knowing who the woman was. Stahl thought about her appearance, and was glad the man hadn't seen her. Diane was too attractive, too memorable.

Stahl wondered if Diane was a product of his imagination. Had he met a pretty woman and imposed on her a set of features and qualities of mind that would make her perfect, rather than simply spending time with an ordinary woman and learning about her? But each day she surprised him. How could he have invented her when he couldn't even predict her?

Stahl watched Diane closely for the rest of the evening, but the scrutiny only made him feel more affection for her. They made love again late in the evening and fell into a deep sleep together.

He woke the next morning about a yard away from her on the edge of the bed. He crawled closer to lie beside her. He studied her face, looked down along the bedspread at the graceful curves of her body where the fabric was draped, and stared at the way her dark hair swirled on the pillow.

Just a casual glance at her showed that she could never have trouble attracting men. How long could she stay interested in him?

She opened her eyes and stared at him. "Well? What do you think?"

"About what?"

"You were staring at me. Am I losing my looks already?"

"No. But I have been thinking. I'm—"

"Oh, shit. Not that. You're not too old. You're not getting me on the rebound. I don't have daddy issues. Or mommy issues either. You're the man of my dreams. Etcetera."

"Etcetera?"

"You know. All the things men like to hear. You're great in bed. The best of my life. Except that's actually true, but don't get complacent." She sat up. "Women don't really think much about those things, you know. We think about them if they cause trouble, like bumps in a road."

"I wasn't fishing for reassurance."

"Hmm?" She seemed to be daydreaming, staring at the wall.

"I said—"

"I know what you said. I was just thinking about what I said. Maybe moving clothes over here wasn't enough. Maybe I'll move in an armoire and a grand piano. Then you won't be able to face the work of throwing me out of here."

They showered and got ready for work. While they sat at breakfast, he said, "Did you come to me because of the danger, the chance you were going to die?"

"Of course. Everything I do is because I'm going to die. But that will be true if it happens eighty years from now. I don't want to waste a day." She got up and put her dishes in the dishwasher. "Got to go. I'm not a captain. I work for a living."

She stepped to the door and stopped. "And I absolutely will be here tonight. Unless our bomber has an exceptional day." And she was gone.

17

The bomb maker was seeing things in gray this morning. He had slept badly, staying up too late, then finally falling asleep for an hour, then waking up again, always in the middle of a nightmare. After one of these awakenings he realized he'd been dreaming about the female bomb technician who had driven the truck in front of him so he couldn't shoot and detonate the bomb vest.

In the dream she stared straight into his eyes, and that had given her complete knowledge of everything about him. He began to run along the streets and became breathless and tired. But every time he stopped, she was there ahead of him, pointing her finger and saying terrible things, which attracted angry people. He didn't wake up but finally acknowledged that he had been awake, listening to the insistent sounds of daylight for some time—birds, a distant train whistle, cars—and swung his feet out of bed.

The bomb maker once had a wife, but now he was alone. He continued to hate her as though he still had her. He smoothed over the sheets and blanket on her side of the bed, and once again noticed that her side of the mattress was still firm, while his side had begun to develop a shallow valley. All he had to do was spin the mattress around, and his side would be the good side. But he never did it.

Her name was Carla. They had met when he worked at a soft drink bottling plant in Illinois. By then he had two years invested in an engineering degree, and she had been in an art therapy program for a year. They were both employed in the bottling plant for the summer because they had relatives who worked there, and it was the sort of place that hired relatives.

Near the end of that summer he got a good look at her after work when she didn't have her long hair stuffed into a hairnet, and her body was not rectangularized by the white coats they wore on the bottling line. She looked at him with her eyes no longer behind protective goggles, smiled, and said hi. After a second of contemplating her voice he realized that she was both women, the one he had worked with and this one. She had straight golden hair, bright blue eyes that looked better unprotected, and a lithe female body. He asked her to go out with him to dinner and a movie, and she agreed and kept agreeing.

After another summer in the bottling plant and another year in school they graduated and got married. The church was the one Carla had gone to as a kid, where she had her first Communion, then seldom entered except on Christmas Eve and Easter morning.

Her parents were not enthusiastic supporters of the marriage. They owned a new-and-used car lot in a southern suburb of Chicago and noticed right away that he didn't own anything, and his parents didn't appear to either. His parents were more supportive because they had been eager for him to grow up and move out of their house. He had always been sullen and solitary, and they didn't like him much. He got a job at a company in Cincinnati that made valves and control systems for pipelines. Moving away from their families was a relief to him, but Carla seemed to dislike the lowering of her standard of living.

After a year of searching in vain for art therapist positions, Carla took a job with a company that sold medical supplies. Her territory included not only Cincinnati but a wider slice of southern Ohio. On Mondays she would put a small suitcase full of clothes in the trunk of her car along with another small suitcase full of samples, order sheets, and inventory lists, then drive off, to return on Wednesday. She would be off again on Thursday and return on Friday.

In her second year, he began to notice that her work schedule became erratic. She sometimes came home from work very late in the evening or even the morning after she was due. She began to be too tired to have sex with him, even when she was home for a couple of days at a time.

He was an engineer, a man accustomed to measuring and evaluating things mathematically. He decided to investigate Carla the same way. He had kept accurate records for tax purposes, so he used them. He plotted graphs comparing her monthly paychecks, which were partially based on sales commissions, with her checks from the previous year. He made another graph comparing the hours she was away at work with the hours the previous year. The results indicated that his subjective impression had been correct. She was away more, but selling less.

One morning he picked up her cell phone while she was in the shower, but found it now had a password. The next day he began to follow her when she left for work. He learned nothing whatever from that practice, so he began to leave his own job early on days when she was working out of the company office and visiting Cincinnati pharmacies. He'd sit in a rental car and wait for her to pass by when she left work. He followed her to a restaurant, but only found she was meeting a group of colleagues that included both men and women having drinks.

Her company's next quarterly sales conference was to be in Cleveland. His study of her movements inspired him to go to the hotel in downtown Cleveland where her conference was held. He went to the front desk with a suitcase, showed them his identification, and asked for a second key card to her room, which he called "our room." Since the name and address on his license matched her reservation, he got the card.

Later, during the string of afternoon meetings of the conference, he went into Carla's room and installed three small digital cameras. Two were electric clocks with the cameras built in, which he put on the two nightstands. The third was a white circular box with a glowing red light that looked like a second smoke detector. He installed this on the ceiling above the bed. Then he went home to wait until the day the conference ended. Early that morning he went to the hotel and waited until he saw Carla walk across the lobby for breakfast accompanied by a man. Then he slipped into her room and retrieved the cameras.

When he saw what the cameras had recorded he sent copies to the e-mail addresses of her parents, four of her female friends, her employers, and another to himself. He sent the videos through a mail service in Moldova that existed to receive e-mails and send them on to their final recipients anonymously. He changed all the locks in the house. He collected all of Carla's belongings, drove them to her parents' house near Chicago, and left them in their driveway. Then he filed for divorce.

For the next week his phone received two or three dozen messages a day from Carla. At first she was all hurt and self-righteous innocence. Then apparently someone made her aware of the recordings he'd made in the hotel room. The next calls carried a freight of rage and professions of hatred, tirades that went on long enough to exhaust his interest. There were threats of arrest, which, after a few days, went away because some expert she or her attorneys had hired couldn't trace the e-mails to him. Next there were detailed recitations of the things about him that had forced her to seek male companionship elsewhere. Finally there were threats that there were "real men" who had heard of his behavior and planned to beat or kill him.

He recorded all the phone messages, turned them over to his attorney, and in a day they stopped. He kept working and saving, living conservatively and quietly. But all the time he was preparing for a change.

In the divorce proceedings he refused to amend his filing to apply for simple dissolution of marriage, which was an option in Ohio. Instead he insisted on a divorce on the grounds of adultery. Since there were no children, both had been employed, and no other complications existed, the pair had to agree to a settlement in proportion to how much money the plaintiff and the respondent had brought into the marriage. He ended up with seventy-five percent.

For some reason Carla felt an irrational urge to end up with the house, either because her lawyer could get it appraised for less than it was worth, or because holding her ground made her feel she had won. He readily agreed, received payment for his share, and moved out. He quit his job in the water valve business and drove a U-Haul truck to California. He was confident that even if she kept her job after the recordings he'd circulated, she would not be able to afford the mortgage and in time would lose the house. That had been about five years ago.

This morning he thought it might be nice to kill her. They'd had no contact since the divorce, so while he would certainly be a suspect, he wouldn't be the sort the police longed for—a husband who was a beneficiary of her insurance, a married boyfriend, a neighbor nobody liked.

He had to think carefully before he took on the project. Carla hated him when he left. And he was sure that over the past five years she would have had some hard times that she blamed on him, which kept the coals glowing.

But he was sure he could kill her without creating a new connection to her. Her family had originally been from Alabama and, like many Southern women, she was addicted to sweet tea. She used to keep a pitcher of it in the refrigerator. It was sweet enough to hide ethylene glycol. And there would be less difficulty if he left the opened jug of antifreeze in her garage. If the jug was gone, this was murder. If the jug was there, this might be suicide.

He could always arrange a methane leak and explosion in her house. If she still had a car, he could tamper with her brakes or cause a gasoline fire. That might be fun. If she had a boyfriend these days, he could get the man blamed for her murder. There were so many ways to do any of these things.

But he was just teasing himself. He wasn't going to do any of it. If her parents were alive—and he had no reason to believe they weren't—they would instantly turn police attention on him. And even if they were dead, the fact that she had been part of a nasty divorce would make the police at least find out where he was living. Contemplating her death had raised his mood, but he would just have to let it go—for now.

He had probably thought of Carla because the person who had ruined his day yesterday had been a woman. But that was yesterday. Today would be different for him and for the woman cop.

He went through his morning rituals. He ate a breakfast of egg whites cooked in olive oil, drank some herbal tea, lifted weights, ran four miles around the perimeter of his property, then walked for a while to get over the shakes that overexertion caused.

At home he took a hot bath and soaked until his muscles relaxed, then dressed in jeans, a T-shirt, and sneakers and went into his workshop to get started. While he was at work, his hours ran as smoothly as a line reeling off a spool. He was alert and completely focused on what his hands were doing.

At some point that morning he realized he'd been pushing himself in the wrong direction. He had begun to use volatile and unpredictable explosives and exotic means of delivering and detonating them. He had been trying to present the Bomb Squad with devices they had never seen before and were likely to misinterpret. Once he destroyed the first fourteen men, he had hoped to take the others out by demoralizing and intimidating them. They would approach a device without being able to think through the ways it might operate, what touching it might set off, what leaving it alone might give it time to do, or what was protecting it from their interference. But working with more unstable explosives and more sensitive switches was risky for the bomb maker too.

And his new tactics hadn't worked. According to the television news, the Bomb Squad was back up to strength with reinforcements from federal agencies. The bomb maker needed something big, another significant bombing, and it had to be flawless, a masterpiece of small deceptions that forced the technicians into making guesses until one of them guessed wrong.

He put away most of the ingredients he had been preparing to mix today. He was not going to rely on the volatility and unpredictability of the explosive to make the bomb deadly. He had lost his way for a few days, but now he would behave as though he were at war. He would use the best components, the most powerful charges, and the most reliable explosives.

He would go back to using Semtex. He went to the locked cabinet where he kept the raw ingredients. Semtex was a mixture of two explosives: PETN and RDX. He would have to start by making supplies of these two compounds.

He brought out ammonium nitrate, acetic anhydride, paraformaldehyde, distilled water, and boron fluoride. He was going to have to do lots of stirring and heating and cooling for the next part of the process, which had to be done within very narrow temperature ranges. When he finished making the PETN and RDX he would have to let them dry completely. The process would take a few days. At the end, he would have to combine the two. He would carefully grind the two substances into fine powder so he could combine them. After a few hours he reached the point where his intermediate explosives were drying and then quit for the day. He spent time ordering a number of chemicals to replace the ingredients he'd used. He ordered them from six different companies under six different corporate names.

He would spend the days while he waited for the process to be completed on his next project. He had watched the police press conference on television, but had not heard any names. There were just "three brave bomb experts." But he could see that the one driving the truck was a woman. She had sergeant's stripes, but she looked young for a sergeant. Her bomb truck had said TEAM ONE. He would find her.

He questioned the search engines in various ways, asking for images of the LAPD Bomb Squad; news organization reports of any public events attended by members of the squad; any interviews with bomb experts; any reports of public relations visits to schools or job fairs, hospitals or charities. And then, after several days of searching, he found the right image—a picture of a female police sergeant and the bomb-sniffing dog Aristotle at a visit to John Nance Garner Middle School, near the alley where a student had seen a homemade bomb. The text said she had gone there to give the students a lesson on what to do if they saw anything that looked like a bomb.

The picture was absolutely her. She was talking to kids in front of a glass case displaying inert fireworks, pipe bombs, hand grenades, and other things that went boom and they shouldn't touch. There was no name given for her. Maybe the service that police unions hired to scrub the Internet of police officers' names had removed hers, or maybe she hadn't let it appear in print to begin with. But the paragraph hadn't omitted the name of the school, the publication, or the woman who had written the article and taken the picture. The writer was also listed on the school paper's website as an editor.

He drove all the way into Pacoima to make the call at a pay phone. After a few tries he reached the woman who had written the article. He identified himself as a teacher at Grant High School who wanted to arrange a similar visit. She remembered very clearly the name of the woman police officer. "It was Diane Hines," she said. "Sergeant Diane Hines. She was so pretty and sweet the kids couldn't take their eyes off her."

Diane Hines had no website, no Facebook page, no Twitter account, no other obvious place where he could learn about her. He knew she had done more than enough to have her name on the Internet over the past few days, but there was no mention of her. She didn't want to be found. But there was no question now that he could find her.

18

When Diane Hines left work the next evening she drove to her apartment. She had been sleeping in Dick Stahl's condominium for six days now and was delighted to be there, but what she was doing wasn't exactly living with him. Their relationship was still like a date that never ended, just got interrupted every day during their shift, and then resumed at night. Most of her clothes and her other belongings were still at her apartment in Sherman Oaks, and her mail, usually just bills, was still delivered there.

She stepped into the foyer of her building, a creamy white-and-yellow place that looked like a lemon meringue pie, climbed the three steps to a small landing, unlocked the room where the mailboxes were, and entered. The mail system was a good one, because the only access to the room was by using an apartment key. It would be very difficult for a mail thief to follow a tenant into the lobby and then into the mail room too.

Diane unlocked her box, took out the stack of mail, dropped the newsprint ads into the trash barrel, and shuffled through the envelopes as she relocked the door. For a year after college she had been a dealer in Las Vegas working at the blackjack tables. Her dexterity with cards and envelopes still made her fingers feel good, but she had found that the glamour of staying up late under the glittering chandeliers of a casino faded quickly. The job never changed, and when she realized that all she was doing was trading her share of sunlight for money, she quit and drove to Los Angeles.

She slipped the envelopes into her overnight bag and went to the stairs. She was a believer in incidental exercise. She never took an elevator if she could use the stairs, never sat when she could stand, never drove when she could walk. In the six days since she had unexpectedly found herself drawn to Dick Stahl she had found little time for the kind of physical training she had been doing since the academy. She wondered if she could get Dick to run with her. He obviously was used to getting exercise somewhere.

As she completed her quick survey of the mail, it occurred to her once again that she could easily have let the mail age in the mailbox for another week. She always paid each bill within a day or two, but every bill she ever got was due, at the earliest, three weeks later.

On the third floor she walked along the quiet carpeted hallway and tried to remind herself of the things she wanted to pick up while she was here. Maybe she would do a quick load of laundry while she wrote checks for her bills. Then she could mail them on the way home—no, she corrected herself, on the way to Dick's. This was home. She opened her apartment door and flipped the switch on the wall.

The light didn't go on. She was not going to elevate this discovery into an emergency, but she was not going to step farther into the apartment, either. She had a flashlight app on her phone, so she turned it on. The room looked as she remembered it. She turned the phone toward the doorknob and the frame. There was no indication that anyone had been in her apartment. But she still felt odd, and then she realized what was bothering her.

Most times when she had turned on a lightbulb and it had burned out, it happened right then. It had given a pop, sometimes a flash as its filament burned up and the current couldn't complete its circuit anymore. It was only when she had lived with other people—her family, her roommates, or someone—that she hadn't seen and heard the end of each bulb. This was because someone else had done it already, and usually that person was on the way to find a replacement. There was nobody else here. Or there wasn't supposed to be anyone.

Diane needed more intense light. She reached into her purse and grasped her Glock 17. Over the years she had fired it only during training and monthly requalifying, but it had a special flashlight mount under the barrel, and she carried it in her purse with the flashlight attached. She turned it on. The beam of light was powerful and narrow. She swept the living room quickly, moving the circular beam around the room. Things looked just as she remembered.

There were no visible electrical devices that she had not bought and placed here. There were no boxes or bags that she didn't own. There were no new lines of insulated cord, no trip wires, no glowing electric eye beams. She turned her flashlight on the sideboard where she kept her big flashlight. She bent to study the floor as she stepped toward it, moving her weapon's flashlight beam up and down in front of her to search for thin wires, side to side to spot any sign of unevenness in the surface to indicate a pressure pad switch under the carpet. All was clear.

She slowly pivoted on the carpet and ran her flashlight around the room again, holding it on anything that might have changed, anything that might hide part of a firing circuit.

And then she realized that there was one thing she had not looked at, and it was exactly the sort of place where a bomber might hide an antipersonnel weapon. She lifted her pistol toward the light fixture on the ceiling. A bomber might make sure the light wouldn't go on. He might have predicted that as soon as she noticed the light didn't work, she would no longer think of that circuit as existing. Without a working bulb, it was useless, so there was no reason to think about it. In her mind it would cease to exist.

The powerful flashlight beam on her weapon settled on the frosted glass dome of the ceiling light. She didn't see the round shape of the bulb inside. There was no bulb at all. She backed up to try to shine the light into the side of the frosted dome.

Something inside the glass dome of the light fixture suddenly gave off a small dull flash, and kept flashing rapidly. She knew what it was—a small metal piece was spinning in the dome. She would never have seen it without the powerful light, but now the metal spinner was reflecting the light as it spun. A bomber had put in a fuze that worked like the ones in some aerial bombs, and wired it into the light circuit. The propeller-like metal spinner was turning and moving up a threaded tube until a striker lined up with the initiator and released the spring to trip it.

The device had probably been spinning since she'd switched on the light. She looked back at the apartment door and saw she had strayed too far inside. The dome was practically above the doorway, and she saw that the spinner had nearly reached the top. She dashed into the dining room, dived forward on her belly, and rolled to the side to get under the big, heavy maple sideboard. Facedown against the wall, she opened her mouth and clapped her hands over her ears. She spent an instant thinking he had been clever to place the mechanism under the bomb, because when the explosion blasted downward, it would obliterate the fuse and the initiator, turning them into shrapnel along with the glass, and driving them through her skin and into her body.

The air turned to an invisible hammer, a noise so loud it was felt rather than heard pounded downward into the apartment, and Diane Hines stopped thinking.

19

She felt pressure, as though heavy weight had been piled on her. The air seemed gelatinous. It was labor to breathe, and when she tried harder her lungs felt full. There were important things wrong with her body. The animal in her felt that somehow she had wasted her chance to be alive.

The quiet was frightening. She couldn't hear her own breathing. She tried a few times, but still didn't hear it.

She knew she had been moved somewhere. She began to concentrate on identifying her location, trying to orient herself, but she couldn't open her eyes. She tried again and again.

A long time later she awoke again and had the impression she was blind. The world was dark except in her dreams. But then she moved her head slightly and she could see a glow. She looked to her left and up toward the ceiling and caught a glimpse of two flat screens on stands with blue backgrounds and yellow numbers. She noticed that the reason she couldn't move her left hand was that straps held it to the metal rail of a bed, and there were tubes running from the back of it through an intravenous hookup.

For a time, she had parts of thoughts but lost her grasp of them because they were wisps. When she tried to concentrate on them and let them develop, they shredded and drifted away. She could hear sounds now, people moving around out in the hallway, the rattling of carts. She couldn't remember why hearing should be such good news.

The next time Diane awoke, there was a woman in blue scrubs and a white coat in her room. Diane felt she needed to test the impression to see if she was real. "Hi," Diane said hoarsely.

The woman said, "Hello." She had an Indian accent. "How are you feeling, Miss Hines?"

"Not good," Diane said. "Are you a nurse?"

"No. I'm Dr. Majumdar, a neurologist." She took a small instrument out of her pocket, gently lifted Diane's eyelid and bent to look into the eye, then released the eyelid.

"What happened to me?"

"You were in an explosion." As she spoke to Diane, the doctor looked at the blue screens above Diane's head, and then at her. "It's not necessary to bring that experience back in any detail just yet. I should tell you that there's a police officer who comes every evening to sit with you and see if you're ready to talk to him. Your nurses tell me there have been quite a few others too. You have many friends."

"I forgot."

"The friends?"

"That I was a police officer." She paused. "Everything, really."

"That's normal. You had a traumatic brain injury. There was bleeding and you had an operation to relieve that. You were put into an induced coma to speed up the healing. You're doing very well." As she spoke, she wrote notes on the clipboard that held Diane's chart.

She set it aside and then lifted the blanket. She moved her light, thin fingers to Diane's arm, her side, her leg. It was like a small bird landing, only to fly to the next spot and rest for a moment.

Diane said, "What's the bottom line?"

"The bottom line? You mean the cost?"

"No. I'm alive, but what have I lost that I won't get back?"

"I think you'll have a good recovery."

"I have a brain injury and a broken arm and what else?"

The doctor sighed. "Several fractures, ribs, fingers, a shoulder dislocation, which was corrected immediately. Much of your body was bruised by the concussion, and there are abrasions and a few burns along your back. You were slammed against a wall by the explosion, so your nose was broken, but it was reset by a plastic surgeon. The bones, I'm told, are doing well."

"Thank you," Diane said.

"Dr. Hollskein is the attending in your case, and he'll talk to you at length and answer all your questions in a day or so. In the meantime you're going to feel discomfort. When you feel that way, buzz the nurse, and she'll give you something for the pain."

"Thank you."

Later a nurse came in, and Diane realized she already knew her. At some point she had simply gotten used to the nurse without being really aware of her. She looked at her this time and felt accustomed to her without any memory of meeting her.

Diane said, "You've been taking care of me. Thanks."

"You're welcome. But it's a team of people, around the clock."

"I know. But you're here now."

"Anything you need?"

"I want to call my mother and tell her I'm alive."

"Okay. But that could be an anticlimax. She calls every day to see how you're doing."

"Only once?"

The nurse smiled, went to retrieve the telephone, and then set it on the tray table where she could reach it. "Dial nine." She walked out. Diane called and she and her mother spent a long time crying, so only the two of them could have understood each other. Her mother had flown to Los Angeles from Miami and come to see her every day for a month, just sitting in the room and then returning to her hotel. In the end she'd had to go back. She'd been back in Miami for only a short time. They laughed and talked until Diane was tired, and her mother had run out of things to say. When they hung up, Diane fell asleep.

Hours later the nurse came in and gave Diane a sponge bath. When Diane had been changed, the nurse said, "You have a visitor waiting. His name is Captain Stahl. Are you okay to see him?"

"I don't want him to see me like this."

The nurse smiled. "Oh, come on, Diane. The last of your facial bruises and the swelling and burns cleared up weeks ago. You look great." She went into the bathroom and brought a hand mirror. "Here." She held the mirror and folded Diane's hand around the handle carefully, because some of the fingers on that hand were still splinted with metal braces.

Diane didn't look just yet. "Weeks ago?"

"Three at least. And the captain has been here at least once a day for as long as you have. He's seen you many times when you looked a lot worse than this."

Diane looked at the mirror. The discoloration, scrapes, and adhesive tape she expected were gone. Her hair must have been shaved, but it had grown in to about half an inch. Her skin looked scrubbed and devoid of makeup, but there was nothing else. "It looks like I lost some weight, anyway."

"He's waiting. Can I bring him in?"

"Okay."

The nurse went out, and the door had barely closed behind her before it opened again and a tall, trim man about forty-five years old stepped in.

"I've seen you before," she said.

She saw his face go flat. He said, "Yes, you have. Do you remember who I am?"

"Of course I do," she said.

"I was afraid you wouldn't. How are you feeling?"

"My memory started coming back pretty quickly. It's odd, though. Things seemed all to be there, but I didn't want to start digging through them. That felt like such a big job. Somebody mentioned I was a police officer, and that seemed so foreign to me. But pretty soon there were bits and pieces—images, memories, like a dream. What I remembered didn't make any sense. None of it seemed like anything I would do." She paused. "Are you my supervisor?"

"Yes. Temporarily, anyway."

"The nurse says you were here every day."

"I was."

"How many days?"

"Forty-two, I think."

"Oh, my God. It doesn't feel that way. I would have guessed a week."

"They put you under for a while."

"They told me," she said. "Just not how long."

"They needed to. You've been through a lot."

"So why have you been coming here?"

His face seemed to go blank. "It's complicated."

"I'll pay close attention. I've got all day."

"I'll start with the easy answers. Several reasons. You're a very highly skilled bomb technician. The bomber we're after tried to kill you by planting a device in your apartment. You obviously figured out the mechanism in time to take shelter in the only place where you would be somewhat protected. You were lucky to survive, but you were also smarter than the bomber."

"I feel like shit. Does he?"

"I hope so, but we haven't caught him yet." He looked closely at her. "You're the only trained tech I've known who lived through anything that big. You might know something or have seen something that will help us catch him."

"This bomber was why you came here yourself? Every day?"

"Well, no," he said. "I could have sent other people to talk to you. Our third teammate, Elliot, for instance. He's a very good cop and a very good bomb tech."

"So why?"

"You said you remembered me."

"I do."

"We were close," he said. "But I think we should talk about that another day, when your memory tells you it's the right time."

"I thought so. I just wanted to make you say it in case I imagined it or got you mixed up with somebody else," she said.

"You didn't," he said. He took a card out of his wallet. "They probably have a few dozen of these lying around here, but here's another." He set it on her tray table. "Call me anytime you want to talk. About anything."

20

The bomb maker read another article about himself in the *Los Angeles Times*. It was around thirty percent true. Everybody seemed to have figured out that the bomb maker was working alone—the police, the newspapers, the television newspeople, the FBI. They were right about his preference for relying on himself, but not about his purpose. He was doing all the work alone, but he'd had a backer since the beginning.

For half his life he had read and watched news reports about terrorist groups. Some were from the Middle East, some in Asian countries, some in Europe or South America. He had begun to keep track of radical factions in all of those places. The Internet was full of reports about them.

One day about two years ago, he had decided to reach out to them. He began by composing a draft communication to the leaders of terrorist factions explaining what he could do for them. He offered to obliterate the Los Angeles Police Department's Bomb Squad. He explained that he was a businessman, not a person with religious or political motives of his own. He simply wanted ten million dollars. He figured that his frankness would keep everything simple and unambiguous.

He used Tor to get into the dark web and began his search. He spent a long time exploring the dark web on his home computer. By definition, the invisible web was all of the sites that search engines didn't detect, so he had to manage without search engines. He found bulletin boards and sites and communications for a great many groups, and for individuals who claimed to have connections or colleagues or followers. He found killers for hire, people selling themselves or others for sex, offers of drugs of every kind and quantity, and guns. He had no way of knowing who or what was real, so he searched for bits of information he could verify by reading neutral sources, and made lists of contacts he could revisit to check for consistency. Whenever he found a new one, he wasn't sure if it was a criminal enterprise or a police agency from an unknown country searching for criminals. When a group disappeared, he didn't know if the members had been caught or if the group had detected a trap and moved on.

Most people on the dark web had or wanted bitcoins. He wanted cash. After a few months he had made contact with thirty-nine groups who declared themselves enemies of the United States and who he believed were real, or had channels to real groups.

After he made contact a few began to try to recruit him. The tone of his responses was tentative and cautious. He was patient, and eventually some of the groups began to send him literature, announcements of meetings, and other information that indicated they weren't imaginary. Others disappeared.

He waited months before the first serious and relevant query reached him. It was from a person who called himself the Messenger. It seemed to him a name like that hinted at a Middle Eastern group, but there was no telling. The Messenger offered to send emissaries to discuss his offer. They would meet with the bomb maker in Canada. When the Messenger specified the exact time and place of the meeting, the bomb maker bought his plane ticket.

The bomb maker met the pair of emissaries at a restaurant in Niagara Falls, Ontario, on a terrace overlooking the cataract. It was a fair, warm, sunny day in July, and they took a table far from any other. The emissaries were a pair of men who seemed to be enjoying their visit to the falls. Both wore what looked like golf clothes—T-shirts, one yellow, one blue, pressed khaki pants—and low-heeled Italian driving shoes and aviator sunglasses. They talked about the water hurling itself off the cliff into the gorge and watched the tourists from many countries who were spending the afternoon swarming the steps and paths above the falls and taking pictures. He tried to start a conversation about business twice, but each time one of the men would put a hand on his forearm and shake his head.

At some point he realized they were not alone. There were at least three similarly dressed men standing at various points where they could watch the bomb maker and his companions outside the restaurant. One of them wore a backpack, and he wondered what was in it.

When they finished eating, the two men asked for the check, paid, and stood up. They took a terse leave of the bomber and then walked off in the direction of the parking lots a distance from the river. Two other men, including the one with the backpack, arrived and conducted him to a viewing area close to the crest of the falls. They could barely hear each other over the roar of the rushing water. At that point he realized the expected order of things was reversed. The first two men had been security specialists evaluating him. They had probably screened him for insanity or fraud, checked him for weapons with a magnetic device, and given any opposition forces a chance to move in.

One of the two men who took him close to the water handed him a business card. It had a phone number written on it. He said, "When you're ready to begin, call the number. The one who answers will arrange your payment."

"I want the money delivered to me."

The man shrugged. "All right, then tell him that and give him the location when it's time."

The five men he saw all had dark hair and dark eyes, but they spoke with no accents. They never introduced themselves. They made no reference to any country, religion, organization, or government. A couple of times they spoke to each other, but the roar of the rushing water was so loud and they had their faces so close together that he heard nothing. They could have been speaking any European language, or Farsi or Hindi or Pashtun, or Tagalog, or anything else.

The only questions they asked were practical. How far was he in his plan to eliminate the Bomb Squad? Did he want some of his payment in merchandise? Drugs or diamonds? How much money did he need right away for supplies? Would one hundred thousand dollars be enough?

He said he wanted nothing to do with drugs or diamonds. Money for expenses would speed things up, but he could still do his work without it. Yes, a hundred thousand would be a big help.

The other man took off the backpack he was wearing and set it down. They talked for a few more seconds, and then the first man said, "We'd better be going. Call the number when it's time." The two men turned and walked away.

The bomb maker felt his heart beating with excitement, and his mouth was dry. He stood still until they were out of sight, then picked up the backpack and put it on. When he went to his rental car to leave for the American side of the river he was agitated. He decided to sit in his car for a few minutes and wait for his breathing to return to normal before he started the engine.

He was tempted to open the pack, but he knew what was inside. It would be a hundred thousand dollars, because these guys were the real thing. They were emissaries from the leader of a powerful faction. But then he remembered he had to drive back across the border. He unzipped the pack and confirmed what he already knew. Inside was a stack of bundled American money. At the bottom was a cell phone in its box, the protective cellophane gone, but the phone clearly new.

This car had rear seats that could be tipped forward to extend the trunk by a few feet for carrying long loads. He tipped them forward and hid the money in the spaces in the back under the rear seats, then restored them to the upright position. He folded his jacket and stuffed it into the backpack to replace the money, then set the pack on the passenger seat. He knew the customs officials at the border would not be unaware of the places for hiding contraband, but they would have no reason to suspect him of anything.

He thought about the men who had given him the money. He assumed they were genuine terrorists. Everything the men had done made him respect them more. He was in an alliance with them, but at this moment he had no idea who they were or where they were from. All they had needed to accomplish their purpose was to give him a business card with a phone number, but they had gone much further. They had staked his work.

The number on the business card was an American phone number. There was no country code, and the area code was 213. That was Los Angeles. As he drove back toward the bridge that arced over the river, he thought about the implications. They had people in the United States already. They were ready, waiting for his call.

The men they had in the United States had to be sleeper agents. That was very wise. They were probably training for an attack. Maybe they would mount attacks in other cities at the same time as his, so everything happened at once. Maybe their people were out in the desert in Arizona, New Mexico, or Nevada firing weapons and perfecting battle tactics, concealment, and escapes. Maybe they were even training in explosives.

He hoped they weren't. He had a proprietary feeling about explosives. He was their expert, and he didn't want to be easily replaceable. He hoped they weren't fanatical. When fanatical groups got involved, it was usually to perform suicide attacks. Fanatics gave him the creeps. They didn't seem to think anything was a victory unless they got killed doing it. But this group seemed calm and polite.

After he crossed the border at the end of the bridge, the US customs officials glanced at him and waved him on. It was a beautiful day, and the bridges were packed with cars inching their way home from Canada. He drove to his hotel. During the drive he had been hoping that when he got a chance to really examine the money and the backpack, there would be something besides the currency. He had seen paper bands around each ten thousand dollars. Maybe there would be a bank's mark on one or a notation from the counting that would give him an idea of his sponsors' location or language. But the money was like the men. It told him nothing. He packed the money into a priority mail shipping box and mailed it to himself in California.

He drove to the Buffalo Niagara International Airport, turned in his rental car, and flew back to Los Angeles. The next morning he returned to his workshop and began to concentrate on his work again. As he made more Semtex he assessed his progress.

It had been over a year, and he was still at the same task, but he wasn't unhappy. He was going to be paid ten million dollars for doing what he would have done for free. He was enjoying being a bomb maker. He had not obliterated the female bomb technician in her apartment, but he had essentially killed her. She wouldn't be defusing any explosive devices again. The news reports had been vague about her injuries, but he knew she must have used up all her luck just to be alive. She must have broken bones, internal injuries—certainly no ability to hold a hand steady. No doubt she was held together by pins and screws.

Thinking about her distracted him, and he felt the urge to find out about her. He found a photograph of her in the newspaper, and then another, but they were both out of date now—taken before he had blown her up. She had been pretty. That would be over too, like her career.

He found some more articles, and read them. They were just rephrasing the same information. Then he found one that quoted Dr. Devi Majumdar, Cedars-Sinai Medical Center. "She's in stable condition, doing as well as a person can do with such severe injuries."

He repeated, "Cedars-Sinai Medical Center."

21

The man who came into Diane's hospital room the next morning was easy to spot as a police detective. He was short and broad shouldered but had a narrow waist. He wore a sport coat and a necktie, something few men did during Southern California summers, particularly when the sun was hot and the sky that deep cloudless blue.

This one opened his coat so she could see his captain's badge, and said, "Hello, Sergeant Hines. I'm Captain Bart Almanzo, Homicide Special. I wondered if we could talk for a few minutes. I promised the nurse I wouldn't tire you out."

"Hi," she said. "I've heard of you, of course. Pleased to meet you."

"I'm in charge of the murder of the fourteen bomb technicians," he said. "We've got a few issues that came up recently, and I thought it would be better to talk to you here instead of waiting. Do you think the person who put the bomb in your apartment is the same one who killed the fourteen at the house in Encino?"

"Yes," she said.

"I imagine you've already talked with Captain Stahl about the technical stuff."

"Captain Stahl was here last night, but we didn't get into that too deeply. I was kept unconscious until a day or so ago, and I'm just sorting out impressions and memories. We'll talk more about it later on, I'm sure."

"Did he agree it was the same bomber?"

"Absolutely."

"Why are you both sure?"

"In this city we have lots of scares and a small but steady supply of actual bombs. Most of the bombs we see are rudimentary—black powder in a pipe, or a few sticks of dynamite, or nitrate fertilizer mixed with motor oil. Sometimes there will be a grenade from some old war. I got a land mine once, and someone I know got a mortar shell. Now suddenly we have a few that are all complicated, well designed, insidious, and psychologically astute. The bomb in my apartment was one of those."

"What sort of bomb did he use in your apartment?"

"He built an initiator that looked like a small version of the fuzes they put on bombs they drop from airplanes. It was cylindrical, and it had a little piece of metal like a propeller that spun around. In the real ones, when the bomb is locked onto the plane's rack, there's a length of stiff arming wire attached to the bomb rack that keeps the propeller from spinning around. When the bomb leaves the rack, the arming wire stays, and then the propeller on the fuze is free to turn. As it spins, it lines up a striker with the initiator. You can set the fuze to go off when it hits the ground, or just spins a set number of times. The wire keeps it from blowing up on or near the plane.

"He hid a small bomb inside the glass fixture for the ceiling light in my living room. He had a couple of ways to make the bomb go off. When I stepped inside and turned on the light, it didn't go on, but there was no pop sound or flash. That didn't seem right. So I used the flashlight attached to my Glock to scan the dark room for traps and triggers. When I was looking for the actual bomb it occurred to me there was one place I was sure not to look—in the burned-out light fixture. When I raised the flashlight to look, I saw a propeller spinning inside the glass dome. I'd started the initiator's arming sequence when I turned on the light switch. By then all I could do was take cover."

"Should we be contacting the manufacturers of military fuzes?"

"No. I'm positive he made this one. I'm not sure what turned the propeller. There might have been a small electric motor spinning it on a screw, or it might have been the spring mechanism of an old-fashioned metal windup toy. The spinner seemed to be the kind of thin, cheap metal that those toys had—usually tin."

"How did you take cover?"

"I dashed to the next room—the dining room—dropped to the floor, and rolled under my antique wooden sideboard."

"Is that what all the wood in the photographs came from?"

"I haven't seen any pictures, but probably. The sideboard was made of maple planks over an inch thick. It's so heavy that when I had it delivered, it took five men and two wheeled dollies to get it into the building. And I had it full of stuff."

"What sort of stuff?"

"Things everybody has but seldom uses. I had a few metal trays—pewter, brass, stainless steel, some candlesticks, the good silverware in its carrying case, some pots and pans, and a waffle iron. And of course, all the good tablecloths and napkins and trivets and things you use once a year."

"Do you think the sideboard is what saved you?"

"I don't really know, but it couldn't have hurt. I'd have to look at the blast pattern, see what's embedded in the floor and walls and furniture, and maybe figure out what quantity of explosive would have fitted in the light fixture. You should probably ask Captain Stahl about that. I'm sure he will have looked, and his judgment is much better than mine."

"I've heard he knows his explosives. Is he a pretty good boss?"

"We all have the greatest respect for him."

"That reminds me. There's another bit to clear up, and now is probably as good a time as any."

She waited. He behaved as though he were approaching a small, wild creature that might get away if he moved too quickly.

They stared into each other's eyes for a few seconds, and then he said, "You had a leather bag jammed into the space under the sideboard between you and the bomb. That may have helped too. You remember it? It seemed to be an overnight bag."

"A travel bag. Yes," she said. She sounded like a liar, even to herself. This suddenly seemed to be going in a bad direction.

"It contained some of your clothes. Can you tell me why? You were at work all that day, and you were scheduled to do a full shift the next day."

"I was going downstairs to do laundry later. It made a good laundry bag." She kept her eyes on him as she added, "The net ones you can see through make me uncomfortable. I don't like people looking at my underwear and everything. It's just a bit too much sharing."

Almanzo looked at her sympathetically. "You understand that when the crime scene people arrived, there was good reason to believe you were another homicide victim, not a survivor. Your apartment was a crime scene, and they had to go over everything carefully."

"Of course."

"Is there anyone other than the bomber who might have entered your apartment that day? Another male?"

"Not that I know of. I haven't given any friends a key, and the landlord has to notify me before he comes in."

"Did you have your boyfriend over, or anything like that?"

"I don't have a boyfriend."

"You understand that nobody on the force wants to embarrass you. But the specialists went over everything. There was male DNA on some of the clothing in your bag. What your cell phone bill showed was that at ten on the night after the bomb was removed from the gas station in Studio City, you called three one zero, five five eight—"

"Yes I did," she interrupted. "Do you know whose number that is?"

"I told you, every lead gets checked."

"I was calling the commander of my unit, who is also the supervisor of my three-person team. I had never met him before that day, but we had both been through a horrific, scary experience, and I wanted to talk to him about it."

Almanzo looked at her for a second. "Good enough for me," he said. "That is as far as I go. I respect you for immediately telling me the truth. But I've got to say one more thing. A secret is something only one person knows. In a homicide investigation everything gets collected, and a lot of eyes get to see it. Even on the smallest matter, do not get caught saying anything that contradicts the evidence."

"I won't. Thank you for letting me know about this."

"I'm leaving my card on the table here. I'll also give one to the nurse at the counter out there. If anything I need to know comes to your attention, give me a call, night or day." In a moment he was out the door.

She wasn't sure what to feel about her relationship with Dick Stahl. When she woke up from her coma she wondered if she'd dreamed what had happened. This morning she felt confused about it, but unable to think about anything else for long periods. She knew she had been very interested in Dick Stahl before she was hurt, but now the whole thought of the relationship seemed distant, as though her injuries had made her into someone else.

She had begun to think about him again after they'd talked. But then Captain Almanzo had drifted in and taken the oxygen out of the air. She felt alone and in trouble. She felt an urge to call Dick, and maybe that meant she still had real feelings for him, but she didn't have a phone except the hospital phone. If she used it, Dick's number would be listed on her hospital bill. She began to think about ways to get a new secret cell phone.

Diane knew she had to get her mind under control, and not make things worse for her or Stahl. But it seemed to her the world wasn't paying attention to the right things. The whole police force was looking for a mass murderer who was not even close to being identified or located. But they were not too busy to go after two police officers who might be getting too close.

When the nurse came back and gave her the tiny plastic cup of the nauseating purple liquid to put her to sleep, she was glad to drink it.

22

Stahl had just arrived at the office after a late lunch hour and sat down at his desk when a call on his radio distracted him. Team Four was on its way to a school in Brentwood, where someone had found a suspicious package in the cafeteria. Stahl stood and walked from his office and through Andy's on his way out.

"I'm going out with Team Four to that call at the school."

"Got it," said Andy.

As Stahl hurried toward the elevator to the parking lot he was already thinking about the fastest way to Brentwood in midafternoon. He had chosen to go to the scene because a school was the sort of place this bomb maker might pick for his next attack. Stahl was aware that a school was also the most likely place for a false alarm. Kids made crank calls and staged misguided hoaxes, and only a very tiny number planted homemade devices. This was most likely a kid's backpack with his sneakers and the remains of his lunch inside. But if it wasn't, he wanted to see it.

Stahl got into his unmarked police car and drove. During the weeks since Diane was injured he had been going to the scenes of bomb calls more and more often. He'd carried a tool kit and a bomb suit in the trunk of his car in case he wanted to go downrange and examine the device that prompted the call.

Diane's injuries had made him try to do everything and be everywhere. Part of the reason was that without her, he felt anxious and restless. Another part of the reason was that in the back of his mind he believed that not even an expert bomb technician was going to be as good as he was.

He had spent years at Eglin teaching military Explosive Ordnance Disposal specialists how to spot and defeat the most sophisticated devices, and since then he'd gone back for the refresher courses required to stay certified. He had kept up with whatever was newest and most formidable. Other people were almost certainly doing that too, but they couldn't match the breadth of his experience.

This bomber seemed to him to require his personal attention. Everything he did was odd—eccentric and unfamiliar, but at the same time teasing and sadistic.

Diane's bomb had been like that. The bomber had wanted to do more than just hurt her. He wanted to fool her, make her stand still where the bomb would be most powerful, and give her a moment or two to realize she had caused her own death. What Diane's attack seemed to have done was change the bomber's rhythm. Maybe he had been so pleased with his work at her apartment that he hadn't been feeling the need to hurt anybody else right away. He had gone quiet for over a month.

All that time Stahl kept waiting and wondering what the next attempt would be. Stahl had gone on around twenty bomb calls and found nothing that seemed to be the murderer's work. There was no device that would have presented a problem for any of Stahl's twenty-seven technicians. The devices that weren't fake were so crude that they would not have detonated if they'd been left in place forever.

Sometimes Stahl concocted stories to account for the bomber's inactivity. The man had to be living somewhere far from other people, where his neighbors didn't see or hear any of his testing or smell the chemicals, many of which had to be heated and cooled and reheated—and mixed with extreme care causing no friction, no buildup of static electricity, and no percussion. The bomber had been on a trend since his first crime, making and using more and more unusual and undependable mixtures in his bombs. Maybe on the day after rigging Diane's apartment he had been making his next bomb and suffered an accident. Maybe he had neglected to ground himself often enough and shuffled his feet. That could build up a static charge in his body. Maybe this time he had sent stray voltage along the metal housing of his device, set off the bomb in his hands, and blown himself to atoms. Stahl hoped so.

Every morning when Stahl woke up he spent a second or two hoping that when he turned off his phone's alarm he would see a text or an e-mail on the screen telling him a bomb maker had blown himself up. So far there was no such message.

It was Stahl's job to assume the bomber had been busy preparing something bigger and more lethal. One possibility was that he was building many Semtex-powered devices. What was stopping him from planting fifty bombs in fifty places at once? Stahl knew this man was more likely to plant a hundred bombs than fifty. Each scene would have one to cause preliminary damage and a second one to kill the technicians and paramedics who would come later.

All the bomber had to do was keep the members of the squad moving fast from one call to the next to the next, until somebody got too tired to think and made a small mistake.

This bomb maker was versatile too. He could make bombs that looked exactly alike, but were triggered in vastly different ways. He could put one in plain sight and another under the only path to it. If he wanted to he could attach very sensitive bombs to immovable surfaces—bridges, staircases, large stone or steel monuments in public parks—with epoxy cement. There was no limit to what this kind of bomb maker could do. Each time a bomb was found, a bomb tech would have to walk up to it and decide what to do with it.

Stahl turned onto Williford Avenue and saw Team Four's bomb truck just pulling up to the front of a large brick building that a sign identified as John Jay High School. The truck turned into a driveway and a police car that was parked across the entrance backed up to let it pass. Stahl approached before the officer could move back across the entrance, held up his identification, and followed the truck in.

He parked some distance from it and walked the rest of the way to join Team Four, who were climbing down from the truck and taking out equipment before entering the school. As Stahl approached he considered what he could see. This was a rich neighborhood. The houses he passed on the way were big and shaded by tall old trees.

He spotted Sergeant Paul Wyman, the supervisor of Team Four. Wyman was barely out of the truck when a middle-aged woman in a navy-blue business suit stepped up to him.

Stahl heard her say, "I'm Julia Cortez, the principal. All of the students have been evacuated to the next street over, where they're waiting with the faculty in the supermarket parking lot. We've activated the phone tree to call their parents to pick them up."

Paul Wyman said, "Very good. But we'll need to double-check that the building is empty before we deal with the device."

"I thought you might," she said. "I can take you to where it is."

"No, thank you," Wyman said. "Just describe what was found and the exact location and we'll take it from there. We have procedures that we need to follow."

Stahl was pleased with the way Wyman was handling it, so he stayed a few yards off and kept listening. The principal said, "It's in a black gym bag in the school cafeteria, which is in the back wing of the main building. This morning the teacher who was going to monitor the first lunch session saw the bag. He opened it to see if he could find the name of the owner and return it. Usually there will be something with the student's name. This time what he found was a kind of bundle with a cell phone and wires and batteries. He left the bag and locked the cafeteria doors, then called me." She handed Wyman a key. "This is the master key. It should open every door."

As the members of Team Four prepared to enter the building, Stahl said, "Mind if I go in with you and take a look?"

"Not at all," said Wyman. "We can use the help."

"Good."

The four police officers put on bomb suits and went in the front door of the main school building. Wyman sent Neil and Welsh to the main hallway to begin the search for stragglers or possible additional suspicious objects. They opened doors on either side of the main hallway and walked the perimeters of the first pair of classrooms, then moved on to the next pair of rooms. From time to time, one would call out: "This is the police. The school building has been evacuated. If you are still in the building come to the front door and gather in the parking lot. This is the police . . ."

Wyman and Stahl checked the rooms off the side corridors. When the four had made it all the way through the building they met where they had started. "The main section is clear," said Welsh.

"The side sections are all clear," Wyman said. "The captain and I will head for the cafeteria while you and Neil check the other buildings."

"The cafeteria is down this hall near the back door," said Welsh. "The doors are on the right."

"All right," Wyman said. "The captain and I will take a look and then we'll meet at the truck."

The two technicians went out the front door while Stahl and Wyman walked to the cafeteria. The room looked like the cafeteria of the middle school Stahl had attended over thirty years ago. There was a stainless steel and glass hot table three feet out from one wall, and the rest of the room was filled with long synthetic veneer folding tables that looked like blond wood, with five stackable molded plastic chairs on either side. They were all arranged in perfect order, with twenty tables to accommodate two hundred students at a time. Only one chair was pulled back from its table at an angle. It was on the far side of the room near where the hot food line would have been in an hour.

Wyman and Stahl approached, and Stahl stepped to the fourth aisle so he could see the one chair. "Damn," he said. "It's him."

Wyman said, "How can you tell?"

"The gym bag. It's just like the one he left on top of the elevator in the women's health clinic."

"Do you think he's using the same kind of device?"

"It doesn't sound that way. Didn't the principal say it's got a phone taped to it? This is the first one like that. Let's take a look."

He stepped close and peered into the half-opened gym bag without touching it. There was a beige brick of plastic explosive with a set of lead wires for a blasting cap running into it. He could see the cell phone and the corner of a lithium-ion battery. "The wires are the same color and style as the last ones—a number eight, probably from the same batch."

"I was thinking," said Wyman. "If we get the containment vessel up to the back entrance, we could just pop it in—even hand it out the window from here so nobody has to carry it far."

"We can't do that this time. It's him."

"What should we do, then?"

"Let's get the jammer in your truck going."

Wyman reached for his cell phone to call the others, but Stahl held his arm. "No phones, no radios until the jammer is running." He let go of Wyman's arm. "What model do you have with you?"

"TSJ-MBJ110."

"Perfect. It's been tested recently, right?"

"Once a week. We keep it charged and tested."

They went out the back door of the school and headed for the bomb truck. As they did, Stahl focused his mind on the jammer.

This model jammer was designed for the military to prevent any radio signal, including a cell signal, from reaching a bomb and detonating it. The jammer had its own ten-thousand-watt AC generator, its own cooling system, and a battery backup. The jammer created a quiet zone for 150 meters around it, blocking every band from 20 to 250 megahertz. Once it was in place and operating, Stahl could go to work on the bomb.

Neil, Wyman's second in command, set up the jammer in the central hallway of the school, plugged it into an outlet, and switched it on.

Stahl turned on his cell phone and waited for a signal, then put it away. "I get nothing. It's operating. Thanks, Neil. Now go back to the truck, call a Code Five Edward and stand by while we figure out what we've got to worry about."

"Yes, sir." He went out the back entrance and headed for the truck.

Stahl and Wyman went into the cafeteria and Wyman stepped up to the gym bag.

"Don't touch it just yet," said Stahl.

"The jammer's working. You tested it yourself."

"Right," Stahl said. "But this is the guy. Our guy. He doesn't do just one thing. He's well informed enough to know that if we suspected a phone trigger we'd use a signal jammer. He didn't hide the phone."

"But he hid everything in the bag."

"Think for a minute," said Stahl. "Why did this guy put the bag here? Not because he wants to kill a dozen middle school kids. He wants to kill some bomb technicians. So I'm guessing the phone isn't the only trigger. It's the bait. He's hoping that once we neutralize the phone, we'll think we've solved the problem. We'll try to put it in the containment vessel."

"That's the logical thing to do. We can't detonate it in a school."

"So far he hasn't planted anything that didn't have a trap," said Stahl. "So let's see what he's rigged to make normal procedures suicidal. Let's start by checking for connections to anything else in the bag—wires, layers of an insulating material that are spring-loaded to pop out when someone touches the device and complete the firing circuit, pressure pads, tilt switches. He's used all of those."

They took out their flashlights and leaned over the bag, not touching it as they strained to see inside from every possible angle.

After a few minutes Wyman said, "No wires, or anything."

Stahl said, "Agreed." He lay on the floor and rolled onto his back to look up under the plastic chair seat. "Take a look at this, but don't touch it."

Wyman lay down on the other side of the chair and rolled to position the window of his helmet so he could see. "What is that?"

Stahl said, "It looks like the sensor mechanism from a burglar alarm. As long as the magnet on this side is touching this sensor, nothing happens, because the magnet is holding the circuit open. If the magnet gets moved, an interior spring pushes the sensor down and the gap in the firing circuit is closed."

"So if we disconnect the battery, we're done."

"Let's not assume that'll do it," Stahl said. "I'm not sure the battery has enough power to operate this."

"You mean the battery is just another decoy?"

"Maybe not, but let's see if there's another power source." Stahl reached into the kit and took out a multimeter. He put the leads to various spots and watched the dial on the box. "There's power running through these two metal legs of the chair."

He looked at the legs carefully, and then at two other chairs. "The feet of this chair are strangely clean—much cleaner than the others. No dust at all." He touched the grout between the tiles of the cafeteria floor with his finger. Next he took out a knife from the kit and scraped the grout. It crumbled and began to come out.

"This grout is new. It hasn't been here long enough to lose the moisture and set properly." He worked at it a bit longer and then lifted his blade. "See the wire?" He pried up a double strand of narrow-gauge wire. "Let's look for the other end of it." He got to his knees and followed the line of fresh grout with his finger. It led to the nearest wall. He pointed to a small double wire with white insulation that ran a few inches up the white wall to the white cover of an electrical outlet. He used the knife to unscrew the two screws that held the cover to the wall, and saw that the two wires split and connected to the sides of the outlet. "Here's the power source."

"Can we disconnect it?"

"Yes." He unscrewed one connection to the socket to free one wire, capped the end, and then freed the other wire. Then he took up the wire that ran under the grout. When he reached the chair he tested its legs again with the multimeter and found no current. He cut the two wires to the battery. Then he pulled the blasting cap out of the block of Semtex.

When Stahl had finished, he noticed that Wyman was looking around the room.

"Do you see something else?"

Wyman said, "If you hadn't shown up, I would have died in this room."

"Maybe," said Stahl. "But now you're less likely to die if you face this again. You just met this guy. Work on getting to know him, and how he thinks. Never forget that what he wants is to kill you and your team. Not some kids or a gas station attendant. He wants the tech who's trying to defeat his bomb."

"I was completely fooled," said Wyman. "I never saw any of it."

"Now you're somebody this guy has to worry about. Pass it on to your team."

"Thanks," said Wyman. He knelt to begin picking up the tools.

"Leave everything where it is, including the jammer," said Stahl. "We need to get the dogs in to sniff the rest of the school for explosives. He could have put another one in some kid's locker."

"I'll make the calls and get the locker keys."

“Right. If the dogs alert on anything, have somebody drive out of the zone and call me. If they don’t, you can turn the place over to the crime scene people. All we need is a print or some DNA, or a sign of where he bought the battery or the bags.”

Stahl clomped along the hall to the back door. He went to the bomb truck and said, “You’d better go in and help Sergeant Wyman. But don’t touch anything until he’s briefed you.” Then he went to his car, took off the suit, put it in his trunk, and drove.

23

Stahl decided it was too late to drive back to police headquarters now. The day shift had ended and he wanted to make it to the hospital to see Diane before visiting hours ended. He knew that by now Andy had left his desk, as usual, clear and clean with everything he had been working on filed in its place in one of the locked filing cabinets, and gone home.

He drove home to his condominium, walked through to the master bedroom, and turned on the light. He snatched a sport coat and jeans from the closet and tossed them onto the bed. He showered and dressed as efficiently as possible, then went to the garage, got into the plain police car, and drove.

He glanced at the clock on the car's dashboard. Visiting hours started at seven on Diane's floor, and it was after eight. He increased his speed a little so he could make it all the way across the wide intersection at San Vicente before the light changed.

He had felt as though he were falling behind during the day, and this was the culmination. Defeating bombs was slow work. It took as long as it took, but he was also the boss, the one who had administrative duties and responsibilities, and even on a good day they kept him distracted. He had meant to talk to Diane on the phone during the day, but that had been impossible. Since he returned to the force, he had been trying to control everything around him, and he was wearing thin.

The need to control had been strongest on bomb calls. The deaths of the fourteen horrified him so much he'd found it difficult to let any of his remaining technicians touch a bomb. Each time he went out to observe their work and give advice, he hadn't been able to resist going downrange himself. There had always been something about the device that made him feel everyone would be safer if he handled it.

This wasn't the technicians' fault. They were all properly qualified, trained, and certified. Some of them had been on the squad for over ten years, and all had served a number of years as Los Angeles cops or federal agents before then. He wondered if they were talking about him yet. He hoped not. They still seemed to see his willingness to go downrange himself as a positive quality. But it was time to quit doing that. He was going to make a conscious effort to loosen his grip and act like a supervisor, which was his real job. He would touch a device only if he was convinced the killer had planted it.

From now on, every week he would bring one team at a time into a conference room and give each an intensive review of everything the squad had learned so far about this bomber's work. Frequent updates would do the most to help the teams handle the devices they encountered in the field. It occurred to him that it would be a good idea to include some of the homicide detectives too. If they knew exactly what to look for, they might find this guy.

He nodded as he agreed to his own proposal, and then his mind returned to Diane. He realized she might be part of his solution. She had seen the bomber's work more often and more closely than anyone else but Stahl. Together they had studied the placement, the hardware, and the explosive substances and talked about every aspect of the scene—the power sources, the blast radius, the selection and origins of the parts, and the bomber's preferences. She could probably teach an intensive class for the technicians as well as he could. Maybe he would mention the idea to her tonight, if he had a chance.

Maybe he should save it for another visit, when her recovery was more complete. He should probably just drop in as though he were a good supervisor coming by to visit a brave wounded police officer, and then leave. He must not look to the doctors and nurses like what he was—a high-ranking public official who had been engaged in a secret sexual relationship with a colleague he supervised. Her injury had turned the idea that he was going to be off the force in a couple of weeks into a fantasy. He'd had to stay because the bomber was still out there, and now he had to stay to protect her.

Stahl drove up the hospital driveway and into the parking structure. He glided up and down the rows of spaces with signs indicating they were reserved for doctors, then up another level, and finally onto the visitors' levels. When he found a space, he took a picture with his phone so he would remember where he'd left his police car.

Stahl took the elevator down to the ground floor, where he could enter the main building. He strode across the busy lobby, then got into the elevator. Just as the doors rolled shut he saw three members of the Bomb Squad come in the front door together. They were Team Two—Curtis, McCrary, and Bolland. It was nice they'd come to visit Diane, but it was a bit of a disappointment. He knew they would have to stop at the reception counter to find out where to go and to get visitors' stickers, so he might still have a little time to see Diane alone.

When his elevator doors opened and he stepped out, the elevator beside his arrived and Elliot emerged. "Hi, boss." They shook hands, and walked toward Diane's hallway together.

Stahl said, "This is pretty interesting. I just saw Curtis, McCrary, and Bolland downstairs."

"What's the latest on her condition?" Elliot asked. "Have you heard anything?"

"Supposedly her recovery is better than normal, but what's normal for having a bomb go off twenty feet from your head?" said Stahl.

"That would be deceased," said Elliot.

"That's been my observation," said Stahl. "If she's ready for a bunch of visitors, she's got to be doing great."

They reached the nurses' station at the end of the hall, and one of the nurses Stahl had met before was on duty. "Gentlemen," she said. "Go to the waiting room down the hall, and do what its name implies. Wait."

Elliot and Stahl went to the waiting room at the end of the hall. Stahl saw that all of the two dozen or so seats were taken. About fifteen of the people in the room were from the Bomb Squad. He leaned in and addressed the group. "What's everybody doing here at once?"

Elliot took a sheet of paper from his pocket. "Haven't you seen this?" He handed it to Stahl.

It was an invitation printed on good stationery that bore the name, address, and logo of Cedars-Sinai hospital. The text said, *"Dear members of the LAPD Bomb Squad, Sergeant Diane Hines cordially invites you to her Coming Out (of a Coma) Party, which will be held on September 15 at 8:00 p.m. at her current residence, Floor Five of the Cedars-Sinai hospital. Refreshments will be served. No RSVP necessary."*

Dick Stahl read Elliot's invitation and thought about it. The fourteen remaining members of the original Bomb Squad were Diane's friends. When the new squad members read the invitation they might see the evening as a chance to become closer to the original Bomb Squad members and to each other. He said, "I hadn't seen this before." He looked around. "And I don't see Hines."

Bolland said, "The nurse told us she wants to get dolled up before she sees us."

"'Dolled up,'" Judy Welsh repeated. "There's an expression you don't hear much anymore." She touched her hair as though she were arranging it.

"That's because you don't see it much anymore, either," McCrary said.

Welsh grinned. "If you could see what Diane and I look like when we go off watch and clean up, it would fuel your adolescent fantasies for the next five years."

That brought loud laughter and a few side comments.

A moment later Elliot appeared behind Stahl in the doorway. "The nurse was about to come down here and tell you all to keep the noise down. I headed her off, so don't get me kicked out of here."

Stahl had a vague sense that this gathering wasn't something Diane would agree to. Maybe the nursing staff had decided it would be good for her, and made the arrangements.

Stahl heard footsteps on the hard floor behind him and turned. Wyman and Neil walked up.

Wyman said, "We used the dogs and searched every locker, everyplace where you could hide a device in the school. The crime scene people are still running tests, taking more pictures, and collecting prints. They'll call if they find anything for us."

Stahl nodded. "Okay." But he was distracted. He had come here expecting to be the only one. This larger gathering had an odd, premature feeling.

The nurse from the desk appeared behind them. She was some kind of supervisor, and she was middle-aged. Stahl guessed she was the one who had said "dolled up."

"Excuse me, gentlemen," she said. As they turned, she slipped past them and into the room, where she saw Welsh and Terranova. "And ladies."

The room was silent.

"A while ago the big sheet cake, soft drinks, and coffee you ordered were delivered to the floor. That is against the rules. We're grateful, and we love you all, and we especially love Sergeant Hines. We're going to let you have a quiet—and I mean quiet—visit with her in this waiting room. Where's the boss?"

She leaned in farther and saw Stahl. "Oh, there you are. You're responsible."

"I'll try to live up to that," Stahl said.

"I'm going down to the break room to cut the cake. If it's loud down here, nobody gets any."

"Need any help?" said Elliot.

"From a bunch of cops?" she said. "Hardly."

She turned and hurried off. As she approached the nurses' station she grabbed a hospital orderly by the arm and made him push the cart that held the cake and the drinks. Stahl saw her turn to the left a few doors down.

Stahl held up both arms and waved them urgently for attention. "Can anyone tell me who arranged this party?"

In her room across the hall from the nurses' station, Diane sat in her wheelchair. The nurse lifted Diane's feet onto the foot pedal as though they weighed nothing, and then straightened her gown and put a clean blanket over her knees. She took Diane's hairbrush out of her hand and brushed her hair, as though it were long enough, and then held the mirror while she put on her makeup. Diane said, "Thank you so much, Sonja. I'll be okay from here."

Sonja said, "Okay." Then she disappeared into the hallway.

Normally Diane would have gone to the waiting room with a walker, but she decided she was not ready to try to step into a crowd of friends and comrades, including some big men with whom she had been on a hugging basis when they met at after-hours gatherings.

She stared into the mirror and shrugged. She didn't look very different from before, she thought. The last bruises and burns had faded, and somehow the swelling had all gone away. She aimed the wheelchair toward the doorway, approaching it from the side to reach the push pad on the wall, rolled out of her room, gave the wheels of her chair a spin, and passed the door of the room beside hers just before it happened.

24

The shock wave blew off the break-room door and punched out the wall behind it where the counter and cabinets were. It turned the air in the hallway into a hard, expanding force that reached the waiting room in an instant, even though it had to bat down the walls of four other rooms to get there, bringing along a growing load of beds, visitors' chairs, monitoring equipment, and other things no longer identifiable or even separable. The sixth wall, the side of the waiting room, was only partially dislodged, but it was possible to see steel items protruding through it in places.

The air in the wing was now a suspension of powdery dust from demolished drywall, acoustic tiles, and masonry.

Stahl found himself on the floor eight feet from where he had stood. He moved a hand tentatively, then a foot, brought himself up on one knee, and finally came to his feet. He could see in the milky haze that there were other human shapes in the room, and most were beginning to move.

He could see three crawling on hands and knees to stay below the clouds of dust, and there were also several on their feet, moving toward the doorway.

Stahl breathed in through his shirt and called out, "Is anybody in this room hurt? Anybody hurt?" Two other voices called the same question from other parts of the room, but no answer reached his ears.

"This is Stahl. Start looking for casualties."

He made his way to the door and felt a cool breeze. The lights had gone out in the middle of the floor in the vicinity of the nurses' station. In the hallway a grid of metal frames that held ceiling tiles had come loose and was now leaning, still partially suspended by wires. Above it, Stahl could see the complicated pattern of I beams, pipes, and conduits for electrical cables. This usually unseen layer above him was all sprayed with a surface coat of grayish fireproofing material.

His eyes adjusted, and after a second he realized the reason was the same reason he could breathe more easily now. The explosion had blown out a part of the outer wall, so there was a big gash open to the night sky. There was a steady breeze of cool air flowing down the hallway, clearing the floating dust away. Stahl shook his head hard and ran both hands down his face to get rid of the dust in his hair and eyebrows, and as he began to trot, he brushed dust off his shoulders.

He tried to run up the hallway to Diane's room, but he felt off balance and clumsy. He wanted to get there but he couldn't seem to find it. He sloshed into icy water, and realized that the water was flowing down the hall from a broken sprinkler system somewhere ahead. He could hear what sounded like electrical sparking, so he knew he had better try to find a switch quickly, but he couldn't see a panel. He looked at the number of the room nearest to the gaping hole in the wall. The number was 568. Diane's room had been 572, but it seemed to be gone. He stopped, his mouth gaping, took a few steps forward, then a few back, but he couldn't make out where one ruined room ended and the next began.

There were other people running now, lifting debris to see if there was anyone beneath it. Some of them were members of his Bomb Squad, but there were others emerging from the stairwell at the end of the hall. They ran to gurneys and wheelchairs as they arrived, grabbed them, and pushed them forward, hurrying to patients' rooms in an otherworldly race, a scramble to get a patient and run.

Stahl began to move again. He hit his phone button for the headquarters and began to talk. "This is Captain Stahl. There's been a large explosion on the fifth floor of Cedars-Sinai hospital. There are numerous injuries and at least two deaths. The outer wall on the north side of the building facing Melrose has a breach about ten feet wide. Request fire and rescue teams, Code Three. Dispatch Team Four of the Bomb Squad, and tell them to bring three bomb trucks."

Stahl came to a place where ceiling tiles, boards, and other debris had fallen and partially blocked the hallway. He could see one wheel of a wheelchair, and a bit of the blue leather seat beneath it. This was an opportunity to get one more patient off the devastated fifth floor and down to safety. He lifted a sheet of wallboard and threw off some tiles and what seemed to have been a wooden cabinet. The chair was upside down so its armrests and seat back were down and the wheels up. As he pulled the chair from the wreckage he saw her.

She was lying facedown, her head toward the waiting room door as though the force of the explosion had thrown her forward.

He touched her carotid artery and felt a strong, normal pulse. Without thinking he shouted, "Medic!" It was a yell that came from ten years ago and ten thousand miles away. He heard it and shouted, "Doctor! I need help over here."

25

The bomb maker sat in front of his television and studied the picture of the hospital on the screen. The cameraman was down on the sidewalk across the street with the reporter, so the camera was tilted upward. He could see a hole in the side of the hospital building that looked like a cave and a sheet of water pouring out of it like a mountain waterfall, making the bricks glisten and then splashing into a pool at the foot that flowed into the street. It looked to him as though his bomb had ripped a major water pipe apart, and the authorities had been unable to shut it off. He hoped the water wasn't putting out any fires.

The hospital was big—six stories on the side with the hole in it. The reporter had said there were 958 beds in the hospital and that some of the patients were being evacuated and moved to other facilities. When the station switched to the helicopter shots he could see a few people being loaded into helicopters on the roof. When the shot was at street level, he saw ambulances lined up along Melrose.

The woman reporter who was so skinny and tall entered the frame. "I've just been told that one of the events at the hospital tonight was a small party consisting of members of the LAPD Bomb Squad. They had come to pay their respects and celebrate the progress toward recovery made by an injured colleague, Sergeant Diane Hines. My source indicates that at least fifteen members of the twenty-eight-person squad were present on the floor where the explosion occurred." The center of her forehead right above her nose pinched her brows together. "We have no word yet of the names of any casualties, or if any of them were police officers."

"*Were*," the bomb maker said. He clapped his hands, and then held them together as though he were keeping something from getting away. There had to be fatalities. There had to be. This was only the first report, and the newspeople were already talking about the Bomb Squad, not the 958 patients. There had to be fatalities. The force that blew out a wall of that reinforced brick building must have taken people with it.

The bomb maker got up and paced across the room in front of the big screen. The picture switched to the anchor desk at the studio, where the two anchors glared at their camera. They were a man and a woman so ill matched they appeared to be on a blind date, but they both had the same wrinkle in the center of their foreheads that the street reporter had. They were both listening to something coming to them through their earpieces, and they didn't like the sound of what they were hearing.

The bomb maker stood still and listened for an announcement, but the woman began talking, and it was only a repetition of the information they had released so far, translated into the clichés that populated reporters' brains. There was a large explosion on an upper floor of Cedars-Sinai Medical Center tonight, wreaking havoc in the building. Fire, police, and ambulance personnel had responded immediately. No information about the condition of the building or any of its occupants had been released yet—or, as the woman ignorantly put it, "as of yet." But a joint press conference of hospital and police spokespeople was expected shortly.

The bomb maker's heart beat harder. They didn't seem to know yet how he had done it—how he had gotten them all into one room at the same time. They didn't seem to know he had set up the bomb in the school in Brentwood just to get the squad agitated and occupied all day while he made his preparations.

The hospital was always going to be today's event. He would have been delighted if he could have taken out one bomb team at the school as a warm-up, but he had never felt as emotionally invested in the school as he was in the hospital. He had wanted them all.

He executed the hospital party meticulously. The designated guest of honor was the ideal choice. Obviously she had been popular with the rest of the squad even before he decided to destroy them all. He had injured her terribly when he rigged her apartment. The squad had been worried about her, and they had missed her. His idea of her throwing her own Coming Out (of a Coma) party was perfect.

Of course they had come. Who would turn down an invitation like that? They adored her. And now, the party had been a triumph for him. There must have been one or two bomb teams on duty, but that meant at least two teams must have been present for his surprise, and possibly three. This was as good as the booby-trapped house in Encino, and much more of a scare for the good people of Los Angeles. He didn't take his eyes from the television until the newspeople quit after 2:00 a.m.

Stahl slept three hours on his office couch, showered, and put on another suit he kept in the office closet for emergencies. He was at the headquarters pressroom for the afternoon press briefing, standing behind the chief of police on the platform. The chief opened the gathering by stepping onto the podium to the clicking and flashing of many cameras recording his grave, determined expression.

"Last night's tragedy was a disgusting waste of innocent lives." He looked at his notes. "Erin Kajanian, a fifty-three-year-old supervising nurse at Cedars-Sinai Medical Center; and Dale Monet, a twenty-three-year-old orderly, died in the cowardly bombing of the hospital. They were in a fifth-floor break room to cut a cake to help celebrate the promising recovery of wounded police officer Diane Hines with some of her off-duty friends and colleagues."

The chief's voice sounded strained. "We will always embrace them both as members of our police family. We mourn them as our own. The term 'LA's finest' would have little meaning if it didn't include citizens like them. Let's observe a moment of silence in their honor." He bowed his head and the room fell silent.

Stahl could see that nearly every head was down. One of the exceptions was an older reporter from Channel Nine who was familiar with the chief's choreography. He knew the signal that would end the silence would be the sound of the chief taking his first step off the platform and heading quickly out the door. Stahl saw the chief's military pivot in place for his first step.

"Chief!" called the reporter. "Will you take a question?"

But the chief was almost out the door, and pretended not to hear him. His two aides were behind him.

Deputy Chief Ogden was already at the microphone. "If you have questions, Captain Stahl, commander of the Bomb Squad, is here, and he's best equipped to answer them."

Stahl's tired mind had been occupied when he heard the words "Captain Stahl." He looked up at the expectant faces of the reporters and the glinting one-eyed stares of the cameras.

A young, red-haired woman near the front waved her hand in a way that reminded Stahl of the girl in all his high school classes who was always breathless with the wish to be first with the right answer.

He said, "Yes?"

"Have you identified the bomber yet?"

Stahl was stunned. How could she not know? "Not yet."

Her face seemed to transform itself. Her eyes were like marbles, and her mouth acquired a displeased half smile that seemed venomous. He noted that she had fooled him. "Captain," she said. "You were hired to fill in for the murdered commander of the Bomb Squad nearly eight weeks ago. Are you any closer to stopping the mass murderer than you were on your first day?"

"Any closer? It's hard to tell. I haven't had a chance to speak with the homicide detectives on the case for over twenty-four hours. I was in Brentwood yesterday defusing an explosive device in a middle school, and by the time I returned I didn't get to ask for an update. I plan to catch up today."

"We were informed that the reason so many Bomb Squad personnel were in one place last night was for a party. Don't you think the people of this city deserve better than that?"

"They certainly deserve to be safe from a person who likes to place bombs in public places. Since the first incident, the Bomb Squad and the investigative branches of the LAPD and local, state, and federal officers have been working nonstop to keep citizens safe and apprehend the bomber. We've prevented several of the killer's attempts during that time, and rendered safe a number of his devices."

"Don't the people deserve to be informed of what's going on?"

"When it's safe to release information, we will fill you in. My job is to neutralize bombs before they injure or kill people."

"Is it true the bomber invited you all to a party last night, and put a bomb in the cake?"

"We're still investigating exactly what happened and how it was done."

Another male reporter, named Todd Tedesco, whom Stahl had been surprised to see outside the studio because he was an anchorman, asked, "Is there a time when you'll simply say, 'This is it? If I haven't caught the bomber by this date, I'll resign and give somebody else a chance?'"

Stahl said, "As you know, I was asked to take on this job temporarily to keep the squad functioning while it's being rebuilt. I've always planned to leave as soon as my services were no longer needed. I don't believe that's a goal we've reached yet. I also serve at the pleasure of the chief of police, who can remove me at any time."

Todd Tedesco turned and glanced at one of his colleagues, Gloria Hedlund, who often shared the desk with him on the local news. Stahl realized that he was trying to yield the floor to her. She jumped up and inhaled to speak. They were ambushing him, but he decided the best way through this was to let them ask their questions. He nodded to her.

Gloria Hedlund had the big eyes and pursed mouth of a long-haired house cat. When he looked at her, he acknowledged that at one time she must have been very beautiful. She pounced. "The chief said this hospital party was for Sergeant Diane Hines. Is that accurate?"

"Yes, the squad was there to visit an officer who was wounded by a device set in her apartment, and to let her know we were glad she was recovering."

"And I understand the bomber set up the party. You allowed this to happen, and in fact attended. Was something clouding your judgment?"

"As I said, I was busy yesterday defusing a bomb in a school. I wasn't aware when I arrived at the hospital that other officers would be there."

"Sergeant Hines seems to be pretty important. Do you have a special relationship with Sergeant Hines? There's a rumor you're being charged with an inappropriate relationship with an officer under your command. Is she the one?"

"Nobody has charged me with anything."

"Just to clarify, you're not aware of any charges, filed or contemplated, by the police department against you for sexual harassment or fraternization with a member of your command?"

Stahl could feel rage building in his chest and moving upward. "I can't know what anybody in or out of the department is contemplating. You're the first one to mention it to me."

She was frustrated, not wanting him to slither away. "Maybe I should be more direct. Have you had sexual relations with any member of the police force?"

"Maybe you should be *less* direct," Stahl said. "I was asked to answer any questions I could about the hospital bombing. Apparently you and the last reporter have no questions relevant to the case, so right now I'm going back to work. Good afternoon, ladies and gentlemen."

He took long steps out the door and away from the pressroom, and headed toward the Homicide Special offices. He was still feeling heat around his neck, but a sensation like cold in his chest and stomach—anger and dread. As he walked along the open floor to the office section of the building, he controlled and isolated the feelings. He had learned to separate himself from distracting emotions many years ago and gotten very good at it over the years, but times like this still caught him by surprise.

He could see that the detectives in Homicide Special were busy. He knew they were probably shunting excess cases back to the divisions where they'd happened, so they could devote more time to the bomber.

Some of them were working on flipping through loose-leaf murder books, slipping new pages into the binders and clicking the jaws closed. Others were making phone calls or conducting people into conference rooms. But he knew most of the detectives would be performing tasks today that focused on the bomb deaths. The device in the hospital would have added two more binders, and they would reside on the desk of whoever became the lead detective on the case.

By now someone had probably entered the essentials of the hospital bomb into the ATF's Bomb Arson Tracking System, hoping to find other incidents that were similar to this one. Entering it also put the incident out there for experts in other agencies to notice and think about.

There might already be a few pieces of the bomb in the crime lab being examined for fingerprints and chemical traces. Stahl had his own expectation for the device. It would be a series of small batteries connected to a number eight blasting cap, a spring-loaded switch that would complete the circuit when the box was opened, and a charge of homemade Semtex. There would be something else. A bomb that would blow out a ten-foot stretch of hardened concrete and brick wall with rebar supports would make the sheet cake heavy. There could have been more Semtex connected to the initial charge. He remembered seeing a cart—not for moving a patient, but the kind institutions used to deliver food. Maybe the lower shelf had been full of explosives.

Stahl arrived at Almanzo's office and knocked on the window. Almanzo was, as usual, working at his desk wearing suit pants and a perfectly pressed snow-white shirt with a .45 caliber pistol in a holster. When he saw Stahl he popped up and stepped to the door. "Come on in, Dick." He closed the door and waved at one of the empty seats facing his desk. "I was hoping we could talk today."

"Me too," said Stahl. "Have we learned anything since the hospital bomb?"

"I want to be sure you got my message."

"What message?"

"I guess you didn't. The crime scene people going through Sergeant Hines's belongings found some male DNA on her clothes. They've been able to identify it."

Stahl stared at him for a moment. He felt as though he'd been punched. "Thank you. That explains something I was just wondering about." He forced himself to hide his shock. "How about the hospital bomb?"

"We're waiting to see if anything survived the blast—prints, blood, or something that was shielded from the heat and the power of it. I'm probably kidding myself, hoping something didn't get burned off or blown away. But there could be a serial number or a marking that will tell us something."

Stahl shrugged. "It's always worth checking. I'll send some technicians to the lab as soon as I know who's coming in today. Everybody who wasn't on duty last night was at the hospital."

"Thanks, Dick. What do you think the bomber is doing right now? Will he take another month off?"

"Month off?"

"Yeah. After the explosion at Diane Hines's apartment, he didn't strike again until last night."

"As of last night I don't think he was taking time off," Stahl said. "I think what he was doing was resupplying his arsenal. He had used a lot of explosives up to then. I think he was in his workshop or lab or bunker or whatever it is, making more high explosives. His favorites are plastics, usually a homemade version of Semtex. Making it is the hardest part of what he does, and the most dangerous. He has to make most of the ingredients, and then combine them right, or they won't become Semtex. The ingredients are mostly explosives in their own right. Some are volatile and unstable, so he has to work in slow motion, also making sure they don't get too hot or too cool, too wet or too dry. He has to heat some of them to make the chemical changes occur, which means he's got to have a source of heat, one of the things that can set off an explosive. He has to grind some of them from cakes into powders without setting them off. At the same time he's got to avoid sparks, short circuits, static electricity. He can't drop things. But the batch he used last night at the hospital means he succeeded in making plenty. So now he's coming after us again."

26

Diane Hines woke and sat up. She felt disoriented for a few seconds, and then saw the shapes in the room—the table on her left that swiveled over the bed, the open door to the tiny bathroom, the monitors. She was in a hospital. It was another one, but still a hospital.

She was clearer now. She hadn't gone over what happened yet, but she was sure the memories were still available to her. She remembered the nurse coming in to tell her that the Bomb Squad was in the waiting area to see her. She remembered trying to make herself presentable. When she had done what she could—a little makeup, brushing her stubble of hair—she wheeled herself to the door of her room and out into the hall. And then there was the terrible noise. All the bomb techs in the world knew that noise because it was the sound they heard when they destroyed a bomb in a controlled detonation. The noise had been in her dreams for years. After that explosion, she remembered Dick above her yelling at an intern to help him put her on a stretcher.

After a time, she had been wheeled through dark night air, and she remembered a ride in an ambulance, but without being able to see anything except the roof of the vehicle above her. When the ambulance stopped she was pulled out on the stretcher at the back of a building. The back of this hospital looked like the back of every hospital, a roofed-over spot for the ambulances to unload, a set of double doors that huffed open automatically, and then a long series of ceilings and fluorescent lights gliding by overhead.

She had seen more of the city's hospitals from the back than most people ever did when she had been a young street cop, taking in injured suspects, victims, and bystanders after some act of violence or poor marksmanship.

It was night again, so she assumed she must have slept from around 8:00 a.m. for the next twelve hours. Sometimes she thought that with the induced forty-two-day coma and all the other drugged sleep after that, she would never have to sleep again. Staying awake would be the only way to get back all the time she had lost.

Diane looked at herself. There were bruises, but nothing to indicate she had sustained any serious new injuries—no tubes, no wires except for blood pressure and pulse. She felt her body and found no casts, seriously painful spots, stitches, or bandages. She knew from practice where the nurse's call button would be, so she felt for it and pressed.

In a moment, a nurse arrived in the doorway. She was about forty and looked like an athlete, probably a runner. "Hello, hon. Is everything all right?"

"I don't know," Diane said. "What hospital is this?"

"Valley Presbyterian."

"Do you know who I am?"

The nurse stepped closer. "I hope *you* do." Diane could see she was joking, but she waited. "You're Diane Hines. You were transferred from Cedars early this morning."

She lifted Diane's left arm to point to the plastic bracelet. "Are you having trouble remembering things?"

"No," Diane said.

"I guess you're checking up on us. We hardly ever mix up names and give anybody the wrong operation—just when things get slow and we need a laugh. Are you feeling all right? Any dizziness, vertigo, or nausea?"

"No," said Diane. "I was in an explosion and got blown around, but I seem to be getting used to that."

"Yeah, I saw that in your paperwork. Let me bring you some water." She glided out of the room on silent rubber shoes.

A moment later she was back with a plastic pitcher of water and a paper cup. She swung the side tray beside Diane's bed and showed her a smaller paper cup with a pill in it. "Your chart says you can have a sedative if you want it."

"Can I hold on to it for later if I need it?"

"Sorry, we're not allowed to do that. Just press your call button and I'll bring it whenever you want."

"I won't. Have I had any visitors?"

"There was a man from the police department who called about the visiting rules around an hour ago. Let me see if I can remember his name."

"Was it Captain Stahl?"

"That's the one."

"What *are* the rules?"

"If you want to see somebody, visiting hours are twenty-four hours a day. If you don't, then there are no visitors allowed. You're under observation, and they'll keep up your physical therapy, but you'll probably be out of here tomorrow or the next day."

"What time is it? After the first explosion they took my watch and phone."

"It's almost ten. If you want a phone, there's one right over here."

"Thanks."

"Press the call button if you need me." The nurse left and closed the door.

Diane remembered being afraid to call Dick from a hospital room, but that seemed like a minor issue now. She dialed Dick's cell phone number. It was interesting to her that she had remembered those eleven digits so easily. Her hands seemed to do the remembering, even though in the first blowup she had lost the names of close friends, childhood pets, and probably her memory of several college courses her parents had scrimped to pay for.

She was aware that the ringing noise she heard was not the actual sound of his phone ringing, just a ring-like signal to reassure the caller that the system was trying to complete a connection. The ringing stopped. "The party you are calling is unavailable at this time," said another female voice. The voice was better than Diane's, a little lower and softer, a mature but sensual voice. It made her jealous for a second; even though it was a recording triggered by a computer with a database of sentences, the words were somebody's voice. "If you would like to leave a message, wait for the tone."

"Hello, Captain," she said. "This is Sergeant Hines. I've been moved to Valley Presbyterian hospital. My number here is," and she read the number off the phone's sticker and then hung up. She set the phone on the swivel table beside the bed where she could reach for it without spilling her water pitcher.

The door opened and Dick Stahl came in. He was looking at his phone. "Hey, Diane. Did you just call me?"

"About a second ago," she said.

He stepped up to her bedside, leaned over, and kissed her on the cheek—an easy, friendly peck. "What did you want?"

"That, for starters."

"Really?"

She nodded. "Since I woke up I've been kind of lonely." She looked at him. "I'm glad you're alive."

"Thanks," he said. "Likewise. They tell me you didn't get hurt much worse by the bomb this time. How did you accomplish that?"

"I haven't figured it out yet," she said. "I had just left my room and given a big push to the wheels of my chair toward the waiting room, when I felt that hard puff of air hit the back of my head, back, and shoulders. And the noise came, and it was insane, and I was moving fast, and then I was down and things were flying along the hall past me. All this was in the first half second, you know?"

"Yes," he said. "I didn't see anything we can use, did you?"

"I don't think so. I never saw the device or any kind of trigger. The area behind the nurses' station appeared to me to be the most likely location."

"Did you see who brought the cake and drinks?"

"No," she said.

"Just for the record, you didn't have anything to do with arranging that get-together at Cedars, did you?"

"Me?" she said. "No. I thought it must be you. When the nurse told me about it I was a little annoyed. The last thing I would ever have wanted was to have the whole squad come at once. But now I think it must have been the bomber."

He frowned. "That's what it looks like."

She said, "I haven't had a chance to talk to you, but I had this really disturbing visit from Captain Almanzo yesterday."

"He told me," said Stahl.

"Well, it seemed important to tell you about it before anything else happened, and then, when I kept getting calls from the police department, I thought it must be on the same subject—maybe even calling me in to talk about it. I ducked the calls. I told the nurses to make an excuse for me. But it must have been Andy."

He gently rubbed her arm. "We'll deal with this if it gets to be a problem. Until then, forget it. They know you survived, so there's no reason for them to investigate your private life."

He pulled the lone visitor's chair beside her bed and they sat together and talked for two hours. Stahl got quieter and quieter until Hines realized he'd dozed off. She said, "Hey, Dick?"

He blinked his eyes. "Hmm?"

"You're exhausted. Have you even slept since the explosion?"

"I got a couple of hours this morning."

"Go home and get some sleep. You don't know what you'll have to face tomorrow. Please."

He stood and stretched, then leaned over and gave her a soft, gentle kiss. "See you tomorrow." He walked out the door and closed it.

When she was alone again she kept thinking about him. The day after the fourteen men were killed and he showed up to take over, she thought he was probably a good, simple guy. By then she had spent a year being trained on military bases and more years working in police stations, and had met a lot of men like him. They seemed to find their way to those places in abnormally large numbers. They were mentally resilient and brave and physical, and not very hard to understand. But later that first day, while she was working with him on the car bomb in the gas station, she started to realize he was more complicated than they had been.

She had spent most of that day watching him work and serving as another set of hands for him, always following his calm, clear instructions. She had become intrigued by him. At the end of the day, she had seen him take the last and worst and deadliest part of the device into his arms and carry it all alone. Her emotions—fear, admiration, gratitude—overwhelmed everything else.

And then she had openly, unabashedly thrown herself at him that same night. She had some trouble remembering what had happened before she met him. She had no problem remembering everything that happened that first day. Usually if she'd been drinking, details would be a little hazy the next day. But that night, after she'd had two powerful glasses of single malt Scotch, the inebriation sharpened her impressions and sensations rather than dulling them. The liquor had removed the surrounding distractions. The night had occurred in a mental tunnel. Her eyes had seen only him, and her ears had heard only his voice and hers.

Lately she had been going over the six days after that in her memory. It felt as though she were holding a piece of fabric in her hands and moving it slowly, inch by inch, examining it so closely that she was able to follow each horizontal thread as it went over the first vertical thread and under the next all the way from one seam to the other.

The part that remained remarkable to her was that on the first night they had both known they were very likely to die in days or weeks, and they had each accepted the other as the ideal person with whom to share those days and nights. Her impulsive attraction to the nearest wise and brave man had turned into something huge and real.

When she got blown up in her apartment, she had been more than injured. The doctors had switched her brain off artificially, and her consciousness ceased to exist for all that time. Dick had lived those forty-two days, but she had not. The doctors saved her by giving her a taste of death.

What now? She had been trying to ask that question since she was allowed to come back. Since she was revived. That was just the right term. She had been allowed to live again. What was supposed to happen next? What did she want to happen?

She thought back to the day when she opened her apartment door intending to face the dull necessity of doing her laundry and paying her bills. What had she been thinking just before thinking was cut short? She had not been making any decisions about the future. She had been intending to move a few more outfits to Dick's place on that trip. That was it. She had not seen the need to make bigger decisions. She had known only that her shift for the day was over and she was planning to spend the night with Dick. Everything in her mind was about the next few hours.

She had made a choice. She'd thought, "Don't think about the man who may kill you. He's been there all along, and he'll always be there. Think about paying your bills and getting clean clothes, and dinner tonight, and Dick. Be alive now." And then she'd actually thought, almost making a joke on herself, "Boom."

27

The bomb maker saw the cars coming a long way off. The road was flat and broad and straight, a model highway. But a strong east wind had been blowing for a couple of days, and now the wind had stopped, leaving sand and dust across much of the black asphalt and on the shoulders, so all he saw at first was two tan clouds like long tails. His mind had to supply the vehicles ahead of them like the heads of comets, but then he could see them, two black cars moving fast.

He stared at them, trying to make out any features he could. They could be the FBI or the ATF or some other agency. This was certainly the way they would come, fast and obvious as they traveled up the road from Los Angeles. Probably there would be other vehicles from the opposite direction, and then off-road vehicles crawling over the hills from behind his land on the old mine roads. When they converged to surround him, they would probably bring in a helicopter so he would know there was no way to be unseen, and no way to outrun them.

He went to the control box he had mounted on the wall of the coat closet near the front door, looked out the peephole toward the road, and waited. On three walls of the closet he had put steel plates from the floor to the six-foot level. The inner side of the closet door had a steel plate on it too, so they couldn't just fire at the house with high-penetration rounds and hit him through the walls. The peephole was hidden behind the upper part of the black metal mailbox he had mounted on the porch wall outside, so he could look without anyone seeing the lens.

He opened the control box, where he had installed a board of toggle switches that activated the firing circuits of mines he'd planted in various places. One set was where the driveway met the highway, and there were others in rings around the house at a hundred yards, seventy-five, fifty, and twenty-five. He had mines down the center of the driveway every ten feet. He could activate any of the mines individually, or sweep down a whole row of toggle switches with the side of his hand.

He believed in explosives. They were reliable and instantaneous and merciless. He didn't have to aim them; he just had to look out and watch to see when an attacker reached the particular rows of shrubs he had planted at various distances from the house. He had planted the rows of shrubs in front of his mines so attackers would choose them as places to take cover.

The bomb maker had also prepared in other ways for an attack. He had a pair of H&K MP5 rifles that he modified to restore them to fully automatic fire, and several thirty-round magazines for each. He had only one pistol in the closet, a Sig Sauer .45 with two magazines.

He didn't imagine that if this turned out to be a visit from federal agents he would escape. He wouldn't, but getting him would cost them a great deal. The number of corpses he made would be an expression of his value.

The two black cars slowed and stopped at the end of his driveway. Then they stayed there while the clouds of dust and sand slowly drifted away. Even at this distance he knew that the engines were still running because none of the windows rolled down. The Mojave Desert in August was a very hot place to sit in a closed car without air-conditioning. He remained motionless, watching them not move and thinking that the last hour of his life had begun.

He heard a phone ringing. He felt for his cell phone in his pocket and looked at it, but the screen was black. Had it been the house phone? He opened the closet door cautiously, because he knew that calling him would be a great way to lure him out of a hiding place. He ducked low and hurried to the phone on the other side of the living room. He heard the ring again, but it was not this phone.

What was the matter with him? The men in Niagara Falls, Canada, had given him a cell phone. The ones in the car must be those men. He ran. He had hidden the phone in his kitchen inside a cupboard and run the charging wire down through the cupboard to the outlet under the sink to keep the battery charging. As he picked up the phone the ringing stopped. He was sweating, the kind of sweat that felt as though it had been squeezed out of him. He stared at the telephone, trying to remember the number they had given him to call. He pressed the button to get the opening screen. The phone had been programmed with that number. Just as he raised his other hand to touch the screen the phone rang again. He swept his finger across the screen. "Hello?"

"We're at the end of your driveway and we want to talk to you. Come out to us. Don't bring anything with you."

The bomb maker took everything out of his pockets and put it on the kitchen island. He set the phone down with his wallet and keys and walked to his front door so he would be visible when he stepped outside.

He opened the door, used the button on the doorknob to make it lock automatically, and closed the door. He had a key hidden under a pot among some potted succulents near the closest ring of land mines, so he knew he wouldn't have to break in later.

He went down the steps, holding his hands a few inches away from his sides so they wouldn't think he had a gun or knife. The walk seemed long, and he felt self-conscious being watched.

When he reached the car, the back door swung open and a man got out. He was tall, with close-cropped dark hair and dark skin. He patted the bomb maker's legs, belly, and back, then lifted the bomb maker's arms and ran his hands up and down his sides. Finally he ran his index finger around the inner side of the waistband of his pants to check for anything hidden under his belt. Then he ushered the bomb maker into the backseat of the car, got in after him, and closed the door.

The tint of the car's windows was so dark he had not been able to see its inhabitants from outside. These four were not the ones he had met in Canada. All but one looked younger, maybe in their mid-twenties. They were all in good physical condition with muscular arms, flat bellies, and buzz-cut hair. The only exception was a man in the front passenger seat whose head was shaved. He seemed older. They had a military look, and their expressions were set and unchanging, but the older one half-turned in the passenger seat to look directly at the bomb maker.

The driver shifted and drove onto the highway for a mile or so before the bald man said, "We'd like you to do something."

The bomb maker waited. He could not have said what country these men were from, but he sensed it was an old-fashioned place, and traditional cultures always seemed to him to be prickly about formalities. He tried hospitality. "You're welcome to come to my house to talk in comfort. I have cold drinks and comfortable furniture and air-conditioning."

"We don't know you that well."

"My new friend beside me just searched me for guns or recording devices and found none."

The bald man said, "We can't know what you have in your house. You could have both. Or maybe the authorities have been watching you all year, and they've put transmitters in your house without your knowledge. The result would be the same."

"Believe me," said the bomb maker. "If they knew who I am and where I live, they would have brought an army. I've been killing police officers for weeks." He knew he should stop talking.

The bald man sighed. "If they learn about you later, they'll search your house for fingerprints and DNA. If we don't go there, we don't have to worry about that. But we didn't come here to argue."

"Why *did* you come?" Instantly he realized that this could have sounded disrespectful. So he added, "What can I do for you?"

The bald man smiled, and his teeth looked odd, with spaces between them, but straight and even. "Good. That's the right attitude."

"Thank you."

"You and we are at war with the United States, and that's a serious thing. We understand that you set off a bomb at a police party last night. How many did you kill?"

The bomb maker resisted the temptation to deceive or exaggerate. "I don't know. The television news said only two."

"Both police?"

"No. Nurses. Or one nurse and a young orderly."

"Is there a chance they just haven't told the public about other deaths or very serious injuries?"

"It's possible. Sometimes more people die later. But we can't count on it."

"No matter. You disabled a hospital. We saw pictures of the building. A hospital can be as important as a few bomb technicians. And you'll get the others."

"Yes," said the bomb maker. "I will. What happened was—"

"We don't care what happened. You kill or you die. Learn from your mistakes, and try again. And I want you to do something else for us."

"What is it?"

"We're going to need weapons. We didn't want to risk bringing any here ourselves, but we don't need to. You're an American citizen. You can buy them for us."

"What kind of weapons?"

"We need fifteen Kalashnikov rifles, fully automatic. We need fifteen pistols. Ammunition and high-capacity magazines."

He knew he would have to be careful now. "I'm a bomb maker. I don't have an armory of guns."

"Of course not," said the bald man. "But you'll buy them for us."

"This could take some time," the bomb maker said. "There are laws, even for citizens, and the government is very careful about that kind of weapon. The ammunition for an AK is hard to find, and has to be bought in small lots. Each of the rifles will have to be altered, the trigger and sear mechanisms replaced with hand-tooled ones so the rifle will fire on full auto."

"Yes, yes, yes," the man said. He was getting impatient. "So do what's necessary."

The man lifted a small day pack off the floor in front of him, swung it over the back of his seat, and tossed it onto the bomb maker's lap. "Here. You'll need money for the guns and ammunition. I don't want you using any of the bomb money. Buy and transport everything yourself. Don't bring in other people. Use the cell phone when the guns are ready for us."

He stared at the bomb maker hard, as though he were trying to decipher a form of script he had never read before. "Don't get caught." He tapped the driver's arm and the car pulled onto the shoulder. "Go home and do your work."

The man who had let the bomb maker into the car now slipped out and stood holding the door open. He watched the bomb maker get out and swing the day pack over one shoulder. The bomb maker moved slowly, hoping to hear one of the men in the car say something to another, so he could hear the language they spoke, but they said nothing and looked ahead through the windshield, not at him.

The man got in and closed the door, and the big sedan glided back onto the highway like an alligator sliding into a river. A moment later the second car slid onto the road and accelerated after it.

When he was alone, the bomb maker swung the day pack around to his belly, unzipped the main compartment, and looked inside. There were stacks of hundred-dollar bills, all with paper bands as though a bank had banded them. One probably had, but there was no printing on the bands. He estimated that the hoard was another hundred thousand dollars. He closed the pack.

The sun was bright and fixed just past the highest point of its arc. The two cars were already out of sight. He turned toward his house and began to walk. It took only about three minutes before he wished he had brought a hat and sunglasses. The sun on the desert seemed almost white. He judged that he was two miles from home and would be there in forty minutes. When thirty minutes had passed he still couldn't see the stretch of road where he lived, so he revised his estimate to three miles.

He knew very well why they had left him out here. If he had been the sort of man who got scared and changed his mind, he might call the police or FBI and turn them in. He wasn't the kind of man who panicked, but these people weren't fond of risks.

After another ten minutes he saw houses he recognized—both abandoned—and after another mile, he found his own. He turned and walked up his driveway, found his key, and let himself into the bath of cool air in the dim interior of his house.

During the walk he had been thinking about the guns. He would have to do some planning and some traveling to fill the order. He wondered about his backers. Did they know everything about this country, or nothing? Were they able to assess what was difficult for him and what wasn't? The only thing he could be sure of was that they wouldn't care.

28

It was after six, and Stahl was at his desk trying to stretch the squad's schedule slightly so there would be an overlap at the beginning and the end of each team's shift. So far the bomber hadn't noticed those weak periods during shift changes, but Stahl couldn't believe he wouldn't. He wanted every moment covered, and if the bomber struck during the half hour of double staffing, Stahl would be able to hold over the finishing shift and send out the fresh shift to handle the emergency.

There was a knock and he saw Andy through the clouded glass of his door. "Come on in."

Andy said, "There's a call from Dave Bushman at the *Times*. He needs a comment on the questions the Channel Ten people asked at the press conference."

Stahl took a deep breath and blew it out slowly. "Tell him the department has a press office."

"I did, but he said he's doing you a courtesy."

"Okay." He held up the page he had been working on. "Take this. It's a design for a new schedule, with each shift staying on a half hour later so we never have that gap between them. Which line is Bushman on?"

"One." Andy took the schedule and closed the door. Stahl took the phone receiver from its cradle and pressed the button that was flashing. "Dick Stahl."

"Hi, Captain. This is Dave Bushman at the *Times*. I wanted to give you a chance to comment on the record about the line of questioning we heard from Gloria and Todd from Channel Ten today. Would you like to make a statement?"

"Not at this time, Dave. I appreciate the chance, but this isn't the moment, and I may not be the person to answer."

"Can you clarify that? Are you confirming or denying?"

"I'm pretty sure we'll have a statement within twenty-four hours. But for now, I guess the answer is that I don't have anything to say at this time."

"All right," Bushman said. "I hope that works out for you."

"Thanks."

Andy appeared at the door again, and Stahl beckoned to invite him in. Andy said, "They're about to run the story on Channel Ten. They just gave a teaser and went to commercial."

"Are you watching TV?"

"I'm streaming Channel Ten on my laptop."

"Want to bring it in?"

Andy hurried out to his desk, lifted the open laptop, brought it in, and set it on Stahl's desk. He hit the key to make the television image fill the screen. When the commercials were over, the faces of Gloria Hedlund and Todd Tedesco appeared. Gloria Hedlund's big blue eyes widened and her perfect mouth turned upward in a smirk as she said, "A well-known public official has come under suspicion of violations of police regulations and city standards of conduct."

Todd Tedesco sat beside her staring into the camera and wearing the expression of stern disapproval he displayed during each night's most serious stories.

Gloria said, "Our story involves Captain Richard Stahl, the recently appointed commander of the LAPD Bomb Squad." Stahl's picture, a frozen image from the press conference a few weeks earlier, filled the screen. "And it involves this woman, a bomb technician who was seriously injured in a bomb blast about a month and a half ago." Stahl recognized a frozen image from the press conference when Diane's name had almost been revealed on camera. It was now on a split screen beside his. She looked beautiful.

"Here's what happened at a police department briefing earlier today." There was a shot of the police press room, where Gloria Hedlund stood and said, "Sergeant Hines seems to be pretty important. Do you have a special relationship with Sergeant Hines?"

Stahl and Andy sat through the rest, which ended with his stepping down from the podium and out the door. Even though three reporters from Channel Ten had spoken, Gloria Hedlund said, "The captain seemed a bit uncomfortable with my line of questioning. At the moment we don't know why that is. It's all too familiar to see an older male public servant with an exalted rank who suddenly gets touchy about his relationship with a young, pretty woman under his command. We believe Captain Stahl should know that and—innocent or not—be willing to answer questions from the public about his conduct. This is Gloria Hedlund, Channel Ten News."

Andy sat paralyzed for a few seconds.

Stahl said, "I'm going to get a call in a minute. You should get out there and answer it quickly to show you're on the job."

"Yes, sir." He took his laptop and went back to his workstation. A few minutes later, Stahl saw Andy pick up his phone. Then Andy turned in his swivel chair, saw that Stahl was watching him, pointed at the phone, and held up two fingers.

Stahl looked at the phone on his desk and picked up the receiver. "Captain Stahl, Bomb Squad." He listened for a moment. "I'll be there in a minute."

* * *

Stahl had to sit for only about five minutes in the waiting area outside the office of the chief of police. He used the time to type a few reminders to himself on his cell phone screen. He knew it was possible that these notes and reminders were things he would be passing on to his successor, and that made them more urgent. Some of them were ideas he had devised to solve technical problems he'd noticed over time, and there was no reason for the next commander to repeat the same work.

The chief's door swung open and Deputy Chief Ogden looked out. When he saw Stahl he nodded and held the door open for him. Stahl walked to the door, took the hand Ogden offered, and shook it.

Ogden gave Stahl a smile that seemed to be intended as a reassurance, but Ogden's nervous manner was unusual.

When Stahl stepped in, he saw the chief stand up from behind his large wooden desk and walk around to greet him. It took a few seconds, and during that moment Stahl took note of the fact that the room held several people he didn't know.

The chief shook Stahl's hand, but he didn't smile. "Dick," he said.

"Yes, sir," said Stahl.

"Thank you for dropping everything to come in. I've been meaning to tell you how grateful we are for the help you've been giving us during this crisis. It's clear to everybody that you've saved innumerable lives—police and civilian lives—in the past few weeks. Deputy Chief Ogden is closer to the scene, of course, because you're in his command. But he tells me you've been proving day after day that you're still the best bomb expert we've had. People say you've raised morale a hundred percent just by your example, and taught your technicians a whole lot of essential techniques and information."

"Thanks, Chief."

"I wanted to be sure I said that first, so you and everyone else know without a doubt that I have nothing but admiration for you." He paused. "Have you heard the story that Channel Ten just ran on its local news tonight?"

"I did."

The chief said, "When we knew there would be a story, I invited these ladies and gentlemen to watch it with me." He held his arm out to introduce a middle-aged black woman in a navy-blue business suit. "This is Gwendolyn Barker, the chairperson of the police commission. You know Deputy Chief Ogden." He passed him and pointed to a small man in a light gray suit. "This is Robert Minoso, our liaison with the city attorney's office. And this is Nora Zorich, assistant DA." She was exactly what Stahl expected of a prosecutor—very thin, wearing a black suit, sharp-featured, with dark eyes behind severe glasses.

Stahl shook hands with each of them. "You've assembled quite a team."

Nora Zorich said, "If you'd like to have an attorney present, we can call and ask the union to send one."

Stahl said, "I don't think that's necessary, but thank you. Let's go ahead with our discussion."

The chief said, "I'm going to ask you a question. You don't have to answer it, but I hope you will. Is there any truth to the accusation from the newspeople?"

"Absolutely."

"Pardon?" said Robert Minoso. "I'm not sure I heard correctly."

"Yes," said Stahl. "From the evening after the bomb we dismantled and destroyed at the gas station in the Valley until the day Diane Hines got injured in the trap at her apartment, she and I were engaged in a sexual relationship."

The mood of the room seemed to become charged, full of potential energy like a courtroom. Gwendolyn Barker leaned forward. "Are you saying that the relationship is over?"

Stahl said, "No. But we hadn't been together for very long before Sergeant Hines was attacked. About six days. She was severely injured and was in an induced coma for forty-two days before the doctors felt it was safe to bring her out of it. I think she'll need time to assess our relationship from her present perspective and decide whether she still wants to pursue it. I'm hoping she'll decide she still wants to, because I do."

Gwendolyn Barker looked disappointed. Robert Minoso said quietly, "Are you aware that city and police regulations prohibit this conduct?"

"Yes," said Stahl.

"I don't know what to say," said Minoso. "You've put the city in a difficult position. The city is liable for penalties and damages for sexual harassment, possibly for creating a hostile work environment, and on and on."

"I'm very sorry," said Stahl. "Mostly for the embarrassment I caused. But I wouldn't worry about Sergeant Hines. She isn't going to go after the department."

Minoso looked deflated. "I'm sorry to have to take a different position, Captain Stahl. Like the chief, I've been very glad you agreed to help. But I've handled these cases for the city for years. We settle cases every year that started out in similar ways. Right now you're saying to yourself that Sergeant Hines loves the police force. I'm sure she does, and I know she's risked her life repeatedly to save other officers. But what we have to worry about isn't today. What if, five years from now, you've broken up, and she's been passed over for promotions, or disciplined, or even fired? She won't love the police force then. There are statutes of limitations on most of the injuries she could sue for, but under the continuing violation theory, her attorneys could get around those limitations. Plenty have figured out how. We're paying damages to plaintiffs from years ago all the time."

"I'm sure you understand that neither of us intended to put the department in a difficult position," said Stahl. "We had expected that the bomber case would be solved and I'd be off the police force by now, and Sergeant Hines would be able to continue her exemplary work for the rest of her career. She's never had any violations of police policy before, and wouldn't have except for my failings as a supervisor."

Nora Zorich, the assistant DA, said, "Captain, I want to state my agreement with the others. I'm an admirer. And I'm more of an admirer since I've watched your behavior today, both in telling us the truth and in speaking of Sergeant Hines with affection and respect that prove to me this wasn't a supervisor taking advantage of an employee. I'm positive that everyone in this room wishes we could apologize to you for invading your privacy, then forget the issue—or really, advise the chief to let it go. But we don't have that option."

"I understand," said Stahl. "I'll go write my resignation and make it effective tonight so it can be released in time for the eleven o'clock news. It will be phrased in a way that makes it clear the force didn't tolerate my conduct and that the chief acted immediately the evening he heard about it and called me in. I do request that no action be taken against Sergeant Hines."

The chief said, "Damn it. We can't afford to lose either of you. We need help. Who wants to bust a woman who's a hero to the department for having a normal private life?"

Gwendolyn Barker said, "I have an idea. It's unorthodox, but it's a way out."

"What is it?" asked the chief.

"You accept Captain Stahl's resignation. Then the police commission contracts with Mr. Stahl's security company to provide his services during the crisis. Sergeant Hines probably won't be back on active status for months. If she comes back while he's still here, she won't technically be under his supervision, because he'll only be a civilian consultant and not a sworn officer. We hire outside experts, lawyers, and contractors all the time. Why not hire Mr. Stahl now? And that's his punishment—that he's off the force, with no rank."

The chief said, "Do you buy that, Dick?"

"Yes, sir."

That night Dick Stahl was waiting in Diane Hines's room at Valley Presbyterian when she returned from a walk. She had a cane, but she was walking normally when she stepped in.

She came to him, presented herself for a hug, then kissed him quickly on the lips and sat on the bed.

"You're recovering fast," he said.

"Yes," she said. "Pretty soon they'll kick me out of here."

"I've been thinking about that."

"Why?"

"Lots of reasons," he said. "Nobody has talked to you about your apartment, right?"

"No."

"That's because it isn't there anymore. It's been gutted and they're planning on rebuilding something, but it won't be ready soon. I'd like to invite you to move into my place with me."

She studied him. "Why?"

He met her stare. "Well, there are actually three reasons, but let me mention two out loud. Keep in mind you don't have an apartment. The reasons are that I want you there, and that my condominium is probably the safest building in Los Angeles, particularly with two veteran cops in it."

"You're worried he'll try for me again?"

"It has crossed my mind, but right now I'm just using that to make my place seem inviting."

"Have you forgotten that living with you would get me fired? Or are you assuming I'll never get well enough to handle a bomb again and be on disability forever?"

"I'm not assuming anything now," he said. "And by the way, we're caught."

"Captain Almanzo? He told?"

"No, he didn't. But a television reporter got a leak, probably from the crime scene people, and sprang it on me at a press conference today."

"So I'm hours away from getting fired for being a slut?"

"No," he said. "Your job is safe. I resigned from the force today. They're going to hire my security company so I can keep working as a consultant on the bomber case while you recover."

"Jesus, Dick. I caused this. I'm sorry."

"For what? I wasn't going to be a career cop."

"For having humiliated you."

"I'm not humiliated."

She frowned. "I've been planning to go stay with my mother in Florida for a while. I have a perfectly nice mother, you know. I think I never mentioned her because we were having a wild fling and it seemed weird to bring her into it."

"What's her name?"

"Grace."

"Pretty," he said. "Was it a wild fling?"

"Hell yes, it was," she said. "Every minute we weren't working we were fooling around or drinking."

"Good for us," he said. She could see that his face looked sad.

"Did calling it a fling hurt your feelings?" she said. "Be honest with me."

"I didn't think about putting it in a category before. During those few days, my life consisted of getting through a tough day, and then making up for it with you at night. It was death all day and life at night with you."

"I know what happened, and I understand everything up to the point when my apartment blew up. But what now? I've been trying to figure out what happens next. I think I need you to tell me what you're thinking."

"We move you into my place. We try to stop leaving things out when we talk. We don't pretend that being together was a fling."

"Okay," she said. "Tomorrow when you come, bring me some of the clothes I left in your closet. All I own now is this nightgown with nothing in the back, and I have to hand it over when I leave."

29

The bomb maker would have to be leaving in a few days, so he began with the drill press. He would have to order it and get it delivered before he left. That way it wouldn't be left boxed up and sitting in the driveway while he was gone. He also wanted to keep this purchase as distant in time from the other purchases as possible.

He found a drill press advertised online that was almost new. A metalworking business had gone under, and the shop equipment was being liquidated. This one was perfect for precision work. It was laser guided, with a one-and-a-half-horsepower motor that turned at 4,200 rpm, and it had a work light over the oversize table. He had to drive to Santa Ana to pick it up, but that meant he would be able to install it in his garage workshop right away. When he got to Santa Ana he also saw a lathe for sale, so he bought that too, and set both up in his shop.

The next day he planned his trip. There were a surprising number of AK-47 rifles for sale by licensed dealers across the country, but he couldn't afford to let them make background checks. Instead he looked for gun shows in states where a seller who didn't earn most of his living as a gun dealer didn't have to report sales.

In a couple of hours he had plotted a route between large gun shows. He would start in Las Vegas; go next to the Crossroads of the West Gun Show in Phoenix at the Arizona State Fairgrounds; then stop for a show at the Tucson Pima County Fairgrounds, one in Tucumcari, New Mexico, one at the Reno-Sparks Convention Center, and then one in St. George, Utah. He added a few running across Texas in Lubbock, Houston, and San Antonio.

He judged he would probably have what he needed long before he ever got near Texas. And if he didn't by then, he could continue on through Louisiana, Mississippi, Alabama, Georgia, and Florida. None of those states required private gun sellers to report anything to anybody.

When he was ready, he packed a suitcase and put it in a metal storage box in his van. He also had four empty metal storage chests running along the floor. He had locks for them, but to start out he didn't use those. Sometimes a lock just attracted attention.

As he drove along Interstate 15 toward Las Vegas he reviewed his strategy. He would walk around the show looking for AK-47s on the tables. He had selected big shows, so there would be at least a hundred tables with guns of all kinds lying on them. It would be fairly easy to tell which sellers were licensed gun dealers with lots of merchandise and which were private collectors with a few pieces they wanted to get rid of for cash or trade for something better. He would select a likely seller and watch for a while. Sometimes a licensed dealer might be willing to run checks on customers for a nearby collector, or even serve as a middleman for a modest cut of the profit. The bomb maker would watch and see if anything like that was going on before he inquired about an AK-47.

After his first circuit of the Las Vegas show, he made his first inquiry to a man about sixty-five years old who had a row of AR-15-style rifles of various makes with a range of configurations. Beside them he had five AK-47 rifles. The bomb maker said, "Can I take a look at your AKs?"

The man nodded, and said, "Help yourself."

The bomb maker was excited. He could feel that, of the usual three positions, the selector lever had only two: the Safe position and the third, lower one that permitted semiautomatic firing. There was no fully automatic position. The older man said, "They're semiauto only. You can't bring one into the country until it's been modified."

"Where are these from?"

"What used to be Yugoslavia. All of them were made for the army, but they were never issued."

The bomb maker could see from the wear patterns that two of the rifles had been fired a lot, and carried in the field. The wooden butt pieces and forestocks had lighter places where being touched had rubbed and discolored them. The bomb maker decided not to mention that. He said, "How much for all of them?"

"A thousand apiece."

"I'll give a thousand each for these three," he offered.

"No thanks, they're sort of a collection, and I want to get rid of the lot."

"How about eight hundred each for all five? That's four thousand bucks, in cash."

"All right," the man said.

The bomb maker counted out the cash and the man began bundling them up in a tarp for him. The man threw in four extra thirty-round magazines, but charged him three hundred more for the five hundred rounds of 7.62 × .39-mm ammunition. He made three trips to load his car.

A couple of days later at the Arizona State Fairgrounds he noticed a woman selling off a collection of rifles and pistols. Her sign said: DIVORCE SALE. Each of her weapons had a sticker with a price written on it with a magenta-colored marker. She was about forty years old, blond with skin that had been in the sun too much. She wore tight jeans and a Western shirt with pearl snaps instead of buttons. When she turned in his direction he saw she had blue eyes that were almost startling in her reddish face.

"Sorry about the divorce," he said.

"Not me. How can I help you?"

"I like AK-47 rifles. You don't have any, do you?"

"I got one," she said.

"Oh?" he said. "I didn't see it."

"Bobby?"

A man about fifty-five who sat at the next table looked at her.

She said, "You going to be around for a while, Bobby? Can you watch my table?"

"How long were you thinking of?"

"Half hour or so."

"Sure."

The woman tapped the bomb maker's solar plexus with the back of her hand. "Come on." She started walking fast along the aisle in front of her table. The bomb maker followed her outside onto the vast parking lot and up to a red pickup truck. He veered toward the cargo bed, but she got into the driver's seat. "It's not back there. Get in."

He climbed into the passenger seat and she drove across the lot, turned right, and then drove into the lot of the closest hotel. She jumped down. "It's upstairs."

He followed her into the hallway and into an elevator. She took him to the third floor and through the door of a room that was littered with clothes, an open suitcase with the clothes mixed up and hanging out of it, and several gun cases and some cardboard cartons. She dragged a gun case into the center of the floor, unzipped and opened it so he could see the AK.

"Where's it from?"

"It says Bulgaria on it."

He looked at the lower receiver and saw something written in the Cyrillic alphabet and some Arabic numerals. "Can I touch it?"

She smiled. "You can touch anything you can reach."

His eyes met hers. "A half hour?"

She shrugged. "So it won't be a long courtship."

He stepped close and put his arms around her, and she leaned into him to kiss him. He pulled the sides of her Western shirt apart so the snaps all opened, and then she was working the buckle of his belt apart while he unhooked her bra. She shrugged it off and backed onto the bed. He pushed her over and tugged off her cowboy boots, so she could wriggle out of her tight jeans.

"You've done a cowgirl before," she said.

"No, you're my first."

She laughed. "Cowgirl is the name of a position, dumb ass. It's a joke."

He flopped onto the bed beside her, naked, and touched her, his hands moving everywhere, arousing them both.

"Use a condom," she said.

He paused, panicked.

"In my purse," she said wearily, and nodded toward the desk across from the bed.

He swung his legs off the bed, stepped to the desk, and riffled through the purse. He felt a familiar square packet and the ring shape inside, tore the pack open, and unrolled the condom onto himself before he returned to the bed. As he began to find his way she thrust her hips forward, clutched his buttocks, and seemed to climb his body to take him in. The sex was eager and rushed, almost violent.

It occurred to him that he had not had intercourse with anyone since he caught his wife cheating and threw her out of the house. It explained to him why he felt so excited. But then the thought of her made his lust for this woman less compelling, and he found the distasteful memory of his marriage was helping him control his sexual urge, delaying the end.

He tried to reestablish a friendly feeling about this woman. He tried their one joke. "Cowgirl."

She giggled and pulled away, pushed him on his back, and straddled him.

"Oh that," he said. "I didn't know there was a word for it."

"But you've done it?"

"Of course."

"Then shut up and do it again. Hard."

About ten minutes later, her little cries and moans increased in frequency, and he speeded up to help her. When she climaxed, he let himself go too.

She lay still on top of him for a count of ten, then craned her neck and squinted to see the electric clock on the nightstand. She disengaged from him, crawled off the bed, and began putting her clothes back on. "Old Bobby will be wondering what's taking so long. He's an old guy and has to pee a lot. I watch his table when he goes, so he had to watch mine."

The bomb maker sat up and began to dress too.

She pulled on her right boot, stood, and stomped once to make her foot settle into it. "Do you still want the AK?"

"How much?"

"A thousand."

"That's the price for brand-new."

"This is brand-new."

"It's been fired, right?"

"Once or twice."

"Then it's not brand-new. It's secondhand." He stood, picked up the rifle and examined it, opened the chamber, and then set it down on its open case. It was in very good condition, but it had been fired a few times.

She sat beside him and put her hand on his thigh. "You just got free sex that you had no right to expect, and didn't even know was coming. If you were a gentleman, you would appreciate that and give me the benefit of my generosity. If I weren't a lady, I could claim you forced me, get somebody to kill you, and take all your money."

He laughed. "You can have the thousand. Want to go out to dinner tonight?"

"Gee, I'm sorry, but Bobby is a relative of my ex-husband. Some kind of half-ass cousin, but he calls him his uncle, which isn't possible. He'd be capable of causing trouble."

"Want to give me your cell number so I can give you a call another time?"

"Nope. It's been fun, but I don't want to get hooked up and moved in with my next guy and then have you calling me up in a month. You know what I mean?"

"Sure," he said. He reached into his pocket, pulled out a stack of hundreds, then counted out ten on the bed. Then he put another hundred down and said, "Here's a hundred for that carrying case."

She snatched the pile of bills from the bed and folded them into her jeans pocket. "Thanks. Take your AK and the case, and then we never saw each other before."

He zipped the rifle into its case and stood. She stepped close, pecked his cheek, and said, "Too bad we didn't have more time." Then she stepped to the door and held it open for him to leave. When he was out, she closed the door and gave it an extra tug to be sure he hadn't done something to jam the latch so he could get in again. Then she turned and hurried into the staircase without looking back.

The bomb maker walked to his van and drove. He had a feeling about this transaction. If he went back into the show, she would see him, and other people would probably notice she was looking at him. Only bad things could come from that. She had been right. It was time to move on.

He went to the gun show in Tucson and picked up another AK-47 in very good condition. Two days later he found two, in Tucumcari, New Mexico, and drove on into Utah. He stopped in St. George for the next show.

After a day at the show without finding another rifle, he was sitting at a table in a bar across the street from his hotel eating a steak dinner. Sitting next to his dinner plate was a glass of bourbon. He had come in mainly because the bar was close to the gun show, and he guessed that drinkers there for the show would rather choose a bar that was in walking distance. There were only five restaurants serving alcohol here on the north side of the Grand Canyon in any case. The liquor law in Utah required it to be served only to members of private clubs, so he had to pay two dollars to join the fictitious club.

The drink sat untouched while he ate his steak. He had bought the drink only because having it would make him look relaxed and ordinary, and if he needed to, he could sip it later to prolong his time in the bar.

There were a couple of groups of men who were there for the gun show. He seldom lifted his eyes from the table, but he eavesdropped first on one group and then on the other, listening for information he could use. After a time, another group of three men came in, and he concentrated on them.

After they ordered, one of the men said, "So, I rented him the old house on the edge of the arroyo. It was the farmhouse from the days when that plot was a separate property. After the arroyo got all filled in with sediment and ran out of water, nothing got planted there except in wet years, but our family kept up the house. He stayed there for twelve years. He was a good tenant, a quiet guy, very steady. He'd worked over at the insurance company for at least seventeen. And then he died. He told me when he retired that he had no relatives left. He'd had parents and siblings, the last one a sister who was much older than he was. He'd had a girlfriend for a while, and she died too. He was eighty-four when his heart attack came, and he was still filling in at the insurance company doing paperwork.

"I paid for his funeral because I figured nobody else would. Then it turned out he had left a will saying whatever was left in the house I rented him was mine. Two days later I went into the house. I figured I'd better empty the refrigerator and cupboards and start cleaning to prepare for another tenant.

"I went down to the basement to look around for anything else I had to get rid of, and what's down there? He's got canteens, backpacks, ponchos, sleeping bags, all in desert camouflage. The rest is all guns and ammo. He was apparently waiting for the end of the world."

"He was a survivalist?" one of the others asked.

"Yeah. He never told me, never talked politics or anything like that. Of course the smart ones don't tell anybody. They think the government or the Chinese or somebody will come and take them out. They don't want to make it easy. He had ten AK-47s and about a thousand rounds of 7.62 ammo for them. There were a lot of manuals, maps, contraptions for cleaning water to drink, and that kind of thing."

"Ten AK-47s. Why did he think he needed ten?"

"Beats me. I guess he didn't want to be without one. They weigh eight and a half pounds. At his age he couldn't carry ten, let alone the ammo."

"What are you going to do with them?" said a third man.

"I'm selling them tomorrow at the show. I've got some extra magazines, ammo, and stuff, so I could probably get ten thousand for them."

The bomb maker waited while the conversation turned to other subjects. He kept watch in case the man with the rifles got ready to leave and he could talk to him outside. But first one, then the other man got up, said good night, and left. When the last man was getting ready to pay and leave, the bomb maker approached the table. "Excuse me," he said. "I happened to hear some of what you said about the AK-47s. I just happened to be looking for some."

"You found the right guy," the man said. "I'll have them at the show tomorrow morning. Table seventy-four. My name's John Sutton."

"Are the ten rifles the only things you're selling?"

"Yes. They're not anything I bought. I inherited them."

"That's what I thought when you were talking to your friends," the bomb maker said. "You know, you could save yourself the admission fee and the rental of the display space if you wanted to make the sale to me tonight. Then we could both save another day's expenses. Hotel, food, and everything can add up."

"I guess that's true," said Sutton. "You mind telling me what you want ten identical rifles for? Are you a dealer?"

"No. I plan to take them to Texas, where I want to open a rifle range. There would be nothing but Russian arms—Tokarev pistols, AK-47s, Makarovs, some old Nagant revolvers. I think a lot of people would like that."

"Maybe," said Sutton. "I guess time will tell. I like your other idea, though. Maybe we can make a deal tonight and be ahead of the game. What do you want to offer for the ten rifles?"

The bomb maker thought about his problem—finding AK-47s with no histories and getting them to his house without having his name on any government list. These, if the story Sutton told his friends was true, were probably brand-new, and he was far ahead of the schedule he had devised. "I'll give you the going rate in cash tonight. No haggling. What everybody seems to ask is a thousand a rifle. I'll give you a thousand a rifle. Ten thousand cash for the lot of them."

Sutton looked at him for a moment, and whatever doubts he had seemed to fade and disappear. "All right."

"Where are the guns?"

"In my room at the hotel across the way. You staying there?"

"Yes," said the bomb maker.

"You bring the money and we can load the guns into your vehicle right away. You got a truck?"

"A van."

"That'll do it," said Sutton.

They shook hands and walked out of the bar. When they reached the street they looked up and down and saw that there were long breaks in the traffic. At the right moment they stepped into the wake of a semi and strolled across to the hotel parking lot.

Sutton said, "Bring your van over here to the nearest spot to this door, and I'll start bringing the guns down."

The bomb maker trotted to his van as soon as Sutton went inside. When the bomb maker got into the van he removed one of the rifles he'd already bought, inserted a loaded magazine into it, and set it down across the passenger seat. Then he sat still for a moment. He scanned all the windows and balconies, then the dark spots around the hotel. He saw a room on the fourth floor where two men stood on the balcony looking down on the lot. They were the same two who had been in the bar with Sutton. He watched for a few seconds, then pulled his van into a space near the door to Sutton's corridor. He went into his suitcase and found a banded stack of hundred-dollar bills that had the numerals "10,000" and stuck it in his jacket pocket.

In a moment Sutton came out with a two-wheel dolly that held a box. When he moved up behind the bomb maker's van, they lifted it off the dolly into the van. The bomb maker looked into one end of the box and saw five muzzles and into the other end and saw five rifle butts. He pulled one out at random and examined it, then said, "Looks good. Want to get the others?"

Sutton said, "What's to stop you from taking off with those five while I'm up there?"

"Okay, let's go together." He locked his van.

They walked into the building with the dolly, took the elevator, and walked to a room on the fourth floor. Sutton opened the door and loaded the second box on the dolly.

The bomb maker examined the other five rifles and said, "Here's your money." He handed Sutton the banded stack and then stepped back to look out the window so he could see his van. "Feel free to count it."

Sutton leafed quickly through the stack. "They're all hundreds. That's good enough for me." He put the money in his coat pocket and started to wheel the guns out.

The bomb maker said, “I’d be careful from here on. People in the hotel will have seen us hauling these guns out. They’ll know you must have gotten a lot of money for them.”

“Don’t worry. They’re the only guns I’m selling, not the only guns I have.”

They took the rifles down and loaded them in the bomb maker’s van. They shook hands, and the bomb maker drove off. He turned into the parking lot of a diner far down the street just before the city road met the highway, and pulled in between two big semi trucks.

While he waited he loaded a second thirty-round magazine for the AK-47 he’d already taken out and set on the seat beside him. In a few minutes he saw Sutton, the man who had sold him the weapons. Sutton drove past the lot, but didn’t see the bomb maker’s van. He was busy looking in the rearview mirror of his pickup truck. Then he swung up the westbound entrance to the interstate. After about two minutes another truck pulled up the ramp after him. The driver was one of the men who had been in the bar with him hours ago.

The bomb maker shrugged. He had warned Sutton. Looking for a buyer for ten military rifles was a dangerous task, but obviously it wasn’t as dangerous as the time after the sale was made and everybody knew you must have the cash on you.

For the first couple of hours he wondered if Sutton was going to make it home, but after that he forgot because he didn’t care. He had nineteen rifles, four more than he needed to keep his employers satisfied, and nobody knew his name.

When he stopped for a snack and a cup of coffee outside Salt Lake City, he went to the case where he’d been storing the .45 pistols he had bought. He hadn’t been paying much attention to them along the way, just buying a good one whenever there was one in the inventories of the private sellers. When he counted, he came up with only thirteen, so he headed southeast and bought his last two at the Houston show. Once he had all of the AK-47s and the .45 ACP pistols, he knew how many extra magazines and boxes of ammunition he could pay for in cash, so he bought them from a wholesaler at the show. He drove homeward in a leisurely manner, not taking any chances of being stopped by police.

30

The bomb maker drove his van into his garage and closed the door with the remote control. He cleared his AK-47 rifles to be sure there were no forgotten rounds in any of the chambers, and then he examined them closely and carefully. They had all been cleaned and covered with a thin protective layer of gun oil, and at least ten of the nineteen had never even been fired. He locked them up, then carried his suitcase into the house.

He went to sleep and got up early the next day to begin work on the next stage. His clients had never said anything about the serial numbers of the weapons. Why would they care? They seemed to be terrorists, and if their guns were ever in the hands of the authorities, they would already be dead. Tracing the weapons could not harm them. But tracing any of the guns to a previous owner might lead to a description of the bomb maker, and maybe a surveillance shot of him, or even his van.

The next stage of the bomb maker's work was purely for his own protection. An AK-47's serial number was stamped on the lower receiver. He put on latex gloves, took the first AK-47 apart, clamped the lower receiver on his new drill press, aimed the bit at the right spot, and turned on the power.

Removing a serial number was difficult, because the process of stamping the number into the steel made microscopic changes deep in the metal. After filing or buffing it was still possible to bring back the number. The only way that really worked was to set a drill on the surface and drill all the way through. There had to be nothing left to read.

When he finished the first rifle, he put it in a fresh, clean metal box and began to work on the next one. Removing the numbers took two days. In the end he had fifteen AK-47 rifles with no serial numbers.

He cleaned another steel storage box and went to work on the .45 ACP pistols. The Beretta numbers were on the left side of the receiver. The Springfield, Smith and Wesson, and Sig Sauer pistols had a variety of locations—either side of the receivers or on the underside. He went about the work patiently and drilled all of them off.

At the gun show in Houston he had bought a fully functional replica of the original trigger and sear mechanism for the AK-47. Now he went to work duplicating enough of these parts for all nineteen rifles.

Ten days later, when he had finished modifying all of the weapons, he went back to cleaning. In the end he had nineteen fully automatic AK-47s with no serial numbers, each loaded with a clean thirty-round magazine and supplied with two more, and fifteen loaded .45 pistols with two spare magazines each. Every magazine and bullet had been touched only with rubber gloves, and each weapon had been cleaned and kept free of his fingerprints.

The day after he completed the weapons, he returned to his work on his explosive devices. He had already decided not to tell his clients the guns were ready. He had to be in control this time, but his clients were not controllable people. If he turned the guns over to them right away, they would begin to pressure him. As soon as they had weapons, they would be impatient to launch their attack. He didn't even know what they intended to attack.

He thought about them again. They never seemed to give him any information that would make it easy to identify them. They never complained about a specific grievance, a hatred that would tell him where in the world they had originated. They were all young, tan-skinned males who could be from a wide variety of places, and they spoke with practically no accent. They never spoke a language to each other besides English, or addressed any of their companions by name. There was no Jose, no Raj, no Ahmed, no Singh, no Zog, no Chou, no Pepe. Everything they wore or used seemed to have been bought in the same American stores where everybody else shopped. They had taken to paying him regularly since they'd arrived, and it was always in American hundred-dollar bills. The money had made him trust them, but it had not given him any information about them.

He knew he needed more time to work now. He would delay the revelation that he had the guns and return to work on his bombs.

Before he had been sent off to buy weapons, he had been engaged in making a supply of explosives and detonators. The hospital batch had been as good as, and maybe better than, the others. One quality of a good mix was stability, and another was power. The bomb he delivered to the hospital had been intended to cause total destruction to one patient room inhabited by Diane Hines and about a dozen visitors.

Instead, the head nurse and an orderly had taken the cake bomb into a break room to cut and plate it. The bombing had been a failure, but the explosive charge had been magnificent. It had blown through both walls of the break room, including an outer wall made of structural concrete, steel I beams, and an outer shell of bricks and mortar. He had failed in his mission, but his bomb was much better than he expected, and it was the first use of the newest batch. It was wonderful stuff. Over the next few weeks he would incorporate as much of it as he could in devices and then get started on making more. He couldn't expect to get paid until he fulfilled his promise to kill off the Bomb Squad. He needed to make something they didn't expect.

The exceptional power of the new batch of Semtex gave him the idea of building a few small antipersonnel bombs. He began to plan and make drawings for the new designs. He drew a few bounding mines, based on the Bouncing Betty bombs the Germans made in World War II. After the war, the Soviet Union, China, and the United States all made their own versions. They had a trigger that freed a spring beneath the bomb. When the spring was free the bomb would fly upward about five feet and detonate, sending steel balls outward in a ring with a kill zone of about twenty feet.

He needed some other designs. Now that he had a new drill press and a new lathe, he went to work on a set of antiwithdrawal fuzes. He based one on the M123 fuze the air force used. The fuze had a set of exterior threads that fitted into a threaded receptacle on the bomb. The original fuze had two ball bearings embedded in the thread. In the original, when the fuze was screwed in, the bearings slipped into two recesses, making it impossible to unscrew. Instead of the ball bearings, he used a moving collar, which a bomb technician would try to unscrew. Once the fuze was in, the collar would unscrew one turn and then free a spring-loaded pin to stab against the detonator and initiate an explosion in the main charge. He devised an improved hiding system for antipersonnel mines by inserting a bounding mine into a tube and burying the tube so it hid the mine below ground level and then acted as a launcher.

He devised antipersonnel weapons as systems. He could install one mine alone, but each one had the capability of being connected to one or more others, so touching one bomb would set off others nearby.

Each day he would pursue new ideas, some of them his own, others adaptations of devices used in wars. He was particularly pleased whenever he was able to make a device that looked like an old classic design but build in a trigger that worked differently from the original. He loved to imagine a bomb technician following the procedures in an old military manual to render a device safe, then blowing himself to pieces.

While he worked he recorded the local television news reports. One night after a long and productive day he returned to the house, showered and changed his clothes, sat down, put the VTR on fast-forward, and began to speed through the reports. He could be fairly certain that if the image on the screen was a crowd of children, a bear in a swimming pool, a group of people in front of a movie theater, or anyone smiling, it had nothing to do with him. When he saw the chief of police on a podium he stopped the speeding image and backed up.

He was feeling mildly optimistic. Had some other cop died without the bomb maker's help? As he backed the sequence to its start, he kept wondering. The beginning was a pretty blond woman in her forties asking a question. Then he saw that the person answering was Captain Stahl. Had he been the one to die? Was it possible?

The bomb maker pushed Play when the police chief appeared. "It's my sad duty today to announce that I've had to accept the resignation of one of the finest police officers and bravest men I've ever known. Captain Richard Stahl has served with the highest distinction every organization he's joined in his adult life. In just the past two months he has been personally responsible for saving the lives of many citizens and police officers. We thank him for his service. Thank you for coming."

The blond woman with the smirk looked suddenly desperate. He saw her begin to talk without producing any sound. In the background another reporter could be heard yelling, "Can you tell us the woman's name?" Another called out, "Will the woman be fired too?" But the chief was a master at evading a follow-up question. He was out the door by then.

The blond woman was now standing close to the camera, facing it. "The chief of police appears to have followed up on our interview of Captain Stahl yesterday afternoon." She was taking credit for what had happened. "This is Gloria Hedlund, Channel Ten News."

The bomb maker pressed the remote control to freeze the image and study the blond reporter's face. Her expression—triumphant and vengeful—reminded him a little of his ex-wife, Carla.

31

Before Dick Stahl left the station that night he took the purse the police had been holding for Diane Hines. It contained her wallet and credit cards, her driver's license, and her police identification. The outside of the purse was blackened on one side and had holes where metal had sliced through the thick leather.

In the bottom he found her car keys. He used them to pick up her car at the police impound lot. The battery was dead after all the time that had passed, but the cops at the lot jumped it for him. He got in and drove it to his condominium. He packed a set of her business clothes in a briefcase and drove it to the hospital with Andy. While Andy waited outside in the driver's seat, Stahl went into the building.

When he reached her room and knocked, she said, "Get in here." When he entered, she said, "Nobody knocks but you. I'm really glad to see you. I've been hoping to beat the reporters out."

"Good idea." He lifted the briefcase. "Your clothes are in here."

"In your briefcase?" she said. "That's a little odd."

"Your overnight bag is in an evidence room. But this is doing the job. Andy's out in your car waiting for us. The reporters haven't seen that car yet."

"You'll get yourself in more trouble."

"No I won't. Andy doesn't work for me anymore, and he's off duty, a guy doing a favor for two friends."

"Okay. You want to go away for a few minutes?"

"I'd be happy to help you get dressed."

"Don't be overconfident. It isn't the same as taking them off. I've already asked the nurse to help me. She's bringing the discharge papers."

He held up both hands. "I was just trying to be helpful."

She stared at him for a moment. "I sure hope you don't end up being sorry. When this started I wasn't thinking of it as a long-term arrangement, and you weren't either. If this starts to feel like a bad idea, please tell me right away."

"Did your mom tell you to say that?"

"No. She told me I had no business doing this in the first place, implied that I was disgracing the family, and wants me home with her as soon as possible. She seems to have forgotten I've never lived in Florida, but at least it means I'll have someplace to go when you find a new girlfriend and cast me out on the pavement outside your stronghold."

"Can't hurt to have an eager parent," he said. He took out his phone and hit a key. "It's me. The discharge papers aren't here yet. Have you seen signs of unwanted attention? Good. I'll call you before we roll the wheelchair."

She laughed and called out: "Thanks, Andy."

In a few minutes the nurse arrived with a clipboard with several sheets of yellow forms, several white, several pink, and one green. Diane signed and initialed for a few minutes, and then the nurse brought in a wheelchair. Stahl left to wait outside while the nurse got her ready.

He made a call and Andy had the car at a side entrance of the building when they arrived. In another minute or two they were on the road. Andy drove them to the driveway of Stahl's building, and Stahl got out to punch in the codes to open the gate and the garage so Andy could pull Diane's car into the space beside Stahl's. Then Andy handed Diane her key chain with her car key and fob and the condominium key Stahl had put on the chain so many days ago.

She stepped up the stairs to the garage entrance for the condo, and said, "You don't have to do that, Andy."

"Do what?"

"Hover behind me like you're my spotter at the gym. I can climb steps again." She unlocked the door.

"Sorry," he said. "Morrissey is picking me up in a minute, so I'll leave you here. Congratulations on getting out of the hospital. I know I'll see you soon." He hurried off to get out before Stahl closed the garage entrance.

In a moment Stahl caught up with her. He pushed open the door and they stepped into the kitchen. "Oh, crap," she said.

"What's wrong?"

She turned around to face him. "Can't you smell it, or are you pretending?"

"Smell what?"

"It smells exactly the way the most expensive whorehouse in the world must smell," she said. "No, I guess this perfume is even too expensive for that." There were tears welling in her eyes. "I'm completely blindsided. Why would you make me want to come here, when you've had other women here with you all this time?"

"Wait," he said. "You're jumping to conclusions," he said. "It's—"

"It's what?"

"I think he means it's a misunderstanding." It was a woman's voice, and Diane knew instantly it was a woman about fifty years old. A thin, attractive woman about that age came out of the spare bedroom wearing a dark suit and carrying a covered hanger. Her makeup was heavy, as though there were some kind of daytime party in the spare room. "The perfume is mine. And don't worry, dear, they never replace you with an older model."

"Who are you?"

"I'm May Hedges. Bloomingdale's asked me to serve as your personal shopper. Mr. Stahl explained your predicament. Having your apartment blown up is bad enough, but having your closet destroyed is unthinkable."

"I'm Diane," she said, her face reddening.

"Would you like to have a look at what I've picked out for you?" She put her arm around Diane and ushered her into the hallway to the spare bedroom. "This is sort of a starter wardrobe. Mr. Stahl showed me the clothes that survived, so I knew your size and the sort of thing you liked."

The bed was covered with clothing boxes, all opened and tipped upward to display blouses and sweaters, lingerie and T-shirts. The closet was hung with about a dozen outfits—dresses, suits, skirts, pants, jeans, jackets—and there was a row of about a dozen pairs of shoes, boots, sandals, and sneakers. "If there's anything you don't love, I can take it with me when I go, then bring better choices tomorrow."

Diane looked at the clothes, and then at Stahl. "No, there's nothing here that I don't love."

"Mr. Stahl explained you were still recovering, so I included sets of sweatpants and T-shirts and comfortable things for wearing around the house. They're in the drawers."

"Thank you," said Diane. "I love it that you brought jeans and things, which are what I wear most of the time."

"I'm glad you like them. But I've presented you with a lot to think about as soon as you walked in the door." She pointed at the business card on the dresser. "There's my card. Just give me a call if anything isn't right, or you'd like something I haven't thought of, or for any other reason."

Stahl said, "We appreciate your care and your excellent taste. Do you have a tally now, or—"

She laughed and held up her hand. "Your bill will reach you soon enough, Mr. Stahl. Meanwhile, here's a card for you too. I'll be happy to come back anytime."

When she was gone, Stahl joined Diane in the bedroom. She was sitting on the bed staring at the wall. "Oh God," she said. "I made such a fool of myself."

He shrugged. "My fault. That's the danger of surprising people."

"I was just so shocked. I couldn't figure out why. If you'd just said nothing, I would have been on a plane to Florida, but you talked me into coming."

"Did you actually like the clothes, or were you just trying to get rid of her?"

"Some of each. Give me a while to look at them after I pull myself together. Right now I kind of want to start over." She stood up from the bed.

"Take your time," he said. "Right now I'm going to pour myself a drink. You want one?"

"I'm off the pain medicine, so I guess I could. But aren't you on duty until eight?" She followed him out to the living room.

"Not anymore. That's why I want a drink."

Her eyes followed him as he walked toward the kitchen cabinet where the bottles were kept. "So what you're saying is that I'm going to want one too?"

"Yes."

32

Gloria Hedlund held her handbag and briefcase on the sides of her body, as she had when leaving work for the past twenty-five years. She had still been getting work as a model when she started at Channel Ten, and she had kept up all the tricks—use the loads you have to carry as free weights for exercise, watch your posture, think about the wrinkles your face is making, never forget what sun and alcohol did to skin. You never had to have anything repaired if you didn't damage it first.

Her modeling agents had taught her to make her body a temple, and she still worshipped at it. She was long past modeling anything, but it didn't matter because the money would have been negligible compared with what she made now. But she still did dance exercises, still ran, and still worked out on the machines. On her days off she did the things that took time—swimming and riding a bike.

Even on nights like tonight she never neglected her skin. She followed the same regimen of cleansing, hydrating, and lubricating with lotion that she did on the early nights. The days like today were the ones that did the most damage. They made a person's forehead hold those washboard wrinkles for extended periods of time, and she'd always had to fight that habit of pursing her mouth that made more wrinkles appear above her upper lip. She was about ten years older than she looked.

Today had been one of the hardest for personal reasons. She was hired twenty-five years ago as just another beauty contestant who would be sent out into the rare rainy weather in Los Angeles to behave as though standing around in the rain made sense. They used to send her to spots like Mulholland Drive or the Griffith Observatory or the beach, even though it was raining just as hard on the sidewalk outside the station. Each year when the ski slopes opened they sent her two hundred miles into the mountains so she could interview people stopped along the uphill highway to buy gas or put on tire chains. And when that happened she had always liked it, because at least she was talking to real people on camera.

Gloria Hedlund had outlasted the others of her era, and she had thrived. After the years of being part of "team coverage" she had gotten to be one of the occasional weekend anchors at the studio desk when the first-string news readers had their nights off. Then she spent another eight years as a weeknight anchor before she got to where she was now, not just a news reader, but a real journalist.

Lately she had begun looking professionally at Dick Stahl. When she first learned of him about five years ago, she sensed something about him she didn't like. Was he a real person? He had started out as a soldier, then became an army explosives expert, then the head of the LAPD Bomb Squad, and finally the owner of a private security company. His bio had the clean smell of omission that life stories of public figures in Los Angeles sometimes had.

Even her first search of the newspaper archive had been very LA. Stahl had a clientele that included a lot of Hollywood people, a few high-profile defendants in court cases, the principals in nasty big-money divorces. There were photographs of him in the backgrounds at parties that huge real estate companies or banks held, and there was no question he was there working.

As far as Gloria could tell, Stahl had never been willing to speak to reporters. That alone had made her suspicious of him. He was an expert in the false politeness that cops used to ensure not that they would never give offense, but that they could never be accused of it. He was also sure of what he could do to get a press reporter, photographer, or television newsperson out of his way when he was leading a client somewhere. When she was doing her research about him she had seen it on unaired video. Some large male reporters tended to use their size and weight to keep a celebrity or a suspect blocked where he was for questions or pictures. Dick Stahl was not someone who made that easy. He simply kept going, never quite stopping, his hand on the client's upper arm, always smiling.

She had watched footage of Stahl taking a client out past David Wainscott from Channel Seven a couple of years ago. David was very big and intimidating, and he had planted himself in the only path through a crowd, the space between a car and the curb. Stahl came along smiling and saying: "Excuse us please. Excuse us. Thank you. Thank you very much." At the last moment, David Wainscott seemed to realize he had put himself in a position that should have been effective, but also made him very vulnerable, and Stahl wasn't reacting the way Wainscott had expected. He wasn't stopping.

There was nowhere for Wainscott to sidestep or even turn his body, because his feet were too long to let him pivot in the narrow space. He was going back or he was going down. The camera showed Wainscott wince in pain as Stahl stepped on his instep, and then David staggering backward and bumping into the reporters behind him, stepping on their feet and then falling backward onto two of them. Stahl never stopped, simply kept up his progress, stepped past Wainscott and around the car, put the client into the backseat, and slid in beside her. The door slammed and the car pulled ahead and picked up speed. A careful slow-motion examination of the footage showed nothing actionable. Stahl hadn't hit, pushed, threatened, or even stopped smiling.

Her distaste for him five years ago wasn't hatred. She just filed him in the back of her mind as one of the cops and former cops who knew how to avoid letting his client be trapped and forced to respond to uncomfortable questions. She made sure there was never any mention of his name on her airtime to give him free publicity, and went on.

As soon as Stahl had returned to her attention two months ago with his odd history and insider connections she began to keep track of him. She wasn't after him. And as he helped rebuild the Bomb Squad and began to take apart bombs that she was assured would have killed anyone else, Channel Ten had to give him the adulation everyone else was giving him. But she kept watching and listening.

And when she realized what the rest of the story was, what he had been hiding, the information clarified everything for her. She had seen this kind of thing before. God, had she seen it.

This was just like what had happened in her first job after college. The news director at Charlotte was a handsome man about forty years old named James, who had once been a reporter at the network. When he hired her, things had seemed just fine. He worked with the reporters as a team leader. He occasionally took the evening news staff out before the show. After a while, sometimes it was after the show. But inevitably, there came a time when there were only four of them, and then one at a time, the others left. After a couple of drinks, he said he wanted her to date him. She had begun to walk the tightrope—not rejecting him outright, but not agreeing. She said she was too busy, and then she was too tired, and then she had plans. He never gave up, never missed a chance.

Then one day she was called into the owner's office. The owner said, "I'm truly sorry, Gloria. We had hoped Jimmy had started growing up, but apparently he hasn't. He's been bothering and pressuring you, hasn't he?"

She was so relieved she nearly cried. She hoped they weren't going to fire him, but as time passed he had become more insistent. She said, "Yes. I didn't want to complain about him, because most of the time he's nice."

The owner sighed. "Well, we can't have that stuff going on here. I've ordered your severance check and included a bonus for the extra trouble. Melinda has it out at the desk, along with some things for you to sign."

"*My* check?"

"We can't fire Jimmy. His contract is too expensive, and it has penalties. We'd be paying him to keep the station in court. Look, there won't be any blame for you. We'll make sure you have terrific references."

It had taken her three years after that to work her way back up through two small stations in Kentucky to a major station in Atlanta. By then she was twenty-six. Even though Atlanta was a place where she could make extra money modeling, she took few assignments. She worked over sixty hours every week and learned everything she could. She became a good reporter. She also kept everything professional. Even in the one instance when she was attracted to someone in the newsroom, she turned him down.

In another four years she was almost thirty-one, and she finally made it to a low-level slot at Channel Ten in Los Angeles. This time the man was the station manager at Channel Ten, Mike Tomlinson. She was grateful for the second chance, and when he asked her out, she went. While they got to know each other better, she even had hopes that they were going to have a nice relationship. But when Tomlinson felt comfortable enough to be frank with her, he told her he expected her to be attentive to his wishes. The next time he asked her out, it was to his apartment. She refused.

Mike Tomlinson said simply, "Okay." At first she was relieved. He reverted to being perfectly professional. He met with her only in company with other people, and issued orders to the group together so everyone would know what the others were doing. The rest of the time he never spoke to her. Messages came through underlings and colleagues. Things stayed that way for two years.

She was thirty-three years old by then, and she understood. The stories she was assigned were the same sort she had been doing as a beginner in Charlotte, and less important than the ones she had done in Kentucky. She was still doing some modeling, but as she aged, there were fewer offers.

The Fourth of July came on a weekend that year, so the holiday was celebrated on the following Monday. She switched with Claudia Shin so she could do Claudia's Friday early broadcast and take what amounted to a four-day weekend. She drove to San Diego and checked in at the Hotel del Coronado. She liked it because Channel Ten wasn't shown in San Diego. People who saw her on the beach seldom recognized her.

She spent two days lying on the beach—always under an umbrella and wearing 100 SPF sunscreen—walking vast distances morning and evening with her feet in the surf, and thinking. She evaluated her life. She had been a television newswoman for over ten years, and she was still about at the level where she started. She was skilled enough and she was still beautiful enough to be at the network, but her time was nearly over to qualify for the jump. If she didn't get promoted at Channel Ten to a slot where she'd get noticed within two years, she'd have missed her chance.

After two days of thinking during the day and drinking on her balcony at night, there had been about three times when she had decided on suicide. Once she had stuck to it long enough to walk to a sporting goods store in town, bring back a nasty-looking fishing knife, and run a warm bath, but she passed out before she'd used it.

Near the end of the second day she called Mike Tomlinson, the station manager. She was told he couldn't take her call just then, but someone would call her back in about ten minutes. His secretary had been saying that for two years. Gloria said never mind, and called the private cell phone number he had given her two years ago.

"Yes?" he said.

"This is Gloria," she said.

"I thought you were off this week," he said.

She closed her eyes and made her voice sound cheerful and soft. "I was sitting here on my balcony at the Hotel del Coronado wondering why you never called me again after that one time."

He paused for a moment. Maybe he was looking at his phone to switch on a recording and protect himself.

She thought about it, but she didn't care.

He said, "I made overtures because I was attracted to you. You made it clear you weren't interested. Since I'm not a psycho, and didn't want to put pressure on an employee, I've left you alone."

"Well, maybe that wasn't the last word. Maybe we should get together soon and talk about it. As I said, I'm at the Del Coronado for the next couple of days. What do you think?"

Within a month she had been promoted to weekend anchor with Todd Tedesco. When Jerry Zingler had a stroke she became a weeknight anchor, a job she'd held all the years since then. The relationship with Mike had gone on for a few years, and she had begun to think he might be planning to marry her, but then he married another woman. When that marriage ended after a few years he was with Gloria a few times, and then married a second wife. Now and then—after a Christmas party or when they were away at a conference—he still occasionally knocked on her hotel room door. She tolerated it and acted cheerful on those occasions.

She was ashamed. She hadn't been a naïf right out of college. She had by then been a professional for over ten years. And she had been the one to suggest the arrangement. All it had taken was seeing the situation clearly. She felt she'd been driven into a dead end. She was humiliated and cheated and hated what had happened to her, what she'd had to do. And she was confused. She was a victim who was making three million dollars a year and winning awards, but she felt worthless.

At the studio today she had felt as if she was reporting her own story. She had been trying to protect that young policewoman from what happened to her. As soon as the police chief ended his press conference announcing that pig Stahl's firing, she had begun to get nasty e-mails from viewers. Every one used the word "bitch." The viewers all had other things to say, but that word seemed to be required.

She knew all about the demeaning crap Diane Hines was being subjected to by her wonderful new boss. Was that supposed to be tolerated from a public official? Apparently. She had begun to screen her e-mails for the word "bitch."

Gloria got into her Ferrari, stepped on the clutch and started the engine, let the car coast backward a few feet, and then touched the brake. The bomb kicked the spinning, flaming car upward to light up the night air, turning the dead body strapped into the driver's seat over and over with it.

33

The bomb maker's special phone rang. Since the terrorists had turned up, he had moved it from the kitchen cupboard and kept it close. He opened his eyes and stretched his arm to the nightstand beside his bed to pick up the phone. "Yes?"

"We're up the road about five kilometers. We'll be there in five minutes."

He looked at the phone. "It's three a.m. What do you want at this hour?"

"We want to talk to you." The man hung up.

All the bomb maker could do was put on the clothes he had taken off only a couple of hours ago and prepare for an unpleasant talk with them that was sure to culminate in some awful new task or condition they wanted to add to the bargain. He went into the living room to wait.

In a minute he saw the same two cars with what seemed from a distance to be two men in each. They pulled up at the end of his driveway, and the phone rang again.

"Yes?"

"We're coming in. Turn off anything you have that will hurt us."

"What would that be?" He was hurrying to his front closet to switch off the mines, but he didn't want them to know there was anything to switch off.

"You tell me."

"I don't have anything like that. Come ahead." He had reached the closet, and now he swept the side of his hand down the toggle switches to turn off the firing circuits and closed the door. As he completed the action he saw their headlights brightening and coming closer. He shut the closet door to hide the panel.

The headlights went off and he opened the front door.

The car doors swung open and the four men hurried to the porch in the darkness and filed inside. They were smiling, but it was the same kind of smile he expected to see if they were about to kill someone in a particularly cruel way. In a moment they had crowded into his foyer. The man who was in the habit of speaking for the others hugged him. "Wonderful night," he said. "You pulled off another one."

"I don't know what you mean," he said impatiently.

"The woman! That television reporter. Tomorrow the newspapers and television stations will be full of stories about it. We heard about it on the radio."

The bomb maker had felt a half second of hope that something had happened he knew nothing about. Now he knew it was only the television reporter, so they'd brought him no information at all. He had needed to bomb something to keep the panic growing in the city, and he hadn't been ready to do anything more difficult. He expected people in the city might think this meant something, but he hadn't anticipated any reaction from his clients.

He said, "She was nothing. Easy. While I'm busy working I need something to keep the pot boiling. Do you know that expression?"

The four men were pleased. "Brilliant," one of the men said. "They'll be confused, and not know where to look next."

He had, of course, assumed that this would be the reaction of the authorities, but he hadn't considered it brilliant. Maybe it was. He noticed that two of the men were surreptitiously looking around his workshop in the garage. They weren't searching, just snooping. He said, "Please remember this is my workshop. You're surrounded by high explosives, some of them in very volatile stages of manufacture."

The one who usually did the speaking looked around at his comrades. "Did you hear and understand?"

The others muttered affirmative words and nodded, but the bomb maker reflected that he still had no idea what their first language was. It made sense that a sophisticated conspiracy would avoid sending people to the United States who couldn't speak English, but he was disappointed and frustrated. Maybe they were from several countries that spoke different languages, and English was their only common language.

He was exhausted. He also hated the fact that his clients had presumed to take the right to drop in on him whenever they felt like it. He couldn't let them feel welcome at all hours, but he couldn't risk a confrontation of any kind with these four men. Anything violent they did in overpowering him might set off an explosion. He thought hard, but he could think of only one thing he could do that might help keep them friendly and under control.

"What time is it?" he asked.

"Three nineteen. What difference does it make?"

"I asked for a couple of reasons. One is that I haven't had much sleep. The other is that I have a surprise I've been saving for you, and I think this might be a good time to give it to you."

"What is it?"

"I'll show you."

The bomb maker went to a seven-foot cabinet at the end of the room, but instead of opening it he reached up and took a small padlock key off the top. He walked to the row of steel storage boxes along the wall and unlocked two of the padlocks and removed them.

The men gathered around him as he lifted the first lid and revealed the nineteen AK-47 rifles and a couple of layers of loaded thirty-round magazines. He stepped back, and the four men surged in and picked up four rifles. They handled the rifles as though each had spent years carrying an identical one at all times. They ejected the magazines, opened the chambers, and examined them. Then they looked down the insides of the barrels, using the light of the open chambers to see the condition of the rifling. A couple of them took a bullet out of the cardboard ammo boxes and used it to partially dismantle the weapons and touch the inner surfaces to be sure they were clean, were oiled, and showed no worrisome wear or corrosion. The more they looked, the happier they appeared to be. Just over two-thirds of the weapons were new and the others were barely broken in. They sighted down the weapons and a couple of them made hasty guesswork adjustments to the unused sights before they set down one rifle and examined another.

The spokesman held up his rifle so the bomb maker could see the lower receiver, and pointed at the line of drilled-out steel. "Did you do this?"

"Yes," he said. "That's where the serial number was. If one is lost or stolen, we don't want the authorities to be able to identify it or where it came from."

"But isn't drilling a serial number a crime?"

"Yes. Having a weapon like this is a crime anyway."

The man nodded. "Yes." He examined the selector lever. "Have you modified these yet to be fully automatic?"

"Yes," said the bomb maker.

The man handed the rifle back. "Test them."

He took the rifle, as though he were agreeing to do the tests. "It will take some time, and I'm working with bombs now."

"Then we'll do it. There's no point in getting the bombs ready if we don't have the weapons for what happens afterward. Do you have the pistols?"

The bomb maker hesitated for a second. He had wanted to hold back something so he could delay them if he needed to. It was clear that he couldn't. He opened the second storage box and the four men examined the pistols. They were satisfied with those. They held them up, pointed at the ceiling, and one of them gave a whoop, but he didn't fire. The others answered the whoop and laughed, but didn't fire.

For a moment he could picture these men raising their weapons and firing celebratory volleys into the sky above a desert city. But as he watched them, he also could imagine them in a tropical jungle on a rounded mountain stronghold wearing dark green fatigues and T-shirts. One who was larger and heavier might easily have been from the Balkans or central Asia.

"If you want to move them, the roads out here are empty from the time the bars close until just before dawn."

The leader of the group said, "Oh, I almost forgot. We came to congratulate you, but also to bring you some more money." He turned to one of his men and said, "Go get the money."

The bomb maker waited while the men carried the weapons to the door and out to the cars. Then one of the men came back in and set a shopping bag down on the floor at his feet, turned, and went out to join his companions. The bomb maker could see it was the usual piles of hundred-dollar bills, so he didn't bother to pick up the bag. He went and stood by the door until he saw the vehicle pause at the end of his driveway, then turn and drive off.

He was wide awake now. He was always tense in the presence of those men, but this time he had been actually afraid. There was a hint of pent-up violence in them. He realized that giving them guns was making them a hundred times more powerful, but he was too afraid of them not to. What did he have left to appease them next time?

34

Morning came earlier at Stahl's condominium than it had in the days before the explosion in Diane's apartment. She was awake and out of the bedroom by five. She put on the bathrobe he had ordered for her, went to the kitchen, and made coffee. She liked the fact that there were skylights above and windows opening onto a narrow garden with a fountain, which made the stone wall outside look as though it were made of water. She was too much of a cop to be uninterested in how the security was maintained. She had to go all the way to the window to look up and see that there were horizontal bars above the garden to prevent intruders, and she supposed there were bars or barriers on the roof to prevent anyone from reaching the skylights.

She sat down in the kitchen with her coffee and played with her new phone. It was late enough in Florida to call her mother, so she did. Her mother's number rang a few times, and she decided she must be too early. Her mother's phone was still turned off. That was the way she left it for the night because it made noises while she was trying to sleep. She sent her mother a text to tell her she'd try again later.

She thought about Dick now, and as always thinking about him seemed to release strong feelings of affection. The response still surprised her, but it also pleased her. She hoped it meant that the direction her life had taken was right. She wasn't quite ready to formulate a more confident statement for herself. That would be too close to saying the words aloud. Once people said things aloud, what they said tended to become sure and settled.

Not much was sure or settled. The reason she had become a bomb technician was not that she was cocky or had no fear of death. It was the opposite.

She wanted to live to be old and had always worked hard to deserve to be alive. A person who risked his life every day for others and who worked to gain the knowledge and skills to do it well must have a claim to living. She had not been overconfident, but she had been optimistic—until the evening after the car bomb in the Valley. That night, she had lost that feeling.

The new captain, the middle-aged man who had come from nowhere that day to stand in for the fourteen men who'd been murdered—an absurdity in itself—had behaved as though the substitution were natural. He had stepped in and taken charge. He had begun to study the booby-trapped car at once. He looked at the car as a single explosive device and saw the device in three dimensions and all its complexity, approaching it from above, below, all sides. He had picked up alterations and signs she hadn't seen at first, and provided ways around the traps that she didn't know.

She had realized within fifteen or twenty minutes that her only chance of making it to the end of watch that night was to do what he asked and to make herself be what he wanted. She had to see with her perfect vision into a dim space and extract the component he wanted out, reach into the hell-made contraption farther because her hands and arms were smaller and thinner, remove the component more gently because her tactile sense was keener and her fingers were less callused. She had concentrated on seeing exactly what he saw and thinking what he thought. Sometimes she watched his eyes to see what they were focusing on.

By the time they had worked their way down to the heart of the contraption—the shaped charge so big it was intended to blow a crater into the pavement and set off the gasoline tanks—she was practically an extension of his mind. It made perfect sense to her that he would strap the charge to his chest and take the long, lonely walk into the concrete riverbed. She was fully aware that carrying the charge was crazy, even suicidal. But taking it below street level was the most effective way to render the bomb harmless, and he was the only one who had enough experience to have a chance of doing it successfully.

At the end of that day, after she was safe and clean and sitting in her apartment alone, she had felt lost. She was relieved and afraid at the same time. She knew that what had saved them—saved her—was that he'd been able to practically read the bomb maker's mind. She had seen how he did it, followed his steps, but was positive she could not have initiated them. If she came upon a similar device tomorrow, she would probably die.

She'd had an urge to talk to somebody, but nobody who hadn't been there could understand or have anything useful to tell her. What did she need to know? What was she supposed to expect, to look for, to fear, to do? She realized that what she wanted to know was the future. She knew there was no place to find it, but she also knew the idea wasn't idle, because there was one person who knew so many other things that he was closer to the future than anyone else. And he had probably learned things dismantling that bomb during the day. She knew he had. Of course she was drawn to him.

She had gotten ready—perfume, pretty underwear, the skirt and blouse she had been saving. She took a great deal of care with her hair and makeup. She thought clearly about why she was choosing to put forward this version of herself, when she could instead put on a clean, pressed uniform. It was because she needed to look as appealing as she could, and she needed to make it clear that her visit wasn't an official errand that should have been handled at work.

She had admitted to herself just as she arrived outside his building that part of the attraction all along had been sexual. She had brought the bottle of Scotch thinking it was an afterthought, but it had really been premeditated. She had thought of it twice in the hour before she left home in the hope that it would set a nonbusiness tone. But the tone was one in which sex would be more likely. In the end she had insisted on the sex—thrown herself at him because sex was the opposite of death, and death might win in a day or so, and because she needed to be as close to him tonight as she could be.

During the next few feverish days while they fought the bomb maker every day and spent every night in each other's arms, she felt as though she were living a whole life in an accelerated form. It had been like riding a runaway horse. She was not in charge at all, rather clinging to the horse and trying not to fall.

Boom. That was the instant everything had changed completely. She woke up six weeks later, on the far side of a chasm. All the unself-conscious abandon and lust and hero worship were knocked into a pile back there with those six days.

Her limber, athletic animal self was gone. She wondered if she would ever walk right, whether her hearing would ever fully return. Whenever she moved to test for pain, she always found it. The notion of sexual attraction was as far from her mind as it could be. She thought about the discomfort of breathing with so many broken ribs, of regaining the full extension of her limbs.

She had told Dick she remembered everything that happened between them. She knew that to him it meant she remembered and didn't regret any of it. What she felt was probably worse. She mourned those times, yet hadn't found a path back to the way she felt the first week with him.

One of the things that had made the relationship happen was her confidence that it would be temporary, a few days of madness that would end with the death of one or both of them. Two days ago Dick had felt hurt when she called it a fling, so she promised she wouldn't.

But keeping her promise was hard. She didn't know what would happen now. She didn't know what could. As the days went on, she had been wanting time to stop so she could catch up with her lost forty-two days. But every day Dick did more to help her and protect her and support her while she recovered. She felt as though she were running up a debt to him.

She knew she should be leaving him right now and taking a plane to Florida to be with her mother. But the things that made her want to leave were the same things that made her want to stay. He was a better person than she had thought. He cared about her. At the moment she didn't have anything to offer him in return. She knew much more about him now, and felt closer to him, but it was all so different and so inferior to the way they had started.

Diane checked her watch. It was already after 6:00 a.m. She looked around her at the kitchen. She got up and wiped the counters, ran the dishwasher Dick had forgotten last night. She got the pans out and set the table for breakfast. Every move she made was slow and careful and self-protective. She held herself erect and bent at the knees to pick things up because her spine seemed tender today. When she ran out of things to do, she went to the guest bathroom and showered.

She looked around for clothes, then put on a pair of jeans and a new T-shirt Dick had bought for her from May Hedges. She glanced at herself in the mirror, then looked harder. The least she could do was try to look good when he woke up. She opened the makeup kit May Hedges had brought.

The cell phone Stahl had left on his nightstand was ringing. He picked it up and looked at the screen, but the extension wasn't familiar. "Stahl."

"This is Bart Almanzo, Dick. Have you seen the news?"

"No," he said. "What news?"

"Gloria Hedlund's car blew up in the Channel Ten parking lot at around one last night."

"Just a scare?"

"She was in it. She's dead."

"And nobody called me when it happened?"

"Your resignation was already in. I don't think they could."

"Who's been to look at the wreck?"

"Your guy Elliot. He's still at the scene now."

"Has he said if this was our bomber or somebody else?"

"He told my detectives that it was the same guy."

"Damn. Elliot is good. He's seen most of the devices, and he'll know the guy's work. But this is a change. The victim should be a member of the Bomb Squad, or at least some kind of cop."

"I'm on my way over there now. I'll pick you up on the way."

"I'm not sure I'd be welcome today."

"Then I'll just say you're with me. It should be sufficient, since you'll be with me."

"Give me ten minutes."

Stahl showered and dressed quickly. When he came out into the living room, he saw Diane was in the kitchen.

"Wow. You're up early."

"I thought I'd make us some breakfast," she said.

"I just got a call from Bart Almanzo."

"Almanzo? Who's dead?"

"Gloria Hedlund, the TV reporter."

"The woman who outed us is dead?"

"Yes. Somebody wired her car. Elliot thinks it's our guy."

"Do you think I ought to go?"

The surprised way he looked at her betrayed the fact that it had never entered his mind. "If you want to see it, I'm sure he'll be glad to take us both. I'm not sure there's much point in either of us going if Elliot's at the scene, but he asked."

"Then I'll skip it and see Elliot another time."

"Have you got your phone?"

She turned around so he could see the outline of the phone in the back pocket of her jeans. He leaned close and kissed her. She didn't turn her body toward him to allow an embrace, but he didn't notice. He went into the bedroom and came back with a metal box the size of a book with a combination lock built into it. He punched the numbers and it popped open to reveal a Glock 17, two spare magazines, and a box of fifty nine-millimeter rounds.

"I want to give you this before I go. I know your gun and badge didn't travel to the hospital with you, and you probably won't get them back until you're on active duty again. This is what you're used to, right?"

"You know it is," she said. "Get out of here now."

Almanzo had already pulled up outside. Diane watched the security monitor as Stahl trotted out to the street and got into the plain car.

She sat down at the kitchen table and picked up the Glock. She looked it over, released the magazine, and checked the chamber, then loaded the magazine with the first seventeen rounds and set it down again. It had been typical of Dick Stahl to give her this. He realized that she was going to be unarmed and alone, and that the bomb maker knew she wasn't dead yet.

She knew that if she had told him the things she was feeling right now—the disappointment at being left here, no longer considered a police officer because she had been hurt—he would have been shocked. He would patiently explain why hers was the wrong reaction, explain that she was irrational to imagine an officer who was on medical leave would be included, and explain that a man who cared about her the way he did would never do anything to hurt her feelings intentionally. Several men had told her that in the past, and they'd all found ways to hurt her feelings.

* * *

Almanzo drove the police car along the quiet street toward Century Park East. "How's Sergeant Hines doing?"

"Glad to be out of the hospital," said Stahl. "She isn't fully recovered, but she's eager to get back to work."

"Do you think she wants to go back to the Bomb Squad?"

"I wish she wouldn't," Stahl said. "But she probably will if she gets back her manual dexterity and nerve control. Getting good at EOD takes a long time and a lot of field experience. It's hard to let go once you've done the work. She made it clear she'd be willing to take a look at the Hedlund scene if we wanted."

"You and Elliot both said it was weird that Hedlund was the victim. Why do you think the bomber picked her?"

"I don't know. If I were to guess, I'd say our boy has been busy. He hasn't done anything since the hospital. That must have taken a big charge and a lot of work, risk, and planning. He might be feeling he's under pressure to keep the tempo up and keep the city off balance while he makes more bombs and prepares for something bigger. He picked a well-known person who has been reporting on him, and on us. So it counts in his mind as a win. That makes it a defeat for us."

"You think that way even after she made a big point of getting you fired?"

"I wish she hadn't done that. But if I hadn't done what I did, she wouldn't have."

Almanzo drove in silence for a minute. "Did you and Sergeant Hines stay home all last night?"

"Yeah." Stahl studied him. "We did."

"Please don't look at me like that, Dick," Almanzo said. "It was a murder. Any question that can be asked has to be."

"You're right, of course. We got Diane sprung from the hospital around seven in the evening, and then my assistant, Andy, drove us home in Diane's car. A cop named Morrissey picked Andy up from my place and drove him home. I had a lady from Bloomingdale's waiting for us to show Diane some clothes I bought her because there was nothing left of the clothes in her apartment. I still have her business card. Her name is May Hedges. By the time that was over we were both tired. We had a drink and went to sleep. If there's any doubt we never left, the twenty-four-hour security guys at my building keep a log and retain the recordings from the surveillance system."

"Okay," said Almanzo. "Sounds tight to me."

"I can guess where you were last night," said Stahl.

"That's right. I was home asleep until one fifteen, when my guys got called in to look at a murder scene and I learned who the victim was."

He pulled up to the Channel Ten studio on Melrose. As he turned up the short drive beside the guard gate, they could both see that the parking lot was full of reporters, photographers, and free-lancers held back by a pair of police officers inside the yellow tape. Some of them began to move as soon as Almanzo's car appeared, instinctively aware that a car like that probably held ranking cops. They hurried to get close while the car was held back by the lift gate. When the bar lifted they were already holding cameras within five feet of the car on both sides, getting shots of the two men inside.

When Almanzo stopped outside the tape, they began to yell. "Captain Stahl! Didn't you resign?"

"Can you tell us what happened?"

"Are you a suspect?"

Almanzo nodded to Stahl and stepped forward to head off the small crowd. "My name is Captain Bart Almanzo, commander of Homicide Special. Captain Stahl has come at my request to assist me in this examination of the scene. This is an ongoing homicide investigation, so neither of us will be answering any questions at this time."

The group could not have failed to notice that Stahl was walking off while Almanzo was keeping them occupied. Almanzo stopped when Stahl was far inside the yellow tape. Then he ducked under the tape and trotted to catch up.

Elliot was beside the burned wreck. He had the hood up and he was taking photographs of the engine compartment. He looked up. "Captain!" He stepped closer to him to take off a glove and shake his hand.

Stahl said, "I hear you think this is our guy again."

"I'm pretty sure it is. It doesn't make sense to me as a strategy, but there it is. We found fragments of a homemade mercury rocker switch on a stand like the one he used at the gas station. So I started to look for his other trademarks, and I found that two backup charges had gone off too. There was one using the circuit for the brake lights, and another backup with a set of lithium batteries using the solenoids that locked the doors as the switch. It was a toss-up which circuit would go first."

Stahl turned to Almanzo. "That's him, all right." He said to Elliot, "Where did the car go up?"

He pointed at a spot behind a reserved parking space. "Over there."

"It figures. Backups to the backups, and far more explosive than he needed."

When Almanzo went to talk with his two detectives, Stahl said to Elliot, "I'm sorry I had to resign, but I won't abandon you guys. I'm trying to come back to work as a consultant, which is probably what I should have been in the first place. If you need me before then for any reason, call me. The same for the other teams."

"Thanks, Captain."

"Not captain anymore, and that's one part that won't be coming back. It's just Stahl now."

35

The bomb maker had a bad start that morning because of the night before. First he had needed to spend the evening making a main charge of the right sort. He had seen the target in publicity pictures at the wheel of a silver Ferrari. At first he thought the car must be part of an advertisement, but it appeared again in a shot on her personal website. She had parked it in the garage of a house. Only the open garage door and a part of a brick facade were visible, so the house could be anywhere. But the plate number began with GH, so it had to be Gloria Hedlund's.

He scrapped the design he had been drawing, and designed a smaller version that could be made flatter and attached under the chassis of the low sports car. Then he decided to use a few yards of wire and two more detonators to connect the charge to the brake light and to the solenoids that locked the doors electronically.

He knew that studio lots were expert at keeping people out, so he hot-wired the tow truck parked in back of a closed gas station where he'd stopped a few times in Bakersfield. He set the sun visor at a low angle to block a security camera's view of his face, then drove the truck to LA and up to the gate. He angled his hat's brim down to obscure his features. He said he was there to jump a battery in the television parking lot, although the explanation would probably not have been necessary, because a tow truck was its own explanation. The guard waved him in, and he drove to the television station's parking lot.

He had no trouble finding her parking space behind the station because of the distinctiveness of the silver Ferrari. He had no real trouble setting the main charge or running the secondary wires to the brake light through the trunk and to the solenoid that controlled the right rear-door lock. The process took five minutes.

He was able to drive off the lot in the tow truck over forty minutes before the explosion. Then he drove back to the gas station, popped the ignition lock back into the column, and walked away. His car was parked a block from the station. The hardest part for him had been driving home from Bakersfield.

It couldn't have been more than two hours after he was in bed when his employers, the terrorists, had come for their night visit. This time he had gotten rid of them by giving them the guns and ammo he'd been saving. It had been a costly tactic for him. He had hoped to use the terrorists' lack of guns as a way to keep them fairly harmless and peaceful while he completed his plans and mixed the rest of the explosives necessary to carry them out. He'd planned to string them along for a month or more while he gave them one or two weapons at a time, then doled out the ammunition as slowly as possible. But when he assessed the situation that night, he decided to give in.

They had been jumpy and emotional. They were on a mission in the middle of a crowded city surrounded by an enormous metropolitan area patrolled by about twelve thousand police, twelve thousand sheriffs, and an unknown number of FBI, ATF, border police, airport police forces, and Homeland Security. They had asked him for arms for fifteen men. The numbers were small enough to persuade him that they didn't intend to accomplish anything but an hour or two of slaughter before they died. They were a suicide squad, whether they knew it or not. How could he be sure they paid him before it was too late?

He was tired and had a pounding headache, and his schedule had him working with difficult chemicals in big batches today. He wished he could close everything down and take a nap, but he couldn't. Now that they had the weapons he'd bought for them, there would be no way to keep them controlled, or even predictable. If they were motivated by religion, one of them could have a vision. If they were motivated by politics, or even were being paid for murdering people, one of them could develop the notion that a neighbor was suspicious and was spying on them or something.

He had never seen any of them engaged in anything that looked like a religious practice. They didn't bow to the east in front of him, or cross themselves, or wear religious medals or talismans. They never wore anything with writing on it, or read books in front of him.

When he was searching for a sponsor he had tried to reach the leaders of any group that identified itself as having committed a terrorist act anywhere in the world. But he had not been told which group these men belonged to. They could be on some familiar mission, or they could be doing something never done before. They could be working to weaken an American city so Russia, China, North Korea, or some other country would be accused. Or they might be a small secret group that wanted to draw out some other group that was a threat in their own country. They could be anything or its mirror opposite.

There just wasn't any way to know whether their plan was rational, let alone comprehensible. He supposed nothing intended to end in a suicidal battle was rational. The whole suicide dimension put him at a terrible disadvantage in dealing with them. In any confrontation, he was the one who would be bluffing. They would be the ones prepared to push their point of view to the extreme of death: you must do as I say or I will kill you even though it kills me too.

It bothered him that they had a kind of sincerity he didn't. A man who was planning to die for a cause might be crazy or deluded, but he wasn't cowardly or selfish. The bomb maker acknowledged himself to be both.

No matter how useful he was to them, how good he was at the job he had undertaken, he was not their brave and noble comrade in arms. He was a mercenary, a person whose loyalty must be bought on a continuing basis. And in this case they also saw him as a traitor to his country. That undoubtedly made him even less deserving of respect. They ordered him around without much regard for his dignity. There was even a danger that they might kill him because they thought he was contemptible.

He began to consider various ways of getting out of California, which he would have to do whether things went badly or they went well. He could buy airline tickets for flights leaving each day from the four major airports—Los Angeles International, Ontario, Long Beach, and Burbank. He supposed the safest way would be to reserve one flight from each airport each day. The flights didn't have to be long, so he could cut the cost by picking cheap flights—say, a hundred dollars. That would bring it down. If he had a ticket for one cheap flight at one airport every day, it would be $36,500 a year. If he booked all four of them for three months it would be the same price, $36,500. There might be some sort of open-ended ticket he could keep renewing for even less, or something else that was less likely to be noticed by the authorities. He decided to work out a travel plan and implement it. He would also look into the idea of having flights from airports farther away from Los Angeles, in case he needed an airport after an attack, when local ones were likely to be shut down. He would also have to think about hidden cars and other ways to get to an airport.

Maybe his house was his call to a bluff, as it always had been. He was comfortable spending most hours of every day inside this enormous bomb. Think you're tough? You're a pure-souled fearless fanatic who smiles as he provokes death? Come stand beside me while I work in this munitions dump.

He kept at it all day and into the evening, making the substances he would need. When he finally gave himself permission to rest, he meticulously cleaned, locked up, and showered, then put on clean clothes before he washed the ones that might have specks of volatile substances on them. When he played back the evening news, he was shocked.

The news anchor said, "A source close to the mayor's office said today that a preliminary investigation had begun in the murder of Channel Ten's Gloria Hedlund. The source confirmed that one person of interest is former police captain Richard Stahl, the subject of Miss Hedlund's final on-air exposé."

36

The next day the bomb maker watched the television news while he ate his lunch, and he could see that the story had begun to grow and flower since last night. Matt Jeffrey was interviewing a retired prosecutor named Etsky on Channel Twelve. Jeffrey said, "Why are the police investigating Richard Stahl for the murder of Gloria Hedlund?"

"I hadn't heard it referred to that way. In a murder of a high-profile public figure, the police have many leads, and many possibilities. They plunge into the investigation and try to eliminate as many people as they can right away. The last I heard, Mr. Stahl was a person of interest, not a suspect."

"Aren't those just two stages in one process?"

"Sort of," said Etsky. "Generally, there are many persons of interest, but only one becomes a suspect. Even then, a suspect is innocent until proven guilty. We're far from a trial, and the police haven't released any information they've found pertaining to him."

"We do know some things. He's a man who hadn't been on the police force for eight years, but who was appointed to take over the Bomb Squad after the mass murder of half the squad. The chief jumped over the heads of fourteen serving Bomb Squad members to make him their boss. Stahl immediately proceeded to defuse at least four very large and complicated bombs, almost single-handedly."

Etsky said, "Yes, I can see what you're wondering about. It's not unheard of that a public official might come in and save the day in an emergency, and then turn out to be the one who caused it. There have been fire officials who set fires, either to expand their reputations or to create a need for their services. And, of course, there have been police officers who committed crimes and pretended to solve them."

"I'm just thinking, who would know better how to defuse a sophisticated bomb than the man who built it? Just wondering if you've heard anything from the police about that."

"No."

"And there is the fact that on the very day Richard Stahl was forced to resign by Gloria Hedlund's reporting, Gloria was killed with a bomb."

"That could be a coincidence," Etsky said. "These bombs have been planted all over the city for about two months—long before she reported on Stahl."

"But loss of a reputation is enough to make a man want revenge. It does provide a motive, doesn't it?"

"Some people would say that. But a motive is a subjective thing. For some people, thinking someone is staring at them is a motive for murder. For others it takes much, much more."

"But not everybody has the makings of a bomb on hand. It's a very small percentage of the population. Because of all of the bombs that have been defused, wouldn't the squad have access to lots of explosives kept for evidence?"

"Now we're straying far beyond my field of expertise. I've never prosecuted a bombing case, but I'm not sure they keep explosives for evidence after they've identified them. They do keep some explosives of their own for detonating suspicious devices."

"I'm just pointing out that he had the motive. He had the means. And the explosion occurred after one a.m. Mr. Stahl had finished his final day of duty on the police force six hours earlier. Six hours. That's the opportunity."

The television screen filled with a shot of the interior of the studio, and the new anchorwoman said, "Thanks to Matt Jeffrey and former prosecutor Etsky for that interview. We'll be back in a moment with more news."

The bomb maker switched channels to see what the other local stations were covering at noon. Channel Ten was running interminable coverage of the death of its reporter, Gloria Hedlund. It kept showing the shot taken by the surveillance cameras on the studio roof. He could see the flash and the nearby cars bounce once from the detonation, and then the Ferrari spinning into the air and falling in flames. He was pleased to see that the anchors didn't show the tow truck, which had left forty minutes earlier. They didn't seem to have made the connection.

After that they showed a report giving a biography of Gloria Hedlund, with pictures from early beauty contests across the South and a much younger Gloria looking like a blond goddess in front of groups of shorter, darker, and nearly identical contestants. Then there was a succession of shots from television stations in Charlotte and other cities, all the way up to shots from Los Angeles, taken twenty-five years later.

The bomb maker set the schedule control to make sure the local news was recorded beginning at five o'clock, and then turned off the TV. He had work to do this afternoon.

He had learned that in addition to killing the woman reporter, his bomb had succeeded in neutralizing the best bomb expert, the commander of the only opposing force that mattered to him, and making him a suspect. It was time to press his advantage. He had been working on some devices, and now it was time to finish them and put them into the field.

The surprising developments surrounding Dick Stahl had changed everything. The bomb maker had killed Gloria Hedlund only because he wanted to keep up the atmosphere of panic, and for that he needed to kill someone known to the public. He had chosen her only because there was something about her he hadn't liked. But now Stahl was out for good.

Stahl had been the man he feared most. Stahl had ruined his car bomb at the gas station, rendered his elevator bomb a waste of effort, and correctly read the bomb he'd planted in the school cafeteria. Stahl had nearly rebuilt the Bomb Squad to full strength faster than the bomb maker could destroy them.

The bomb maker examined his work, selected the devices he felt were ready, and went to his car. He opened the trunk and placed the metal toolbox inside it. The box had a lining of bubble wrap, then a layer of Styrofoam bits, and then a four-inch layer of foam rubber. There was a second four-inch layer with four oblong holes cut into it so he could set a device in each one without it moving or bumping another. On top of that was a plain metal tray, which held a few light tools, rolls of wire, tape, and boxes of screws. They made the box look harmless, but they were all things he might need. The springs and shock absorbers of the car kept the ride sufficiently smooth to give him some confidence.

Driving around with a load of explosives in his trunk introduced a few unavoidable risks. He could be hit by a drunken driver in another car. He could drive into a sinkhole so deep it would jar even his padded box enough to set off a charge. He could have a taillight burn out and get pulled over by a cop who then got suspicious.

The Los Angeles police had automatic license plate readers mounted on patrol cars. The main purpose was to spot cars that had been reported stolen or had outstanding warrants. But there was a computerized record of every plate scanned. He was sure that by now, the homicide detectives would be looking at the numbers scanned near the times and places of his bombings. If two or three of them matched his car's plate, they might take him in.

Tonight he was driving the sedan because he hadn't used it in any of the bombings. He parked on a side street near the subway station in North Hollywood. He sat for a few minutes while he put on his black makeup, then he put on his knit cap and clear glasses. His clothes were baggy so they would hide the devices he was going to hold close to his chest beneath them. He went to his trunk, took out the pair of bombs, hugged them under his coat, and walked to the escalator. He rode it down to the first floor of the subway station, bought a tap card by putting cash into the machine, and went to the next escalator. He rode it down to the platform level and waited. He saw the train on the southbound track arrive, let off a few passengers, then rattle away. He set his watch's timer, walked to the space behind the elevator shaft at the end of the platform, lowered himself down to the tracks below, and began to trot.

The third rail was easy to avoid. It was on the farther, inner side of the train bed. He knew he had ten minutes before the next train would come. He ran steadily for a hundred yards and then climbed up onto the walkway in the dimly lighted tube and ran more easily and faster.

When he reached a spot where a switch track was installed to shift a train onto another branch of the tunnel, he placed the first bomb. It had a detonator that would be set off by shock, a main charge of Semtex, and a timer that would set off a smaller backup charge if twenty minutes went by, so at least the tracks would be torn up.

He climbed back up to the maintenance walkway and resumed his run. When he was about a quarter mile farther down the track, he set the second bomb down on the walkway, where it would be seen.

Now that he had no burden, he ran harder. He reached the Universal City station, pulled himself up onto the platform, rode the escalator to the floor above, and then went up the second escalator to the street. He walked back almost to the first station and then to his car. He drove off.

The bomb maker knew exactly where his second spot would be, and he drove right to it. The second spot had a number of features he liked. It was public, but it wasn't infested with a thousand witnesses and a hundred security cameras. Even in the dark he could see that in the daytime it would be pleasant and verdant, and it had bare dirt.

Griffith Park's buildings, he was sure, would all have security cameras. But the bomb maker intended to stay far from buildings. Unless he was very unlucky, there would be no police cars with license readers or anything else.

Fern Dell was a wooded garden within the park. He entered Western Canyon Road at Los Feliz, then drove until he reached the picnic area. He parked as far as he could from the road and searched for the exact place.

He went to the trunk of his car and took out the posthole digger he had brought. He worked quickly and dug nine holes, each about the size of a large tomato can. He brought one to the spot to be sure it matched. When he had the nine holes, he went back to the car to begin moving components. He slipped them into the eight holes and connected the holes with insulated wire, then connected each of the holes to the main device.

When he was finished, he buried the wires, covered the holes with their plastic tops, carefully smoothed dirt evenly over all of them, and took his tools and wire back to his car. He drove all the way home while it was still dark, trying to beat the traffic that would begin to clog the freeways at dawn. It was a two-hour drive even late at night.

He made it home, exhausted, at about 6:15 a.m. He parked the car in the empty bay at the side of his garage and went to bed. As he lay there he wished he could see his work when it was set off, but he knew that was out of the question. If the device didn't kill everyone close enough to see it, then it didn't work.

37

"It bothers me. I'll admit it," Stahl said. "I don't want people to think I would rig a newswoman's car to blow up. But I don't know what to do about it except wait. Either we'll catch the real bomber, or the normal workings of Homicide Special will make it clear to everybody we couldn't have done it."

"They already have enough evidence to prove that now," said Diane. "I don't think everybody's convinced. But I guess that's the least important worry we have."

Stahl drove with Diane to the office of his security company on Sepulveda Boulevard. They parked in the outdoor lot and walked around to the front of the office building. She looked at the red brick, the strange glassed-in set of exterior steps, and up ahead at the row of office doors along the balcony above. "Wow," she said. "That is one ugly building."

"It's cheap. And the office is upstairs beyond the balcony where you can't see it from outside."

"If you ever call and say you're staying late at the office, I'll know you're lying. Nobody could stand to."

"It's not as bad inside."

"I'm sure. How could it be?"

"I was going to ask if you wanted to get into the security business. I haven't spent time on it in months, and I could use the help."

"I'll consider it, if the money is right. But only until the police take me back."

They took the elevator beside the top of the concrete steps, got out at the third floor, walked past the long row of offices, and then stopped at a door that faced away from the balcony.

She looked at the door. It read: NO-FAIL SECURITY in corroded brass letters. "How do you ever get customers?"

"It's sort of a word-of-mouth business. If people need my kind of help, they ask around."

He opened the door and they entered the waiting room. Diane saw that the receptionist, a pretty black woman about thirty years old, was behind a wall of bulletproof glass. Stahl waved his hand at her, and she reached for a button. There was a buzz and Diane heard the sound of a bolt retracting in the steel door.

They went through the interior door, where another woman about forty-five with long blond hair sat at a desk in a large office. She looked up and saw him. "Dick," she said.

"Hi, Valerie. This is Diane." He turned to Diane. "Valerie runs the business."

"The money part, not the part that matters," Valerie said. "I'm a certified public accountant. Pleased to meet you."

Valerie glanced at the receptionist. "And this is Clarissa, who does everything else."

Diane stepped to the receptionist and held out her hand. "Diane."

The receptionist smiled. "It's a pleasure. But I'm surprised to see you two here this morning."

"Why?" said Diane. "He said you were expecting us."

"That bomb business in the subway. I really thought they'd call you in."

Stahl had his phone out, looking at the screen. "Nothing. Don't tell me they're that stupid." He dialed a number, then said, "This is Dick Stahl. Is Deputy Chief Ogden available?" He listened for a moment. "I see. Can you tell me where it is? Thank you."

He turned to the others. "Somebody set off a bomb on the tracks in the Red Line subway in North Hollywood and it caused a wreck." He looked at his phone for a few more seconds. "I'd better get over there. Are you up to coming with me?"

"If I wait here you'll get there faster," Diane said. "And I don't want to be part of the news story."

He gave her a quick kiss on the cheek. "I'll see you as soon as I can."

As the casualties of the subway crash were brought to the surface by elevator and escalator, they were loaded into ambulances and driven north on Lankershim Boulevard toward Valley Presbyterian, east to Providence Saint Joseph in Burbank, or south toward UCLA. The rescue was rapid. One moment there were thirty ambulances lined up along the curb near the station, and ten minutes later there were none. The police and sheriff's deputies kept the traffic moving across the nearby intersections, and kept a lane free for emergency vehicles.

In the sky a swarm of helicopters circled, the throbbing rotors and growling engines making it hard for the rescuers to hear a human voice. The cops and EMTs had to rely on practiced procedure and hand signals to get the patients away.

Dick Stahl pulled his car into the parking structure of a nearby supermarket and trotted to the mouth of the subway. When he got there he saw Judy Welsh, the agent from Raleigh who had been assigned to Team Four.

She was near the parked bomb truck talking on a device with a wire that ran down into the escalator pit. Stahl assumed they had set up a hard connection for communication so they could maintain a no-cell-phones zone. Cells didn't work very well belowground anyway. As he stepped up to her she looked up. "Captain Stahl!"

Someone on the other end said something, and she replied, "Yeah, it's him, big as life."

She heard something else and she said, "Captain, they want you downstairs."

"Thanks, Welsh." He turned and ran to the entrance to the subway, then down the steps because the motor had been turned off. When he reached the first floor down, he saw that there was a command area set up just inside the turnstiles where Elliot and another bomb technician were leaning over a video unit.

Stahl stepped close. "Hi, Elliot. Are you the supervisor of the scene?"

"For the moment I am," he said. "Wyman and Neil are downrange. The damaged train cars are being towed to sidings to the north of the station so they'll be out of the way. While that goes on, they're trying to be sure there's no other explosive device down the track between the location of the crash and the next station, which is Universal City."

"You're sure it was an explosive device, and not a crash?"

"Yes," Elliot said. "The first car was charred, pitted, and scratched from the blast, and the surface tests positive for nitrate compounds. The tracks had been subjected to heat and lateral force. They're bent and have to be replaced."

"How far have Wyman and Neil gotten?"

"They've got two thousand feet of communication line on a wheel, and there's plenty left, but they're past the wreckage."

Stahl said, "Not to second-guess anything, but why Wyman?"

Elliot shrugged. "No choice. He's the ranking supervisor on this scene, and he decided to go. I was just suiting up when he got here and took charge."

"Mind if I hang around?"

"I'd take it as a favor," Elliot said. "As soon as they reconnect themselves to the line, we can see what else they find."

"I'm pretty sure there will be something," said Stahl. "This guy always leaves something for us to disarm. What do you know about the hookup for the first explosion?"

"I think the bomb was fairly small, placed between the left rail going south and the track for a switch to divert a train into another tunnel for maintenance. So when the front wheel of the train passed over the spot, the bomb went off under the front of the first car. It must have killed the driver instantly, and then derailed the first three cars. The railway people were able to tow everything behind that out of the way because it was mostly undamaged. They're working on clearing the cars that were derailed, but there's no telling how long that will take. They may have to use cutting torches and move them out in sections."

There was a sudden change on the screen in front of Elliot. They saw hands appear. Then there was Neil's voice. "Team One, this is Neil. Wyman says he's found a second device on the maintenance walkway on the left side of the tunnel."

"Want to tell him anything?" Elliot asked Stahl.

Stahl said, "Hey, Neil. This is Dick Stahl. Tell him not to touch anything until he's shown it to us on the video feed. I think I'll be able to identify what it is."

Neil said, "He says he's got it identified."

Stahl said, "Remember, this isn't about stopping a subway train to disrupt the morning commute. He's trying to get us to make a mistake. If you find—"

There was a sudden bump that seemed to come up into the vault of the station from the train level below. It felt like a giant hammer hitting the bedrock foundation, and almost simultaneously there was a rush of air. It was similar to the feel of air forced out of a tunnel ahead of a train when it approached at high speed, but it came harder and hotter, filled with fine particles that stung the skin. And then the sound arrived, a deafening vibration that lasted a couple of seconds, shook solid rock and concrete, and made squares of tile drop from the walls and ceiling.

In another second it was gone, as though it had passed down the tunnel to the rest of the system. Stahl and Elliot looked at each other with the same horrified expression. Wyman had guessed wrong.

38

Late in the afternoon, long after the bomb technicians, firefighters, structural engineers, metro engineers, train specialists, and others had declared the emergency over and the scene safe, the mayor arrived. He came with his entourage—a photographer, a public relations officer, a political spokesman, a driver, and a bodyguard. Both the driver and the guard were on-duty police officers, but the mayor liked them to dress in identical black suits, which were a little like the livery of servants. Both men were muscular and formidable, but neither was quite as tall as the mayor, nor was any other member of the retinue. Experts had advised the mayor never to allow himself to look short in a photograph, because the taller man almost always won an election.

The police chief and Deputy Chief Ogden were both taller than the mayor, but in their uniforms, with their pistols and badges and utility belts crowded with gear in black leather pouches, they looked more like instruments of the mayor's power than colleagues. He always walked a couple of paces ahead of them, trying to look like their commander in chief.

The flat, paved area above the subway entrance held satellite trucks from the four major local news channels parked at odd angles, each of them with booms and dishes extended and a reporter and camera operator standing by. The reporters needed to stand in the foreground to provide teasers and superfluous commentary while the camera operators followed the mayor around.

Television cameras were like sunlight and water to the mayor. He stood straighter, and his eyes and facial muscles assumed the look his underlings called "resolute." He seemed to drink power from the microphones.

At this moment he was giving the reporters a somber procession, a portrait of the city's wise leader walking the scene to survey the damage. The camera operators took in the sight and transmitted it to their studios, and the reporters spoke in reverent tones, knowing the mayor would be out again soon to give them the chance to question him, to ask him respectfully how the people of the city should feel about today's developments. They knew he was as aware as they were of the need to get the interview transmitted in time to make the early evening news, so they trusted him.

As soon as the entourage had traveled down on the escalator to the platform, the chief checked to be sure the newspeople were too far behind to hear. Then he said to the mayor: "I'm sorry to get into this right now, Mr. Mayor, but we're on an emergency footing. We've lost two officers, an engineer, and three civilians. You'll recall that when we let Dick Stahl resign, we made an agreement with the police commission to approve a contract with his security company to let us use him as a civilian consultant to the Bomb Squad."

"I remember the idea, but I never signed off on it," the mayor said.

"After what happened today, I'm convinced we ought to make a move on this now."

The mayor got to the bottom of the escalator and waited while the chief and Deputy Ogden glided down. "You're telling me that having Stahl on the payroll would have prevented this? Would he have put on a bomb suit and gone down there to defuse the bomb himself?"

"I don't know what he would have done, sir, and that's exactly the point. He knows the best ways to approach an explosive device, and we don't have anybody else who knows it as well. We know he personally defused three very large and complicated devices during his few weeks as commander, at least a couple of them so big that there was no point in wearing a bomb suit."

The mayor's expression became brooding and resentful. "How do you know he hasn't been setting these bombs himself and then taking them apart? He would know just how to do it because he put them together. I'm not the first one to wonder about that, either. At least two of the reporters up there have said as much."

The chief was frustrated, and his voice turned hard. "He's been cleared of any suspicion. Homicide Special found that there was no chance he did any of these crimes. None. Zero."

Deputy Chief Ogden said, "He wasn't even in the country the day the fourteen men were killed. He was in Mexico. I was in his office and saw him arrive from there the day after it happened."

The chief said, "He's got alibis for every bomb. He was in front of the TV cameras defusing a bomb when—"

"What about Gloria Hedlund? What was he doing when she blew up?"

"He was at the station, from the time of the press conference until seven, with other police officers present while he cleared his office. And then he was with Sergeant Hines all night until morning, when Captain Almanzo woke him."

"She's Stahl's girlfriend, for Christ's sake. And she had reason to hate Gloria too. You call that an alibi?"

"She's a sergeant on the police force. And she's also a victim of the bomber with severe injuries."

"I don't believe having Richard Stahl inside our government and giving his advice to our police would have done anything to prevent this."

"We just lost a bomb technician supervisor with twenty-two years of experience. He wasn't good enough to outsmart this bomber. Stahl has done it repeatedly. We have the best explosives expert in the West still willing to help us. We'd be foolish not to take his help."

"I'll do better than that," said the mayor. "Call the FBI again and ask them for their very best man to be assigned here on temporary duty. We'll pay his salary and expenses, and he can be in charge of all bomb-related activity. We'll give him all the support he wants." The mayor shrugged. "Problem solved."

As the mayor moved ahead, Deputy Chief Ogden said to the chief: "Mind if I go back up for a minute?"

"No," said the chief. "Calling Stahl?"

"Yes. I think I should tell him."

"Right. But let him know we're going to keep trying."

39

Steve and Debbie Garrick drove into the parking lot beside the picnic area in Fern Dell at 12:15 p.m. on Saturday. They were in their Suburban, and when all the seats were installed and the kids were strapped in, they could carry both of them, six of the boys from the baseball team, their equipment, and the picnic supplies. Haley and Ron Steiner had the rest in their van, and they would be along in a few minutes.

They had been practicing all morning at a field in Griffith Park, and now they were all hungry. Debbie tugged at the big cooler of food she had made before dawn and pulled it toward the back door. Then she tapped it on top so the boys knew she wanted it out. As the two Morales boys and Henry Cooper lifted it, she watched her son, Dennis, try to help. He wasn't as strong as those boys, but at least he had the alertness and hustle to get in on the work.

Debbie stifled the feelings that surfaced unexpectedly. She had been a star softball player in high school and college, and later she played in a women's hardball league for three years. She had gotten used to keeping to herself the fact she was so much better at baseball than her husband, Steve, and now their son too. But that didn't mean she'd forgotten.

The problem she faced had been being a woman. She had fallen in love with Steve at the age of twenty-four, and in a year Steve had passed the bar exam. He wanted to marry her, but she knew if she married him she would have to drop out of the league. She couldn't be his wife and travel with a baseball team. Her team had played in a championship series in Venezuela the previous season, and there were signs that they were good enough to keep competing at a high level. But baseball was a game, and being Steve's wife was a future. She tried various methods of putting him off. She told him she was perfectly happy to keep having sex with him regularly while she was home without getting married, and would even live with him for the entire off-season. She made an argument that this would probably be the future pattern for most male-female relationships. But he was a good lawyer. He lined up all his arguments and then marched them past her in review—children, house, financial security, shared risks and rewards, and the near certainty that if they remained single, one of them would meet someone else and move on.

She still had a better arm than Steve, and she was fairly sure she could still outrun him, maybe even by a larger margin than she could at twenty-six, because of her jogging and taking care of the kids every day. When she and Steve were coaching the baseball team she always took the secondary role. Steve would instruct and give pep talks and she would demonstrate. She pitched batting practice, popped fly balls into the outfield for the fielders to drop, and hit grounders for the infielders to bobble.

Her life had not been a disappointment. It was just that her hands still longed for the feel of the horsehide in the precise diameter of the regulation ball. She loved the smell of the glove leather, the grass, and the exact shade of reddish dust in the infield. None of those things had anything to do with Steve.

She was in her mid-thirties now and would have been at the end of her career, probably already a step slower toward first base. And women's baseball had not grown into the sensation everyone used to assure each other it would be by now.

She moved close to the place where the cooler sat on the other table and reached to open it. Her glance passed over a shiny cylinder shape on the ground beyond the table, and she thought the boys must have knocked one of the stainless steel thermos bottles off the table or dropped it while unloading. As she walked around the table to pick it up, it looked less like one of hers. Then she saw wires and looked more closely.

"Okay, guys," she called out. "I'd like you to step back to the car. Walk exactly the way you came, in a straight line, and then go to the side door and get in."

She called out, "Steve, can you help me, please? We need to move the picnic to another spot."

She could tell he heard something in her voice that nobody else's ears would pick up and that something was off. And here he came.

The bomb truck arrived with a police cruiser in front and another about two hundred yards behind. Sergeant Ed Carmody got out of the passenger side of the truck and looked in each direction. He spotted a family of—no, too big to be just a family. There were three mothers and two fathers. All boys. Baseball.

He moved toward them smartly. He saw one mother in particular whose blond hair was in a ponytail that protruded through the back of her baseball cap. She had great legs and when she threw a ball to one of the boys at the far end of the lot she threw like a guy, with a little snap to the release at the end and a loud smack when it hit leather.

She saw him long before he got near, and trotted up to him. "Did you see it yet?" she said. "Is it a bomb?"

He read in her eyes a concern for the boys who were her responsibility. She looked along her shoulder at them like a pitcher holding runners on base.

He said, "I haven't seen it yet. My men are taking a preliminary look before I go in and deal with it." He hadn't realized he was gong to deal with it until just then, but now he was.

"Do you go in with those big bomb suits?"

"That will depend on what we see. Sometimes there's something to worry about, and sometimes there isn't." He looked into her eyes.

"How far should we pull back?"

He smiled. "Far enough so that if this weren't LA, you'd be a couple of towns away, ma'am. I'd suggest you take the boys home now."

"Really?"

"If you don't, then later one of the mothers will take you to task for it, and I'll bet you know just which one already."

She smiled and cupped her right hand beside her mouth. "Steve!" she shouted. "Let's round them up now. We've got to get out."

Her husband made a couple of arm-swing herding gestures and the boys scrambled in the open door of the Suburban and the sliding door of the van. They began the business of buckling seat belts and settling in.

The woman said, "Good luck with that thing."

"Thanks," Carmody said. "Good luck with the team. What's their record?"

"Four and six, but we're building."

He watched her trot off to join her husband. He waited while the three vehicles took a slow turn like elephants forming trunk-to-tail into a caravan and then lurched up the gravel incline to the road and headed for Los Feliz. This time when they reached the city street, the second police car moved across the opening in the gate and stayed there.

Carmody was over forty, and he had been in uniforms most of his life. He had been a marine until he was wounded in Fallujah in the Iraq War. Then he went to EOD school and served two more tours, which was what he'd calculated he owed the country in exchange for the training. After that he became a Los Angeles police officer.

He'd had a theory once that he would be happy if he married a good woman. But when he became a civilian, he tried it three times and it never worked out. He kept throwing his marriages away, and then being surprised that he'd been so easily distracted.

He would run into a woman who was very pretty, usually married, but had that small spark of interest anyway. He would try to charm her, succeed, get caught by his wife, and end up signing papers. He'd been much happier, but for shorter periods of time, since then.

These days most of the women were like that baseball mom, except that they had been interested in Ed Carmody, which she wasn't. But who knew? Maybe the sight and sound of him would grow on her too. It had happened before. The ones who didn't seem interested would show up in a day, a month, or even a year, having experienced a change of some kind, and be in a playful mood.

There was still the bomb—if it *was* a bomb. Carmody made his way to the end of the parking lot near the picnic tables where the vans must have originally parked, and watched his two teammates study the device from about ten yards away. Marshall was carrying the video camera and documenting the scene, using the zoom lens to get a better look.

Carmody got into the truck and watched the video screen to see what had caused all the concern. When he saw it, the image was more than familiar. The object looked just like an M904 nose fuze for a five-hundred-pound aerial bomb. He knew all about that model. When he was in the military it had been the standard fuze for the standard bomb dropped by fixed-wing aircraft. The M904 held a powerful explosive charge for initiating the trinitrotoluene, but it was safe and reliable.

He said, "Okay, you guys. Do you recognize the fuze?"

Marshall said, "It looks like an M904 nose fuze."

"What's it attached to?"

"It looks like it's inserted into a canister about the size of a big thermos."

"As long as it's not screwed into an Mk 82 five hundred pounder, we ought to be able to take it out."

Rogers said, "Maybe we ought to just blow it up, like Captain Stahl said in his e-mail. This isn't a bad place to do it. Nothing but trees and a parking lot."

"There's no need to scare the crap out of everybody in Los Feliz. I'll suit up and disconnect it. Come on back."

He was already breaking out his suit, and Rogers and Marshall returned and helped him get it on. They helped lift the helmet up and over his head, and Carmody heard the small ventilator fan begin to whirr to clear his vision screen and cool his head and face. He walked to the place where the others had been looking.

Now that he was in the suit he had to communicate by radio. He knelt down and said to the transmitter, "It looks just like an M904. I'm going to take it out and then render the device safe. Please double-check to be sure the area is clear of bystanders."

"Check," said Rogers.

"Is the road clear? No cars allowed in or out?"

"Clear," said Marshall.

"Code Five Edward called?"

"Code Five Edward in effect."

Ed Carmody turned his body to bring the clear plate in front of his eyes around to sweep the parking lot and the foliage surrounding it. The three bomb technicians were alone in this beautiful, quiet place. "I'm going to remove the fuze."

He knelt and touched the fuze. It wasn't screwed in, just inserted and taped to stay there. He looked at it closely. It wasn't quite the way he remembered the M904. Was its housing a lighter metal? He cut the tape that held it to the canister, and then lifted the fuze away. There was a sudden resistance. It was only then that he saw the thin lines of wire under the fuze, like a spiderweb gleaming in the sunlight that leaked through the canopy of the tree above him. He realized that the fuze was a decoy. The canister was too.

He set it back down, but lifting the wires had set something off. He saw a small disk fly up from the dusty ground a few feet away, spinning like a flipped coin and revealing a round hole in the ground. A cylinder shape shot out of the tube in the hole. It rose six feet into the air and then hung, poised there for a second before it would fall.

Carmody half turned and shouted, "Get down!"

Then, at the top of its arc, the bounding charge detonated. There were nine bounding charges in the air, each wrapped in tape that held ball bearings in place until its charge made them fly outward in all directions.

The nine bounding charges had been made by hand, and they were intentionally not uniform in weight, size, or power. Some rose only three feet, others seven, and the charges detonated over a period of nearly two seconds as Carmody saw light for the last time.

40

Diane Hines had finally reached the stage in her recovery when she was able to do exercises. The designers of Stahl's condominium building had equipped the subbasement with a workout room full of weights and exercise machines and a twenty-five-yard indoor swimming pool. She could see that Stahl had been right about the designers. They had misjudged their buyers. During Diane's first fifteen visits she never saw anyone in the pool or the workout room but Stahl.

The rest of the owners were not people who spent much time in the building. Many of them occupied their condominiums only about ten days a year, when they were in Los Angeles on business, and lived in other countries the rest of the time.

The building was perfect for Diane. There was a short hallway off the entrance to the condominiums with an elevator that worked with a key. She took it to the subbasement level of pool, showers, locker rooms, and exercise room. When the elevator arrived and the doors opened, the lights and air-conditioning came on automatically, and she would go in and do her workout. In the third week of workouts, she had begun making noticeable progress toward the way she had always been.

Stahl had spent most working hours at his security company lately, but when he came home he would go down to the subbasement with Diane to lift weights, hit the heavy bag, and swim before dinner.

Today she had done more work than usual in the morning, partly to beat the loneliness she felt when Stahl was away.

After Diane moved in, she had gone online and bought a stack of manuals to help her prepare for the police detective exam. She didn't exactly hide the manuals, but she didn't show them to Stahl, either. She kept them on the dresser in the spare bedroom. She knew she was delaying a conversation because she wasn't sure what she wanted to say to him about it. She wasn't sure she really wanted to transfer. She just didn't want to be declared unfit to be a bomb technician and have her career end for lack of alternatives.

Now Diane carried her books into the kitchen. She set the books on the table, but didn't open one immediately. She realized that what she was fighting was her transformation from a trained and trusted professional to a kept girlfriend. What she had to do was to keep from fighting *him* about it. She checked the time on the big white face of the wall clock. One thirty. Then she gave in to the temptation to turn on the television.

There were helicopters at different altitudes circling above a tree-choked park. There was a parking lot like a gash in the green, with the herringbone pattern of diagonal stripes to define parking spaces. And across the lot was a black bomb truck with a containment vessel on a tow rig behind it, and all the windows blown in.

The bomb maker was back in his garage workshop, taking dried cakes of highly explosive PETN and gently rolling them into powder on a wooden board, like a baker working in slow motion. Every minute or two, he reached up and touched a device that looked like a trapeze suspended from two wires that led to a bracket in the ceiling, then out through the back wall of the garage. The wire ran to an iron spike he had driven a couple of feet into the ground outside. Each time he touched the device, any buildup of static electricity bled off him to ground.

Things seemed to him to be improving steadily now. Apparently the hype about the legendary Dick Stahl had some truth to it. For weeks it seemed that nothing the bomb maker could do was good enough. Stahl destroyed every device. But he was disgraced and under suspicion now, kept away from the Bomb Squad, and the odds, the numerical rules of the universe, had reasserted themselves. People could be deceived, even induced to deceive themselves, more often than not. He had just done it twice—in the subway and at the park.

The ring of the cell phone he kept plugged in deflated his good feeling. What the hell did they want now?

He stepped to the long workbench by the wall and picked it up. "Hello?"

"We're at the end of your driveway."

He hung up, went to the front closet, turned off the mine circuits, then closed the door, went to the entrance, and unlocked the door.

He watched the three big cars make the turn into the driveway, switch off their headlights, and navigate the long gravel drive using the lights of his house. It was usually two cars, not three. He didn't know what the reason for the extra car might be, but he felt a mixture of dread and annoyance.

Didn't they think three big SUVs driving along the desert highway and up to his house might cause people to wonder? Even on desert roads, people drove past once in a while. When they saw anything unusual, they were less likely to miss it or overlook it than they would be in a city.

He opened the door and waited for the men to get out and come to the house. He listened harder than ever for non-English words, for whispers or signs. In the light from the doorway he studied them. He looked for jewelry, for print or script stenciled on anything. He looked for tattoos, sniffed for alcohol or food. He detected nothing that identified them as coming from a particular part of the world—or eliminated any part of the world.

As they came in he stood in front of them and said, "I need to remind you to use extra caution when you are in my house. The whole house is full of detonators, large charges, and chemicals that explode or burn. Watch where you step, where you sit, what you touch."

The man with the shaved head came inside just then. He called out: "Did everyone hear what he said? Were you listening? Don't touch things. If you don't know what it is, leave it alone."

The fifteen men crowded into the living room and overflowed into the dining room and even into the hall. All gave a nod or a thumbs-up, but none of them spoke. They clearly had been trained to function as an infantry platoon, traveling in silence except when the platoon leader asked a question that required an answer.

The bomb maker noticed that the first four men in the door had come in and checked for unseen people behind furniture and doors. Then they'd taken positions by the windows, looking outside from beside the curtains now and then.

His observations told him very little. The men were terrorists, or guerrillas, or jihadists, or special operations troops, or insurgents, or something. They clearly wanted to bring death and destruction to Los Angeles, but he had no idea why. It was usually some sort of revenge or anger, wasn't it? They were undoubtedly wise not to tell anyone like the bomb maker the exact nature of their motives or their mission. If a person they needed didn't agree with them, then it was possible he might opt out, or even betray them.

When they came crowding in tonight he hated it as much as he always did, and maybe more this time because having fifteen of these men in his house was dangerous. Five were a crowd for his small, clean, quiet house. Fifteen were worse than three times as much trouble. There were not enough places for them to sit. There was no reason for them to be here. This was an awful imposition.

He hated them, but he wasn't going to betray them. They couldn't be expected to know that, but it was true. Before he left for California he had cut himself loose from all loyalties, and he'd never formed any in Los Angeles. He had come from the Midwest and was still as much a stranger in LA as these men were. He'd had no political or abstract opinions since he was in middle school. He had learned during his adulthood that the only goal that made much sense was having money, and even that had limits. He didn't want an enormous fortune. He simply wanted enough.

He studied the men who came close to him, paying special attention to the ones he had never seen before. It brought him no closer to discovering their nationality.

He had no interest in knowing their ideas. All he wanted was enough money so he would never have to do anything again to get more. He didn't want these men to distrust him on the basis of his principles or beliefs, because he didn't have any. He was the most trustworthy conspirator of all, a man who didn't think about utopia or heaven but thought just about having money.

The bald man edged close to him in the crowded space and leaned near his ear. "You've done it twice this week. First you killed the ones in the tunnel, and then the one in the woods. That's four more kills for you."

"I know," the bomb maker said. "Did you bring me information I don't know?"

"Yes, we did," the man said. "We've tested all of the guns you bought for us, and sighted in the rifles for three hundred meters. They're all excellent weapons."

"That's good," said the bomb maker. For the first time since his shopping trip, he thought about the danger he had been in. If the weapons had been defective or damaged, he might be dead. Then it occurred to him they might be about to ask him to buy more guns. He clenched his teeth and waited.

"We've been training for over a year, and spending time getting familiar with the region. We've rented houses where we stored supplies, clothes, food, and cars. If things go wrong we can stop, rest, and start over again. When we came back from the desert, we learned you had killed more bomb technicians."

"I did," he said. "I'm trying to cut them down to the level where the best ones, and the ones who know the city, are gone."

"You've done very well. Who is the best one left?"

"It doesn't matter," he said. "I not only killed most of them, but I got the best bomb expert they had fired."

"Is that Richard Stahl?"

"Yes," he said. "But he's gone."

"Gone? Has he moved to another city?"

"It doesn't matter where he is. They made him resign, and they won't let him go near a bomb ever again. You came all the way here again. This time you interrupted some very delicate and dangerous work. You must have something else you wanted to talk to me about."

"We came to tell you we think it's time."

"For what?"

"I told you we tested the guns. We have what we'll need—ammunition, supplies, cars, safe houses. We're ready now."

The bomb maker's heart began to speed up. "I didn't get you enough for a battle."

The bald man made a gesture as if to brush away a cobweb. "We didn't want to make you do everything. We sent out men to buy much, much more ammunition. Now we'll each have as many loaded magazines as we can carry, and still more in cars nearby. We're ready."

The bomb maker was nervous. "We've never talked about when you'd be ready, or what you want to do. I assume you have a detailed plan."

The bald man nodded. "We would never tell anyone in advance what we're going to do. You've done very well so far. Now we need you to plant a great many bombs in many places, and very large ones in a few particular places. This is the remaining thing we have to ask. It will have to be done within a short period, so you'll be busy."

The bomb maker said, "Well, those are things I will be able to do. What you want is smaller than what I've already done. But—"

"But? But what?"

"Before the big day comes, you'll need to deliver to me the ten million dollars your group promised me."

"We'll get it for you as soon as you've planted the bombs and set the detonators."

"That wasn't the agreement I made with you in Niagara Falls. I must have the ten million dollars before the final day begins. Once I have it, I'll make this city into a little corner of hell for you. Until I have it, I'll keep making my preparations, as before."

"What's going to stop us from killing you tonight and taking your bombs?"

"My bombs are all designed to fool the best set of civilian bomb technicians in the world. You already know that. If you think you can do anything with them, go ahead. If you make a mistake, the detonator initiates the explosive, but you have lots of men."

The bald man's eyes were on his, and they never blinked or turned away. The bomb maker kept his gaze steady, robbing the bald man's stare of power by counting seconds to distract himself.

The bald man said, "All right. We'll give you your money first."

The bomb maker said, "Then I'll do the rest of the job. I'll need time to assemble the devices I've been working on, and mix the rest of the explosives. We should agree on a day when everything will happen."

"When will your preparations be ready?"

"Three weeks. You can use the time to go over all of your plans, fix anything you're worried about, and obtain the money."

"We can get the money by then," the bald man said. "You realize that once we give you the money, I'll have to assign men to watch you twenty-four hours a day until bombs begin to explode?"

"I suppose I can accept that."

"You will."

41

Diane Hines and Dick Stahl stood at the memorial service for Sergeant Edward Carmody at Forest Lawn cemetery. Hines wore her police uniform, Stahl a black suit that looked a bit like one. A solitary police bagpiper was up the hill from the grave playing "Going Home—the Fallen Soldier." There had been one at the service for the fourteen men who died together in the first explosion too, and a week ago, for Neil and Wyman.

He seemed to Diane to be the same piper. He wore a Black Watch tartan, and he was good at the instrument, a big blond man with strong wind and quick fingers. She watched the seven men and one woman shoulder the casket to the grave. They handled their burden with little strain, and it reminded her there was probably a lot less of Carmody inside than there should be.

Shrapnel from the bounding mines had torn Carmody apart, Elliot had told her. There had been a decoy fuze attached to a dummy cylindrical charge and nine bounding charges loaded into launchers made of tin cans. There would probably be the forty pounds of bone—fifty, maybe, for a man Carmody's size—and whatever muscle was still on the bones or they could collect from the surrounding area, which wouldn't be much after the storm of steel balls cut through him. There would be nothing of the five quarts of blood, of course. That would have sprayed the grass and soaked into the floor of the wooded glen.

Rogers and Marshall said Carmody had known what was happening to him. The design had given him a second or two to see and hear the charges pop into the air a few feet before they detonated. She knew what that foreknowledge felt like. Not good. The second she'd used to roll under the big wooden sideboard, Carmody had used to warn his friends.

She studied the crowd. There were a couple of attractive women about forty years old in full formal mourning black. They were probably ex-wives. That was another side of Carmody. When she was promoted to the Bomb Squad and had returned from training, Carmody had paid a lot of attention to her for a few days. He had asked her to an Italian restaurant that was an old landmark. When she made inquiries about him she learned he was married.

She looked at the two women and wondered if the wife at that time was one of them, or someone else who wasn't here. At least Diane didn't have to feel guilty today. She had turned him down. She tried to figure out which one was the earlier wife, the one Carmody had cheated on with the other. They both seemed to be about the same age, so she gave up. They looked as though they had made their peace some time ago, because otherwise there was no reason to sit together. There had been at least one more wife who didn't seem to be present.

The leader of the firing party shouted his order and the eight men stiffened, snapped their rifles to their shoulders, raised them at once, and fired. The air was still, and she watched a cloud of smoke drift away over their heads. Then there was the second volley, then the third.

She caught Dick Stahl looking at her from the corner of his eye. She knew he was thinking about how close she had come to being the one in a box. She pretended she hadn't seen, and focused instead on the dead man. She mentally said good-bye to Carmody. It was like waving to a friendly acquaintance as he walked away for the last time. She had given enough thought to his failings. They were erased now.

The chief, the priest of Carmody's church, and one of his teammates said the words that people filling their roles always had to say—competing value systems expressed by people who didn't seem to notice the contradictions between them.

The firing party, the color guard, and the pallbearers marched through the cordon of uniformed police officers, and then the members of the LAPD, sheriff's department, and highway patrol, and all the nearby police forces moved off too. The woman left sitting near the grave with a couple of others had the folded flag from the coffin on her lap. She seemed to be Carmody's mother. A woman who was probably a sister had her arm around her.

Hines took a step and felt Dick's big hand close on her arm so he could keep her from falling. "I'm fine," she whispered. "Don't touch in public." She wasn't tottering on high heels. She was wearing a police uniform and sturdy, spit-shined shoes with wide soles.

He realized she was right, so he moved his hand quickly enough to disguise the touch as an accidental brush in a crowd. They didn't seem to have drawn attention. They began to walk toward the remaining group of Bomb Squad members at the edge of the row where they had been seated.

When the two reached the group, the squad members surrounded Stahl to shake his hand and enveloped Hines in gentle hugs.

They all said they were sorry about Carmody and would miss him. Then Stahl, Hines, and the others began to walk toward their cars.

As they passed near the low dais where the high-ranking police officials and civilian dignitaries had sat, Deputy Chief Ogden separated himself from the others and caught Stahl and Hines.

"Hello," he said to them. He patted Hines's shoulder, a gesture that seemed to her to be prompted by the inherent maleness of the police uniform they both wore. "Sergeant Hines, you're looking well. Are you feeling better?"

"Yes, sir," she said. "Thank you for asking."

He shook Stahl's hand. "Dick," he said, "I've been watching for you." He glanced at Diane again. "Sergeant, would you mind if I borrowed him for just a few moments?"

"Of course not, sir. I see a couple of bomb techs over there that I missed." She stepped off toward Elliot, who had just turned away from the grave.

Stahl walked with Ogden. "What's up, Dave?"

"There's no reason for you to come with me. It's just me asking a friend for another favor."

"What's the favor?" Stahl asked.

"That black limo over there idling in the drive is the mayor's."

"It looks a lot like the hearse."

"Your lips to God's ear. Will you talk to him?"

Stahl slowed down for a moment, then stopped. "I don't see much point in that."

"I said it was a favor." Ogden said. "If it was something you'd do anyway, it wouldn't be a favor."

Stahl nodded. "All right."

Ogden conducted Stahl to the side of the road and up to the rear door of the limousine. He opened the door so Stahl had to duck inside, and then followed him in. Two rows of seats faced each other in the black interior. On one side sat the police chief and the mayor. On the other were Ogden and Stahl.

Stahl said, "Hello, Chief. Mr. Mayor."

"Good to see you, Dick." The chief smiled and spoke to Stahl, but the mayor was silent. The chief went on. "I hope you're well."

"I'm fine," he said. "I just wish Carmody and the others were."

The mayor seemed to feel insulted, and he sighed impatiently. "I have to tell you, Mr. Stahl, that the chief talked me into waiting around to hear what you have to say. I wasn't eager."

"I wasn't either," said Stahl. "And I'm not sure what you've waited to hear me say."

"I'm here because I've been told repeatedly by these gentlemen that you have incontrovertible alibis and other evidence to prove you couldn't have had any fault in anything that's happened. After some discussion I agreed to accept that."

"Sir—" Ogden said.

The mayor said, "Let me talk. I've been told repeatedly that there are only two men who understand those bombs—you, and the bomber. And now that you've got free time, the pace seems to have accelerated."

"Interesting observation," said Stahl. "I have a business that keeps me busy most of the time, and I've had to ignore it for a while. Now I'm catching up with the work."

The chief said, "Mr. Mayor, we asked you to meet Mr. Stahl because we're desperate. We just buried an experienced and very competent bomb team supervisor, and there are two bomb technicians who will be hospitalized for a long time, and may never be able to serve again. It's our considered judgment that Mr. Stahl is our best chance to defeat this bomber, and to ensure we don't lose anyone else before then. The city is in terrible danger as long as the bomber is at work."

The mayor smirked. "What do you think, Mr. Stahl? Are you the only one who can save us?"

"No," said Stahl. "Nobody is the only one."

"But you think you're one of the few who can."

"It's a question of doing your best to outlive a bomber. You try to avoid the traps he sets, and to destroy the substances that power them without making a mistake and getting killed. The longer you do that, the more likely he'll make the first mistake with the explosives, or he'll be seen, identified, and arrested."

"Are you saying these men would be alive if you had still been there to supervise them?"

"I would have ordered them to take fewer chances."

The mayor looked triumphant. "You do think so, don't you?"

Stahl stared into the mayor's eyes. "I do."

The chief said, "Sir, maybe this isn't the—"

"And you think it's my fault."

Stahl said, "I managed to get myself in trouble by breaking a police regulation. I did that by myself. I'm willing to help with the bombings, and I'll do it free."

The chief said, "Mr. Mayor, we have an assurance from the police commission that they'll approve an agreement to have Mr. Stahl work with us as a civilian consultant."

"You know I'm aware of that idea," said the mayor. "I can't appear to be providing a way for city employees to get around rules, and especially laws. The appearance of wrongdoing is as bad as wrongdoing."

"With respect, I don't think it is," said the chief. "Having him with us is almost sure to save the lives of police officers and civilians."

The mayor said, "I didn't mean as bad for you. I meant as bad for good government and the future of the city. I'm an elected official, and any future opponent would bring this up for the next thirty years. I've listened. Now I've got to get back to city hall and do my job."

Stahl got out, and so did the chief and deputy chief. The black limousine drove off toward the road that led down the hill to Forest Lawn Drive and the 101 Freeway.

The chief said, "Damn."

"Sorry, Dick," said Ogden. "Thanks for giving it a try with us."

The chief shook Stahl's hand. "Something may work out yet. I'd really appreciate it if you wouldn't leave town on some long business assignment without telling us."

"I won't," he said. He turned and walked back along the row of graves to the spot where Hines was talking to Elliot and a few others. When he got there, he could see the others were watching him for some hint of what had gone on in the mayor's limousine. He said to Hines, "Ready?"

"Sure."

Before they left, he said, "Take care of each other, guys. Use Andros and explode any devices from a distance. Stay alive."

As they walked to the place where Stahl had parked his car, the sun was almost below the hills to the west, and the sky was reaching its most fiery red-orange. Hines looked back toward the section they had just left, and she could see the cemetery crew pushing the dirt into the grave.

42

On the drive away from the cemetery they didn't speak much. Stahl drove west, but instead of turning south toward the west side where they lived, he took Barham to Ventura Boulevard into Studio City. He turned into the plaza just before Laurel Canyon and parked. The sky was dark now, the deep indigo that lingered in the west during early evening in the Valley. She looked up at him. "Du-Par's?"

He shrugged. "Funerals make me feel hungry. I think it's probably the body trying to fight back, to be alive."

They walked in the front door. Anyone who stepped through the glass doors could see the place had a long history. Its fiftieth anniversary cups were now almost antiques. There were old photographs framed and hanging on the wall that proved the layout had reached approximately its current configuration sometime in the 1950s, and the more recent remodeling had only added a half room that looked like the other one. The simplicity of the diner hid the fact that deals to launch big-budget movies had been make over breakfast at the big table in the back, and it was still an easy place to spot stars. Du-Par's was always open.

Hines stepped in ahead of Stahl and picked a booth. "I've been here on three Thanksgivings. All the older cops got the dinner hours off on big holidays. My partner and I had turkey here."

Stahl said, "I used to come here when I was assigned to North Hollywood too. I don't think I was ever here on Thanksgiving. It didn't matter when I was here, though. I always ordered pancakes."

"Yeah," she said. "Those are good. Are you going to order some now?"

"I don't know."

"Think about it," she said.

"Why?"

"I'm pretty sure you'll give me a taste."

A waitress in a white uniform appeared. She and the other waitress looked exactly as their predecessors had years ago, except a few of them used to wear lace handkerchiefs folded into corsages pinned to their chests. Hines wondered when that custom had disappeared. When Stahl asked for a stack of pancakes and a pair of fried eggs, Hines ordered only the eggs and some coffee. The waitress walked off, and Hines said, "The pancakes were a good decision."

Just as the food arrived, Hines's cell phone buzzed. She pulled it out of her purse and said, "Mom? I'm sorry, but I'm in a restaurant. I can't talk." She listened. "You're right, Mom." She looked at Stahl across the booth. "It's very fancy. Decadent. He treats me like a queen. I know it's late there, so you can go to bed. I won't be out of the restaurant for a while, but I'll call you tomorrow." She slid the phone back into her purse.

"You're lying to make me look good to her?" Stahl asked.

"She thinks I need to be cared for and babied twenty-four hours a day. If she thinks you're not doing it, she'll be on the next plane from Miami."

"She can come anytime, you know."

"I know," Hines said. "And I appreciate it. I just don't want her to yet."

"Why not?"

Hines cocked her head. "Things haven't worked their way out to what they're going to be yet. Too much is still in the air. Having her here would make it her business too, and she's a person with opinions."

"What hasn't worked out?"

"Life hasn't found its way to normal yet."

"What do you mean?"

"I don't know if I've got a career or a disability payment. I'm trying to figure out if I can go back to the squad, or if the department will want me back at all. I haven't been charged with violating Police Regulation 271, but they could do it. And you and I are still a work in progress."

"We are?"

"I'm willing to take the career questions from her. Either way, she'll be fine with it. She's always hated it that I'm a cop. But I'm not ready to have the conversation about you yet."

"Thinking of dumping me?"

"I think about the opposite," she said. "It's been about two months since I moved in with you. The ambience is not that different from being in one of those long-term care places. I spend a lot of time lately wondering when you're going to rip my clothes off and carry me to bed again."

"I didn't know you were ready for that kind of thing. In working order and feeling frisky."

"I'm maybe not feeling like a peak performance yet, but maybe you could just gently peel the clothes down or lift them up off me or whatever is called for. That can be pretty erotic too. Or just show some prurient interest. I think it might help morale around the condo quite a bit."

"It's already lifted mine in a matter of seconds."

"I'll bet," she said. "It'll be even better if I'm not wearing a police uniform to start. You know, I love my mother, but before we figure out what normal is going to be, maybe we shouldn't invite her into the middle of it. You agree?"

"Completely," he said.

She finished her last bit of egg and eyed his plate. "Are you ready to share your pancakes?"

"Yes." He pushed his plate in front of her. "Have at it."

"You're not afraid I'll get fat?"

"It's not really my job," he said. "I don't want to be that guy. Besides, you work out like you were an NFL linebacker."

She poured a bit of melted butter on the pancake, lifted her fork, dipped a morsel of pancake into the pool of maple syrup, and closed her eyes as she ate it. "I've missed these too." She put the fork down. "Let's go home."

He picked up the check, slid out of the booth, and held out his hand. "Did you mean that about the clothes?"

"Take me home and find out."

They drove home over Laurel Canyon. Just as they reached Mulholland Drive at the crest of the hill, the radio said, "We have a late-breaking report on the bomb crisis. Sources close to the mayor's office have indicated that in the wake of the latest booby-trap attacks, the mayor will ask Richard Stahl, the bomb expert who was forced to resign two weeks ago, to return and take over the Bomb Squad, possibly as early as tomorrow."

Stahl tapped the power button to turn it off.

"That's quite a story," Hines said. "I wonder where it came from."

"Somebody probably saw me get into the mayor's limo at the funeral and drew the wrong conclusion."

When Stahl reached their street he kept going and circled the area looking for suspicious cars or trucks parked near enough to the condominium building to indicate it was under surveillance. Stahl checked nearby buildings to see if there was any sign of lenses or directional microphones in upper windows.

She knew immediately what he was looking for. "How long have you been doing this?" she said.

"Since I moved in. Since the bomber singled you out as the one he wanted to kill first, I realized what a good habit it is, so I do it more often."

"I think he tried for me because I'm a woman."

"Really?"

"Yes. I humiliated him when I blocked his rifle shots at Elliot and Crowell with the truck. The only other person he targeted personally was Gloria Hedlund, also a woman. With everybody else it was just a matter of who answered a particular emergency call, something he couldn't predict."

"He doesn't seem to like women much."

"No, he doesn't," Hines said.

"And I'll bet women don't think much of him, either," said Stahl.

"No, but I'm probably not the most objective one to ask."

Stahl said, "I think he's living alone in someplace that's remote enough to test explosives and initiators. That would keep his social calendar kind of empty. Besides, it would be really hard to explain to another person what he's doing with all the chemicals. What you have to remember is that he's doing it voluntarily."

"True," she said. She watched the upscale houses glide by, all of them under big old trees at the back of green, closely trimmed lawns. The houses all sat at the ends of long driveways and had big garages, so there were very few cars parked on the streets in this area. The only multifamily building was Stahl's condominium, the sort of place that was half submerged in its lawn, and had a modern look that made it seem more like an art installation than a dwelling. The parking was underground and invisible. "Looks clear tonight."

"Agreed," Stahl said. "I hope I didn't make you feel nervous."

"I'm not," she said. "This is just another reason to stick to you like a suntan. Whenever I'm with you I feel safe. Let's enter the confines of your paranoid palace."

They stopped at the gate and drove inside while it closed behind them. They waited while the barred entry to the garage lifted to admit them. Just as Stahl pulled into the space beside Hines's, his phone rang.

"Stahl," he said.

"Hi, Dick. This is Bart Almanzo. My guys just finished watching all the video of the funeral today. I'm afraid nobody spotted the suspect. There was no face that had turned up on an earlier video."

"You used the same officers who watched all of the other videos?"

"Yes. Even though by now almost everyone in Homicide has seen all of it. We'll be getting more tape from businesses along the way, but we blanketed the cemetery with cameras, so it's unlikely we missed anybody."

"Sorry to hear it," Stahl said. "The breaks aren't falling our way today."

"Yeah, I heard about the meeting with the mayor. It was on the radio, backward."

"How did you know it wasn't true?"

"There's a growing faction of people who are connoisseurs of the mayor's stupid decisions. This one is already getting famous. I heard it from a gentleman who is high up in the union. Take care of yourself."

"Just what I plan to do," said Stahl. "See you."

Stahl and Hines went inside through the kitchen entrance and Hines set her purse on the table in the living room. Stahl called over his shoulder: "Scotch?"

"And ice. I'll be back in a minute."

She went into the spare room and hung her dress uniform in the closet, then pulled a sweatshirt on over her head and put on shorts.

They sat on the couch to sip their drinks. They kissed gently and then drank some more. After a few minutes together Stahl said, "Does that outfit mean I won't be tearing your clothes off tonight after all?"

"I hope you're not disappointed. But I've had that pistol belt strapped to me all day, and heavy shoes and all. You're welcome to take this off me if you want. It doesn't take as long, so you won't get bored."

"Bored? I'm confident that I won't."

They moved into the bedroom and made love in the faint light from the skylight streaming in from the living room. This was the first time since the bombing in her apartment, and so it was like coming together after years apart. At first there was a tentative, cautious quality to their movements. They were like people learning all over again to trust their instincts about what the other would want, and to give the other permission to take chances. But soon they were comfortable again, each of them wanting, taking, and giving at the same time. When it was over, the hour was late.

He leaned over her. "Are you okay?"

"Except for the broken bones."

"Come on."

They moved together and kissed, a long, quiet moment while their lips touched, they closed their eyes, and they breathed the same breath.

Hines woke up lying on top of the sheets, still touching Stahl. His larger body was giving off heat so she hadn't noticed there were no covers. She moved her foot to try to hook the sheet and pull it up without waking Dick.

The movement seemed to bring her out of a dream, and she realized she had not just awakened spontaneously. As she saw her phone across the room light up, swung her legs off the bed, and stepped toward the phone, she saw Stahl turn toward his nightstand, where his phone was lit too.

They both read the message at once. "SECURITY," it said. "Break-in detected. Lock all doors and shelter in place."

"This is for real," he said. "Get dressed."

He stepped into the pants he had taken off at bedtime. She went to the closet and pulled on a black pullover and a pair of black jeans, and stepped into a pair of black flats. She went low, ran to the purse she had left on the table in the living room, and plucked out her Glock pistol and the spare magazine.

In a moment she saw Stahl emerge from the bedroom and step along the wall pushing the .45 pistol he kept in the nightstand into his waistband. He stopped. "Where are you?" he said softly.

"On the floor by the couch. Who sent the message?"

"The building security system. The security guys can send it by pushing a signal on their phones. But if a door or window breaks it comes automatically."

"Why didn't you tell me when you gave me the new phone?"

"I bought it when you were in the hospital and forgot."

She said, "What do you want to do now?"

"Stay put. It's most likely nothing."

"That suits me."

"I'm going into the spare bedroom for a minute."

"To the gun safe?"

"Yes."

She heard the faint sounds of Stahl moving across the room to the hall, and then imagined she could hear the gun safe swing open, a slight rub of the hinges. She did hear it close and lock. She heard some clicks and metallic slides. In a moment his dark silhouette materialized beside her.

She reached for him, but felt the cold barrel of a rifle. She recognized the distinctive shape. "An M4. Thanks. Is the magazine full?"

"Yes. I got one out for each of us."

"You're so thoughtful."

"I've lived here for four years, and I never got an alert message before."

There was a noise, a faint crunching sound above them. In the dim glow coming from the skylight, Hines and Stahl turned to glance at each other. Stahl pointed at the island with the marble top that separated the kitchen from the living room.

Hines nodded, stayed low, and skittered around the counter to take up a firing position on the other side. She charged the M4 and aimed at the skylight.

Stahl moved back toward the spare bedroom, knelt in the doorway with the muzzle of his rifle up, and began to scan the windows.

The sound of crunching gravel came again, then a similar sound from the other end of the roof, and a third trail following that one. He looked toward Hines. He couldn't see her behind the marble-topped counter, but he could see her rifle barrel aiming up at the skylight. He looked at the kitchen. There were no windows in there, only a skylight. The outer wall held a wide stainless steel Sub-Zero refrigerator, a stainless steel eight-burner Wolf stove, a vertical pair of ovens. There was nothing but brick and reinforced concrete on the outer walls.

Stahl stayed motionless and listened. The sounds of footsteps on the roof had stopped.

43

There was the sound of footsteps moving away, and Stahl felt relieved. They must have tested the steel bars over the skylight and realized they couldn't enter through it. Then there was a flare of light from above the skylight like a slow, silent explosion that lasted a few seconds and went out. The intruders had only been stepping back and turning away to protect their eyes. Stahl just had time to whisper to Hines, "Thermite!" Hines understood that the mixture of aluminum powder and iron oxide was cutting through the steel. Hines heard the sound of a steel bar clattering onto the safety glass above them. She moved her finger to the trigger.

The glass of the skylight showered the floor, and the living room was illuminated by the rapid muzzle flashes of an automatic weapon firing down into the room. The bright, continuous flashes looked like the flame of a blowtorch as the shooter moved his weapon back and forth, sweeping the room below.

Stahl and Hines held their fire and waited for a shot. Then a man dropped from the empty frame of the skylight. He landed on his feet near the couch. Stahl fired three rounds that hit the man squarely in the chest and pounded him off his feet to the carpet. There was more wild automatic fire from the skylight, probably intended to keep the defenders' heads down.

Instead, both Hines and Stahl fired their M4 rifles at the skylight as rapidly as they could pull the triggers. The automatic fire from above stopped. They both watched the skylight, hoping the man still up there would be visible for a second as he moved to get a better firing angle.

While they watched, the man they had shot popped up from beside the couch and aimed a burst of automatic fire at Stahl where he crouched in the doorway. Stahl dived back into the spare bedroom and saw a line of bullet holes appear in the bedroom wall as the man fired through it.

Stahl heard a single shot from Hines's M4 near the kitchen and the automatic fire stopped again.

Stahl dashed from the bedroom and nearly overran the man. He could see that the man was wearing body armor under his shirt, but Hines had shot him through the skull while he was firing at Stahl.

He found Hines resting her left elbow on the marble counter at the edge of the kitchen. When a rifle muzzle poked down into the room at the edge of the skylight, she fired four shots at the spot where the shooter must be.

Stahl came close to the counter and beckoned. She moved around it after him and then out the steel door into the underground garage. Stahl let her through, then closed the door quietly so the intruders wouldn't be sure he and Diane had retreated.

Stahl went past the parked cars and along the rear wall of the garage until he reached a door with a pair of surveillance cameras mounted on the ceiling about ten feet to either side. He looked up at the camera to his left, making sure his face was visible to anyone watching the monitor. Then he knocked, waited, and knocked again, but there was no response. He said, "The security guys aren't in there, or they would have opened up for us."

"Where could they be?"

"There's a hallway on this level that runs the length of the building, and a couple of short alcoves off it that go to outer doors."

"Can we get access to them anywhere?" Hines asked.

"Only if they'll open up," Stahl said.

They moved to the metal barrier that had closed the entrance to the garage. Stahl went to the barrier and tried to use a crack between sections to look out at the driveway and the bit of the front lawn near the sunken driveway ramp.

"I can't see anything," he said. He hurried to his car and used the butt of his rifle to break the driver's side window. He reached in and pressed the remote control on the dashboard and the barrier began to rise like a garage door. They both ducked outside, and then up the driveway. As it curved and rose, they saw the body of a man in a dark uniform lying near the side of the building. There was a door open behind him. They scanned the area, but didn't see anyone else, so they trotted to him. When they got there, they could see his throat had been cut.

"I know him. That's one of the security guys. It looks like they lured him out to investigate something and then overpowered him."

Hines pointed at the way his legs had been pulled into the doorway and left there to prop the door open. "Do the security hallways lead to the roof?"

"Yes," Stahl said. "There are stairs at the ends. That's probably how they got to our skylight."

"It looks like they're still in there."

They stepped past the dead man into the short hall to the main corridor and continued across it to the only door. Stahl moved to the left by the doorknob, and Hines knelt in front of the door with her rifle at her shoulder. Stahl swung open the door, but there was nobody visible, so they rushed in together, ready to fire.

There was nobody standing. There were security monitors on the wall, and Stahl moved closer to see if he could spot any of the intruders, but the only monitor that wasn't covered in static patterns or black was the one that showed this room. And then he saw the second body. As he came around a desk, he stepped close to it. The other security guard must have been waiting to hear from his partner when the intruders came in the door behind him and cut his throat too. Stahl sidestepped to keep from stepping in the blood. "Let's head for the roof."

They went out to the long corridor and hurried along it until they reached the stairs to the roof. They climbed to the trapdoor set into the ceiling, and Stahl pointed to a bolt that had been opened and was still open. Hines nodded.

Stahl lifted the trapdoor a half inch and tried to crane his neck to look in three directions. After a few seconds he reacted to something. He threw the trapdoor off the opening, popped up, and fired. Then he pulled the trap closed again while there was a barrage of automatic weapon fire. He closed the bolt and pulled Hines down the stairs with him.

They ran along the corridor all the way back to the control room. He said, "There are at least five still up there on the roof, and maybe others in some of the other apartments. We should get out of here."

"I've got a spare key hidden in the gas cap of my car."

"Why didn't you tell me before I broke a window in my car?"

"I didn't know you were going to do that."

"Let's take your car and get out of here," said Stahl.

"Right."

They left the security control room. Hines went to her car while Stahl slipped out of the garage and moved along the sloping driveway to the lawn. He prepared to open the gate manually when a pair of headlights appeared at the end of the block—then another and another.

The cars were three big black SUVs, but he couldn't see any white markings or police equipment on them. Could they be cops? Three cop cars wouldn't all come in from the same direction.

He crawled to the front of the building near the door propped open by the dead security man's body, and watched from behind the shrubbery. A moment after he reached a hiding place in the foliage men began to appear from the building. He saw three men hang from the edge of the roof and drop to the lawn. The front door of his condominium opened and two men half-carried, half-dragged out the body of the man Diane had shot in his living room.

He heard running footsteps, and five men ran out of the security hallway past the dead guard. He saw other men emerge from dark places all over the property in twos and threes and head for the street.

The two men with the body set it on the lawn only a few feet from Stahl. He knew they were going to get others to help pick it up and take it with them to one of the SUVs.

He crawled out a few feet on his belly, took his cell phone out of his pocket, and reached under the body armor of the dead man. He slid the phone under the man's belt and into the front of his underwear. Then he withdrew, creeping backward into the dark entrance to the building, and became still.

Four men ran back from the edge of the street and lifted their fallen comrade. When they reached the three SUVs that had pulled up at the curb, they loaded him into the rear cargo space of the last one.

The three SUVs began to move. As soon as they were down the block, Stahl got up and ran to the driveway and into the garage, where Hines was sitting in the driver's seat of her car.

She said, "What did you see?"

He said, "They're leaving in three black SUVs. If we don't find out where they go, we'll never find them."

"Get in," she said. "We'll go after them."

"Hold on," he said. "Give me your phone."

She took her phone out of her pocket and handed it to him. "What happened to yours?"

He said, "When I bought our new phones, I programmed them to locate each other."

"I know."

He pulled her door open. "Get out. I need your car."

She got out.

"I put my phone on that dead guy's body, and I'm going to use yours to track it. Tell the cops to get Almanzo and have him track me on your phone." He got into her car, started it, and drove out to the driveway. While he waited for the gate to open he turned on Diane's phone and engaged the GPS locating application.

A map of the nearby area appeared on the screen followed by a red dot with a circle around it. The dot was heading for San Vicente Boulevard. He began to drive up the street toward San Vicente, but not fast enough to intercept the three vehicles, or to pull within sight of them.

Stahl looked at the dashboard of Diane's car. Diane had filled the gas tank recently. He was not surprised. She was a woman who had lived alone for years and learned early in life to keep a car's tank full, change the oil, and keep the tires properly inflated. It wasn't a stupid car. It wasn't sporty and eye-catching. It wasn't cute and underpowered. It was a simple black Toyota Camry with a decent-size engine.

He put Diane's phone in the holder she'd installed on the dashboard for it, so she could talk or use the GPS for directions with her hands free. When he had to stop for the next red light, he reached for the M4 he'd left leaning against the passenger seat. He removed the magazine and looked at the slot along the front to count the copper-jacketed noses of the rounds inside. He'd fired twelve rounds, which left him eighteen.

His Glock 30 pistol held only ten .45 rounds and one in the chamber. He had another ten in his spare magazine.

Stahl had no intention of engaging in a gun battle with these men. He might as well shoot himself here and save the drive. But it felt better to have something to fire if he made a mistake. He might be able to delay his death for a while.

The tracking signal on Diane's phone was strong. He followed a course parallel to the one the dozen men were on. Before long he could see that they were heading northeast consistently, not speeding or taking reckless chances. The symbol of Stahl's phone stopped at some intersections and went steadily through others, which meant they were obeying traffic signals. They were being careful not to appear to be fleeing.

They crossed Wilshire Boulevard, Sunset Boulevard, and Hollywood Boulevard. They climbed into the hills at Crescent Heights, and stayed on the road as it became Laurel Canyon. He checked the screen of Diane's phone often as he drove, careful on the winding road to stay back where the vehicles he was following couldn't see him.

He couldn't be sure the vehicles were together anymore. He had slid his phone into the dead man's clothes. All he had was a fairly reliable indication that he was following a corpse.

44

"Nine-one-one. What is your emergency?"

"This is Sergeant Diane Hines, badge two eight nine six three. I'm at the home of police captain Richard Stahl, Seven Twenty-Three Anthony Drive. We've been attacked by several men armed with fully automatic AK-47 rifles. They killed two security guards here in order to gain entry. They've driven off in three black SUVs, and Captain Stahl is following them using a cell phone GPS program. It's essential that you transmit this call to Captain Bart Almanzo, the commander of Homicide Special."

"Are you in a safe place right now?"

"Safe enough. I'm inside the condominium."

"Then stay where you are until the officers get there."

"I don't plan to go anywhere." She was sitting in the corner of the kitchen using the house phone. Dick was using her cell phone to track his phone, so there had been no better way to call the police to reach Almanzo.

Diane wasn't sure why the police weren't here already. She'd assumed the guards had called 911 right away, but now she thought probably they hadn't. There must not have been time before they were killed. She had called during the thirty seconds or so while she waited in her car for Dick, but nobody seemed to know that either. Had her first call broken up because she was underground in the garage?

Using the house phone was the best way. The computer program that ran the emergency communication system had a reverse phone book, so it identified where a call had originated. The cops would be here soon.

She waited, holding the phone and listening to dead air. Now and then the emergency operator said, "Are you still there, Sergeant?"

She would answer, "Still here."

The operator would say, "Keep standing by. I'll be here with you."

"I'm here," Diane said. "If I have to hang up I'll warn you."

She switched the phone to speaker and set it on the kitchen table where she could hear it without pressing it to her ear. She wanted to keep both ears uncovered so if anything happened in the condominium building she would hear. She kept the M4 she had used to shoot the terrorist on the table with her hand near the trigger guard.

When had she decided to call him a terrorist? she wondered. She deduced that it was when she'd identified the AK-47.

The time seemed too long. She said, "Did I neglect to tell you that this is a life-and-death emergency? Where are they?"

"I'm showing them as all around you, pretty much," the operator said. "They're closing in."

"Tell them I'm coming out." She hung up.

She removed the magazines from the rifle and her Glock, left the guns and ammunition on the table, stood, and walked to the front door. She switched on the porch light over the front steps and opened the door wide without standing in it. She waited until a number of bright spotlights from the cars and police officers all converged on the spot, and then she stepped out with her hands high in the air.

When she got a few steps from the door and onto the lawn she knelt there to wait, her hands still high. She judged it was safe to look around, so she tried, but the bright lights made it impossible. She knew there was a SWAT team out there in the dark behind the lights.

Seconds later she heard the sound of men running in combat boots. The first shout was: "Lie down where you are with your arms spread."

She eased herself forward onto her stomach and let the first SWAT team members approach.

As they dragged her to her feet, she said in a loud, clear voice, "I'm Sergeant Diane Hines, LAPD Bomb Squad, and I need to talk to Captain Almanzo, Homicide Special. It's a Code Three."

They ushered her toward the row of police vehicles that clogged the street. She knew she had to think of a way to force things to start happening. "Get him on the phone now!"

45

The bomb maker had been sleeping soundly for several hours. He had worked longer and harder than he considered wise. For several weeks he'd been stockpiling all the Semtex he could make. Since the night the terrorists said they were ready, he had been building explosive devices.

He had not wanted to deal with these men any longer than he had to. He was sure the terrorists were getting more volatile and dangerous each day. They'd been waiting for a year, and now that they had the guns and ammunition and had practiced in the desert, they were terribly impatient. They could hardly wait to kill someone.

He would once have said they could hardly wait to die but was no longer sure they were a suicide squad. During the last visit the bald man had told him they'd assembled things intended for survival—cars and food. Dead men didn't need food. They seemed to have some notion that they could attack Los Angeles and live. It wasn't a likely outcome, since the city was protected by about ten kinds of local, state, and federal cops, and the terrorists' ignorance about that seemed to be causing cognitive dissonance among them. It seemed to him the reason they were so eager to launch their attack must be that the longer they waited the more likely they would be to lose their nerve.

For the past few days he had been working to shape and wire the immense new batch of Semtex into the right containers. He wanted the smaller ones to look like harmless objects, so they would be easy to leave in the open. Waste containers could go almost anywhere. Luggage could be left in and around airports, train stations, parking lots, bus depots. Potted plants could be placed near houses or in public buildings. Cardboard boxes inside shopping bags with the names of stores printed on them could be left in or around malls, stores, or restaurants. He had been collecting containers ever since he'd begun leaving bombs for the police. He had a good supply of yard ornaments, birdbaths, plaster trolls and statues, electrical fixtures and appliances. He had toys and games, basketballs and hollow aluminum bats. He had a few dozen orange traffic cones that could be filled and armed. He had bought two fire hydrants from a scrap yard and left their faded paint jobs intact so they wouldn't be noticed. All of these devices required extra work, and all required that he see the object as part of a scene and an action, almost like a small play, ending in the triggering of the initiator.

Some of the larger devices had taken the most effort for him. They needed to contain very large quantities of Semtex—tens of pounds and up. They had to be delivered to sites, but some were too heavy to carry. He had loaded one charge into a portable electric cement mixer that had a tow hitch and wheels. He put one batch into a generator made for construction projects. Another he built into the van he used, all set into the bay and then covered with a false floor. There were seven blockbusters in all, each containing five hundred to a thousand pounds of high explosives. He was ready to blow up bridges and buildings, not just a few curious civilians.

But he was still not finished, not ready. He had at least two more weeks of very hard work ahead, and when he dozed off in his chair last evening after watching the news on television, he had forced himself to wake up only long enough to go straight to bed.

Stahl followed the red dot on the phone's GPS map onto the 134 Freeway toward Glendale and Pasadena. He could see from the map that at least the black SUV carrying the corpse was staying on the freeway. As soon as it passed the junction with the Golden State Freeway he was sure it was still heading east. The Golden State could have taken them north toward Oregon or south toward Mexico.

Stahl kept driving, going faster now. He didn't want to gain on them enough to be visible, but he also didn't want to allow them too much distance. At some point they could simply stop, abandon those three vehicles, and take others. If they left the body inside one, he would have no way to find them again. Or they might just stop and dump the body somewhere. He had to be able to catch up with them in a minute or two. He and Diane had been lucky so far—lived through the attack and placed a phone among the assassins—but luck was never limitless.

He needed to be alert, be aware of their speed, and watch carefully for stops. They were on a freeway before 4:00 a.m., and they were in sparse traffic. There should be no need for stops unless something new was happening.

Diane's phone rang. He didn't want to do anything to interrupt the tracking of the corpse, but he knew he had to answer.

"Hello?"

"Dick? It's Bart Almanzo."

"Hi. I'm using the tracking program that's installed in Diane's phone to track the GPS on mine. We're on the 210 Freeway heading east. I just passed Indian Hill Boulevard near Claremont."

"I know. She installed the same program on my phone, so we're tracking you and the body."

"Good. If you call ahead, make sure the cops ahead of us don't block them off. We've got to see where they're going."

"I know," said Almanzo.

"How far behind me are you?"

"About forty-five minutes, maybe more."

"I'll let you know when I get where we're going."

"Do that," said Almanzo.

Stahl ended the call and put the phone back on its stand. Then there it was, the red dot with the circle around it, still moving along Interstate 210.

They passed Victorville, then got off the interstate and moved onto Route 18. They moved along the road at almost freeway speed through Lucerne Valley and then turned north onto a nameless road.

Stahl could tell the road must be good because it was straight and their speed didn't change. Out here that probably meant it was smooth and level. A road curved only if it had obstacles to get around or if it was on a steep hill.

Ten minutes later, the dot on the map stopped.

46

The bomb maker woke to the sound of wheels rolling up the gravel driveway. The SUV engines almost idled as they slowly approached the house.

He stood up immediately, put on his pants, and pulled the shirt he'd left on the chair on over his head. The nearest window was high, placed where the outer wall met the ceiling of his bedroom. He pushed his chair against the wall and stood on it to look.

It wasn't the police or the FBI. It was only the three black SUVs. He swore to himself as he walked to the closet beside the entrance to his house. He turned off the firing circuits and made sure the door was closed so they wouldn't get curious, and then opened the front door.

Tonight he wasn't feeling just the usual irritation at their presumptuous, unwelcome visit in the middle of the night. He supposed that if they had to come, the middle of the night was the best time. But these visits were costing him. He felt the anger as a pressure this time, like someone squeezing his chest and making it hard for him to breathe.

He'd made an agreement with them, and he had been living up to his side. He was doing impossible things, many of them repeatedly, just to speed things up and meet their ridiculous schedule.

In return, they were supposed to go away and leave him alone to accomplish his work.

As he stood there he had a fantasy in which he would throw open the closet, hit the switches to arm the circuits for the mines outside, and then begin closing the switches that would set off the ones beside the driveway where they would have to step when they got out of their cars.

To calm his rage, he reminded himself of the money he had almost finished earning. Usually that worked to distract him from annoyances. But he was so sick of these men that even the huge payment he'd demanded did not seem like enough compensation. They were swaggering and arrogant and brutish. Their bald-headed leader was irritating.

He began to open the front door, but it swung inward into his shoulder and side, knocking him backward onto the floor. Two men carrying a third who seemed limp and injured staggered toward him. He crawled to the side out of their path, and was immediately stumbled over and kicked by the gang of men coming in after them who didn't see him lying there. He was hurt, and the pain frightened him. One of the men turned on the light, and the glare seared his eyes.

His right shoulder was injured. How was he going to be able to do the rest of his work? If he couldn't use his arm properly he could blow himself up. And if he said he couldn't do his work, what would these men do?

Making and planting explosives could be very delicate work, and if something went wrong right now, it wouldn't be some minor problem. The whole house and workshop were filled with wrapped bricks and tubs of high explosives. He looked at the other man on the floor with him.

He could see the man was dead. There was a hole in the side of his temple. Nobody was trying to help him or stop the blood that collected under his matted hair. The bomb maker crawled closer, drawn mostly by curiosity, and saw that the other side of the man's head was much worse. That was the place where the bullet had passed out of the skull—the exit wound. Blood and tissue and bone had been blown out.

"What happened?" he said.

He pushed himself off the floor with his uninjured arm and lurched to his feet with a clumsy stagger. He went into the kitchen and grabbed a roll of paper towels, and then returned to the living room. He knelt beside the corpse and began to wipe the thickening blood off his floor, making a pile of crumpled towels beside the man's head.

He collected most of them and wrapped them in a length of towel to carry them out to the kitchen trash, but stopped and dropped them by the body when he saw the bald man come in the door with two other men in a muttered conversation. The bomb maker heard, "We'll just have to do things more quickly, and fight that much harder. The important thing is to move right away, before they realize the meaning of what happened. We can't give them time to bring in all their men and send for more."

The bald man noticed the bomb maker standing there over the body, holding his right arm. "What's the matter with you?"

"The door hit me and I fell. What happened?"

"That building was like a military bunker. We lost a man trying to get to Stahl."

"Why?"

"Somebody shot him."

"No, why get to Stahl?"

"Because we wanted to be sure the whole plan wouldn't be ruined. Once bridges and buildings began to blow up, they would have brought Stahl back. He was the one who was always able to make your bombs harmless. We didn't want to let that happen again. Not now."

"Did you get him?"

"Probably not."

"Probably not?" said the bomb maker. "What the fuck are you saying?"

In less than a second the bomb maker realized he had not been seeing the situation clearly. The bald man had already been chagrined, and while he had been standing there looking calm, his rage had been growing. His left hand shot outward and clamped shut on the bomb maker's shirt, then held him there to punch him in the face with his right fist. He hit him six times in rapid succession, holding him immobile. When the bomb maker's knees would no longer support him, the bald man let go of the shirt and gave a tremendous push that sent him into the nearest wall, where his muscles lost their strength and his body slumped to the floor. He was astounded. His life had not offered any opportunities to fight that he couldn't escape. He felt shock and pain that he had never experienced before.

The men all seemed to go into motion to fill the sudden silence. One stepped into the bomb maker's bedroom and came back with sheets and blanket stripped from the bed. He and two others began to wrap the dead man in them. Other men turned and went outside.

The bomb maker heard the engines starting, and then the sound moved around the side of his house as the cars were parked out of sight behind the buildings. He hoped none of them swung too wide and went over a mine, but he didn't feel up to getting to his feet, running out there, and shouting warnings.

He felt profoundly harmed. He looked down, saw his own blood drenching his shirt, and knew his nose was broken. Other things inside his face were damaged too, as though maybe a cheekbone had been fractured. He had never imagined what this felt like. He was filled with anger and hatred.

47

Dick Stahl drove up the road slowly, alerted by the GPS that he must be very close to the place where the three black vehicles had stopped. As soon as he saw the house at the end of a long driveway that led far back from the road, he switched off his headlights and pulled off the pavement. He took Diane's phone from its stand, and called Bart Almanzo.

"Almanzo."

"Hi, Bart. It's me. They've stopped. Do you have my location?"

"Yes. We've been tracking your phone. You're on a road that heads north from Route 18, right?"

"Right. This seems to be where they were headed. We passed a thousand places where they could have stopped if they just wanted to lose a tail or dump the body."

"Can you describe the place?"

"The house is ranch style, one story, not big. There are lights on inside. It's maybe two thousand square feet, but it has an attached garage that's about a thousand square feet. It's got space for at least four cars, and a few extra feet besides. I can't really tell the color in the light from inside, but it's white or pale yellow. The three black SUVs are parked behind the garage right now. In front of the house is a long gravel driveway—maybe two hundred feet, and there's a lot of land in the back. It could be a hundred acres, most of it desert brush. I can't tell what's behind that, but along the horizon I see a line like mountains."

"All right. We're still maybe forty minutes behind you," said Almanzo. "The best thing to do is back up and put a few miles between you and that house. We'll be there."

"I'm pretty sure this is the place we've been hoping to find all this time. It's the perfect place to make bombs. There are no neighbors for a mile or two, no sign that people go by here much. It's dark as the basement of hell, with no electric lights to be seen in any direction except the ones in that house."

"Just wait. I'll call the county sheriff's office and some of the local police. We'll cut off the road from both ends and move in."

"We'll lose these guys, and we'll lose *him*."

"Do you still think it's one bomber?"

"It's always one bomber. Somebody designs the devices, and he's usually the only one who puts his hands on them until they're assembled and ready. I'm really surprised he's got all these men with him, but this is where they came. I'll talk to you soon."

Stahl hung up and sat in the car watching the house from a distance. The night seemed to have reached its darkest hour already, but that meant he was running out of time. He would have to accomplish some things before daylight changed everything.

He had to know what was waiting in that house for Almanzo and the local police. He needed to know if a dozen men with automatic weapons and unlimited ammunition were waiting to ambush them, or if they were rushing to change cars and leave for an airport. He couldn't let them do either. Stahl wished there were some way to find out other than walking up and looking. There wasn't.

Stahl looked at the brush and the ground beside the highway. It was dark enough to risk leaving the car and walking. There were yucca plants and tumbleweed, lots of thick, dry spiky plants high enough to disguise the shape of a car, at least until dawn. He released the brake on Diane's car, shifted it into neutral, and let it coast into the brush.

Motion was what the eyes noticed most easily. He walked directly toward the house instead of along the road, and tried to stay among the Joshua trees, which looked a bit like human shapes. He tried to make the best use of the landscape and the darkness.

Soon he was at the edge of the open land around the house. The grounds had been cleared of random desert weeds and brush, so the land looked like white sand under the night sky. Someone had planted dark-colored drought-resistant shrubs in tight rows that circled the house. This was an arrangement that Stahl had never seen anywhere. From the air, the house must look like a huge target. Was that a psychopath's private joke? No, he thought. This man's jokes were cruel.

He couldn't move his attention past the arrangement of shrubs. The rows were about ten yards apart, going from almost the edge of the highway all the way to a spot about fifteen yards from the house.

Stahl walked close to the outer row and knelt just outside the giant circle. He began to brush away the coarse sand from between two shrubs to see anything hidden there. The sun had been down for at least eight hours, but the sand was still warm to his touch. He dug a little bit deeper, where the sand felt cooler and less dusty. He felt a length of insulated wire. He kept digging, unearthing more and more of the wire.

The wire was thick, about a quarter inch, jacketed with a rubbery plastic like coaxial cable. The wire ran along the same course as the shrubs, but just outside them. After a few feet he found a pair of thinner insulated wires that had been spliced to the cable.

He followed them a couple of feet, where they entered a plastic box. He dug around the box with great care, because even working by feel, he thought he knew what must be inside. The boxes were there to keep the rainwater, the burrowing animals, the shifting sand away from the electrical wiring and the explosives. He was kneeling at the edge of a minefield.

He kept digging until he could lift the plastic box out of its hole, set it down on the warm surface sand, and open it by stripping away a layer of duct tape that ran along the side seam. He disconnected the thick wire that carried the electrical power that probably fed off the house's 110-volt circuit, and then explored with his fingers what was left in the box. It was a blasting cap stuck into a few pounds of Semtex with one of its two wires connected to the power wire and the other back out. The way the charge was wired, a switch in the house could set off a mine, or maybe blow a whole row at one time.

He dug at the next place where he found thin wires spliced to the main cable, which was about ten feet away, then disconnected them and unearthed another box. He took up a third, and realized it was not going to be possible to disconnect them all before dawn. Out of caution he examined the next row of shrubs, and realized this row had very thin wire strung about two inches above the ground between very small eye screws in the trunk of each shrub, so a man walking through would trip the wire and be blown up.

If he hadn't been here looking for booby traps, he probably wouldn't have suspected that the wires were a trigger. They looked like the sort of guide a gardener might string to show him where to plant his shrubs.

He studied the second row. There would be a number of buried bombs here. He guessed there would be bounding mines, like the ones that had been used to kill Ed Carmody. A whole assault squad of cops could be killed that way without an explosion big enough to do much harm to the house. Stahl decided that if he lived, he would blow them up in place.

The lights in the house were on, but the shades and curtains were drawn. He was positive now that this was the place he guessed months ago must exist somewhere. He had favored the theory that the bomber was a loner rather than a terrorist, someone acting out of personal malevolence. The men Stahl had followed here had proved the loner theory wrong.

He stacked the three boxes of explosives, picked them up, and carried them along the trail of footprints he had made coming from Diane's car. When he got there he set them down carefully, opened the hood of the car, and began to work. He was pleased to see that the tape the bomber had used to seal the plastic boxes was still very sticky and functional. He also noted that this bomber always used more tape and wire than he needed, possibly to avoid the chance of having a circuit's wires get jostled taut and disconnect. It wasn't just the device's high explosive and blasting caps that could be reused.

48

The bomb maker was lying on the garage floor, his wrists and ankles bound with heavy-gauge wire and duct tape from his own workshop.

The terrorists had completed their inventory of his munitions, his supplies, and his devices. They were carrying the devices, one by one, from the garage into the three black vehicles and his van and his sedan.

As they worked, he tried to talk to them. "You don't have to do this. There's no reason to panic and think we have to launch the attack right away. If they had found you or traced you here, they would never have let you get this far. What you're trying to do is very dangerous for you. I can do it safely."

One of the men, who was with some trepidation carrying a device that weighed about eighty pounds, said, "Shut up."

The bald man came out of the kitchen eating a sandwich he had made from food in the bomb maker's refrigerator.

The bomb maker felt a hot wave of irritation wash over him, but reminded himself he didn't need any of that food. He had always planned to get out of Southern California the minute the first charges began to explode all over the city.

The bald man stared at him, chewing thoughtfully.

The bomb maker knew he had to be strong and prove he was still valuable, not a sad, craven victim, if he wanted to live through this. He said, "I've forgiven you for losing control of your emotions before. That was understandable. If you'll give me the money I was promised, I'll still set all the big devices and place them. They'll be set at the most strategic spots and they'll demolish their targets. They'll be incredible. I guarantee a thousand or more dead."

"Forget the money," the bald man said. "Do you see ten million dollars on me? It's not here, and I have no way to get it. The money is over. Everything goes today."

"You won't be able to do it."

The bald man smiled. "Why do you think we would hire you to kill off the Bomb Squad and not, say, the SWAT team, or the chief, or something? We're all trained in demolition. We can set a bomb ourselves."

"That's even better. Pay me whatever you can, and let me go, and I'll tell you how each device works."

"I'll take the chance of setting the big charges off by putting little ones beside them. That's simple enough even for men who aren't geniuses like you."

"But you don't have to do this yourself. I'll do it better because I've spent years studying it, and I designed all of them," said the bomb maker. "Every one of them is designed to fool the Bomb Squad. You could have men killed with our own devices."

The bald man finished his last bite of sandwich, chewed it, and swallowed. "I once saw a man kill a dog in a desert. He didn't need to shoot it or poison it. He took duct tape just like the kind wrapped around your arms. Then he taped the dog's mouth shut so he couldn't cool his body temperature. It's hot outside here too."

The bomb maker fell silent.

* * *

Stahl had finished his work, and now he returned to watching the house from a distance. There was something different going on. Two more vehicles that had been parked somewhere in the dark area far behind the house had been moved up, and now there were men walking out a back door carrying things to the five vehicles, loading them into the cargo spaces, and then going back inside for more. He moved around to the far side of Diane's car, sat down, and called Bart Almanzo.

"Captain Almanzo's line." It was Diane's voice.

Stahl stiffened. "Hey! What are you doing on this phone?"

"The captain's busy driving and my hands are free. Didn't you know I was in the car with him? I was the one who installed the program on his phone so we could follow you. Are you still okay?"

"Yes," he said. "I was better when I thought you were home surrounded by cops. Where are you?"

"We're just about to Victorville. We've got the local police briefed for this, but it's taking them time to call in their SWAT teams and get everybody moving. The teams are a way behind us."

Stahl blew out his breath without forming words.

"What's wrong?"

"The men I followed seem to be moving stuff into their vehicles. There are five now, including a van and a four-door car."

Diane said, "We'll get to you pretty soon. No more than twenty minutes."

"Not soon enough," Stahl said. "These men are all up, all heavily armed, and by now they're rested, fed, and ready. If the police show up now, it's not going to be a raid. It'll be a battle. And this guy has the land around his house mined. Judging from the wiring, I think he can set at least some of the mines off with switches in the house. Others are booby-trapped."

"Oh, great," said Diane. "You were digging up mines in the dark? Just sit tight, and we'll be there."

"Don't come roaring in here. As soon as you see the lights in the distance, turn yours off and pull over. Call the locals to let them know what's waiting for them."

He hung up. The stream of men going back and forth between the house and the vehicles had dwindled. Now there seemed to be a couple of men standing by the open doors of the vehicles, talking and fiddling with their equipment. He saw one man insert a fresh magazine into a rifle. He had to act before they left.

He checked under the hood of Diane's car. He had about thirty pounds of Semtex in a bundle attached to the wall of the car's engine compartment. He had inserted the three blasting caps in the Semtex, and then attached one lead wire of each blasting cap to a circular saw blade he'd found in Diane's toolbox and taped to the inner side of the grille and the other to a second circular saw blade he'd taped on the front of the radiator. He'd insulated the blades from the metal car parts with more duct tape, and connected the wires to the car's battery. If the front end of Diane's car accordioned to take the force of a collision, the two bare metal surfaces would clap together to complete the circuit.

Stahl judged that the men in the house had reached the stage when they were ready, but were looking around the inside of the house to be sure they'd done everything to prepare and left nothing behind. The men beside the cars had begun to pace or walk back to the house to check on their comrades' progress. The approach of daylight must be bothering them as much as it did Stahl.

For the first time in his life, Stahl hoped the police would be late. When the cops came east up the highway, now they would be blinded by the sun and completely visible to the men at the house. The SWAT team would be here, but not ready to do what SWAT teams were supposed to do—apply military-level force to a civilian-level threat. They would be crowded into trucks, too late to be shielded by darkness, and too early to let the terrorists depart without a fight, but not prepared to win it. Many would die in the first minutes.

And somewhere among the vehicles would be an unmarked police car carrying Captain Bart Almanzo and Sergeant Diane Hines.

Stahl climbed into Diane's car and practiced what he would have to do when the time came—tightening the knot in the cable that would keep the steering wheel immobile, and then jamming the jack and tire iron between the gas pedal and the front seat. He took a few breaths. He had to do this now, before it was too late.

He started the engine. He drove the car up onto the highway with the headlights still off and the engine running low to keep the noise down, and turned toward the house. He was aware of the moment when the men at the back of the house detected the approach of Diane's car. He saw one of them reach into the back of an SUV and bring out a rifle. The man opened his mouth to yell, but his voice was inaudible from this distance.

A second man put his hand on the man's arm and said something to the others. Stahl knew he must be saying, "It's only one car. It can't be the police."

As Stahl turned into the driveway and put the car in neutral, he got the impression that men were running toward the front of the house to stop him. He aimed the wheels of the car up the center of the driveway toward the garage, held it on course with one hand, and cinched the cable tight with the other. He used his right foot to jam the jack against the gas pedal and the other end against his seat, and step out. The last things he did were to pull the shifter to Drive, lock and slam the door as the car moved ahead, and then go low behind it to dash toward the dark desert where he'd come from.

He reached the brush at the right side of the property and kept running hard, staying where the bushes and plants screened him from the house. He sprinted as fast as he could to put some distance between him and the house. He heard rifles firing, as though bullets could stop the accelerating vehicle. When he reached a bowl-shaped depression in the land, he dived to the ground on his belly and clapped his hands over his ears.

Diane's car was moving fast when it reached the garage door. It hit the sectioned aluminum door, and the two metal objects seemed to merge. The car's front end crumpled as it bent the door backward, tore it out of the track, and pushed halfway into the bay as the two saw blades in the engine compartment clapped together like cymbals. The circuit was complete.

What happened next was too fast to be anything but a single event. There was simply an instant when the garage, the house it was attached to, and the cars behind it became motion. There was a bursting, expanding black wall of smoke with a fiery release of chemical power at its core. From the first instant there were boards, shingles, irregular pieces of wood and brick and concrete and glass that flew out in every direction at ballistic speed.

The blast was so powerful and hard that the ground kicked up against Stahl's chest, arms, legs, and face. Dust and dirt were hurled hundreds of feet into the air and held there.

He kept his face down with his hands covering his head, hearing large objects fall to the ground all around him for at least ten seconds. When they landed on the pavement of the highway they made hard, ringing noises. The ones that came down near Stahl thudded and dug into the dirt.

During these seconds, a few large objects came down in the minefield around the house and set off secondary explosions that set off other mines in chain reactions.

When the mines had exploded there came a moment when the sounds all stopped. Stahl sat up and looked around him for a few breaths. The house was gone. The road was covered with things that didn't belong. There was a heater/air-conditioner, a complex steel object like a drill press, a water heater, all charred and smoking. But most objects were only parts of things that had once been in or near the buildings. The remains of cars were barely recognizable dozens of yards away, just assemblies that were charred, bent, and torn apart by the explosives that had been loaded into them.

Stahl stood and began to walk. He saw nothing that looked to him like part of a human body. Either the body parts had been thrown too far, or the force and temperature at the center of the explosion had cremated the men and scattered their ashes.

He realized that dawn had begun as he surveyed the leveled spot where the house once stood. He could see shapes, but no color yet. He supposed this spot wouldn't have had much color even when the sun was high. Nothing was living within a broad circle around him. It would be gray dust and ash until the wind blew it all off the surfaces that remained. The bushes and desert trees and brush were scorched and wrenched out and blown outward. Eventually a person driving by would probably guess something had been here only from the long, straight driveway that led a few hundred feet from the highway and stopped. And even now it would be clean. High explosives had a sterilizing effect.

49

Tucson, Arizona
January

Ace Feiker got out of his car a distance from the back wall of the property, and that put him half a city block from the house. It was just an estimate, because up here on the hills above Tucson there were no blocks. He walked along the empty road. The soundless steps of his black sneakers were long and fast because of the mood he was in. He felt like an ace. His mother had named him Asa, a name from the Bible, but it got shortened along the way, and Ace suited him better anyway.

The nights of killings always made him feel especially energetic. There was a feeling at the start like stage fright, with his heart beating and his lungs craving more air. But then, when the job began, he felt smart and slick and on his way to another win.

He had to be conscious of the passage of time. This was the rich part of Tucson, in the hills north of the city, not far from the big hotels with three golf courses and seven swimming pools, and parking a normal little car—not even new—on the road at night might make someone curious. The servants at big houses and the hotel workers usually parked somewhere on the property.

Ace reached the back wall of the yard, hoisted himself up to the top of the stucco wall, and rolled over it into the hedge, which took his weight like the arms of a mother and bent to release him gently onto the lawn.

Ace knelt where he was, staying motionless while he studied the large residence. The area closest to him was the tennis court. Its tall, evenly spaced lights were safely turned off tonight. In the moonlight he could see that the white markings on the court were bright, and the net was tightly strung, as though somebody in the Omaransky family cared about tennis.

Beyond the court and closer to the house was the pool. Ace could appreciate the pool, because in spite of its size, which was crazy in a place like southern Arizona, the expert landscaping around it made it seem, if not natural, at least a part of the real world, not like the ones with fake rocks and Las Vegas–style waterfalls. The pool house looked like a smaller version of the house—modern, but with a Mexican influence. He moved his eyes along the house's walls, studying every opening to decide which one would be his way in. He adjusted the sling of his FN FAL assault rifle so the weapon was strapped comfortably across his back, and then he stood and walked toward the house.

He liked the skills and methods of his profession—finding his way to the target, executing the kill in a way that wouldn't leave him covered in blood spatter and didn't make so much noise that everybody in the neighborhood woke up and called the police. He hated leaving witnesses alive, but even more, he hated killing four or five extra people free. It was always best to find the easiest way into the building, do the work quietly, and then leave by the same route without opening extra doors or touching anything twice.

He had taken this job only because the money was good. The man who wanted it done had some strong reason to hate Omaransky, but didn't say what it was. He swore it wasn't the kind of thing where everybody would say, "Omaransky's dead? Then Thompson must be behind it." Thompson just hated Omaransky, and could obviously afford to have him killed. So he would be.

Ace went straight to the French doors that led from the pool area to the interior. These French doors were even dumber than most. They were just like the house—everything was the most expensive, with the doors set into a rounded alcove and equipped with a hardened steel precision lock and bolt. Everything had to be made and fitted by hand. But a French door was just a woodwork grid of twelve or fifteen small rectangles of glass, or "lights" as the people who sold them would say.

Ace took out his pocketknife, flicked the blade open, and proceeded to slice its sharp edge through the caulk around the sheet of glass beside the door handle. Then he stuck his suction cup to the glass, inserted the point of the blade under the edge, wiggled it around a bit to wedge it in deeper, and popped the sheet out of its wooden frame. He turned the sheet of glass at an angle to fit it out through the frame, and examined it. Typical. It was the best safety glass, the kind you could hit with a hammer and not break. But you didn't need to hit it with a hammer.

He reached through the empty frame, found the knob that opened the dead bolt, and then found the doorknob.

He was in. He closed the door slowly and carefully. He was in a room that had few furnishings. There were a dozen chrome, steel, and leather chairs, a giant abstract painting that took up most of a wall, three glass-top tables, a polished wooden bench. He didn't care much for midcentury modern, and it seemed stupid for rich people to spend money on things that weren't even comfortable.

He reminded himself it was time to get his job done. He reached into his shoulder bag, took out the suppressor, and screwed it onto the muzzle of the rifle, then charged the weapon to put a round in the chamber.

There was an audible click, but it seemed to come from two places at once. He saw from a change in the light that something behind him was moving to cut off the dim moonlight from the French door, so he went low, spun, and fired a short burst in that direction. But then he realized he was firing under steel slats coming down over the French doors like a curtain. It was too late to get out that way. He spun toward the other door that led deeper into the house and realized there was a curtain of steel slats coming down to cover that door too. Security shutters.

He fired, this time at the steel, but his bullets ricocheted back into the room, hitting the polished concrete floor, the walls, the ceiling while he crouched on the floor waiting for them to stop.

A male voice came to him through a speaker set into the ceiling. "Don't bother trying to get out. You can't."

Ace yelled, "Who are you?"

The voice said, "We're from the security company. We installed the steel shutter system. We've done a lot of the houses around here."

A female voice that seemed a few feet farther from the microphone said, "Boss, how much fentanyl gas is safe to pipe into a room that size?"

The male voice said, "Just use the one-liter aerosol. You remember what happened in that Russian theater when the police tried to rescue the hostages."

"No I don't," the female said. Her voice sounded confused.

"They used too much and a hundred and thirty hostages died. You can always add more if he doesn't go down right away."

"Hold it!" Ace shouted. "Stop! Don't put any of that shit in here. I won't shoot."

"If you want to surrender, you can put your weapons on the floor in the corner of the room, and then back away to the opposite corner and lie down. If you go near them again, you'll still go quietly. It's up to you how it happens."

"I'm doing it," Ace shouted. He got up and went to the far corner of the room, where he put his rifle, his knife, and his shoulder bag on the floor.

In the control room on the second floor of the house Dick Stahl and Diane Hines watched the man on the security monitor. Diane switched off the microphone they had been using and gave Stahl a kiss on the cheek.

"What's that for?"

"I'm just happy. I never thought the security business would be this much fun."

"Here's the best part—calling the cops to come pick him up for us," Stahl said. He reached for his cell phone.

THE END